SHARDS

(The Beginning of "Strings")

a novel 

by James V. Viscosi

"So what kind of character do you want?" Mercy asked.

"I don't know." Bernard inspected the options. "What's a rogue?"

"A rogue is like a thief."

"What, you mean they go around robbing people?"

"Well, sort of, but not like a mugger. More like, you know, Robin Hood or Ali Baba."

"Mmm. What are you?"

"I'm Ambrosia, the elf sorceress."

"Of course you are. I'll be a human rogue. Male. Good."

"Good? You can't be good."

"Why not?"

"You're a *rogue.*"

"So?"

"So you're a thief. You burglarize castles. You waylay people and take their stuff. Does that sound like good behavior to you?"

"You just said rogues weren't muggers."

"It doesn't take any skill to be a mugger. All it takes is a weapon. Rogues are like, like, like gymnasts. Acrobats who steal. Cat burglars. They jump around, they run along tightropes, they climb up walls." She had no idea if this particular game actually presented rogues that way, but she was getting a little impatient. "Trust me, you'll love being a rogue."

"Hmm, I don't know. Maybe I should be a scout. What would a scout do?"

"Help old ladies across the street. Oh, come on. Live dangerously." Before he could protest further, she had made him a neutral male rogue. The computer then prompted her for the character's name.

She gave Bernard a sidelong glance.

"Can't I just call him Bernard?" he said.

"Ambrosia the Sorceress is not going to pal around with someone named *Bernard.*"

"Well, I can't think of a name," he said, sounding cross.

"Fine, I'll make one up for you." She typed *Brannoc* and accepted the character; the screen went black for a moment, then returned to Ambrosia standing alone and motionless in the forest, as if she'd started down the path and then forgotten where she wanted to go.

"Where's my character?" Bernard asked.

"He's probably sitting around somewhere complaining about his name and wondering if he should have become a scout," Mercy said.

This is a work of fiction. The people, events, locales, and circumstances depicted are fictitious or used fictitiously and are the product of the author's imagination. Any resemblance to any actual events, locales, organizations, or persons, whether living or dead, is entirely coincidental.

Copyright © 2012 James Viscosi
All Rights Reserved
www.jamesviscosi.com

Cover Art: "Inhale Exhale - The 7th Hour", by Émilie Léger
Copyright © 2012 Émilie Léger
All Rights Reserved
www.emilieleger.com

Also by James V. Viscosi

Available Now
Night Watchman
A Flock of Crows is Called a Murder
Long Before Dawn
Dragon Stones
(The #1 UK Amazon Kindle Epic Fantasy Bestseller)

The "Strings" Duology:
Shards
Ravels

Anthology Appearances
New Traditions in Terror
edited by Bill Purcell
featuring "The 66th Vampire"

Crossings
edited by Megan Powell
featuring "Draw"

Coming Soon
Father's Books
Television Man

PART ONE

GAME

Chapter 1

Mercedes sighed and rolled over, twisting herself up in a sheet-shroud. She had just checked the digital clock by her bed; its big red numbers decreed that it was 5:56 in the morning, which meant that in four minutes, the radio would come on and force her out of the warm, soft cocoon of her covers. Was she just going to let that happen?

No. She was not.

Mercy closed her eyes and attempted to shunt herself into a pocket dimension, one where time passed more slowly or, better yet, didn't pass at all, where she could get another two or three or twelve hours of sleep before school. She concentrated on this effort most intently, focusing all of her mental energy on making it happen, on forcing a metaphorical crowbar into the cracks in the plaster walls of reality and pulling them apart like a demolitions crew preparing to open a new doorway.

When she opened her eyes, it was still 5:56.

"I did it," she whispered. But she could feel the pressure of Time pushing against her, building, building, relentless as a storm surge against a levee, until something inside her snapped and Time, with gleeful malice, skipped over 5:57 and 5:58 and went straight to 5:59. With a frustrated groan, she pulled the pillow over her head. Obviously her bleary morning vision had taken the eight for a six, seeing what it wanted to see; although if she were going to venture down Hallucination Alley, she could think of better things to imagine than an extra minute or two under the covers.

The appointed hour arrived on schedule and her clock radio came to life, spewing the voice of her cheerful nemesis, Tom Tuttle, morning DJ on the local Top 40 station. She seemed to have caught him in the middle of one of his highly technical weather reports. "Blue skies this morning but cold, cold, cold!" he chirped.

Tom Tuttle could afford to be chipper. Tom Tuttle didn't care how cold it was outside. Tom Tuttle was sitting in a nice warm studio, quaffing an enormous mug of hot cocoa, and at the end of the day he would be chauffeured home in a flying car with heated seats. Or something like that.

"A mass of arctic air is moving down from Canada and it'll send temperatures plunging when it gets here!" he continued, projecting a slightly crazed enthusiasm, as if he were a huckster attempting to hawk bottles of frigid air to gullible buyers for use as cooling devices come the heat and humidity of summer. "The high will be near thirty but don't expect it to last very long. Brrrrr! Keep those furnaces running, everybody! And if it's been a few years since you had your furnace serviced, why not call our friends at——"

"Sorry, Tom, no sale," Mercy said as she hit the button to turn the radio off, cutting him off in mid-pitch. Having thus once more vanquished her sworn enemy, she rolled over onto her back and looked at the ceiling, her eyes tracking a spider as it scuttled along a rafter, passing through a reflected moonbeam and vanishing into the protective darkness of a corner. "I know just how you feel," she told it. "I hate mornings too. But at least I don't have to eat flies for breakfast."

If the spider sympathized, it didn't write her any messages in its web to let her know. It had better things to do.

Mercy threw herself out of bed and padded softly across the room to her large mirror, where she clicked on the light. Here was another reason to hate mornings: Every night, she went to bed a girl, and woke up a zombie. Her hair, the color of the sand on some nondescript beach (not one of the famous ones, like Coronado or the Riviera, but some dull and anonymous beach that cuddled up to a small, cold lake way out in the boreal forest), lay limply against her skull and trickled lazily down the back of her neck to gather in a muddy puddle at her shoulders. Her eyes, puffy from sleep, or the lack thereof, looked too big for her face, never more so than in the shadowy semi-darkness of the early A.M. Perhaps because they had been crowded out by her eyes, her nose was too small and her lips were too thin and even her ears, which she knew were anything but miniature, seemed tiny amid their veil of fur. It was as if all of her other features were terrified that her massive peepers would spot them and muscle them right off her face. What would she look like, going around with no nose, mouth, or ears, just eyes and skin? That would be trippy. She could almost hear Vice-Principal Dobbs chewing her out. *We require our students to come to school with their faces on, young lady!*

Ha. That would be awesome.

She smiled, reached up, and turned off the light.

~~~~

Mercedes waited on the sidewalk in front of her house, rocking back and forth on her boot heels, clutching her backpack to her chest. She wore a baggy purple sweatshirt and old, faded jeans and canvas tennis shoes, just to spite her nemesis Tom Tuttle. No gloves, no coat, no socks. Suck it, Tom.

"Hey, Edsel!"
~~~~

She sighed. It was tough when your name was associated with a brand of luxury automobile, but you looked like something that had been dragged out of a used-car lot out behind the junkyard. No one teased her about her name anymore—being seniors, they were above such childish antics—but some of the old nicknames had stuck, and unfortunately, *Edsel,* always among her least favorites, was still in occasional use. The voice that had just uttered it was also among her least favorites. The correlation was not coincidental.

Mercy glanced toward the corner where the Maple Avenue extension crossed her street before terminating in a heap of dirt and a faded sign announcing a new subdivision that had never been built. Jack Kinsey and Warren Oates, her auxiliary nemeses, had stopped their mountain bikes there to indulge in a bit of baiting. "Don't you two have to pedal your tricycles off to kindergarten?" she called.

"We'd rather ride a Mercedes," Warren said.

"Yeah? Looks to me like you can barely handle a bike."

"We can handle more than that!"

"Oh really? Finally got your learner's permits? Sorry, but you'll have to practice on somebody else."

"Uh-oh, Warren, here comes Edsel's boyfriend," Jack said, pointing up the street, where her best friend Bernard had just come out of his house. She and Bernard had been buddies since fourth grade, although he had, for reasons she couldn't really fathom, recently developed some sort of romantic crush on her that he thought she didn't know about. She couldn't help but worry that it would mess up what had been a long-standing and perfectly satisfactory platonic relationship, as boy/girl stuff was wont to do. Maybe she should snap a picture of her morning self in the mirror and give it to him to tape up in his locker; that ought to cure him.

While Bernard paused to turn his key in the front door, she turned back to Jack and Warren. "Why don't you two shove off before you forget how those things work and have to spend five more years with training wheels on?" The two of them exchanged a glance, then saddled up and rode off in the general direction of school. That had been too easy; she didn't like it. As Bernard's footsteps crunched toward her, she watched her two nemeses vanish into the woods. Evidently they were really going, not planning to come back around and circle them like a couple of sharks sniffing at a diver with a bleeding hangnail.

"Hey," Bernard said. She glanced at him, then back at the spot where the mountain bikes had disappeared, then, startled, back at

Bernard. "Nice double-take," he said.

"I see you broke your glasses again."

"Is it very obvious?"

"Well, maybe it wouldn't be if you hadn't fixed them with electrical tape."

"It was all I could find."

"And the only color you had was *pink*?"

He shrugged. "It was in my mom's craft drawer."

"What does your mom need pink electrical tape for?"

"How should I know? For making robot Easter bunnies, maybe."

Mercy shook her head. "You're not doing yourself any favors, my friend." As they began walking up the street, she added: "You should have used duct tape. That would at least be semi-cool."

"I don't think we have any duct tape."

"*Everybody* has duct tape."

"Who needs to tape ducks together?"

Mercy snorted, blowing out a cloud of steam. She kept a wary eye on the woods as they neared the path, but it looked like her friendly neighborhood jerk-offs were not lying in wait. Too cold for them, perhaps; after all, reptiles were known to become sluggish in chilly weather. She and Bernard turned right, leaving the sidewalk and starting down the well-worn path through a forest remnant that had been left standing as "green space," though at the moment there was nothing green about it; the trees were fully denuded of leaves, and summer's verdure was well on its way to becoming a sludgy precursor to topsoil.

"You know what, Bernard?"

"What?"

"I wish this path went on and on and came out somewhere else."

"Somewhere else besides school? Sure, who doesn't wish that?"

"Not just somewhere else besides school. Somewhere magical."

"What, you mean Disneyland?"

"No, not Disneyland!" She smacked him on the shoulder. "You're being obtuse on purpose, just to annoy me."

"I know, I know. The world bores you. You want to fall down the gopher hole and end up in Wonderland with Alice."

"*Rabbit* hole. Alice fell down a *rabbit* hole. Anyway, no, I don't want to go to Wonderland. I want elves and trolls and dragons and——"

"Trolls? Dragons? Don't they eat people?"

"Okay, granted. They won't eat me, though. I'm Ambrosia the

Sorceress. They get fresh with me, they'll be on the receiving end of a fireball."

"Oh, of course," Bernard said, in a *there you go with the fireballs again* tone of voice. She decided to drop it before she got a lecture about growing up and accepting reality. He used to go along with her flights of fancy, but lately he had gotten rather stodgy about such things. She blamed this on the looming prospect of graduation and then college and then, horror of horrors, *work*.

They emerged from the woods at the edge of the athletic field; the school building stood at the top of a low rise across a wide expanse of frosty grass and asphalt like a drab fortress waiting to be stormed, though it was not clear why anyone would bother doing so. It certainly didn't look strategically important or stocked with treasure. "Well, I guess today is not the day that the path leads somewhere magical," Bernard said.

She grunted.

"Can Ambrosia the Sorceress teleport us to homeroom? I think I hear the bell."

Ambrosia the Sorceress said: "Crap."

~~~~

"Effing detention," Mercy muttered, looking up from the inane fill-in-the-blanks ditto that had been assigned as punishment for her fifth tardy appearance at school this month. Fortunately, the month was almost over. Besides, was it *her* fault she had to trudge on foot through the icy forest every day? If they *really* wanted her to be on time, they would send a bus to come pick her up like in the good old days before the budget cuts.

She was alone in the dungeon that was the after-school detention room, except for a leather-clad fellow who was sprawled in a chair a few rows ahead of her. She had thought he was asleep, but now he looked at her. "Did you just say *effing*?" he asked.

"I wasn't effing talking to you."

He raised an eyebrow at that, then shrugged and turned away, which suited Mercy just fine; she was busy concentrating on the clock, trying to get time to speed up. Time, evidently baffled by her inconsistent demands, just ignored her and kept ticking along at its usual rate.

She heard the door open and glanced over her shoulder as Derek Dobbs, Vice-Principal Extraordinaire and her tertiary nemesis, entered. He passed by her desk without acknowledging her existence, heading for her fellow detainee. "Wake up," he growled, nudging the
~~~~

other prisoner with his foot.

"I *am* awake," Leather said.   "Didn't my father tell you to stop kicking me?"   Turning to Mercy, he put his hand to the side of his mouth and said, in a stage whisper, "My father's a lawyer."

Cowed, or more likely just bored, Dobbs wandered over to Mercy's seat. "And how are we doing, Miss Vaccaro?"

"Why, we're just peachy, Mr. Dobbs," Mercy said.

Dobbs crouched down next to her, which meant he was about to give her a pep talk. Joy. "Miss Vaccaro, you don't belong in detention. You're one of the smartest girls in your class. Why do you have so much trouble following the rules?"

At this range, Mercy thought, Ambrosia the Sorceress couldn't miss Dobbs with a lightning bolt if she tried.

The assistant principal seemed to be watching her expectantly. "Sorry," Mercy said after a moment. "Did you expect me to answer that? I thought you were speaking rhetorically."

Dobbs sighed and stood up. "That attitude isn't going to serve you well out in the real world, Miss Vaccaro."

"Then it's a good thing that I don't plan to live in the real world."

"Let me know how that works out for you," Leather called.

"*You* can just be quiet, young man."   Dobbs shook his head and ostentatiously checked his watch. "Another twenty minutes, then you can both leave. Don't forget to check in with the office on your way out." Exit Dobbs, stage left.

When Dobbs was gone, Leather asked: "How come he calls you Miss Vaccaro?"

She cocked her head at him. "Because it's my name?"

"But he doesn't call me Mr. Ulster."   Leather gave the door an unfriendly look. "Why doesn't he call me Mr. Ulster?"

She shrugged. "Couldn't tell you, Mr. Ulster."

He looked back at her. "Miss Vaccaro. You're that girl."

"I'm *a* girl."

"You're Mercedes. Like the car."

"No, the car is Mercedes like me."

"I'm Roy."

"Like the cowboy."

"What?"

"The cowboy." Blank look. "Roy Rogers? Wore a hat? Rode a horse named Trigger?"

"Oh," he said, "you mean the guy who owns the restaurants."

Well, that had been fruitless. "All my friends call me Mercy."

"Not Miss Vaccaro?"

"No," she said. "Not Miss Vaccaro."

"You're smart, huh?"

"Supposedly."

"What are these rules you can't follow?"

"I was late for school."

"Oh." He didn't sound impressed.

"I'm late for school a *lot*."

"Whee," he said.

"Well, what are *you* in for, then?"

"I set fire to my history book in the third-floor bathroom sink."

"Oh, that was you? I heard about that."

Roy grinned. "They called my father's office," he said, rather proudly, "and he told them they could keep me in detention for a whole *month* and it wouldn't help, because I do what I want to do."

"You go, girl," she said.

"Ha ha."

"You're lucky they didn't have you arrested instead of just sticking you in the dungeon."

He seemed genuinely shocked at this notion. "Arrested? For what?"

"Does the word *arson* mean anything to you?"

"It was a history book, not an English book."

"So you're saying you were making a political statement about the book? Protesting its slanted take on history?"

"What are you talking about?"

"I'm talking about your being protected under the First Amendment. How does that sound?"

"Okay, I guess," he said after a moment.

"Can't you stir up a little more excitement than that?" Mercy said. "The First Amendment is heavy duty stuff."

He twirled his finger in the air.

"You're a political detainee," Mercedes continued, ignoring his utter lack of enthusiasm. "Incarcerated because your views don't conform to the mainstream, you languish in this stupid little room. And why?"

Roy, eyeing her with a mixture of curiosity and skepticism, said: "Why?"

"Because you're a mere student!" Mercy slapped her palm on her desk. "But do students surrender their First Amendment rights at the schoolyard door? Do they?"

After a moment, Roy said: "No?"

"Right!"

"Right?" Roy said.

"Wrong."

"Wrong?"

"Wrong." She shrugged. "You're just some bozo who torched his history book to raise some hell."

She lowered her head and went back to work on the ditto.

After a little while, Leather said, "I can see why you don't have very many friends."

~~~~

The last twenty minutes of detention seemed as long as the first forty, as if Time had scornfully decided to apply her earlier request for a slowdown to her current situation, but finally her sentence ran out. Free at last, Mercedes stood and headed out of the room, leaving her fellow prisoner (who appeared to be asleep for real now) snoring away at his desk. She had long since finished answering the questions on the compulsory ditto, and had then proceeded to adorn it with made-up glyphs and sigils that, in the world of her mind, constituted a spell that would cause the paper to catch fire when Dobbs picked it up. *That* would show Leather how it was done. She stopped by the office to turn the booby-trapped ditto in to Dobbs, but he wasn't there so she left it in his mail tray. Her incendiary enchantment was specific to Dobbs, so she didn't need to worry that it would accidentally take out the secretary; not that she was overly fond of the secretary, either, but it wouldn't do to waste magic on a mere assistant.

She exited via a door in the waiting room and struck out across the athletic field beside the school. The wall of trees loomed at the bottom of the hill, dark in the waning day, the branches rattling like old bones left hanging in the wind. The sun floated low in the west, hazy and bloated and indistinct, its color leaching into the pale sky like a slowly dissolving dye tablet. As she passed into the tree-bound realm of brown, grey, and black, the light faded and she hugged herself to keep warm. Tom Tuttle might be her nemesis, but he hadn't been wrong; it was cold, cold, cold this afternoon. She was starting to regret not taking his advice to bundle up. Each exhalation of breath formed a little cloud of steam, like a dragon idly blowing smoke, although had she been a dragon she certainly wouldn't be hanging around *this* dump.

If she froze to death out here, it would, she decided, be charged to Dobbs's account. She hoped he liked being haunted by a blue ghost girl with chattering teeth.
~~~~

In the dim depths of the narrow woodland, passing near a peculiarly shaped mound of leaves, she left the path and tried to kick them into the air; but they were sodden and half-frozen and stubbornly refused to float. "Get up!" she cried, kicking them again. "Get up, fly away! Don't just lie there! Do you want to rot away to nothing?" But Gravity proved no more susceptible to persuasion than Time, and refused to relinquish its hold on the dead foliage.

Was Ambrosia the Sorceress going to accept defeat at the hands of yet another invisible force? No. She was not.

She plucked a stubby branch from the grip of frosted mud and aimed it at the leaves. Now the leaves would dance at her command, their shapes and colors and individuality miraculously restored, a swarm of red and gold and orange flakes swirling like a banner in the air. She would send them spinning around the tree trunks, weaving through the branches, in and out and up and down, a flock of madcap birds, until they finally settled back onto the trees, green once more, the forest restored to the lush fullness of its summer life.

But, of course, none of that happened; the leaves continued to lay there on the ground, limp and still and dead, ignorant of the miracle they could perform if they would only wake up. She sighed and dropped the stick. It was only a bit of wood, not a magic wand; and she was only Mercedes Vaccaro, not Ambrosia the Sorceress. Just like before. Just like always.

"A little old for make-believe, aren't you, Edsel?"

She turned, and there was Warren Oates, leaning against a tree, arms folded across his chest, watching her and grinning.

"Don't you have better things to do than spy on me?" she said.

"I'm not *spying* on you. This is public property. If you don't want people to see you acting like a freak, do it in your house like a normal person."

"That doesn't even make sense—*hey!*" Somebody grabbed her from behind. She struggled briefly, admonishing herself for getting caught with her guard down; she should have known Warren wouldn't be slouching around in the forest without his trusty sidekick Jack. "Let go of me, jerk," she said over her shoulder. Jack just laughed and waggled his tongue at her.

Leaves crunched as Warren approached. She turned her head to glare at him. He stepped up close and put his big hands on either side of her waist, then slipped them under her sweatshirt. His hands were rough and freezing cold.

"What the hell do you think you're doing?"

"Just settling something," Warren said. "See, Jack here thinks you wear this loose baggy crap because you're hiding what you've got, but I say it's because you're hiding what you *haven't* got."

"I'm not one of your harem girls. Let go of me."

"Harem girls?" Warren said. "That sounds hot."

"What about *assault*? Does that sound hot?"

Warren said, "This isn't assault. This is just good clean fun. Stop wiggling, it'll be over faster."

He wasn't going to release her. With that realization, her mind went somewhere else.

She heard herself say, "You have one second to get your hands off me."

"Ooh," Warren said.

"One."

"Careful, Warren," Jack said. "She's count——"

Mercy snapped her head backwards, smashing Jack's face with her skull. She didn't have an enormous cushion of hair like some of the girls did; he took the full force of the blow right on the nose. He grunted and his grip slackened. She kneed Warren in the crotch before he had a chance to react, then broke free from Jack, spun, and backhanded him across the face without even looking at him. By the time he hit the ground, she was facing Warren again.

"You *kneed* me!" Warren said, his voice between a choke and a groan. "You bitch, you kneed me in the *balls*!"

"Where else would I knee you?" Warren was out, she judged; she didn't need to hit him again. She edged around him, moving in the direction of home; he made a half-hearted attempt to grab her elbow as she passed, so she slugged him. Warren went down, blood flowing from a cut below his eye socket.

"You two had enough?" she said.

They both glared at her. Neither one spoke.

"I went easy on you," she said. "Teasing is one thing, but touch me again and I'll show you the *really* hardcore stuff I learned in self-defense class. *Capice*?"

Warren nodded; Jack, still trying to stanch a major nosebleed, didn't seem to have heard her. She backed up the path until she was sure they weren't going to come after her; then she turned and, refusing to give in to the urge to run, walked away.

Chapter 2

HER HOUSE WAS dark when she got there, its windows black as she opened the postbox and absently stuffed its contents into her backpack. Holding the mail-laden backpack by one strap as if it were a handbag, she trotted up the cement walk to the porch. A wooly black cat lay curled up on the woven doormat. Why Warren's cat insisted on sleeping on *her* porch, she would never know. She nudged him out of the way with her foot and said, "Get lost, Ribbit." The cat stalked off, all severely offended dignity, tail straight up and twitching. "Why don't you go home and yack up a hairball on dear sweet Warren?" Mercy said as she unlocked the door. Ribbit, now perched on a nearby railing, watched her balefully with one eye the color of the sun and one the color of the sky.

She pushed her way into the house, closed and locked the door behind her, dropped her backpack, took a few steps into the living room, and collapsed into the first chair she came to. Her knuckles hurt and her heart was still racing. If her parents kept liquor in the house, she would go pour herself a nice stiff drink, but instead she just had to sit there breathing steadily until she finally started to relax. She was glad no one was home to ask her awkward questions.

Once she started to feel better, she distracted herself by retrieving her backpack and pulling out the mail. Most of it was for her parents: Bills, more bills, advertisements, still more bills, a letter from her father's college roommate—she grimaced, hoping the guy wasn't going to come for a visit; every time he did, he pinched her and told her how she was *filling out*, like she was some sort of prize farm animal—and oh, look, more bills! But at the bottom of the pile she found a stiff brown envelope. No return address; no delivery address; just a name. *Ambrosia the Sorceress.*

What the hell?

She turned it this way and that, looking for the flap, but it appeared to be a single continuous surface. What sort of envelope had no opening? Wasn't the whole point of an envelope that it contained something you could get at? Holding it up to the light revealed nothing; the material was completely opaque. She ran her fingers along it, trying to figure out what might be inside, but like a treasure chest the material refused to give up any clue to its contents. It had to be from Bernard; slippery fellow that he was, he might've tucked it into her pack while she'd been cooling her heels in detention, or slipped it into the mailbox underneath all the other junk.

But what was it?

Leaving all the boring mail in a neat little pile for her folks to deal with, she absconded to the kitchen with the mystery envelope. Although their house was nominally a bungalow, at some point in its history someone had taken out the normal flight of steps and replaced it with a wrought iron spiral staircase that ascended from beside the stove in the back right corner of the kitchen. Her parents thought it had been done to increase the available first-floor living space, but Mercy's pet theory was that this previous owner had been a former lighthouse-keeper who'd added the stairs in a fit of nostalgia for his former abode. Sometimes she liked to close her eyes as she climbed, imagining the screeches of seagulls and the crash and spray of waves; this fancy had largely displaced an earlier childhood desire for a switch she could throw to turn the steps into a funhouse-style corkscrew slide for rapid kitchen access.

She entered the bungalow's vestigial second floor through a trap door at the top of the stairs. In addition to her narrow bedroom and a closet-sized lavatory, the space consisted of a nook where the spiral staircase terminated, a crawlspace, and a couple of large dormers. One of these faced the street, the other the backyard; they were well-positioned for catching cross-breezes and for watching storms. The way the nook jutted out from the roofline, it was practically a sail, and any substantial wind caused the beams to groan and creak, while rain made the roof thrum and vibrate. During periods of heavy weather, it was like living in the prow of a sailing ship, albeit one that, sadly, never went anywhere.

Apart from the windows and the narrow aperture that led to her bedroom, the nook was jammed full from floor to ceiling. A chair flanked by a standing lamp, a small computer desk, and a wooden stand bearing a small, heavily-planted fish tank full of cardinal tetras occupied most of the horizontal real estate, while a series of homemade shelving units, their horizontal members growing ever more parabolic under the increasing weight of her books, claimed every inch of wall space. A tiny crawlspace was accessible from a small door that, in her younger days, she had been sure concealed monsters, treasure, or a tunnel to another dimension, and possibly all three. This belief had eventually withered after her father repeatedly demonstrated that there was nothing beyond the door except floorboards, rafters, dust, and boxes full of crap; and now the disappointingly ordinary entrance was itself concealed behind a barricade of old storybooks and outdated encyclopedias that she kept because she liked the pictures.

After closing the trapdoor with her foot, Mercy went to the tank. The timer had already switched the tank light on, setting aglow the red and blue stripes on the fish as they swam around with the aimless determination of schoolers prowling for morsels while hoping not to become morsels themselves. She switched off the filter and sprinkled in some flake food, watching her gaudy pets swarm to the surface like a raiding party of tiny, patriotic piranha; when they were finished, she turned the filter back on. It clattered to life with its usual grinding rattle, spewing a cloud of algae that the tetras attacked with the startled, voracious gusto of creatures who lacked the mental capacity to remember that this happened every single day and was never a fresh cloud of food.

Having taken care of the beasts, she crossed the nook and entered her bedroom. The underside of the peaked roof rose above her head, painted forest-green and daubed with circular blobs of color; below it, the naked beams were painted in red and white candy-cane stripes. The effect was like living in a Christmas tree. She'd adored it when she was ten, but now it seemed rather hokey. Maybe this summer she would drag the stepladder up here and redo it, paint the upper portion of the ceiling like the sky and the lower part like the ocean. She could even throw in a few gulls. That would make the lighthouse-keeper's ghost happy.

She flopped on the bed and tried again to open the envelope. As it had no flap, no pull tab, and no notch, she tried tearing it at an arbitrary spot near one end, but the packaging proved resistant to all such efforts and eventually she had to retrieve a large pair of scissors and just snip it across the very edge of the short end. A thin line of material fluttered off and vanished, along with, she thought, a small puff of powdery multicolored glitter that seemed to simply evaporate; then an optical disc slid out and landed in her lap. She picked the iridescent plastic circle up and examined it. On one side it said, a faux-runic script, *Boot Me.* Hmm. She took the disc back to the nook and sat down in front of her computer. She eyed the computer, the disc, the computer again. Should she? Oh, what the hell; it wasn't like she had anything important on there that wasn't backed up. She inserted the disc and booted the computer. Much humming and whirring ensued and, before long, a block of text appeared on the screen. It said:

AND SO THE FELL GOD USHGALUK, ESCAPING
ONCE MORE FROM HIS PRISON, PURSUED
TYNDALLËAU ACROSS THE SKY. THE TWO MET IN
BATTLE ABOVE THE GREAT FOREST OF TORGON.
FIRE RAINED FROM THE SKY ALL THAT DAY AND
NIGHT, AND GREAT WAS THE BURNING OF THE
TREES. THEN TYNDALLËAU CAST DOWN
USHGALUK; THE EARTH SHUDDERED BENEATH
HIM, AND THE MOUNTAINS SPLIT AND THE SEA
POURED IN. THE WATER BOILED AT USHGALUK'S
TOUCH, AND A GREAT CLOUD OF STEAM ROSE
UP, HIDING USHGALUK FROM TYNDALLËAU'S
SIGHT. STRIKING FROM WITHIN THE MIST, THE
EVIL GOD TORE FROM TYNDALLËAU HIS SHINING
HEART AND SMASHED IT IN HIS IRON HAND,
SCATTERING THE PIECES TO THE FOUR WINDS. A
GREAT CRY WENT UP FROM TYNDALLËAU'S HOST
WHEN HIS BODY WAS FOUND FLOATING IN THE
BOILING SEA; HE WAS BORNE AWAY ON SHIPS OF
WHITE GOSSAMER, TO SLEEP UNTIL THE DAY
WHEN THE BROKEN SHARDS OF HIS HEART
SHOULD BE FOUND AND REASSEMBLED.

AND OF USHGALUK, NO FURTHER TALE WAS
EVER TOLD.

So. Evidently this was an adventure game of some sort. That lent credence to the theory that it was from Bernard, although she still had no idea what to make of the bizarre packaging and utter lack of documentation. Perhaps it was intended to make things more atmospheric, by thrusting the player into some alien world with little information and no idea what they were expected to do aside from not getting killed. She waited a little while for something to happen, and when nothing did she pressed the space bar experimentally, at which point the backstory vanished and was replaced by a new screen:

ENTER CHARACTERS

RACE	PROFESSION	OUTLOOK	GENDER
DWARF	ASSASSIN	GOOD	FEMALE
ELF	BARD	EVIL	MALE
GNOME	CORSAIR	NEUTRAL	NEUTER
GOBLIN	HARLEQUIN		
HALF-TALL	INNKEEPER		
HUMAN	NECROMANCER		
ORC	PALADIN		
PELTISH	ROGUE		
RITTANDIC	SCOUT		
	SHAMAN		
	SORCERER		
	WARRIOR		

Mercy looked this list over; it seemed more or less standard, although she was pretty sure this was the first time a role-playing game had presented her the choice of playing an innkeeper or, for that matter, of voluntarily neutering herself. Neither option seemed particularly attractive. She had no idea what the Peltish and Rittandic races were, but it didn't matter; there was never any question as to what she was going to be. She made her selections, and a moment later the screen showed her the scores for her brand-spanking-new female neutral elf sorceress:

ATTRIBUTES

STRENGTH	50
INTELLECT	95
INSIGHT	81
ENDURANCE	62
AGILITY	75
DEXTERITY	80
CHARISMA	99
ACCEPT	REJECT

Evidently they were using a scale of one to a hundred, in which case her elf was rocking it in the brains and beauty department. Mercy wondered what it would be like to have such scores real life. In addition to being valedictorian, she'd certainly be the most popular girl in school, probably in the county, perhaps in the entire state. People would follow her down the street begging her to throw them her used tissues and offering her modeling contracts. How tedious would *that* be?

She told the computer that those scores were acceptable. Then it wanted to know her character's name which, of course, would be *Ambrosia* (she left off *the Sorceress*, as that was more of a title than a name); then it wondered if she perhaps wanted to enter another character. She had no idea what sort of a situation she would be facing once the game began; it could be a party-based dungeon crawl, a top-down scroller, a first-person slasher, or even something like the ancient text adventure games her father kept trying to get her to play, insisting in a cutely old-fashioned way that her mind would make better pictures than her computer. In any case, she decided to go solo for a while, and add in more characters if she immediately got pincushioned by a gang of kobold archers or whatever. After she told the computer that Ambrosia would be dining alone this evening, the screen went blank and stayed that way for a while as the disk light glowed and the drive whirred.

And then, Mercy found herself looking into another world.

It was as if she were floating behind and somewhat above the character, looking at Ambrosia's minutely-rendered head, neck, and shoulders. The program had given her hair that was blond to the point of whiteness, from which protruded a pair of almost comically pointy elvish ears. Ambrosia was, naturally enough for an elf, hanging out in a lavish forest, surrounded by an extravagant variety of trees; she could even see variations in the color and texture of their bark, the sizes and shapes of their leaves. She stood in a clearing among the plants, surrounded by soft grass and flowering weeds, bathed in yellow sunlight, serenaded by calling birds and chirping insects. Mercy found herself wishing that she had surround speakers hooked up to her machine; she was sure that if she did, she would be hearing the sounds of forest life coming at her from every direction. But this wasn't really a gaming rig, and she had to make do with the tinny speakers it had shipped with.

Suddenly a loud screech sounded from Ambrosia's left; then a very large raptor—not roc-sized, but dwarfing any condor or eagle—sailed into the scene and landed on a nearby tree, which bent slightly under its weight. This creature regarded her platinum-tressed bombshell alter ego with quick, hungry eyes. Mercy didn't like the look of the bird, its long, hooked, bright orange beak and its strong, sharp, equally bright orange talons. It seemed like the sort of apex predator Ambrosia might need to fireball. She started trying to get her character moving into the cover of the trees. The cursor keys seemed like obvious candidates for promoting movement; she pressed the left arrow and the scene rotated to the right around Ambrosia, bringing into view a trail that led down a gentle slope and into the woods. It kind of reminded her of the path that led to school; if she went down it and it emerged onto an athletic field, she was going to be sorely disappointed.

She hit the up arrow and Ambrosia began walking down the path, leaving the clearing behind. Massive trees surrounded her now, depriving the forest floor of sunlight. The path wound in and out among the trunks, and Ambrosia followed it with no further prompting, taking the turns as they came; Mercy just watched, an angel perched on the elf's shoulder. Things were going on out in the woods as she went along; occasionally she heard a branch snap or a tree groan or something crashing through the brush, while the rustling of leaves and the chattering of distant birds were a constant whisper in the background, but she didn't see any more megafauna like the giant bird, which, as she had hoped, did not appear to be following her. Perhaps it had never even been interested in her at all.

She stared at the screen, watching the world move, feeling as if she were riding a small train through the sylvan landscape, as if the trees had begun to tumble out of the monitor, passing by to her right and left, until the walls of her room were lost in dappled shadow. Could she feel the breeze on her face? Could she smell dirt and leaves and rain, the musty bark and moldering stumps and rich loam? Could she——

A hard knock from the trapdoor broke the spell, brought her back to reality. She realized she'd slumped forward in her chair like an overbalanced drunk, her forehead leaving a faint smudge on the monitor glass; there was no wind on her face, no odor in her nostrils, unless you counted the faint whiff of ozone that her computer gave off when it was exerting itself. She leaned back, feeling drained and vaguely disappointed; she must have fallen asleep, maybe from the adrenaline crash after the stress of having to beat the crap out of her idiot classmates. She examined the keyboard, wondering how to save the game. *CTRL-S* did the trick; the disk drive whirred briefly and the word *Saved* glowed and faded across the image of the forest. Look at that, she had saved the world. Satisfied, Mercy shut off the monitor and the computer, leaving the disk in place. Then she called, "Come in!"

The trapdoor opened and her father rotated partway into view through the hole in the floor, stopping partway, so that he seemed to be emerging from the floor like a rising ghost; if he came all the way up, he would have to stoop, and then he would have to complain about his back. He had abandoned his coat and loosened his tie, and was vigorously scratching his neck where his corporate collar had encircled it. "Hi, Mercy," he said. "How was your day?"

Mercedes shrugged. She wanted him to go away, so she could get back to her game, but that wasn't going to happen; it was time to make dinner, which meant she would not be allowed to remain cloistered in her room with her computer unless she feigned illness or said something incredibly rude and inappropriate and got herself banished, and she wasn't in the mood to do that.

"Nothing much happened?"

"Yeah. Nothing much." He didn't need to know that those self-defense classes she had complained about being forced to take had proven valuable after all. "Well, except I was late for school."

"Not *again*, Mercedes."

"Afraid so. What can I say, I wasn't brought up properly."

He frowned. "Your mother and I aren't here to dress you, feed you, and drop you at your classroom every morning. You're not eight anymore."

"I know, I know. Don't worry, I was duly punished in detention. Oh, the trauma. It'll never happen again."

"Uh-huh. Well, that's good. I'd hate to have to confiscate the power cord from your computer and make it available only on a sign-out basis. Which is what will happen the next time you're late." He glanced at her bed. "Did you get something in the mail?"

"Sort of," she said, already plotting how she could sneak an extra power cord out of the computer lab at school. "I think it's from Bernard. He might have felt guilty for contributing to my lateness."

"You two always were a couple of delinquents. What was in the envelope?"

"A game," Mercy said.

"A computer game?"

"Is there another kind?"

"Sure there is," he said.

"Oh, right," she said. "Console games."

"No, see, when I was young, we had these things called board games. We played them with *other people*. In *person*."

"Inconceivable."

"Really! And do you know what else? Sometimes we went *outdoors*."

"I can hardly imagine," Mercy said.

"I know. Seems quaint. Ready to get started on dinner? I'm thinking pasta. You boil the water, I'll microwave the sauce."

"Sure," she said, "claim the easy job for yourself."

Chapter 3

Mercedes stood at the curb in front of her house, rocking back and forth, waiting for Bernard. He finally came out the front door and headed her way. As he approached, she made a great show of checking her nonexistent watch; but when he got closer, she noticed that he was sporting a black eye and dropped the pantomime. "Where'd you get the shiner?" she said when he stopped in front of her.

"Nowhere."

"What do you mean, *nowhere*? Black eyes don't just appear out of nowhere. And don't tell me you walked into a doorknob."

"I walked into a doorknob."

"Ha ha. Spill it."

He said nothing.

"Don't make me beat it out of you."

Nothing.

"I know right where to hit you."

Nothing.

"If you don't believe me, just ask Jack and Warren."

That finally elicited a response; Bernard's eyes widened and he said, "Oh."

"Oh?"

"Ow."

"What?"

"I said *ow*, not *oh*."

"You little liar. You said *oh*. As in *oh, what was that strange noise* or *oh, I just realized something* or *oh, Mercy, you're right as usual*."

He sighed.

"You know you're going to tell me eventually. Save us both some time and spit it out."

"Fine." He looked at the ground, then up again. "I was walking the dog last night and I bumped into those two coming out of the woods."

"Those two ... Jack and Warren?"

"Yeah. They looked like somebody had worked them over with a baseball bat." He eyed her with something akin to wariness. "I take it that was you."

"Could be," she said.

"Yeah, well, I made like I didn't see them, but Warren, he came right over, grabbed my shoulder, and punched me in the face."

She stiffened. "That son of a bitch."

"The funny thing is, Jack looked so scared I thought he was going to pee his pants. Warren seemed like he wanted to hit me again or maybe kick my dog. Jack practically dragged him away."

"Wow. Really?"

"Really. What did you *do* to them?"

"Nothing worse than they tried to do to me." She studied him for a moment, then said: "Come inside."

"But ... school—"

"It's not going anywhere."

"But you'll get detention again—"

"Forget detention." Pause. "Come on, I want to show you something."

As he followed her up the front walk, he said: "This had better be good."

She gave him a backward glance and grinned, but said nothing.

Inside the house, she dropped her backpack on the kitchen table and headed for the spiral stairs. Bernard, though, held back, suddenly looking doubtful. "I don't know about this, Mercy," he said. "You're going to get more than afternoon detention for actually *skipping* school."

"Let them do their worst," she said.

He was already fumbling his keychain out of his pocket. "I think I should—"

"Let me see those," she said, extending her hand. Bernard, ever obliging, handed his keys over. She held them up, inspecting them ostentatiously; then, with a flick of her wrist, they vanished.

"Oh dear," she said. "You seem to be locked out of your house."

"That isn't funny. Give me my keys back."

"Sorry. I sent them to another dimension. I'll return them after you come upstairs."

He sighed and followed her up to the sitting room. She planted him at her computer desk, then fetched an extra chair out of her bedroom and sat down next to him. There wasn't much elbow room, but she didn't think he would mind. As she reached for the power button, he said, "I've already seen your computer."

"Yeah, but you haven't seen *this*." She booted up the computer and the game loaded; this time it went directly to Ambrosia, who was still moving among the trees, right where Mercy had left her. As soon as the forest appeared, the elf started trudging through it.

Bernard said: "What is this, a movie?"

"It's a game, silly."

"It is?" He leaned forward, peering at the screen. "I thought you were in the middle of some dungeon thing where you were stuck in an ice cave."

"*Dungeon thing* lacks specificity, and the ice cave was months ago," she said. "Anyway, this just sort of turned up yesterday. Somebody put it in my bag or maybe out in the mailbox. I don't suppose *you* know anything about it."

"No."

"Are you sure?"

"Of course I'm sure. I was busy getting punched in the face." He leaned back and frowned. "Someone is leaving you presents? Why?"

"You don't have to sound so annoyed that someone is being nice to me. Here, let's make you a character."

She studied the display, wondering how to get a pulldown menu or back to the initial screen. Bernard watched her. At length he said: "Do you actually know how this game works?"

"Not really, no." She started pressing keys.

"Maybe you could, um, read the manual."

"It didn't come with a manual."

"What sort of game doesn't come with a manual? Oh, there you go." She wasn't sure exactly how she'd done it, but a menu had opened over the picture of Ambrosia. One of the items on the list was *Add New Character*. Mercy selected that one, and was rewarded with the original *Create a Character* screen.

"So what kind of character do you want?" she asked.

"I don't know." He inspected the options. "What's a rogue?"

"A rogue is like a thief."

"What, you mean they go around robbing people?"

"Well, sort of, but not like a mugger. More like, you know, Robin Hood or Ali Baba."

"Mmm. What are you?"

"I'm an elf sorceress."

"Of course you are. I'll be a human rogue. Male. Good."

"Good? You can't be good."

"Why not?"

"You're a *rogue*."

"So?"

"So you're a thief. You burglarize castles. You waylay people and take their stuff. Does that sound like good behavior to you?"

"You just said rogues weren't muggers."

"It doesn't take any skill to be a mugger. All it takes is a weapon. Rogues are like, like, like gymnasts. Acrobats who steal. Cat burglars. They jump around, they run along tightropes, they climb up walls." She had no idea if this particular game actually presented rogues that way, but she was getting a little impatient. "Trust me, you'll love being a rogue."

"Hmm, I don't know. Maybe I should be a scout. What would a scout do?"

"Help old ladies across the street. Oh, come on. Live dangerously." Before he could protest further, she had made him a neutral male rogue and moved on to the attributes stage.

ATTRIBUTES

STRENGTH	90
INTELLECT	80
INSIGHT	55
ENDURANCE	90
AGILITY	99
DEXTERITY	93
CHARISMA	50

ACCEPT   REJECT

Bernard, seemingly a little disgruntled over having gotten the bum's rush into criminality, inspected this result. "What are those fifties? Reject."

"Are you nuts? Look at those scores! You want to reject them just because of a couple of fifties in attributes you don't even need?"

"A rogue doesn't need insight?"

"No. A rogue needs strength, agility, and dexterity."

"What's the difference between agility and dexterity?"

She sighed. Leave it to Bernard to analyze all the fun out of a game. "Agility is usually like balance, you know, for running along rooftops and stuff. Dexterity is usually manual dexterity, like for picking pockets and locks. So what if your ugly face breaks mirrors and stops clocks? You can probably dodge bullets."

"Bullets? I thought this was a fantasy game."

She sighed. "Fine. Arrows. You can dodge arrows. This is not a critical life-path decision. If you don't like how the character works out, we can just generate a new one for you."

"Well … okay."

Such an ordeal. She'd hate to see Bernard trying to make a choice about something that actually mattered. Mercy accepted the scores and the computer prompted her for the character's name.

She gave Bernard a sidelong glance.

"Can't I just call him Bernard?" he said.

"Of course not! He isn't from Derbyshire!"

"*Derbyshire?*"

"You know what I mean."

"So what should his name be?"

"I don't know, but it wouldn't be Bernard."

"Maybe humans in that world just have regular names."

"Regular names are boring. Ambrosia the Sorceress is not going to pal around with someone named *Bernard.*"

"Well, what makes *Ambrosia* such a good name for an elf?"

"It's an ancient Roman word. Food of the gods."

"So you're saying elves speak Roman?"

"Latin," she said. "The Romans spoke Latin."

"So you're saying elves speak Latin, and that your character is something that gods eat?"

"Now you're just being obnoxious."

"Well, I can't think of a name," he said, sounding cross.

"Fine, I'll make one up for you." She typed *Brannoc* and accepted the character; the screen went black for a moment, then returned to Ambrosia standing alone and motionless in the forest, as if she'd started down the path and then forgotten where she wanted to go.

"Where's my character?" Bernard said.

"He's probably sitting around somewhere complaining about his name and wondering if he should have become a scout," she said; but then a horizontal line appeared across the middle of the screen, dividing it in two. Ambrosia's locale, scaled down and a bit stretched out, appeared in the top half, while the bottom displayed a cliff wall punctured by the entrance to a cave. Someone, presumably Brannoc, stood outside the opening, peering into the darkness. From the behind-and-above point of view, all that showed was a rather shocking head of pumpkin-orange hair partly covered by a ridiculously large hat, along with ears and a neck that seemed to be more freckle than skin.

Bernard said: "Is that me?"

"I can't imagine who else it would be."

"I look like a scarecrow."

"I don't see any straw. Although that hat looks like he might have stolen it off the poor sap from *The Wizard of Oz.*"

"Ha ha. How do I move?"

"I don't know. Try some keys on the left side there. Maybe E, S, D, and X."

He tapped the *E* key, but nothing happened in his half of the screen. "They don't work. Why doesn't this thing have joysticks?"

"Real gamers use the keyboard."

"Uh-huh."

"Besides, I got this computer for writing."

"Oh, right. All those stories you never let me read."

"And papers for school," she said. "I suppose you want me to let you read those, too?"

"That would be cheating."

"Why should I be the only one of us to get detention? Stop complaining and try some other keys instead of just standing there."

He grunted and continued hunting-and-pecking; meanwhile, Mercy watched as Ambrosia rounded a bend and entered a shadow-dappled glade. Much smaller than the clearing in which she had started, this one featured a good-sized pond fed by a rill that tumbled over mossy rocks into the cattail-filled shallows that rimmed the open water. Ambrosia seemed rather intent on passing by this little tableau, but Mercedes stopped her, then turned her to gaze upon the darkly rippling water. To her left, the path continued on, skirting a few large, oddly-scratched rocks, then returning to the tree-bound gloom. She tapped a few keys, trying to get Ambrosia to look up; the elf did so, revealing a lapis dome smeared with clouds like damp, stretched cotton. The sun was not visible, though she saw an orange tinge low in the sky. Mercy wondered if that meant it was early in the day, or late. She hoped it was early; she didn't want her character to have to sleep alone in the woods. As Ambrosia's gaze came back down to the pond, she spotted a single large, blue-black, webbed claw withdrawing into the water, leaving three furrows in the dirt where its long, sharp nails scraped through the soft earth.

Oh crap.

Mercy started to back the elf up, but then the claw erupted from the water again. This time it had brought a friend. Each vicious-looking talon gripped one side of one of the large rocks, fitting perfectly into the well-worn grooves she had noticed. Muscles bulged in the distended limbs to which the hands were attached; and momentarily a wide-mouthed, many-toothed amphibian hauled itself out of the water, bulbous yellow eyes swiveling to look at Ambrosia.

Double crap.

She fumbled with the keyboard, trying to get Ambrosia out of there. She clearly wasn't going to be able to outrun that thing, but maybe she could lose it in the trees or keep ahead of it long enough that it would start to dry out and give up. Apparently, though, she had hit upon an unfortunate button combination, because instead of fleeing, Ambrosia simply fell down. From the perspective of sitting on her butt in the grass, the creature looked even larger as it clambered up the muddy bank, water coursing down its smooth glossy skin. She wished she knew how to have Ambrosia whip out a fireball wand and reduce the monster to charcoal. But suddenly, a dark-shafted arrow flew onto the screen from the right, it thunked into the creature's thick neck, causing it to bellow like a giant, startled bullfrog. Its rear leg, bending back on itself in an astonishing fashion, reached up and scrabbled at the fletching, trying to get a grip and pull the projectile out. Ambrosia didn't wait to find out if it succeeded or who had shot it; she was back on her feet, and scurrying away down the path. Mercy didn't even have to press anything to get her to do it.

"I think I've got this figured out," Bernard said, momentarily distracting Mercy from Ambrosia's flight. She glanced at his half of the world, where Brannoc had started ambling along the bottom of the cliff. From this new angle the forest edge was visible to his left, while to his right, a sharply-angled curtain of craggy stone lurched into the sky from an apron of rubble and massive slabs of sheared-off rock.

"I'm in that forest," Mercy said. "Maybe. Have you got things under control?"

"Looks like it. How do I find you?"

"I don't know. Come looking for me. You can probably see my character's hair from outer—" She broke off as a massive boulder crashed to the ground scant yards from where Brannoc stood, followed by a shower of smaller rocks, pursuing it like ball bearings pulled along by a magnet. The big stone rolled down the slope and flattened a few trees before being stopped by the resistance of the forest wall. Although Bernard didn't touch the keyboard, Brannoc immediately stopped walking; a moment later his perspective shifted sight up along the palisade, the top of which had become obscured by a gigantic cloud of dust.

"That can't be good," Bernard said.

"I'd get out of there if I were you." Bernard started tapping away like an over-caffeinated telegraph operator; the world rotated around Brannoc, bringing the cave opening back into view. He started running toward it. "No, head for the *forest!*" Mercy said.

"How am I supposed to do that?"

God, it was like adventuring with a six-year-old. "With the same keys you used to turn him around."

"Like I was paying attention to which ones those were." He gave the keyboard a few half-hearted pecks, but if anything that made Brannoc run toward the dark hole even faster. A thickening hail of powder, gravel, and fist-sized stones fell all around him, giving him the chance to demonstrate the value of his superior agility score. "Wow, look at him go," Bernard said. "I mean, me. Me go."

"Nice grammar, Tarzan."

"Cut me some slack, I'm running for my life."

The besieged rogue reached the cave mouth and threw himself inside, just ahead of a massive landslide that quickly sealed him up in the dark. Bernard said: "Oops."

"I *told* you to head for the forest."

"Mmm. Well, I guess I'm stuck here for a while. What's going on in your neck of the woods?"

"I'm running away from some kind of gigantic ugly frog."

"I thought you were Ambrosia the Sorceress. Can't you just like incinerate it or something?"

"Sure, if I could figure out how to cast spells."

"Huh. A sorceress who doesn't know how to sorcer. Interesting." Bernard tipped chair back in his chair. "Well, that was fun. I guess. If we leave now, we can still get to school in the middle of first period. Maybe they won't have noticed we weren't there for roll."

"You really want to go show off that shiner, huh?"

"Well, I can't go home, can I? I'm locked out." He gave her a significant look.

"Oh, right," she said, smirking. "Here, let me return your keys to this dimension." She showed him that she had nothing in her hands, then distracted him with gesticulations while flicking her wrist to bring his keychain down into her palm from its hiding place up her sleeve. But what emerged was not Bernard's keychain. It was a longish piece of wood, thick at the base and tapering to a point, not unlike a stubby pool cue or heft drumstick. Highly polished, it gleamed in the glow of the monitor, almost as if it had tiny reflective threads embedded beneath its coat of lacquer.

She held it up and gawked at it. "What the … ?"

"That's not mine," Bernard said.

"I know that."

"What is it?"

"It's … a wand."

"Why did you have it up your sleeve?"

She looked at it, then at him. "I didn't," she said.

"Uh-huh, sure." He plucked it out of her hand and waved it at the computer. "*Alakazam!*"

The wand exploded, and took the world with it.

PART TWO

THE FIRST SHARD

Chapter 4

SHE BECAME AWARE that she was running through a forest.

It was a sudden sort of thing, as if she had drifted to sleep and been startled back to wakefulness. Her stride broken, she stumbled, fell, and rolled to a stop in a scatter of leaves and bracken. Lying on her back, looking up at the spreading canopy of trees, she took a moment to catch her breath and wonder: Who was she? Where was she? How had she gotten here? She couldn't answer any of those questions; the only thing she remembered was that she was fleeing from something.

She had landed near a stand of ferns that grew alongside a massive fallen tree. It looked like they would provide decent cover, so she crawled through the stems and fronds until she reached the decaying trunk. She rested there, the wood spongy but reassuringly solid against her back, thinking, trying to recall something, anything from before she had fallen just now. She thought there had been an attic room, small and dark and oddly painted, wedged under the eaves of some structure. Had she been imprisoned there? Was she running because she had escaped from that place? The memories seemed vaguely false, as if they belonged to someone else and she might be called upon to return them one day, but at the moment they were the only memories she had.

Frustrated, she turned her attention toward the things that she carried. She wore a belt accessorized with many small pouches and packs; maybe something among their contents would inform her, jog her awareness. She picked through them, but most of what she found appeared to be useless junk. Tiny glass discs? A little box containing gummy, aromatic resin? A sachet full of variegated pieces of string? A small cylinder full of marbles? What was all this crap?

Leaving aside that collection of bric-a-brac, she moved on to a small sheath on her left hip, from which a thread-wrapped wooden pommel protruded. She took hold of the hilt between her thumb and forefinger and gingerly drew the blade to which it was attached, a short, slightly curved dagger with an odd gleam along its surface. She turned it this way and that; the glimmers slid within the metal in concert with the movement, little quicksilver flickers of light. Holding the weapon sideways, she slashed at the thick stem of a nearby fern. The blade whisked through the woody stalk with almost no resistance; the frond fell to the ground, cleanly cut, each severed end perfectly smooth. Mentally filing the dagger in the category of *extremely dangerous*, she carefully returned it to its sheath.

On her opposite hip, she discovered a soft leather holster with a cinched top. She loosened it, allowing her to remove a stubby, tapered, highly polished piece of wood about six inches long. Thicker than her thumb at the wide end, this poker-like baton narrowed to a rounded point. Inlaid scarlet thread spiraled in a helical pattern along its length.

"Magic wand," she whispered. Now *that* was interesting. She held it up and sighted along its short length. A slight ripple seemed to emanate from it, like heat distortion, although the smooth surface was perfectly cool. She waved it around a bit, then pointed it into the air and, without really knowing why, said: "*Alakazam!*"

Nothing happened.

She shook the wand a few times, tapped it with her fingernail, shook it again. The wand remained inert. Disappointed, she returned it to its holster for later review, just as she heard stealthy movement approaching her hiding place. She flattened herself against the tree trunk, hunched down into as small a package as she could make herself, and waited.

Before long, a pair of slim figures crept into view, little more than vague dark shapes through the profusion of fronds. The one in front was bent over and seemed to be paying close attention to the ground. Following her trail, she realized. Were these the ones she was running from? Had they been sent to drag her back to that attic room she gauzily remembered?

The trackers stopped for a moment near where she had tripped. She could hear them murmuring to each other; then they left the path and came toward her hiding place. As they got nearer she became aware that they were both armed with bows; the one in front had his slung across his back, while the one behind was carrying his in both hands, an arrow loosely strung. They were taller than she'd thought at first; neither stood fully straight, intent as they were on following her trail. Their long, thin faces and pointed ears and chins aroused an odd sense of affinity. Somewhat to her own surprise, she realized that she didn't think they intended to harm or capture her, but she didn't want to just pop up from her hiding place and say hello lest she should startle them into doing something rash; so she called: "Wait! I'm coming out."

The two of them stopped and exchanged a significant glance; then the one in back said, "Well, come out, then."

She raised her hands and stood. The ferns reached past her waist, thick and verdant, swishing against her as she moved through them. Her trackers watched her carefully; when she fully emerged from the vegetation, the one in back told her to stop. She did, holding herself motionless while they scrutinized her. Finally the one in front said, "You are an elf." He looked over his shoulder at his companion. "She is an elf."

"I can see that," the other one said.

He turned back to her. "Greetings, my lady," he said. He doffed his hat and gave her a little bow. "We are elves too, as you have no doubt observed."

"Yes," she said. She hadn't realized she was an elf. Maybe that was why these two didn't scare her. "Hello."

"I am Glorian, and my companion is——"

He broke off with a yelp as the other elf whacked him across the calf with the side of his bow. Rubbing the back of his leg, he gave his friend a baleful look, which was utterly ignored. "Never mind *my* name," the second elf said. "Find out what *her* name is."

She said: "My name?"

"Yes, your name." Then, when she failed to answer: "By which I mean how, if one wanted your attention, one would address you."

What *was* her name? She couldn't remember. She had to be called *something*. Mer-something? Am-something? Ed-something? No, she thought, not Ed-something.

The nameless elf arched a delicate eyebrow. "Is this a difficult question?"

She shook her head, then said, "Why do I have to tell you my name if you won't tell me yours?"

"This is not about me," Nameless said. "This is our forest. We live here." He tipped his bow in her direction. "*You* do not."

Ambrosia. That was her name. Wasn't it? She said it slowly, trying it out; it seemed to suit her, but Nameless appeared dubious. "You do not sound very sure of that."

"No," she said. "I mean yes, I'm sure. I'm Ambrosia."

"Ambrosia," Glorian said. "The sweetest drink."

The elf who wouldn't give his name snorted. "Poison can be sweet, too, Glorian." He eyed her coldly. "We do not know who she is or why she is here, or even if she is really an elf."

"What? Of course she is."

"Is she?"

"*Look* at her."

"Oh, I am looking at her. One so fair, who would not? Who

would not want to protect her, take her back to his village, only to discover that he had brought home a serpent in disguise?”

“No disguise could be this perfect.”

“There are glamours that may make one thing look like another,” Nameless said. “You study magic, you should know that.”

“Yes. But the dwarves are not capable of casting glamours.”

“They have gold and gems to hire those who can.”

All this bickering, as if she weren’t standing right there, had begun to annoy her, but this last paranoid fantasy pushed her to speak. “You think I’m a *dwarf?*”

They stopped arguing and turned to look at her. “I believe his implication is that you might be an *agent* of the dwarves,” Glorian said after a moment, casting a sidelong glance at his companion, “not that you *are* a dwarf yourself.”

“Thank you for the clarification,” she said, unmollified. “Why would these dwarves want to make someone look like an elf, anyway?”

“Infiltration,” Nameless said. “Spying. Sabotage.”

“You make it sound like there’s a war going on.”

The two of them exchanged a glance; Glorian started to speak, but Nameless forestalled him. “It seems more than passing strange to find you in our forest, at such a time as this, claiming no knowledge of the present … situation, and with no explanation of why you are here or where you came from.”

She had to concede that the elf’s concerns were not unreasonable, although she was pretty sure she was neither a dwarf nor an agent thereof. “I don’t remember anything from before I tripped and fell,” she said. “I can’t tell you what I don’t know.”

“Did you hit your head?” Glorian cast his gaze about, as if searching for the churlish rock that had dared to collide with her skull.

“No, it’s not that. At least, I don’t think so. Everything from before is just … it’s *gone*, like something is hiding it from me.” She sighed. “I can barely remember my own name, let alone where I am or how I got here or what some dwarves might be doing. I was running from something, I tripped, I fell. That’s where my memories start.”

“Well, we cannot say how you got to the forest,” Glorian said, “but we spotted you in a clearing yesterday. We have been following you since then.”

“Following me? Why?”

“White robe, no supplies, all alone?” Nameless said. “You are completely out of place in the forest. We *had* to follow you. And you are fortunate that we did; otherwise you would be nothing more than gnawed bones at the bottom of a pool now."

"I …" She trailed off; that remark struck a vague chord. "I think I remember … there were rocks, and a pond, and a … a monster?"

"Not a pond, a lair," Nameless said, "and not a monster, just an animal that digs deep waterholes and in order to ambush prey—animals, foolish wanderers—that stop to drink. I … gave it something else to think about."

"Thank you."

He grunted. "I was not pleased at being obliged to harm it in order to protect you. But … you are welcome."

Glorian said, "She *has* been enchanted."

Nameless sighed. "Glorian, please—"

"Wait, hear me out. She is obviously a sorceress—"

"Why is she obviously a sorceress?"

"Look at what she carries."

Nameless looked. "A bunch of pouches, a short blade, a …" His gaze alighted on the holster for her wand, and he trailed off.

"Yes," Glorian said, watching his friend—assuming they *were* friends—carefully. "Do you know what you have in your pouches, Ambrosia?"

"Just some junk. Some pieces of glass, marbles, string, gum."

"That is not junk," Glorian said. "Those are spell components. Foci."

She looked at her pouches, surprised. "They are?"

"Are you sure she is a sorceress, and not just someone who has been rummaging through a wizard's trash?" Nameless said.

"Wizards do not throw away magic wands, even ones whose utility has been exhausted." Then, to Ambrosia: "You have been robbed of your skills and memories, by an enemy or by misadventure, but you *are* a sorceress. I am sure of it."

"Enough speculation, Glorian," Nameless said.

"It is not speculation," Glorian said. "She *is* enchanted. I threw a glamour while you were berating her."

"You cast a spell on me?"

After a moment, Glorian said, "No, I cast a spell *around* you."

"Hm," she said, unimpressed by the distinction.

"But can your glamour tell us what the enchantment is?" Nameless asked.

"It is not that precise."

"Then it is not very informative, is it?"

"No. And that is why we must bring her to Yexandor."

Nameless opened his mouth, then closed it again, looking puzzled and unhappy to have blundered into Glorian's rhetorical snare. Before he could raise an objection, Ambrosia said, "Who is Yexandor?"

"He is our leader, a powerful sorcerer and divinator," Glorian said. "And the oldest elf in Torgonderrer."

"Second oldest," Nameless said. Then: "Very well, we will take her to Yexandor. If nothing else, it will deprive the dwarves of a potential hostage." He pointed a long finger at her. "But there will be no wandering off, and no magic, and you will do as we say until we get to the village. Agreed?"

"Agreed."

"And you will give Glorian your wand and your knife."

Simultaneously, Glorian and Ambrosia said: "Why?"

"We cannot allow you to carry offensive weapons into the village," Nameless said. To Glorian: "You know that."

"But if she wanted to attack us, she——"

"It does not matter what she wants," Nameless said. "If the archers at the gate perceive her to be a threat, they will shoot her."

"Oh. Of course." Glorian looked at her and held out his hands; she sighed and removed the dagger's sheath from her belt, giving it to him hilt-first. He stowed the blade, then accepted the wand from her. Holding it gingerly between his fingers, he turned it this way and that, examining it. "What does it do?" he said.

"As far as I can tell, nothing."

"It must do something," he said. "It is not fully discharged, I can feel that much. Probably you have forgotten how to use it."

"Probably," she said.

"We could try different command words, or gestures, or——"

"Just put it away," Nameless said.

Glorian sighed and slipped the wand into one of his pockets. With Nameless in the lead, Ambrosia in the middle, and Glorian bringing up the rear, they left the path, moving off among the trees toward the deeper woods. Ambrosia glanced back as the little stand of ferns receded into dappled shadow, and caught Glorian looking at her. "What?" she said.

He gave her a thin, sheepish smile. "Sorry to stare," he said. "I just wonder where you came from."

"So do I," she said.

~~~~

It was dark, and Bernard had a headache.
~~~~

He remembered Mercy producing that wand instead of his keys; he remembered taking it from her and waving it around like an idiot. Then there had been an explosion, an extended sensation of falling, and, finally, unconsciousness. Now he had come to, only to find himself surrounded by utter blackness and with a throbbing pain in his skull.

All things considered, it had not been a very good morning.

He lay there for a little while, waiting to either wake up for real or die of carbon monoxide poisoning; when neither happened, he sat up, realized he wasn't wearing his glasses, and started pawing around looking for them. His fingers drew lines through a thick layer of silty dust on top of what felt like rough stone, which was rather unexpected; he didn't think Mercy had any slate floors in her house. Unless he had somehow ended up in the basement? If so, it had been a long, long time since anyone had come down here with a broom.

Speaking of brooms, his searching hands had found a rod-shaped piece of wood. He picked it up; it was a little over a foot long, and ended in a crusty wad of cloth that smelled like tar or pitch.

A torch? Whatever happened to good old flashlights?

Hanging onto the torch, he got himself to his feet. His balance was way, way off and he staggered into a wall, grazing his head on a rough overhang. He caught it and braced himself to keep from falling as he tried to figure out what the hell was going on. He felt *wrong*, all stretched out and wiry beneath clothes that seemed to be crafted of some exceptionally rough fabric. When he ran his hand along the front of his body he realized he was wearing a woven shirt with leather pads at the elbows, wrists, and shoulders, and loose pants with similar protection at the crotch, seat, knees, and ankles. It was as if while he'd been asleep, someone had dressed him like a biker or 1930s baseball catcher as a prank. He wondered what he had on his feet. Cleats? Calf-high boots? Strappy Roman sandals? He was almost afraid to check. When he did—the answer was calf-high boots—he felt something shifting on his back and bumping between his shoulder blades. Reaching around to feel what it was, he discovered a long, cord-bound piece of wood holstered there.

A quarterstaff.

"All right," he said. "I must still be dreaming."

If you are dreaming, then please wake up and go away.

Startled, he looked around, which was pretty useless given that the place remained as pitch black as it had been before that voice had come out of nowhere. "Who said that?"

I did. What do you want with me, demon? Why are you here?

"Sorry, what? Who did you say you were?"

I didn't.

"Well, would you, then?"

Why should I tell a demon who I am?

"I'm not a demon."

He got no response to that, other than a derisive snort.

"Here, I'll tell you my name. It's Bernard Lansing."

Lancing? Fancy yourself a knight, demon?

It took Bernard a moment to figure out what the voice meant; then he said: "No, not with a C like in jousting. With an S."

There was a pause, and then the voice said: *My name is Brannoc, if you must have it.*

"Brannoc? Your name is *Brannoc?*"

Yes. Have you heard tell of me? My exploits are well-known in Banderlund and elsewhere, but I did not know that demons followed such things.

"I told you, I'm not a demon," Bernard said, starting to feel rather aggrieved at the accusation. "And yes, I know who you are. You're a character in a game I was playing."

This is a game to you, then? Why not play with someone else?

"That's not what I meant—" He broke off as he became aware of a faint, scratchy rumble emanating from the darkness to his left. "What's that noise?"

That noise is trouble. The dwarves are coming.

"Dwarves?" Bernard said. "Are these the merry, singing-about-working type of dwarf, I hope?"

Brannoc was silent for a moment, then said: *None of the dwarves I've ever met have been of that variety.*

"Um. Okay. Should we hide?"

Unless you can turn invisible, demon, you will find nowhere to hide in here.

As his unseen companion spoke, Bernard became aware of a glow emanating from his left, where a nearby section of wall had started slowly turning on a pivot. The strengthening illumination revealed a small, pocket-like cavity chiseled into solid rock; it looked as if the entrance had once been to his right, though it was now choked with rubble and completely impassable. The cave continued inward for ten or fifteen feet before ending in what would have looked like a blank stone barrier, if it hadn't currently been opening. Brannoc was right; there were no hiding places. Which sort of made Bernard wonder where Brannoc's voice had come from; nobody was in the chamber except for him.

The door stopped rotating and a trio of short, squat humanoids trudged in through the narrow aperture, clutching black iron weapons, clad in garments that resembled overalls with no undershirts. They spotted Bernard and stopped dead, gawping and blinking, fine dust sifting from their bushy brows. Dense, wiry hair sprouted out of almost every square inch of their heads, from thick lashes that shaded their dark, deep-set eyes to a mane that framed their foreheads and cheeks; a shorter, somewhat finer mat of fur ran along their arms all the way to the backs of their hands. The hue either offset or complemented their complexions, each of which resembled a different type of stone. The lead dwarf had charcoal hair and a granite-red epidermis with dark flecks; the next sported a coif the color of mercury and skin like basalt; and the third could have passed for a marble statue onto which some prankster had glued wads of crimson clown wigging obtained at a local costume store.

"Um, hello," Bernard said.

The granite-skinned one pointed at Bernard and said something gutturally incomprehensible, but quite clearly unfriendly.

"My name's Bernard," he said.

I don't think they care what your name is, Brannoc said. Bernard looked around wildly; the voice seemed to have come from directly behind him, as if Brannoc were right there speaking into his ear, but aside from the dwarves he was quite alone. He was starting to think Brannoc's presence was just in his head.

Of course I am in your head, demon! You stole my body!

Shocked, Bernard said, "I did *what?*"

At that, the lead dwarf stepped forward and made even angrier noises. His companions took up positions behind him, forming a triangle, brandishing their weapons; Granite held a mallet, Basalt a pick, and Marble a flat-bladed shovel.

Wait … those weren't weapons.

Those were *tools*.

The dwarves hadn't come here looking for a fight, he realized, but to work. Maybe they'd intended to clear away the rockslide. Bernard pointed at the rubble and mimed digging it out, then leaving. The dwarves looked at each other and grumbled amongst themselves, the sound like a distant avalanche; Granite started repeatedly smacking his hammer into the palm of his hand. *Whap. Whap. Whap.*

Brannoc said, *That did not help.*

"Doesn't look like it," Bernard said.

Do you know how to handle a quarterstaff, demon?

"I'm not a ... No. No, I don't."

Well I do. So you'd best get out of the way.

"Get out of the——"

Give me my body back, let me fight!

Bernard considered this proposal. If he allowed Brannoc to take over his body——assuming he even *could* allow it——would he be able to reclaim control afterward? Would he end up trapped, a disembodied observer, as Brannoc appeared to be? If he refused and tried to deal with the dwarves on his own, would there be any body left for the two of them to squabble over?

Granite raised his arm, apparently preparing to do something unpleasant with his hammer; Bernard had to make a decision. "All right," he said. "Go. Go, go!"

Suddenly his body was in motion; his consciousness got pushed back until he almost seemed to be trailing along behind, like a balloon tied to Brannoc's neck. In a weird way, it reminded him of the over-the-shoulder perspective from Mercy's game. He seemed to retain a connection to the brain he had left behind; figuring it might be a way to pick up some skills, he paid close attention to the rogue's activities, hoping to learn how he did whatever he was about to do.

In a single continuous motion, Brannoc pulled a short, blackened stick out of a pocket, struck it on the stone wall to ignite it, then used it to light the torch. He flung both of these at the dwarves, causing them to break formation to avoid the flaming brand. At the same time, Granite hurled his mallet, but it was a clumsy throw that Brannoc easily evaded. Bernard stifled a shriek as the flying hammer seemed about to smash him in the face, but of course he wasn't really there and it just passed harmlessly through him and out of his field of vision. As Bernard recovered from *that* little surprise, Granite charged, his hands balled into surprisingly large fists; to Bernard's shock, Brannoc responded with his own charge. Just before dwarf and human collided head-on, the rogue transferred his momentum into a slide through the lubricating dust, as if he were trying to steal second under the outstretched glove of a shortstop. He somehow managed to whip out his quarterstaff and plant it in Granite's stomach, using it to lever his attacker off the ground and pitch him into the wall. The dwarf's skull connected with the stone, the sound like concrete being dropped from a great height onto hard pavement.

As the stunned Granite slid to the floor, Brannoc stood, leaned on his staff, and gave the other two dwarves a hard stare. Tools at the ready, they approached, displaying somewhat greater care than

Granite had.   Brannoc watched and waited, watched and waited, watched and suddenly broke into a sprint, running straight at them. They stopped and braced themselves for an attack, but instead he planted one leather-wrapped end of his quarterstaff on the floor and pole-vaulted over their bushy heads. He landed behind them and took off through the pivoting door they had used to enter. Unfortunately, pushing off the quarterstaff had forced him to abandon it. Bernard felt disarmed and somewhat naked without it, then wondered why he should be so upset over losing a possession that he had only found out about five minutes ago, then realized that it was actually *Brannoc* who felt that way, that the emotion was bleeding across into him. He wasn't sure quite what to make of that, but he didn't like it.

Beyond the opening, a short, rough tube T-boned with a larger passage. Brannoc gave the secret door a hard backwards kick as he passed, sending it spinning rapidly on its pivot, then dashed to the intersection. An iron pipe was bolted to the opposite wall, at about the level of his chest; bluish fire jetted from erratically spaced spigots, providing the illumination that had entered the alcove earlier. In the ghostly light he could see that the cross-corridor looped in from the depths of the mountain, with only a short stretch visible from here. With no clear indication which way to go, he turned right and rounded the corner, only to be brought up short by a ragged wall of unfinished rock. The floor was littered with stone chips and rubble; wherever this tunnel was intended to go, it hadn't gotten there yet.

Brannoc took the setback in stride, doing a half-run up and around the wall to reverse his direction with barely any loss of momentum. He glanced down the stubby passage as he passed by; the dwarves who'd found him were trying to stop the rotating block of stone without getting crushed or trapped. He put on a fresh burst of speed, sprinting around the other corner, following the tunnel as it began a gentle upward slope, then turned sharply to the left. As he went around the bend, Brannoc looked behind him for pursuers, and saw none. Bernard felt an immense relief; they were still trapped under the mountain, but they had escaped the immediate threat.   Perhaps Brannoc really *did* know what he was doing.

After a few zigzags, the passageway ended in a partially-open iron door. This one was relatively conventional; it had hinges and a handle, and was extensively decorated with runic doodles. It looked extremely heavy, as if it were designed to resist a siege, but swung inward easily enough when Brannoc pushed through it. On the other side he found a wide, dark room, some sort of barracks; Bernard saw pallets chiseled into the stone walls, a cooking hearth, tables strewn with cards and dice-like amusements. Brannoc skidded to a stop as at least half a dozen armed dwarves, arrayed in a semicircle and, apparently, waiting for him, began moving in. Oops.

"If you have any powers besides body theft at your disposal, demon," Brannoc said, "now would be the time to use them."

Sorry, Bernard thought, *I've got nothing.*

"Useless thing." Brannoc raised his hands: "I surrender."

Which did nothing to dissuade the dwarves from beating him senseless.

Chapter 5

AFTER LONG HOURS of walking through a dim green twilight permeated by the calls of unseen birds and the rustling of both large and small animals that declined to approach them, Ambrosia realized that the ground, previously level with gentle undulations, had begun to slope consistently downward. The forest thinned; patches of standing water appeared among blackened trunks as the terrain eventually became an outright wetland, replete with cattails and rushes and buzzing insects that flitted and crawled among creeping bog plants the color of tarnished copper. The nameless elf led the way through the marsh, treading carefully along a narrow lip of stone that snaked through the rising weeds. It seemed as if this, too, had once been woodland; here and there the tattered boles of ancient trees loomed from the muck like the broken masts of sunken ships, black with rot, frosted with lichen and drooping moss. The water table must have risen, she thought, turning this region into a swamp and killing off the trees.

Out in the sun after having spent so much time in the shade, the air felt luxuriously warm. Ambrosia turned her gaze toward the sky, sapphire blue, deep and rich as a tropical sea, streaked with high thin clouds made luminous by the sun even as they obscured it. Far in the distance, looming over the vast dish-shaped depression in which the forest grew, a long, craggy cliff wall drew a wobbly line across the horizon; snow-shrouded mountaintops peeked over the top like nosy neighbors behind a fence.

At last, their twisting path brought them to the foot of a steep, forested ridge. Instead of climbing it, they turned left and followed the edge of the marsh to a ravine. Thorny, yellow-berried bushes choked the entrance. The berries looked quite succulent; she reached out and plucked one, but Glorian caught her wrist and said, "Leave those for the birds." She thought this might be reflective of some sort of share-the-earth philosophy, until he said: "They will give you stomach pains for days."

A creek splashed out of the defile, flowing into the bog to create a small eddy relatively free of murk and vegetation. Ambrosia tossed the berry into it; to her surprise, it sank like a pebble. She knelt to peer into the clear water. The bottom was visible, a bed of mud and sand riddled with tiny shells and dotted with squat spinach-green plants. Small, iridescent darters swam to and fro in a mad dash from this rock to that rock, this plant to that plant, as if searching for something that they never found; some of them had gathered around the sunken berry, inspecting it like superstitious peasants who had found a meteorite in their field. She felt an odd desire to feed them, although she was sure she had nothing that they would eat.

"If you are finished adoring your own reflection," Nameless said, "may we continue? The village is nearby."

She stood. "I wasn't looking at myself," she said, annoyed. "I was looking at the *fish*. And I don't see any village around here."

"You are not supposed to." Nameless stepped into the gully, standing on a narrow ledge of crumbling, flaky stone. "Come."

The creek had cut its way through layers of shale until being stopped by a bed of broken slate, creating a series of small waterfalls as it cascaded from terrace to terrace. The ravine narrowed as they made their way up the slippery path; the bushes grew thin, then vanished. Now they were walking just a few feet above the burbling, foamy stream. The walls rose sharply to either side, covered with fallen leaves and sun-dappled ferns and broad plants with red-tinged leaves. They looked unclimbable; between them and the unsteady footing offered by the shale, she wouldn't want to be caught in a flash flood here. Anyone who was would be washed away in an instant.

They reached a spot where the ravine split; the stream gushed out of the left fork, leaving the right dry. A faint but obviously artificial stairway followed the water; Nameless ignored this and went the other way, which quickly became a box canyon with high, rough, dripping walls. It made a sharp turn at an upthrust incursion of black-flecked rock, then steepened drastically, becoming a chute. The way was so narrow that most of it was in permanent shadow; some variety of dangling creeper had taken advantage of this to grow down in great sheets, hanging like tapestries along vast sections of the gully. Subtle ridges in the stone floor provided footing, but still, she found the climb difficult and tiring. The others hardly seemed to notice that the ground wasn't level, except that they had to keep stopping so she could catch her breath, which Nameless appeared to find quite tedious; if he'd had a timepiece on his person, she thought, he would probably be ostentatiously consulting it every time she begged for a rest. As it was, he had to content himself with impatient foot-tapping.

At last the climb ended at a jumble of rocks and fallen trees that formed an impassable plug in the ravine. A trickle of water found its way under the stones, where dust and evaporation quickly overcame it, causing it to vanish after a few dribbly yards. She eyed the pile of debris, finding it of questionable origin, a little too neat, a little too well-packed. "This isn't natural," she said.

The elves exchanged a glance; then Nameless shrugged and said, "No, it is not. We built it many years ago to divert the stream into a small cistern, so we no longer have to go down to the lake for water except when it is extremely dry."

"And if enemies come up the ravine, you can blow it and flood them out."

Glorian looked puzzled. "Blow it?"

"She is speculating that we could destroy the dam and cause the cistern to discharge into the ravine," Nameless said. Then, to Ambrosia: "Yes, we could do that."

"But *would* you?"

Nameless gave her an appraising look. "If necessary," he said.

She nodded. "So where's the door? Behind the vines?"

"Very good," Nameless said. He took hold of the green drapery and parted it like a curtain, revealing a heavy wooden door, black with age and dampness, mounted on a brass rail. Claw-like metal clamps along its edge bit into the stone, holding it fast. Nameless touched the door and whispered something, as if sharing a secret; the talons quivered and then sprang open. He took hold of two of them and used them as handles to slide the door to the left, away from a narrow black opening. Low, steep stairs ascended in a curving path, quickly disappearing from sight. Cool air wafted out, smelling of rock and water.

"This passage leads to the stockade," Nameless said. "There will be archers. Do nothing to inspire them to loose their arrows."

"Um, all right," she said. "Maybe you could go first and tell them I'm coming?"

"Oh, I will definitely be doing that." The elf turned and vanished into the tunnel; after a moment she followed, trailed by Glorian. She waited there, watching as the creepers fell back into place, filtering the light down to a dim green; then Glorian pulled the door shut and the darkness was complete. She heard a faint metallic *snap* as the enchanted locks engaged.

They began to climb, the steps slick underfoot. The arc of the stairs brought the dark shape of Nameless into view up ahead as he lifted a nearly horizontal door, allowing sunlight to pour in. He exited, leaving the way open.

"Remember," Glorian said. "Archers."

"I remember."

"Do not speak or make any odd gestures."

"All right."

"And no sudden movements."

"Maybe you should just tie me up and drag me to the top of the stairs?" she said. That suggestion quieted him down nicely.

Before long, the tunnel came to an end at a slanted protrusion of rock. She stepped out onto level ground. Glorian put a hand on her shoulder, stopping her; dark shapes swooped in, surrounding the two of them. Archers, as promised. Each bow was drawn, each arrow aimed at her. Remembering Glorian's admonition, she didn't move or speak; she almost forgot to breathe. She could definitely see these steely-eyed sentries riddling her with arrows, then going off to have lunch without giving her another thought.

The ring of elves parted to make room for Nameless. He looked at the archers to his left, then at the archers to his right, then at her.

"Welcome to Torgonderrer," he said.

<center>~~~~</center>

Ambrosia's newly-enlarged entourage escorted her along the top of a broad, flat ridge; this was the summit of the steep incline she had seen from the swampy lowlands. About fifteen feet wide, it encircled a broad, shallow depression where the forest seemed more tame and tended than the woods through which she had recently traveled. From here, if she glanced behind her, she could see that the marsh they had traversed eventually opened up into a wide, reedy lake, plied by small boats; but she didn't spend too much time looking that way, because when she did she found four stern archers staring back. She was a little bit worried that she would twitch an eyebrow wrong and end up full of arrows.

Not that looking ahead was that much better; two more archers were up there, walking *backwards* while keeping their bows trained on her. She supposed this must be so they could catch her if she moved her lips in a way they didn't like, which those behind would not be able to see. Nameless was in front of the backward-facing duo; Glorian, bringing up the rear as usual, was behind the forward-facing quartet. They were staying out of the line of fire in case she sneezed and the archers panicked, she thought. How prudent.

Fortunately she didn't sneeze, the archers didn't panic, and they reached a nearby stockade wall with no bloodshed. The fence had a gate that seemed to have been planted rather than built; two large trees grew up from the slope, their branches interlaced over the ridge in an unnaturally symmetrical geometric pattern. A system of ropy vines and cut timbers had been woven through the branches to create a sturdy catwalk that spanned the gap above a set of wooden doors; a net of leather, wood fibers, and what looked like spider silk hung from this platform, weighted down at the bottom with heavy stones. At their approach, the webbing slowly rose out of the way. Her eyes followed its movement upwards, where two elves, obscured behind a screen of foliage, operated cranks at opposite ends of a log shaft, wrapping the organic portcullis around it.

Once the way was clear, the wooden doors swung inward and they moved forward again. As they passed beneath the platform, Ambrosia looked up and saw that it was heavily perforated with arrow slots, which at the moment were being used as spy-holes for curious elven eyes. Apparently they figured she had more than enough bows pointed at her already, and didn't need any more.

Past the gate, the ground flattened out at the bottom of the gentle slope. The trees were thick to the left and right, while a broad dirt track led directly to a tall, steep hill about five hundred yards away. Smaller trails and paths diverged in numerous locations, winding through and vanishing into the forest, but her little band stuck to the main avenue, which headed straight for the looming mesa. As they scuffed along the dusty road, Ambrosia kept glancing to the left and the right, hoping to catch a glimpse of the elves who must live here, but their dwellings were well-camouflaged or deep in the trees and she saw nothing. Mindful of Glorian's admonition not to speak, she didn't ask any questions; although she was intensely curious where everyone was, it would be a shame to have made it to the village only to end up leaving a nasty stain on their nicely manicured street.

At length they reached the hill, passing through a gap in a low rampart that ringed it at the base. She felt something, a ripple or a flicker, when they went through the opening, leading her to conclude that it was warded in some fashion; this inference was reinforced when the archers did not enter, leaving Glorian and Nameless to escort her the rest of the way by themselves. The threat of an arrow in the heart was, it seemed, no longer required.

Once inside the earthworks, Ambrosia begged for and was granted a brief rest. Leaning back against the grassy embankment, she sighted up the slope, which was densely carpeted by fescue flecked with clumps of aging wildflowers in shades of purple, red, orange, and yellow, like random daubs of paint on a rich green canvas. The fragrance seemed to drift down the hill and puddle at the base into a heady mixture of aromas. From here, the butte looked even steeper than it had from a distance; any more of an incline, she thought, and the vegetation itself might have had difficulty clinging to the sides. She could see a path winding around and around the hill, cut into the side to keep its surface level as it ascended like the thread of a screw.

This was an ascent she did not look forward to making.

At length, Nameless and Glorian prodded her back into motion, leading her along the inside of the earthen bulwark until they reached the trailhead, at which point they began climbing. Unlike the dirt paths they'd been on until now, the spiral track was surfaced with crushed white stone brought in from who-knew-where. She figured this must have been done to reduce erosion, assuming it ever rained around here; for all she knew the elves skipped around with magic watering cans tending to the trees and flowers, while forcing inclement weather to pass them by.

They trudged along, gravel crunching under their feet; the path spiraled upward, around and around. When the avenue came back into view, they had risen nearly to the tops of the surrounding trees; she spotted the group of archers some distance away, returning to their posts near the wall. After another few circuits she was able see down into the woods, and could make out a number of paths winding through the forest. Wisps of smoke drifted into the air from what she assumed were dwellings or fire pits; the biggest plume emanated from a large oblong clearing off to the right, the space ringed by evergreens planted in a tight formation. Maybe it was a sort of picnic area, although it probably didn't count as a picnic if you lived in the woods full-time.

At last, they reached the top, where the path ended in a small, sculpted terrace with a bed of raked gravel surrounded by stunted trees in white clay pots. A circular bench ran around the edge of the gravel, with gaps at what she guessed were the cardinal points of the compass. From the largest gap, directly opposite where they stood, a narrower path emerged and meandered across the wide, flat top of the butte, ending at a huge fallen tree with a dark opening in its side. Ambrosia wasn't really interested in such details right now, though; she just wanted to sit down. She stumbled over to the bench and sagged onto it, facing outward, feeling her legs and chest burning with exertion. Glorian and Nameless remained nearby, still standing, neither of them even perspiring. It seemed that when it came to endurance, she had been sorely cheated.

As she gathered her breath, she took a look around. This appeared to be the highest spot in the basin; she could see the forest spreading like an apron in every direction, as if the hill were a volcano that spewed woodlands instead of lava. Directly in front of her, far off in the distance, the ground rose sharply up in a broad cliff wall the color of milk chocolate. Beyond, brown-shouldered mountains thrust upward, steep and craggy, tall enough to scrape frost off the rime of the sky. These jagged peaks formed a barrier of ice and barren rock that curved off to the right before being lost to view behind an obscuring veil of clouds and blowing snow. She had noted this range earlier, but it was much more dramatic from here, where she could see just how vast it really was.

Following the line of the cliff brought her gaze to the marshy lake they had skirted on their way to the village. Its placid water glimmered in the sunlight. A veritable flotilla of small, broad boats traced sluggish paths across the surface as tiny figures poled them through the shallows or hauled up the gleaming contents of fishing nets. Past that, dry land closed in again; the swamp became a narrow stream, a gap in the trees, spilling into a wide river that eased through the forest in the laconic manner of an old, mature waterway until, far off to what she thought was the north, it emerged into the barest hint of a broad green plain.

Nameless said: "Yexandor is waiting."

Ambrosia sighed and got back to her feet. She trudged with them across the smooth gravel, then along the walkway that led to the dead tree. It loomed large as they approached, becoming a curving wall of bark. Off to the right, massive network of roots—long since denuded of the earth that had once anchored it—reared up in a tangled, knotty ball; to the left, the bole ended in a jagged, weathered break, as if when it had come crashing down, its top three-quarters had snapped off and slid down the hill. The fallen behemoth had been so massive that it didn't taper at all along the entire length that remained, but instead ran as straight as a toppled column in some ancient temple of giants.

They stopped where the path widened and ended in front of the arch-shaped hole in the trunk. To either side of it, the bark had been peeled away and strange sigils carved into the wood beneath. She eyed the hollow; the opening was too symmetrical, and the darkness beyond much too thick and impenetrable, for either one to be natural. "What is this?"

"This is Yexandor's home," Nameless said.

"In a hollow tree? Like a woodpecker?" This earned her a derisive look from Nameless; behind her, she heard Glorian choking back a snort. "Now what? Do we just … go in?"

"*You* do," Nameless said, "if you can."

"What is *that* supposed to mean?"

"Do not be afraid. Nothing will happen to you, unless you deserve it." He gestured for her to proceed. She looked at him for a second, then turned and peered at the opening again. She still didn't think it could have formed on its own, but it didn't appear to have been carved, either; there were no tool marks along its edge, or anywhere else for that matter, not even where the strange bas reliefs illustrated the surface. She put her hand on the lip of the arch, then slid it forward into the darkness. Although she could see nothing, her fingers told her that they were still touching something solid. She glanced at Nameless and Glorian, standing side by side a few yards away. Glorian smiled and nodded his head in encouragement; Nameless just looked impatient.

She took a hesitant step forward, then another, entering the cool blackness of the interior. The floor felt slightly spongy under her feet; the moist air was redolent of wood and fresh sap, even though the tree must have been dead for decades if not centuries. She reached out to see if she could find the walls, but they weren't there; and when she looked over her shoulder, the entrance wasn't there either. She was alone in an impenetrable shadow. She thought about turning around, but from what Nameless had said this seemed to be some sort of test, and backing down was rarely the correct response to such things. So Ambrosia continued onward, one careful step followed by another; before long, she caught her foot on something, stumbled, and found herself caught by Glorian's waiting arms. He steadied her and set her upright on the white gravel; Nameless stood nearby, studying her. She looked at Glorian, dumbfounded, then at Nameless, then over her shoulder at the tree; she had tripped over the slightly raised threshold of the archway.

She said: "How did ... ? But I never turned around—"

"Misdirection glamour," Glorian said. "Space is not linear in there."

Ambrosia frowned. "That wasn't a funny trick."

"It was not intended to be funny," Nameless said, "nor was it a trick. Yexandor was examining you."

"But I was only in there for a few minutes."

"It only *felt* like a few minutes. There is also a time dilation glamour." Glorian pointed at the sun, which had moved far from where she had last seen it. "Yexandor spent hours trying to figure you out before he sent you back to us."

"He is ready," Nameless said. A pale, translucent, wavering figure stood just inside the arch, like a picture of an extremely aged elf painted on a canvas of mist. This apparition beckoned for them to enter, then flickered out of existence.

"That's Yexandor?" Ambrosia said, as Glorian guided her back toward the opening that had just swallowed up most of the afternoon.

"Yes."

"Is he a ghost?"

"No, that was just a projection. He is actually quite solid."

In front of them, Nameless entered the tree and vanished as if he had fallen into a tank full of black ink. Glorian sent her in after him. Going in felt different this time, almost like walking through a gossamer curtain; then she found herself within a large, barrel-shaped room chiseled out of the wood. Nameless stood nearby, waiting. She turned; she could see through the archway now, out to the hill and the sky and the surrounding woodlands. When Glorian entered, though, he seemed to materialize from nowhere, so she knew enchantments still operated on the entrance. This whole place was suffused with magic, she could feel it, like prickles on her skin.

They appeared to be in a sitting room, with a few benches carved out of the inner tree trunk and wooden doors in each side wall, but little else in the way of furnishing or decoration. One door was plain, the other adorned with carvings similar to those that surrounded the archway. Nameless went to the ornate portal, which opened at his approach. He ushered her through it, into a lozenge-shaped chamber that must have stretched almost to the splintered end of the giant log. The walls of this room were heavily decorated with painted scenes and bas relief sculptures, giving it a three-dimensional appearance, as if instead of being inside a hollow tree she had stepped into a forest. Its diameter was greater than that of the sitting room, which meant the walls were thinner; in fact, where the reliefs went especially deep, she thought she could see the veined underside of the exterior bark. A hill stood in the middle of the room, carved from the trunk—or rather, left behind when the trunk had been carved out around it—into an identical, albeit greatly downscaled, representation of the mound they had just climbed, down to its verdant slopes and clumps of flowers. She almost thought she could see tiny figures slogging up the spiral road that wound to the top, where a massive tree grew, painted in lifelike colors, reaching to the ceiling to join its spreading branches to the roof. Partway up the tree, within a hole that pierced it all the way through, she saw a small dodecahedron, glowing with an internal blue light. Ambrosia took a step toward it; Glorian took her left wrist in a surprisingly firm grip, while Nameless checked her with an arm across her clavicle. "No," he said.

"Is that the—"

"It is the Illata. Our treasure."

This was a new voice, old, brittle as glass. It came from an elderly elf who had just stepped out from behind the carved tree and was now moving stiffly toward them. He seemed to need a cane, but didn't carry one. As he approached, passing for a moment in front of the gem, it seemed as if it were glowing *through* him, as if he were as translucent as his projection had been. But when he stopped several paces away from her, he looked as solid as any of them. Whatever brief trick of light had turned him into cellophane had faded.

Her impression of him as a ghost had not been that far off, she thought. Shrunken, wizened, with skin like parchment wrapped around crooked purple veins, he could well have been the most withered, decrepit creature she had ever seen, although it wasn't as if she had extensive memories to draw on. He examined her with rheumy eyes the color of wet coal. He cocked his head to the left, then the right, then the left again, like a bird appraising a sparkly object it might want to steal.

"Um," she said. "Hello."

"What were you going to say?"

"I'm sorry?"

"You started to ask a question. *Is that the*, you said. What did you think the Illata might be?"

"I ... I'm not sure."

He watched her with those eyes.

"I think I was going to ask if it was the Heart."

"Were you, now?" There he went, cocking his head again. "What Heart would that be? It must be an important one."

"I can't remember," she said. Then: "It was broken."

"Was it?" Yexandor gave a little shrug. "That is an unfortunately common state for hearts. Perhaps in time you will remember more clearly." He stepped closer. "I think you have a question about *me* as well."

"Oh ... ah, no, I—"

Yexandor chuckled. "The child struggles to be polite," he said, to no one in particular, "but anyone can see what she is thinking." Then, to her: "Ask your question."

"Well ... look at you."

"Yes?"

"You're … you're … *old*."

"Indeed. Older than most, but younger than some." He wagged a palsied finger at Nameless. "Is that not so, Meliander?"

Nameless, no longer nameless, said: "Yes, that is so."

"But don't elves live forever?" Ambrosia wasn't sure where she'd heard this; it was just something she had taken for granted.

"That is a fiction invented by humans and their ilk," Yexandor said, "out of superstition, or envy, or darker motives." His pale face grew stony. "It must seem like immortality to them that our lives are measured in centuries, while their own flicker out in mere decades; some of their *holy men*, in their wisdom, go so far as to claim that we sold ourselves to their favorite fiend in exchange for eternal life."

"If they were truly wise, they would not harbor such beliefs," Meliander said.

"I said they *claim* it, not that they *believe* it." To Ambrosia: "It is true that elves do not show the effects of aging, leading those who are granted less time in these lighted realms to think that we must go on forever. But inside—" Yexandor pressed his hands to his chest and took a step closer. "Inside, the care of years wears us down, as it does every living thing. Even the great trees must one day return to Shandan's embrace; could anyone expect less of we who walk beneath them?"

"I suppose not," she said.

"Indeed. Of course, Shandan *has* made us the longest-lived of the races." He looked thoughtful. "Except, perhaps, for the dragons."

"You have dragons here?"

Yexandor smiled thinly. "Not *here*, no." He took another step forward; the closer he got, the more ancient he looked. "But I have not answered the question you are too polite to ask directly. You want to know why I look the way I do."

She felt herself flush, embarrassed.

"Most elves do not become as you see me; most elves, as they approach the end, simply … fade. But I have spent the greater portion of my life in pursuit of esoteric knowledge, seeking ways to protect what is left of our society, to restore some faint echo of a place and time long since vanished. Without my research, this forest would be thin and drab, this village scrub and brambles. Without my research, the elves would be weak, scattered, scraped thin across the lands of men, waiting to see which would be the last to die."

That all sounded very dire. She wasn't sure what to say about it, if she should congratulate him or offer sympathy for the terrible price that his pursuit of powerful magic—which, she knew, was what he meant by *esoteric knowledge*—had exacted. And the price *had* been terrible; now that he had come so close that she could have touched him without even extending her arm, she appreciated just how badly he had been ravaged. He looked as though his body had been drained of everything soft and fluid, left dry and brittle, a dead leaf just before the wind plucked it off the tree. The *care of years* had not worn him down to this; something else had done it. Still, she saw nothing feeble in his eyes as they glittered from the sunken recesses of his face. She wondered about the lost world he had alluded to, which those eyes must have once looked upon, what wonders it might have held, for him to have sacrificed so much of himself on its altar.

"I can see that you would like to know more," Yexandor said. "Let us talk briefly of what *was* before we move on to what *is*."

She nodded.

"Few of us remain who remember the time before the Breaking, when Shandan turned his attention upon us and found us wanting."

"And some who do remember it would like to forget," Meliander said.

If Yexandor heard that remark, which Ambrosia was sure he did, he chose not to acknowledge it. "In those days, before the great forest burned, when it stretched from sea to sea along the southern peninsula," he said, "the trees grew so tall that if you climbed to their very tops, where the air grew chill and the wind never ceased, you could see from the mountains all the way north to the plains of the Slash, even to the human city of Abacar on the southern shore of the northern ocean. Such trees could never have stood individually without toppling, but they had grown up together from saplings and their boughs interlocked. You could walk for miles along the large branches without fear of falling. We built platforms and lived up there, coming down to hunt and fish—"

"Wait," Ambrosia said. "Is this one of those trees? What we're standing inside?"

Yexandor glanced at Meliander, who said: "*I* certainly told her nothing about this."

"Am I right?"

"Yes. This was one of the few ancient trees that survived the catastrophe, though it fell not long after. We planted the new forest from its seeds. The carving you see there is a representation of what it looked like in life."

"Were *all* the trees so huge?"

"No, but each had its own use, no matter how small. Some bore fruit of such a size that it could hardly be carried. Some had leaves that never fell, but when cut they would serve to repel wind and rain for years before decaying. There were saplings that could be shaped into the finest bows, trees with great thorns that our fletchers made into the sharpest arrows, bark that could be——"

"I hope you are not planning to recite the virtues of *every* extinct plant that once grew in Torgon," Meliander said, "or we will be here until Glorian is as old as you and I."

Yexandor chuckled. At least, she thought it was a chuckle; it might have been a cough. "My friend always did have difficulty with patience," he said. Then, in a different tone: "Perhaps that is why we could come to no agreement when our villages began to encroach upon each other, when our hunters walked the same trails, our fishers trawled the same streams and rivers."

"You ..." She looked at Meliander, then back to Yexandor. "You fought? You two? Over territory?"

"Over territory, over game, over the right of way on paths."

"We behaved like men," Meliander said.

"Worse than men," Yexandor said.

Meliander snorted. "Are you sure that is possible?"

"Men think in the short term. This is to be expected, as the short term is the only term they have. But we elves must be held to a higher standard of behavior."

"As I recall, in the end, we were."

"We must hold *ourselves* to a higher standard," Yexandor said. "But we failed to do so, and when Shandan rendered judgment it was swift and terrible. It came on the very day that Meliander and I and our councils had traveled to neutral ground to discuss ways to end our conflict. We met at the northern edge of Torgon, at the top of a tall, flat hill where a lone, precarious specimen of the great trees grew, its roots clutching the summit like a great hand, reaching down through the soil to its lower-growing neighbors whose branches it could never quite touch."

Ambrosia didn't need to ask to know that he meant *this* hill.

"As we exchanged threats veiled as pleasantries, a great fire came into the sky, hotter and brighter than the sun. The earth shook when it exploded overhead; burning rocks fell like hailstones the size of fists. In that instant vast tracts of the forest were ablaze. From our hilltop retreat, all we could do was watch the flames spread through the forest as far as we could see.

"The fire alone would have been devastating, but it proved only the first part of our punishment. Even while the thunder from the first falling star had faded, a second one, even larger, struck just off the eastern coastline of the peninsula, throwing up waves of a size and fury such as we had never seen. The ocean poured over the barrier islands, then over the shore. It inundated the forest, scoured it of plants and elves and animals as it crossed from one side of our land to the other. Low-lying areas became saline marshes. Trees that survived the deluge withered and died as their roots drank saltwater from the earth. We who had provoked Shandan's retribution were forced to witness it, watching from the heights as our world was destroyed around us."

"You were the only survivors?" Ambrosia said.

"Not quite," Yexandor said. "A few others had endured the disaster, either on higher ground or clinging to debris or just because they were elsewhere in the Slash that day. Most eventually found their way here, to the highlands surrounding the hill where we had come to parley. Since then we have been rebuilding, reclaiming; but the soil here is not like the soil below, and the vast majority of our trees are lost forever. We will not see the like of the old forest again."

"What about that?" She indicated the gem. "The Illata? You have it inside the tree sculpture; is it from back then, too?"

Yexandor smiled thinly. "Yes, it is," he said. "We discovered it in the rubble of the foothills, where Shandan's fire had shattered an ancient tomb. Broken jewels littered the place, along with disks of silver, gold, and copper that had melted and then cooled. Most of it we left, but the Illata was ... different. Special. So—"

"So we stole it," Meliander said.

"We did not *steal* it," Yexandor said, in a weary, chiding tone of voice that told her this was a longstanding semantic disagreement. "By cleaving the cliff, Shandan was *giving* it to us as a token of hope in the face of so much destruction. We only took it because it was offered."

"The dwarves do not seem to think it was offered."

"They have never proved that the tomb was one of theirs."

"The entire barrow had been obliterated. What evidence was left for them to present, aside from the fact that it was located in the foothills of their mountain?"

Yexandor made a dismissive noise. "An accident of geography. They discovered that we had found a treasure and decided it should be theirs. This was all settled long ago."

"The dwarves do not think so," Meliander said.

"Enough," Yexander said. "Let us cease airing our differences in front of our guest." He reached out and took her hands. His grip was light, his skin dry and papery. He studied her face intently, staring at her, or *through* her. Supposedly he had already spent hours examining her when she had been wandering in the dark; hadn't that been enough?

Finally he said: "You are not from around here, are you?"

Ambrosia wasn't sure what she'd been expecting to hear, but that wasn't it. "No," she said. "At least, I don't think so. Are you going to ask me what my sign is?"

Yexandor cocked his head. "Is that a common greeting where you come from?"

She opened her mouth, then closed it, then said: "I don't know."

"Where *do* you come from, I wonder?"

"So do I."

Meliander said: "Glorian is of the opinion that she has been enchanted."

Yexandor's gaze flicked to Glorian and his thin lips twitched into a faint smile. "Oh, she most definitely has been enchanted," he said, "and if I am not mistaken she is not the only one."

Glorian turned bright red.

Yexandor looked back at Ambrosia. He released her hands, reached forward. The skin that stretched across the small bones of his fingers was thin and dusty white. "May I?" he said.

She felt an impulse to shy away; she hadn't experienced any reluctance or discomfort when he had touched her before, and wasn't sure why she did now. Maybe it was because he had felt the need to ask for permission this time. Still, did she really have a choice? She nodded agreement; the ancient elf closed his eyes and his hand began to shimmer, a faint light tracing the edges of his fingers, running along the lines of his palm.

She said, "Um——"

"Do not be afraid. He will not hurt you." Meliander said, putting a hand on her shoulder, though she was hardly reassured when he pulled back hastily as Yexandor's fingers were about to touch her. They brushed her stomach lightly, then gave a little push, firm enough to make her exhale. Yexandor opened his eyes, looking slightly confused; then he frowned and pushed a little harder. She had no idea what he was trying to do. Whatever it was, it didn't seem to be working as he'd expected. He pulled his hand back and examined it, as if he thought he might have picked up some sort of residue from touching her; then he pushed it into her again, harder still, with the same result.

She decided she didn't care for this peculiar exercise. "Would you mind not doing that again?" she said.

Now Yexandor seemed truly perplexed. He looked at Meliander. "Where did you say you found her?"

"Near the edge of the forest, not far from the eastern entrance to Dolvendelve, just before the dwarves set off a landslide to block everything off."

"We did not see her enter the woods," Glorian added. "Her trail just started out of nowhere."

Yexandor eyed her, then reached out again, but this time she stepped away. "Why do you keep poking me?" she said.

"I am not poking you. I am trying to hear your music."

"My what?"

"The music of your strings," he said. "But I cannot get through to them. Something is preventing me."

"I'm not trying to—"

"I know. This resistance is passive, innate; it is something that you are, or that was done to you, not active opposition."

"I was right!" Glorian said. "She *is* under an enchantment!"

"Yes. A powerful one."

"Can you break it?"

"I think not."

"Not even with the Illata?"

Yexandor half-turned to look at the glowing gem, then turned back to Ambrosia. "Perhaps. But it would be difficult, and as likely to kill both of us as to counter whatever magic has been laid on her."

Ambrosia, not liking the odds Yexandor had just laid out, said: "Can we not try that just now, then?"

He nodded slightly. "It would be ... premature, to say the least."

"What should we do?" Glorian said. "Will you let her stay?"

"I need time to think. She may be what she appears, or she may be something else, but I do not think she is dangerous. I will not turn her out into the forest. Not yet." Then, addressing Meliander: "Stay here. You and I must talk." Addressing Glorian: "Stay close to her. Keep her safe, and keep us safe from her."

"I will," Glorian said. He took her elbow and started to guide her out.

"And before you go ..."

Glorian stopped. "Yes?"

"I will take her wand and dagger. For safekeeping." Ambrosia watched in some disappointment as Glorian handed them over; not that she knew exactly what they did or how they worked, but they were far and away the coolest things she possessed. They hadn't come up in the discussion, and she had been hoping to get them back.

Well, at least with Yexandor hanging onto them, she didn't have to worry that they would get stolen.

~~~~

The throbbing pain in his head, not to mention just about every other part of his body, seemed to be waking Bernard up according to some kind of predetermined schedule. After the dwarves had pummeled him—or rather, Brannoc—into the ground, they'd started in with the kicking and the stomping, and he'd been sure they wouldn't stop until he was nothing but a smear on the floor. Bernard had hovered just above Brannoc's shoulder, a horrified, helpless onlooker, not feeling any of what Brannoc must be suffering, until finally the rogue had gone unconscious. At this point Bernard had found himself returned to the driver's seat of their shared flesh vehicle, and got to experience first-hand the effects of Brannoc's beating; the accumulated trauma crashed over him like a wall collapsing, and he'd passed out almost immediately.

After that, the dwarves must have dragged him away and locked him in a tiny cell carved of rough stone, illuminated only by a dim flicker that found its way through the barred window of an iron door a little taller than a garden gnome. If the cell had been vertical it might charitably have been described as closet-sized, but it was much longer than it was tall so it was more like a morgue drawer than a nook for hanging clothes. Bernard couldn't squirm around very much, because his wrists and ankles were manacled to chains attached to anchored rings, but even if he hadn't been tied down he still would have been unable to sit up. Not unless he felt like cracking his skull on the ceiling.

Unable to move and sore all over, he lay there for a while feeling sorry for himself, then finally fell asleep again. The next time he awakened it was to the sound of a key turning in the lock. After a moment, the small, thick door swung outward to reveal a dwarf, or part of one, anyway; short as the fellow was, the cell opening was still only about as high as his chest. The jailor bent over and peered inside; Bernard raised his head as far as he could and peered back, which meant he was looking at the dwarf from between his own clownishly large feet. He was hardly an expert on dwarves, but this one seemed rather bulky and disheveled, with knotty muscles and unkempt hair the
~~~~

color of cracked shale offsetting skin like sandstone. The fellow wore a ridiculously wide leather belt, as if he had just wandered by on his way to a power-lifting contest; the belt was festooned with black iron keys and mysterious gadgets but, Bernard was relieved to see, nothing that resembled the medieval sort of torture implements that frequently turned up in movies during situations like this one.

Bernard said: "Are you here to let me out?"

The dwarf stared at him.

"Is that a no?"

Stare.

"What if I ask nicely?"

Blink, then stare.

"Batman called," Bernard said. "He wants his utility belt back."

That remark earned him a few more blinks; then the dwarf unleashed a torrent of words, none of which sounded reassuring. Of course, his voice was so harsh and stony, he would probably sound threatening even while crooning any random title from Bernard's mother's collection of adult contemporary music. Bernard didn't bother saying anything else; after a little while the jailor glanced up the corridor, then backed away and slammed the door shut. His footsteps retreated, then faded; but before long Bernard started to hear dwarven voices rumbling, sounding simultaneously faint and nearby, as if several of his captors had gotten together and were attempting to whisper. He was pretty sure they were talking about him, but had no idea what they were saying. He hoped it was something about giving him a meal and a hot bath. He wondered if Brannoc would be able to translate, if he were here.

Sorry, Brannoc thought. *I speak elvish, but it's hard to find a tutor to teach dwarvish. I doubt they're planning to bathe and feed us, though.*

"Welcome back," Bernard said. "Did you have pleasant dreams?"

They were pleasanter than this.

"Yeah, well, I'm still finalizing my escape plans."

Let me see where we are.

Bernard remembered from his own experience that while he hadn't seen directly through Brannoc's eyes, he was generally forced to view things from Brannoc's perspective, so he lifted his head and looked around, giving his invisible companion a chance to inspect their cell. The light from the door grate was dim as ever, but his eyes had had plenty of time to adjust. After a little while his neck got sore and he lowered his head again. "So what do you think?"

I've been in worse situations than this.

"Really," Bernard said.

After a pause, Brannoc said, *Well, maybe not.*

Bernard grunted. "I wish I knew where Mercy was."

Mercy? You're unlikely to find any mercy here.

"Not that kind of mercy. This is a girl."

It has been my experience that mercy is to be sought from neither girls nor women.

"No, Mercy is her *name.*"

That's a strange name.

"It's a nickname. Her real name is Mercedes."

That's even stranger. Could this girl get us out of here?

"I don't know."

Then of what use is she?

"She might be a sorceress now."

Might be?

"Yeah, a lot has happened lately, and I'm not sure what … quiet, they're coming."

I am not the one making noise.

Footsteps approached again. The door creaked opened to reveal two new dwarves. They bent over to stare into his slot-like prison. The jailor dwarf stood behind them, talking to them under his breath. Maybe he was selling tickets and giving tours. *Come see the human, first time in captivity!*

The jailor stopped muttering; the two newcomers stepped aside and Bernard's old friend Granite stepped forward. He reached in and grabbed a stubby handle in the floor that Bernard hadn't noticed before, then gave it a pull. The entire bottom slab of the cell rolled out along a hidden track, smooth and silent, until it came to a jarring halt by crashing into the opposite wall. Bernard found himself treated to the unique experience of having three dwarves bend over him, poking and prodding and grunting like an alien surgical team trying to find his tender spots. It turned out they were everywhere.

Finally they stopped examining him and softly conferred amongst themselves, their voices like stones being shaken around in a metal box full of gravel. The larger of the two new dwarves—with glossy onyx skin and shockingly white hair—said the least and was, apparently, in charge; the other two seemed to be reporting to him. Finally the second newcomer, a smaller figure with a copper patina and hair the color of gold, gestured at his bigger companion. "Round-ears, this is Filothandiar, boss of Dolvendelve," he said. "He has questions."

"You speak English!" Bernard said.

"I do not know what is *English*," Copper said after a moment, "but I can make the round-ear talk." His larynx didn't seem quite structured for human tone and language; he sounded harsh and rumbly, but at least his words were intelligible.

"English is … never mind, I understand."

"Good." Copper looked at the boss, who grumbled something that Copper translated as, "What is your name?"

At least they were starting out easy. "I'm Bernard."

Filothandiar's voice rumbled something else. Copper said, "Why are you here?"

"I was out walking along the cliffs and there was a rockslide, and I ran into the cave to get away from it, and then these three dwarves came out and attacked me, and——"

"Slower," Copper said, raising his hands. "Go slower."

Bernard repeated himself at a lower speed. Copper listened, then translated. Judging by Filothandiar's reaction, which was to spit near Bernard's head, the boss found this version of events less than credible. Then, to Bernard's astonishment, Filothandiar started holding his stubby hands up to his ears and mincing around the corridor. Copper and Bernard both stared at this for a little while; then Copper said, "The boss believes you are a spy and an elf-lover."

"That prancing around means elf?"

Copper used his stubby fingers to make crowns on either side of his head. "Pointy-ears," he said. "Elf. Same thing."

"Well, tell him I've never met an elf in my life."

Copper dutifully translated. Filothandiar glared and grumbled, sounding like he was shaking several large rocks in a bag of sand.

"He doesn't believe me, does he?" Bernard said.

"You were outside the elf forest," Copper said. "What business does a human have there except to spy for the elves?"

"Why would I be spying?"

"Spying dwarven strength. Spying to see what we are doing."

"Who cares what you're doing?"

"*Elves* care," Copper said. "They know we are closing up the ways into Dolvendelve, getting ready for war."

"War? With who?"

Copper had been translating right along; now Filothandiar favored him with a look that clearly indicated he thought Bernard was either a liar or incredibly dense, or possibly an incredibly dense liar. Filothandiar gave Bernard's rolling slab a mighty kick, propelling it back into its slot. It slammed against the back wall so hard that he thought his teeth and hair and ears might keep going. Copper bent over to look in at him. "The boss says interview is over."

The door banged shut; Bernard heard the lock being thrown.

After a moment, Bernard said, "Well, that could've gone worse."

How so?

"They could have started kicking us again."

~~~~

"How do you think that went?" Ambrosia said, as she and Glorian descended the winding path from Yexandor's hill. Going down seemed much less effort than going up had been; maybe that was because she was no longer worried about what would happen to her when she got to the top. Of course, going with gravity instead of against it helped too.

"What do you mean?"

"Do you think he liked me?"

"There is little point worrying about that," Glorian said. "He is beyond being motivated by simple likes or dislikes."

"That can't be true. If he didn't care about anything, he wouldn't look and sound that way when he talks about the ... the disaster. He wouldn't have almost killed himself trying to restore the old forest."

"It is not that cares about nothing, just that he would not build a house out of such slender trees as *like* and *dislike*," Glorian said. "You certainly impressed him, though."

"I did, or the enchantment I'm supposedly under?"

"There is no *supposedly* about it; that is settled, you *have* been enchanted. The questions are who enchanted you, and why."

"Those are big questions."

"Yexandor will find the answers."

"You're awfully confident in him."

"Of course I am."

"Why?"

"Because he is *Yexandor*," Glorian said.

She thought this sounded perilously close to saying the sun rose in the morning because the sun rose in the morning, but it was apparent that her minder was starry-eyed about more than just her. She doubted she would get a more critical analysis out of him. "You aren't surprised that he let me stay here when he couldn't figure me out?"

"No. I do not think you are dangerous, and obviously neither does he."

"Why not? If I'm carrying such a powerful enchantment, *somebody* must be very interested in me, right?"
~~~~

"You would have to ask him. The last thing he tried to do failed, but not *everything* did. He was probably working glamours on you from the moment we entered the village. And he took your wand and dagger, after all, so he is taking some precautions."

"I guess so," she said.

"I am confused. Do you *want* to be turned out into the forest?"

"No, of course not. I just … I don't want to bring anything down on your village. Whoever put this spell on me probably wasn't doing it to be nice. I was running away from somebody, remember? He might still be looking for me."

"You only started running when the pond-dweller frightened you. Before that you were wandering around, as if you were trying to decide which way to go."

"I didn't know where I was or where I came from."

"So we have learned." By now they'd reached the bottom of the hill. Glorian paused here. "Would you like something to eat?"

"What?"

"Eat. Food?"

"Oh." Meliander and Glorian had given her some dried meat and dense bread in the woods; it had filled her up without being satisfying. Still, she could hardly complain; her own supplies didn't include anything edible, so if the elves hadn't shared she would have gone hungry. "Yes, please."

He smiled. "Good. I could do with some real food myself."

Instead of going back down the wide central avenue, Glorian took her into the forest, leading her along a narrow, winding path. Before long this brought them to a wall of closely spaced, cone-laden evergreens, their needles a much darker green than the leaves of the surrounding trees. This must be the outer ring of the clearing she had seen from the hill, she thought. The sound of voices and laughter and singing drifted through the pines; the resiny odor of the trees mingled with the savory aroma of roasting meat. A wide dirt track ran to the left and right, encircling the evergreens like a belt; Glorian made to go right, but she put a hand on his elbow and he paused, giving her an expectant look. Rather than speaking, she plucked a cone off a nearby tree, examined it, sniffed it; it smelled of earth and pitch and cinnamon.

"You are studying that as if you would like to eat it," he said, "but real food is just ahead. Is something the matter?"

"No. Yes. I'm just … nervous, I guess."

"About what?"

"It sounds … crowded. In there."

"It should be. This is the time for the evening meal. Would you prefer to come back later?"

She shook her head. "No, it's all right. Let's show everyone in the cafeteria the new kid."

"Cafeteria? New kid?" He gave her an odd look. "I am not sure what you mean, but you need not worry. No one will point arrows at you this time."

She followed him along the tree line until they reached an opening where the boughs had been bent back and woven with flowery vines, tying them up into a colorful archway. Glorian waited for an exiting clump of elves to pass—they went the opposite way, and didn't appear to notice the two of them—then took her hand and led her inside. She eyed the place, attempting not to look like a slack-jawed bumpkin. Several dozen elves were gathered here, the exact number fluctuating as they came and went through various gaps in the trees. Despite what Glorian had said, the space didn't really seem crowded; it could easily have accommodated a group several times larger than was present. "Is this everyone?" she asked.

"Not *everyone*, no," Glorian said. "There are always a few patrols out, and the stockade is always guarded. But this is about as full as it ever gets. Come." He guided her toward the large central fire pit, where a temple of charred logs smoldered, glowing orange from underneath; various sorts of cooking devices and implements stood in or around it, minded by attendants clad in soft leather aprons. Nearby, a low wooden platform supported a small band of musicians playing oddly-shaped instruments, while an even lower platform provided a space where a few elves danced and pirouetted in rhythms that, as far as she could tell, bore little or no relation to the tune being produced. Three or four elves were singing, their voices drifting through the air like spiderwebs wafting on a summer breeze, but she couldn't tell where they were; the harmonies just flowed and blended and became part of the susurrus of the place. Tables ringed the hearth. Diners sat at them singly, in pairs, in groups. They slurped from tankards, tore chunks of bread from loaves with their teeth, used their hands to scoop food out of communal wooden bowls.

Glorian headed for an empty table. Nothing obvious happened as they moved across the hard-packed earth—the band kept playing, the dancers kept dancing, the hungry kept eating—but still, she had the feeling that they were all watching her. Shifting her gaze to the ground, she said, "Glorian?"

"Yes?"

"Is everyone staring at me?"

After a moment, he said: "Staring? No. Noticing? Yes. You must understand, it is rare that a new elf appears, especially one as striking as——"

He broke off and stopped walking; she looked up and saw that they had been intercepted by a tall, rather broad elf, with dark hair and exceedingly bright green eyes. He was looking at her appreciatively. "So this is the little lost one," he said. "You brought back something interesting this time, my friend."

"She is not lost anymore, Orindel," Glorian said, letting go of her hand and throwing his arm around her shoulder.

Orindel chuckled. "Fear not, Glorian, I do not intend to steal her."

"I'm Ambrosia." She extended her right hand; Orindel looked at it oddly, then took it in an awkward grip. "Pleased to meet you," she said. He didn't seem quite sure how to respond, and when she released his hand he examined it as if she might have slipped him a piece of candy.

"Come and sit with us," Glorian said.

"I would like to, but dusk is my time to patrol."

"Another time, then," Glorian said, not sounding particularly disappointed. He watched Orindel head for a nearby exit as if making sure his friend wasn't going to sneak back and talk to her, then deposited her at the vacant table. It appeared to have been carved from a single huge stump, and could have seated at least twelve. Its surface had been planed flat and cut into three concentric sections: A low outer ring that served as a bench, then another ring excavated into a gutter for feet, and, in the middle, a tall circular tabletop. All were lacquered with some sort of preservative, and highly polished.

"What does Orindel patrol?" she asked as she got settled. Glorian remained standing beside her. "Does he go way out in the woods like you do?"

"No," Glorian said. "He stays inside the village, looking for sick trees, injured animals, woodwork that needs repair." His tone implied that while these were all very necessary things, *truly* virile elves went way out in the woods like he did.

Now that she was sitting she felt a little less exposed, and comfortable enough to survey her surroundings. Watching the elves sitting at their stumps, talking and laughing and eating their dinners and listening to their ambient music, reminded her of something, but she couldn't quite focus on it. She closed her eyes and tried to catch hold of an ephemeral memory, an echo of white tile and long tables, of trays and plates and noise and——

"Ambrosia?"

She opened her eyes. "Yes?"

"I asked what you would like me to get for you."

"I don't know what you have."

"Well, there is fish, and nut porridge, and bread, and game——"

"You don't have to read me a menu," she said. "Bring what you would eat yourself and I'm sure it will be fine." Then: "Is it always like this?"

She had puzzled him again. "Is what always like this?"

"The atmosphere. In here, I mean. It seems … revelrous."

"How would you expect it to be?"

"Well there was all that talk about the dwarves. And Yexandor's story, it was so … so gloomy. Like where you live now can't ever measure up to where you lived before."

"Few remember the days Yexandor told you about," Glorian said. "We do not pine for a world we never knew. As for the dwarves, well, they have been shaking their hammers at us for centuries, and nothing has ever come of it."

"Meliander seemed to think the situation was more serious this time."

"Meliander worries too much. The dwarves will cause some trouble along the edge of the forest, we will send them away with arrows in their leathers, and things will settle down again."

"I hope you're right."

"I am. You will see." He patted her shoulder. "You have no memory from before we found you, so you are insecure. You have no idea what to expect from the world, from us, from the dwarves, even from yourself. But you are among friends now. We can help you."

"Can you?" she said. "I feel like someone reached into my head and scooped out a big empty space in my mind. I don't know where I came from. I don't know what I was running from. I'm not even sure *Ambrosia* is my real name." She shook her head. "You told Orindel I wasn't lost anymore, but I am. I *am*, and I don't know how to get back."

"Your memories will return in time," Glorian said, "and if not, then you can start making new ones here, with us." He sighed. "I am not as wise as Yexandor or as experienced as Meliander, and not very adept at magic, and I cannot fill the empty space in your mind. But I *can* fill the empty space in your stomach. I will be back shortly." He gave her shoulder another squeeze, then headed toward one of the fire pits.

Almost as soon as Glorian had gone, a pair of elves—a male and a female—trotted over and sat down on the opposite side of the table from her, as if they had been waiting for her to be left unattended so they could pounce. The male was built more like Glorian than like Orindel, thin and tall, with a narrow skull, hair the color of tree bark, and eyes a shade of green normally found only in new leaves. The female was much slimmer than Ambrosia; dandelion curls framed a pale-cream face and eyes like smoky amber. She didn't seem particularly happy to be dragged over to meet the freak.

"Greetings," the male elf said. "My name is Nebandalex. You must be Ambrosia."

"I suppose I must," she said.

"Allow me to welcome you to Torgonderrer," he said.

"I've been welcomed already, thanks."

"Of course. I trust Glorian has been making you feel at home?"

"He's … trying."

The female elf cleared her throat conspicuously.

"Oh, and this is my partner, Shelliyan," Nebandalex said, as if he'd just remembered she was there.

"Hello," Ambrosia said; Shelliyan acknowledged her with a small nod and a half-smile. "So you two are partners? You patrol together like Glorian and Meliander?"

Shelliyan raised a golden eyebrow. "Not exactly," she said.

"We are partners as in a couple," Nebandalex said. "Together. A pair. Neither of us ranges like Glorian and Meliander." A grin crossed his face and quickly vanished. "And you? Talk under the trees names you a sorceress."

Word certainly got around fast in this village. "I don't really remember," she said. "I'm having a … a problem with my memory."

"Why do they name you a sorceress, then?" Shelliyan asked.

"Um. Well, I do have a wand."

For the first time, Shelliyan looked interested instead of just irked to be there. "May I see it?"

"I'm afraid not. Yexandor has it."

"Do you use it as a focus?"

"A what?"

"Something to concentrate and amplify your power," Shelliyan said, "as opposed to drawing on your own innate abilities. Do you find that you cannot cast glamours without the wand?"

"I don't know. I don't even remember how it works," she said. "For all I know it shoots fireballs, but I haven't used it or cast any spells since I've been here."

"Mmm. I see." Shelliyan had lapsed back into looking bored and mildly irritated.

"Do *you* use magic?"

"No," Shelliyan said, "but Glorian does, and speaks at tedious length about it to those who are willing to listen, and to many who are not."

"Shelliyan is an archivist," Nebandalex said.

"An archivist? Like a librarian?" Her two visitors exchanged a puzzled look. "Someone who keeps track of books?"

"She collects information about the natural world. Her specialty is herbs and fungi, not books or scrolls."

"Books and paper are quite scarce," Shelliyan said, her tone suggesting that this was something any idiot should know, "and those who have them, hoard them."

"She has been making a survey of all the species that can be found in the vicinity of the village, so that we know what grows nearby, and what we should preserve." Then: "We heard you have seen Yexandor. That is a rare honor. He has not come down from the hill since …" He trailed off and looked at his companion. "When was it? Last spring?"

"She does not care when you last saw Yexandor." To Ambrosia: "You must be exhausted after that long trek through the forest. We should let you sit in peace instead of bothering you with——" She gave Nebandalex a scorching sidelong glance. "——*rumors* and *silly questions.*"

"Surely we are not bothering her," Nebandalex said. Then: "Well, perhaps *you* are, being so standoffish."

"You need not humor him," Shelliyan said. "*I* never do."

Embarrassed, Ambrosia said, "Really, it's all right."

"Hmm. It was … interesting to meet you." Shelliyan stood. "I hope you get your wand and your memory back soon."

"Um, thank you."

Nebandalex hadn't gotten up. Shelliyan gave his collar a tug, but he waved her off; after a moment she pivoted and stalked away. Ambrosia watched her go; if she were a cat, her tail would have been straight up and twitching.

"I think your friend is upset with you," Ambrosia said.

"I will make it up to her later. You *did* see Yexandor, then?"

"Yes."

"And the Illata?"

She shrugged. "You can hardly miss that. It's right there in the middle of everything."

"So it is," he said. "So it is. Did you hear the story of how we *acquired* it?"

"Yes," she said, wondering what he was getting at.

"And surely you know that the dwarves ..." Nebandalex trailed off and moved his gaze to something behind her; a moment later she felt a hand on her shoulder. Glorian slid a trencher and large mug in front of her, then sat down next to her and looked at Nebandalex. "Nebandalex," he said, not affectionately.

The other elf tipped his head in greeting. "Glorian."

"Did you want something?"

Nebandalex got to his feet. "Nothing consequential. I was just chatting with your fair friend." He made what she took to be a gesture of farewell, tossed a nod to Glorian, and, without waiting for either signal to be returned, he departed, heading in the same general direction that Shelliyan had gone.

Ambrosia eyed the food. He seemed to have brought her one of everything: A puddle of thick paste that looked like unset plaster but smelled like roasted nuts; a green fish that had been broiled whole, head and all; a hunk of crusty bread; and a steaming, unidentifiable slab of meat resting on a bed of grilled root vegetables. There were no utensils. She found the idea of picking up the fish and biting into its scaly flesh mildly revolting, and the meat looked likely to burn her fingers, so she started with the porridge, scooping it up with a piece of bread. It tasted pretty much like it smelled, although the loaf turned out to contain a large number of odd little seeds that fizzed on her tongue.

Glorian, still looking off in the direction Nebandalex had gone, said: "Was he bothering you?"

Of course he waited until her mouth was full to ask a question. She shook her head and took a drink from the tankard, the contents of which looked like water but tasted like ginger mixed with black pepper and cloves. The unexpectedly strong flavor made her choke. Glorian observed this with some alarm and slapped her on the back a few times, which didn't help. At last her coughing fit subsided, and she turned to look at Glorian with watery eyes.

"You may want to start by sipping it," he said.

~~~~

The clatter of the lock awakened Bernard from an uncomfortable
~~~~

semi-doze.   The oven-sized door opened, revealing his usual jailor, backed up by three dwarves he hadn't seen before.   They rolled him out, then fussed with either end of his platform.   He heard a couple of bolts disengage, then the four of them lifted him up, slab and all, and loaded him into what looked like a long-handled black iron wheelbarrow.   It wasn't long before he found himself being trundled along dim, narrow passageways by a couple of sullen dwarves who looked like they'd rather be almost anywhere else.   He tried to keep track of the route they took, but the twists, turns, and unlit stretches hopelessly confused him and he soon gave up.

Pity, Brannoc thought.   *I was so looking forward to being able to find my way back to that nice comfortable cell after I escape.*

"Ha ha," Bernard said.   "And *how* exactly were you planning to escape?"

There's a lock pick up my sleeve.

Bernard glanced at his left arm and saw the outline of a tiny pocket stitched into the fabric, down near the wrist.   It was perhaps six inches long, and about the width of a pine needle.   "Doesn't do much good when I can't reach it."

That's hardly the only one.

"Well where are——" One of the dwarves made a grumbling noise that Bernard took as an admonishment to shut up, so he did.   Brannoc also fell silent, even though no one but Bernard could hear him.   He supposed that was better than having his head filled with yodeling or something.

Eventually, the dwarves pushed his conveyance into a small, square room, maybe ten feet on a side.   It looked like a dead end, but overhead, a shaft rose into darkness. Looking around, Bernard noted a gap of perhaps an eighth of an inch between the walls and the floor, leading him to conclude that they were on top of a lift. Sure enough, he soon felt a little lurch; the wall in front of him began scrolling downward as the floor was raised by a silent, smooth, invisible mechanism.   Before long they drew level with an opening in the forward wall. The elevator stopped when the floor was flush with the floor of the corridor beyond. He had to hand it to these little guys; they might be irascible and they might look like they were made of rock and metal, but they certainly knew how to engineer with precision.

The dwarves once again took up the handles and started wheeling him forward.   Although many small, dark openings beckoned from each side, they stuck to the gaslit main tunnel. The walls through here were adorned with glittering mosaics depicting dwarves engaged in a variety of productive activities, such as chipping gemstones out of a wall, excavating a tunnel, or carving a block of stone into a column. He didn't see one of them cavorting with Snow White, although he looked for it. At length, they passed through an archway elaborately engraved with armor and weapons; beyond, the mosaics turned warlike, gems and precious metals depicting scenes of carnage. Glittering rubies gathered in pools of impossibly red blood, from which skeletons formed of opals and diamonds stretched beseeching, claw-like hands toward their dwarven conquerors; forests of emeralds fell to silver axes while alabaster elves fled or cowered beneath copper trees. Brannoc, overwhelmed by avarice, kept begging Bernard to turn and examine the images much more closely than he cared to. *There's a fortune stuck into these walls! Let me look! If I could steal just one of those pictures, I could retire in style!*

Bernard wondered what *retiring in style* meant to someone like Brannoc. A hut with a roof? His own private army of pickpockets? The mind boggled.

They had come into view of a large square opening that loomed at the end of the corridor. Another elevator, he thought. A sound like the constant rumble of a low-grade rockslide emanated from the shaft. Unless he was quite mistaken, this noise was most likely being generated by dozens if not hundreds of muttering dwarves, which probably meant he was about to become the main attraction in some sort of violent spectacle, or perhaps a show trial followed by a public execution. He knew how these things worked.

The opening came and went. They stopped in the chamber beyond. As he'd expected, the floor proceeded to rise, pushing them up into a cavernous amphitheater excavated out of the rock. The lift clicked seamlessly into place, forming a broad, unbroken, mostly flat expanse of stone. A ten or fifteen-foot wall surrounded this, topped by tall iron spikes that curved up and inward, connected to each other by horizontal crosspieces. At regular intervals, this barrier supported massive gaslight braziers that provided harsh illumination from every direction, overpowering any shadows on the arena floor. Beyond the black spines, a rabble of dwarves looked down at him, pointing and jabbering among themselves. Many of them were snacking on kebab-style things that, from here, looked like flash-fried lizards, rats, and other small, subterranean creatures, reminding Bernard that the last time he had eaten was … when, exactly? Not that he wanted to consume vermin, but still.

One thing he hadn't realized until now: Brannoc's distance vision was *fantastic*. He wondered which score had determined that.

The elevator had brought him to the center of the arena, which was, of course, the worst place to be in such a structure. Now his minders wandered off and left him unattended. For a while nothing happened; he began to wonder if the evening's entertainment was going to consist of the audience watching him sit there in chains until he fell asleep. But then a dwarven voice boomed through the amphitheater, echoing off the walls and ceiling. Bernard, of course, understood not a word, but a couple of times he thought he heard a mangled version of his name. That couldn't be good.

After the announcements, footsteps approached from behind, but he couldn't turn his head far enough to see who or what was coming. Eventually, a copper-colored dwarf appeared next to his conveyance; after a moment Bernard recognized him as the one who had interrogated him earlier. He held Brannoc's quarterstaff in his thick hands. To his surprise, the dwarf leaned the staff up against the bin, then climbed up and began unshackling him.

Bernard said: "What's going on here?"

"A test."

"A test? What kind of test? Algebra?"

"You fight the champion. Put on a show. Entertain the dwarves." He shrugged as if to indicate sheepish embarrassment that his cohorts were so easily amused, but what could one do?

"Why should I want to entertain them?" Bernard said.

"You rather be in dungeon forever?"

Once the manacles were undone, Bernard stumbled down from the contraption, nearly planting his face on the rock floor. This elicited a round of laughter from the observers, although Copper didn't seem amused. The dwarf tossed him his quarterstaff; to his own astonishment, he managed to snatch it out of the air before it bonked him in the face. That had to be Brannoc's influence, as Bernard was notorious for not being able to catch anything that was thrown at him, from footballs to pillows, even when given a heads up.

Bernard tried a few experimental spins of the staff. It felt nicely balanced and comfortable in his grip, although if he actually tried to use it he would probably kneecap himself. He leaned it up against the crook of his arm before he could have an accident. Rubbing his sore wrists, working out kinks in various muscles, he said: "What do I get if I win?"

"You get to not die."

"Well, gosh."

Copper shrugged. "You win, maybe the boss will let you go."

"He will?"

"I said *maybe*."

"All right." Bernard assumed what he thought might be a combat stance. "Let's go. Where's your weapon?"

Copper found this immensely amusing, and was momentarily disabled by mirth. When he was able to speak again, he said: "You are not fighting *me*, round-ears. I am translator, I am envoy. I am not champion." He looked around, a little bit unhappily, and added, "Not supposed to be arena announcer, either, but they send me because I can talk to you, can explain."

"Oh, of course," Bernard said. "Then, who——"

"You will see. She will be here soon. Quiet, now. Must address crowd." Stepping away, the dwarf walked in a slow circle, hands raised, until the babble of voices receded to a murmur. Once he had silence, Copper bellowed an announcement in the dwarven language; the audience cheered and clapped as the little dwarf turned back to Bernard and squeezed his beard with both hands in what, apparently, was some sort of salutation or goodbye gesture. Then he toddled off across the arena and disappeared through a narrow, dark doorway that opened in front of him, closed behind him, and vanished so thoroughly it might as well never have existed. The applause continued the entire time Copper was leaving and culminated with most of the audience leaping out of their seats—not that they got any taller, but he could hear their feet hitting the floor—to begin hooting, clapping, and stomping. That could only mean their favored contestant had arrived. Resigned, Bernard looked around until he spotted his foe. She was the biggest dwarf he had seen yet, nearly four and a half feet tall. She had translucent skin the color of amethyst and hair a light shade of purplish-pink, a combination that made Bernard think of those little plastic trolls you saw in novelty shops and hanging from rearview mirrors; she was clad in armor made of overlapping black iron scales attached to a dense chain mesh. It covered her torso from her neck to her knees, where a pair of greaves took over, protecting her shins down to her boots, leaving her head and long, muscle-knotted arms bare. Her massive hands clutched the shaft of an enormous hammer. Bernard had seen such implements before, but only in sepia photographs of sweaty men driving railroad spikes or trying to impress their girlfriends by ringing the bell at the top of a carnival attraction. He gripped his quarterstaff tightly, wondering if it would shatter into splinters after the first blow, or if it would merely snap in half.

The dwarven champion paused beside the wagon, sizing him up; then she grinned, showing teeth that looked like gemstones. She raised her hammer and swung it in circles over her head, then brought it crashing down on the cart. There was a crack and a crunch and the cart broke into pieces, the platform flipping over a few times, one wheel rolling lazily away, eventually spiraling around and toppling over like a coin in some distant part of the arena. The assembled crowd of dwarves clapped and cheered and hooted; he just goggled at her. Those little plastic trolls never did anything like that.

In his head, he heard Brannoc's voice: *My turn now?*

"She's all yours," Bernard said.

Chapter 6

BY THE TIME Ambrosia finished her supper, she had gotten the hang of quaffing the strongly-flavored beverage——a blend of sap from various trees, boiled down, diluted with water, and spiked with herbs, according to Glorian——without choking. She never overcame her squeamishness about eating an intact fish, scales and head and tail, but Glorian had relieved her of that responsibility by devouring it himself. Now the bread and meat were merely pleasant memories and the remains of her porridge had congealed into a gummy encrustation. Just about every elf who had entered, departed, or spent any time in the dining area had stopped by for greetings and introductions, though she had quickly given up on trying to remember their complicated, multisyllabic names. Too bad she didn't have a guestbook and a pen; she could have made them all sign in. Glorian, playing the role of resident societal expert, made sure to tell her a few facts about each one's personality, place in the village, claim to notoriety. By scrutinizing his face and paying close attention to his tone of voice as each new visitor approached, she'd concluded that some sort of factionalism was at work in the village. He never whispered explicitly derogatory comments in her ear, and was perfectly civil to everyone who came over; nevertheless, a small but substantial percentage received a noticeably cooler reception than the others. Nebandalex had been the first and, perhaps because he had imposed himself on her while Glorian was off fetching food, most obvious example, but he had hardly been the last. She suspected the division had something to do with the situation regarding the dwarves and the Illata, but hadn't yet had the opportunity to seek clarification.

At last, the steady procession of curious bystanders wound down, and Ambrosia began to think she and Glorian might be able to leave; but just then Meliander appeared at the table with a small plate of food and sat down.

Glorian eyed him. "I was beginning to think you had gone back out on patrol without me."

"I have been with Yexandor." Meliander gave Ambrosia a significant look. "There was much to discuss."

"Me?" she said. "You were talking about me this entire time?"

"Not the *entire* time, no," he said. "We *do* have other things to be concerned about just now. But yes, you were one topic. Where you might have come from, what you might be, what to do with you."

"What I might be?"

"Yes. Yexandor is not sure of the answer, but he does not believe that you are truly an elf." Meliander, apparently a daintier eater than Glorian, took a small bite of bread, chewed it well, and swallowed, all the while looking at her thoughtfully.

"If I'm not an elf, what am I?"

"We do not know, but Yexandor thinks you might not be from this plane of existence."

"Yexandor thinks she is some kind of … of *demon*?" Glorian, scandalized, inspected her as if searching for horns.

"He was careful to point out that not everything that comes from beyond is demonic in nature, Glorian."

"So I'm from another dimension?" she said.

"Possibly."

"Then why do I look like an elf?"

"You do not look like an elf. Not really. Have you seen any female elves that bear you more than a passing resemblance?"

She thought about that for a moment. "I guess not."

"No. You have not. Our females are much slenderer than you, and shorter, and none has hair like yours. You are a caricature of an elf, or an idealization."

"You're saying that someone or something dressed me up like an elf and sent me here? Why?"

"We do not know. Yexandor is consulting the Illata for help."

"I don't understand. What would the Illata know about it?"

"The Illata is a power source. It knows nothing itself, but serves to amplify the abilities of the one who uses it." Then, darkly: "These days, Yexandor can do little without it. I think it sustains him, even as it kills him."

"That is why he hardly ever leaves his tree anymore," Glorian said.

"He could just carry it with him, couldn't he?"

"One does not simply *carry* the Illata," Meliander said.

"Why not?"

"The stone invites … retribution."

"Retribution?"

"Death. Immediate, if one touches it with bare flesh, and——"

"He could put it in a pack. I have plenty that could fit it."

"——slow and lingering if one merely stays near it." Meliander used a finger to stir his nut porridge. "Yexandor will not bring the Illata down from the hill, lest its radiance sicken the rest of us as it has him." He shook his head. "That accursed crystal. I wish we had never found it."

"But then where would we be? Living in hovels, eating berries and bark? Living out in the Slash, in the cities, among *men*?" Clearly Glorian found this prospect horrifying.

Meliander made a helpless gesture. "Who can say? But we would not be where we are now, an armed camp, facing a needless conflict with the dwarves."

If they were going to start batting around *what-ifs*, this conversation would never end, and she would never get any sleep. "So how long will it take for Yexandor to figure out what's going on?" Ambrosia said, hoping to steer the topic back to something that might be answerable.

"How tall is a tree?" Meliander said. "He will have answers when he has answers. But he does not believe that you pose a threat, and he finds your situation intriguing, so you need not fear being put out of the village. He will have you back to the hill soon, to study you further, but for now Glorian will continue as your escort, and acquaint you with the village and its inhabitants."

"He's been doing that all night."

Meliander tipped his head, gave her a canny look. "As you say." Then, to Glorian: "She is exhausted. Take her out of here and let her get some rest."

Glorian nodded and stood, offering her his hand; she took it and allowed him to pull her to her feet. He led her to one of the festive archways, pausing a number of times for goodnights and farewells and see-you-soons before finally reaching the exit. He let her go through first; beyond, the path was dark and quiet. Glorian slipped past her, taking the lead again as they headed off into the woods.

"Are we going to your ..." She trailed off, wondering how elves referred to their abodes; surely they weren't called houses. "To where you live?"

"Yes, to my platform," he said. "It is not far."

"Where am I ... is there an extra ... ?"

He gave her a backward glance, his face pale in the dimness. "You may have my hammock. I will string a rope bed for myself, or sleep on the floor."

"I didn't mean—what?"

He had stopped suddenly, and was looking around. "I thought I heard ... never mind, nothing is there." He started to turn, then suddenly crumpled to the ground as if felled by a blow to the head. She opened her mouth to shout for help, but never got a word out; something hit her hard across the back of her legs, the blow knocking her to her knees. A second, sharper strike to the back of her head sent pain flaring from the top of her spine down to her feet and up through her skull.

And the night went from dark blue, to purple, to black.

~~~~

Brannoc's method of fighting a stronger, slower foe turned out to involve a lot of ducking, dodging, running, and jumping. He couldn't win this fight through force, that was obvious; perhaps he hoped to keep evading his foe's attacks until she became tired and started making mistakes. If that was the plan, it didn't seem to be working; wearing her down would probably take only slightly less time than waiting for her to die of old age. From his vantage point as a disembodied presence floating just behind and to the right of Brannoc's head, Bernard always trailed along a hair after his body. Several times, this had given him the unsettling experience of seeing Amethyst's massive weapon come straight at, and then through, his face. If he had been a helium balloon tied to Brannoc's shoulder, he would long since have been popped.

The arena turned in circles as Brannoc did a backflip to avoid a low sweep of the hammer, then continued cartwheeling across the floor while his foe pursued as fast as she could. This tumbling routine left him standing in the center of the amphitheater, near the smashed cart and his abandoned quarterstaff, which he had left behind as a useless impediment to maneuverability at the beginning of the match. It was worthless against Amethyst's armor and dense body structure; hitting her with it would be like trying to smash a granite statue with a wooden dowel. No doubt the dwarves had had a good chuckle about that when they'd returned his weapon.

He paused there catching his breath while Amethyst came lumbering along, keeping a careful eye on her approach. As she drew closer, he started picking up pieces of broken wood and iron; when he had a good armful, he began to retreat toward the wall, throwing bits of scrap at her as he went. The ones that found their mark just bounced off without doing visible damage to her armor or her skin, but she seemed to find this strategy annoying; she made a face and, putting on the dwarven version of a burst of speed, closed the distance between them. Brannoc winged the last of his makeshift projectiles just as she charged, swinging the hammer around in a slanting uppercut which, if it connected, would send his head into the left field stands. He was ready for this, though, and instead of dodging fell back fractionally, then grabbed the shaft as the weapon whistled by, seizing it just below the head. He only held onto it for a split second, but that
~~~~

was long enough for its ferocious momentum to yank him off the ground. He let go and went flying through the air, spinning like a trapeze artist; somehow he managed to parley this into a mostly controlled landing at the base of the inner wall that encircled the arena. Bernard's head was left spinning; if he'd been in control of Brannoc's body, he would be vomiting right now.

Amethyst came trudging over, sort of resignedly, as if she had decided this game wasn't fun anymore. When she finally arrived, she stood there looking at him, fidgeting the hammer back and forth between her hands, probably trying to decide what would be the best way to squash him without giving him the chance to embarrass her with more circus aerobatics.

Too bad he didn't have a stick of dynamite he could toss at her.

Suddenly she raised the hammer over her head and charged. As she brought her weapon down, Brannoc jumped up and back, planting his feet on the side of the wall; an instant later he sprang forward to land on the dwarf's shoulders. He hopped from there to the top of her head and then, using her skull as a platform, back-flipped to the inner the wall. He ended up perched on a narrow strip of stone, wrought iron bars behind him, an angry-looking Amethyst staring up at him from the arena floor.

On the other side of the inner wall, a narrow aisle encircled the arena, followed by another wall and, beyond that, the stands. He could see a number of openings in the second wall that might be ways out, but the gaps in the barrier were too narrow to allow egress. He took off running along the ledge, bent over to avoid cracking his skull on the bars as they turned inward overhead. He stopped beneath the first brazier he came to, perspiring in its envelope of heat. As Amethyst toddled along to catch up with him, Brannoc eyed the fiery pot. It appeared to be removable using the proper tools, which, of course, Brannoc did not have. Losing interest, he started to move on, but then Bernard noticed a round tube that came out of one of the spikes and ran into the bottom of the brazier. *Wait,* he thought.

Brannoc paused.

I think that's a gas line.

"A what?"

A gas line. My dad has one going to the barbecue on our patio.

"What is a barbecue?"

Never mind. I'll explain later. Bernard thought fast, trying to figure out if they could use this; Brannoc, meanwhile, kept casting glances at the approaching dwarven bruiser. *Try to get her to throw her hammer at us so it hits the torch. When she does, get us out of here as fast as you can.*

"Why?"

If we're lucky, it'll explode.

Brannoc was dubious. "Why would her hammer explode?"

Not her hammer, the bowl of fire.

"Oh, of course."

Brannoc obviously thought this idea was idiotic, but he had nothing better to offer and they couldn't keep running forever. He pressed his back to the bars, panting and sweating, waiting for Amethyst to arrive. When she did, she stood below them, gazing upwards. She gave her hammer an experimental sweep, but her height plus the length of the weapon's shaft left her a foot or so shy of the top of the wall. Realizing this, she let the hammer drop and started swinging it back and forth like a pendulum, apparently trying to decide what to do next. The audience, bored with the standoff, started voicing its disapproval; Bernard might not be able to understand their language, but boos were universal. Hearing this, Amethyst put her hammer aside to ham it up for the crowd a little, pointing at Brannoc and raising her hands as if to say *What can one do?* She mimed someone cowering and running away, prancing around in circles and looking behind her fearfully, as if she were being chased by a ferocious dog.

Bernard sensed that this parodic act stung Brannoc, could feel his body tense as he prepared to jump down at Amethyst, grab her hammer, and bash her head in with it. This was not at all the way Bernard's plan was supposed to be playing out; Brannoc was meant to bait *her* into doing something rash, not the other way around.

So Bernard took over Brannoc's body.

It wasn't difficult at all; he just settled back in, like slipping on a well-worn glove. The fact that the glove already had a hand inside it didn't seem to make much difference. Once he was back in control, he could feel the fatigue burning in his arms and legs and chest, the hammering of his heart, the roaring of blood in his ears, the ache of unhealed injuries that had been exacerbated by all the exertion. Brannoc had obviously pushed himself close to the point of collapse; perhaps his exhaustion had made it easier for Bernard to reassert control.

Did that mean Brannoc could do the same thing to him when he was in a similar state?

Well, he had other things to worry about right now. Taking hold of the warm iron, he leaned out from the wall and shouted: "Hey, rock-head!"

Amethyst halted her performance, turned, and looked up at him. Bernard used his free hand to flip her the bird; she cocked her head at him, evidently puzzled by the gesture. He stuck out his tongue and blew a raspberry at her. This elicited a few blinks, and then she razzed him back. Her thick tongue proved ill-suited to generating the proper sound, but that didn't stop her from adding it to her repertoire when she resumed her impersonation of him, mincing around with both middle fingers in the air, making noises like a defective whoopee cushion. Bernard quickly began to feel ridiculous. Amethyst wasn't going to fall for his taunting, he realized; she'd doubtless been in the arena dozens if not hundreds of times, and far from being infuriated by schoolyard antics, she turned them against him, making him look silly in front of the crowd. He would have to think up a different strategy.

That was hardly a strategy, Brannoc said.

Suddenly something clanged into the iron barrier behind him. Startled, Bernard let go of the railing and nearly fell, barely catching himself by hooking a knee around one of the bars. He cast a baleful look at the audience; it appeared that a spectator in one of the lower rows had become bored or irritated enough to throw something at him. Others picked up the idea, and shortly a veritable barrage of crap was bouncing off the fence: Food, bones, metal plates, even rocks. Who hauled *rocks* around with them? Did the dwarves bring them to the arena in sacks just to fling them at contestants they didn't like?

The booming voice came back, shouting something in dwarvish. The clatter of incoming material ceased, but whatever had just been announced didn't make the audience happy; they started hooting derisively and stomping their feet. The voice boomed something else and the noise stopped instantly, replaced by a low murmur as the spectators grumbled amongst themselves. Bernard, clinging to the bars, the top of his head getting toasted by the underside of the brazier, watched and waited; it wasn't long before a rough voice from below said, "Round-ears!"

He spotted his old friend Copper, scuffing along the aisle on the better side of the wall, kicking junk out of the way as if irritated by a mess he would have to clean up later. When he arrived, Bernard said, "What's going on? Is the fight over?"

"Fight?" Copper snorted. "Looked to me more like jumping and running away."

"You fight your way, I'll fight mine."

"I told you, I talk, not fight. Filothandiar says contest is a draw.

Says come down from there, come talk to him."

"Talk to him?"

"Yes."

"Last time he just yelled at me."

"I see. So you want me to tell him you rather stay here and keep *fighting*?"

Was this some sort of trick? Bernard glanced at the arena, where Amethyst was watching him; she had picked her hammer up, but was leaning on it like a gardener taking a break from hoeing. When she noticed him looking at her, she stuck out her tongue and razzed him again, but didn't make any threatening moves.

"Okay, I'll come down," he said.

Copper folded his arms and waited as Bernard knelt down and began climbing off the wall. He slipped almost immediately and landed on his backside on the arena floor. The audience thought this was just about the funniest thing they had ever seen; they laughed so hard he almost expected the vibrations to cause a roof collapse. Feeling sore and ill-used, Bernard slowly got back to his feet. A little way off, Copper waited beside a door that had been completely invisible before it opened and would be again after it closed. He headed that way, trying to ignore Amethyst as she trailed along behind him, mimicking his stiff walk and somehow making it look like a panic-stricken retreat, much to the crowd's delight. She didn't follow him out of the arena; she was probably going to hang around for a while and bask in the adulation of her fans. In any case she would have been superfluous, security-wise, as Copper had a couple of bruisers waiting nearby to make sure Bernard didn't try any funny business.

The four of them went through a small doorway beneath the stands, leading into a baffling warren of low, dim, narrow tunnels. Other than in one or two stairwells where he briefly had the space to stand up, Bernard was forced to remain stopped as they navigated the labyrinthine passageways in what seemed to be an upward-trending path. He attempted to draw Copper into conversation a few times, hoping to discover what Filothandiar was planning to holler at him about this time, but the dwarf remained stoutly uncommunicative. He didn't bother trying to engage the muscle. Brannoc, sullen over having been given the boot during the match, wasn't talking either, so except for one time when they passed near a jabbering group of exiting spectators, they walked in silence.

Eventually they passed through an iron door that apparently kept the rabble out; the dark halls beyond were rather sumptuously decorated with wall hangings and reliefs, and they didn't encounter any more proletarian riffraff. Bernard, walking in the middle with Copper ahead of him and the two bruisers behind, being led through empty corridors in isolation and utter quiet, felt like a condemned prisoner on his way to the electric chair, or whatever the dwarven equivalent was. The steam chair, maybe. He kept telling himself that if the dwarves wanted him dead, they could have just left him in the arena. After all, it wasn't as if he'd been winning.

I was doing fine until you *took over,* Brannoc sniffed. Bernard let that one go by, and Brannoc went back to sulking.

Eventually the corridor turned into a spiraling ramp that wound sharply clockwise around a central shaft of rock. Emerging at the top, they entered a wide chamber carved into the rock where, happily, Bernard could straighten up without breaking his head open on the ceiling. To the left, instead of a wall, the room was open to a vast empty space. After a moment he realized he was in a skybox, looking down upon the arena. The stands were almost empty now; Amethyst was gone, and a few dwarves were doing maintenance work, cleaning up the wreckage of the wheelbarrow and patching spots where Amethyst's hammer had knocked chunks out of the wall or floor. He wondered if one of them had picked up his quarterstaff.

"If you are done staring out window, Filothandiar would talk to you now," Copper said.

Turning, Bernard saw the onyx-skinned dwarf sitting on a large seat chiseled out of the stone. A tiny dwarf—a child?—stood next to him, holding an enormous mouth-horn and staring at Bernard with unblinking eyes. On the other side of the throne, a table held the remnants of a meal, reminding Bernard once again that he hadn't eaten in … how long? A day? Two? He tried not to start drooling.

The dwarven boss rumbled something in that distant landslide voice of his. "Filothandiar was very impressed with your performance," Copper said.

"Um, okay," Bernard said.

"You have passed the test."

"Test?"

"Yes. I told you it was a test. You forget? I did not see you get knocked on the head."

"Okay. But I still don't know what the test was for."

"It was to see if you can do the job he wants you to do."

This was getting weirder and weirder; first they beat him up and imprison him, then they throw him into combat, and now they were offering him an employment opportunity. "You want me to do a *job* for you?"

Copper blinked a couple of times. "Do you not hear good? All that booing in arena hurt your ears? I can talk louder."

"No … No, I can hear fine," Bernard said. "I'm just surprised is all. What sort of a job are we talking about here?"

"You are burglar, right? Creep in and steal things?"

Bernard didn't feel quite comfortable agreeing with that characterization, but that *was* what Brannoc had come here for; and the way Copper had said it, he figured it must play into whatever they wanted him to do. "I've … been known to do that, yes."

Copper looked at Filothandiar and nodded; the boss nodded in return. Turning back to Bernard, Copper said: "We want you to go into the forest and steal the Brisindeld for us."

"Steal the what now?"

"The Brisindeld."

"What's a Brisindeld?"

"Is a gem. Big, glowing."

"And it's in the forest?"

"Yes. In the elf village."

"So … you're jewel thieves?"

"Dwarves are not thieves! Elves took it from *us* a long time ago! We think maybe you can find it and bring it back."

Bernard considered this. "How long ago did they take it?"

"Why that matters?" Copper said.

"Well I'm just curious, if it's been years and years, why all of a sudden you're asking some random person to go get it back."

"Are you *some random person?*" Copper said. "No. You are not. You are a *robber* who sneaked into our mountain hoping to steal from dwarves. But dwarves catch you. Yes, we catch you. We watch you in arena. You look to us like an opportunity. Like we were *meant* to catch you. Like you were *sent.*"

"No one sent me here."

"So you say, but maybe you were sent without knowing it. Maybe you will succeed for us where others fail."

"Others? What others?"

Copper suddenly looked nervous, as if thinking he may have overstepped. "I am not sure I am supposed to tell you that," he said, glancing at Filothandiar; the onyx overlord sat in his big chair, watching them, evidently expecting Copper to hammer out the details of their arrangement or declare it untenable on his own while he,

Filothandiar, picked nuggets of meat off the cold bones of his meal.

"Nobody else understands what we're saying, right?"

"No."

"Then don't worry about it. I guarantee *I'm* not going to tell on you." Copper still seemed reluctant to elaborate on his comment, so Bernard said: "Look, if I'm going to do this, I need to understand the situation. So I wouldn't be the first one you sent?"

"Not first, no," Copper conceded. "We sent … others. Before."

"And what happened to them?"

"Some come back without gem."

"And the rest … ?"

"Not come back at all."

"They died?"

Copper shrugged.

"When was the last time you tried?"

The dwarf considered this. "A year I think? Almost."

"Who did you send that time? Another thief?"

"No, Rittandic magic-using type. It told us it could infiltrate elves and bring back gem. It got inside elf village and we received information from it for a while, but then we never hear from it again."

"So … Hold on. Did you say *it*?"

"Yes, it."

"Is that what non-dwarves are to you? Just *things*?"

Copper blinked at him a few times. "You not know how it is with Rittandics?"

"How *what* is?"

Evidently this marked Bernard as a provincial hayseed. "Sometimes Rittandics born not male nor female," Copper explained. "They have no, what would you say, parts of either kind. Everyone calls them *it*. Is not an insult."

"No *parts*? How would that even *work*?"

Copper made a dismissive noise. "You think I ask?"

"Huh." Those poor Rittandics must love going through life being referred to as if they were inanimate objects or animals of an unknown gender. "Well, so, what did they do to him?"

"Unknown."

"What will they do to *me*?"

"Nothing," Copper said, "unless they catch you."

~~~~

Ambrosia came groggily awake. She tried to sit up, but couldn't; she seemed to be strapped to something solid, like a wooden plank or
~~~~

table. A gag, leather by the taste of it, kept her from crying out; a blindfold, also, she thought, leather, prevented her from seeing anything. She twisted her body left and right, hoping to loosen her bonds or make some noise, but the fetters didn't offer enough play and the rigid backing was too heavy for her to shift. If anything, squirming around only made the knots get tighter. She gave up struggling and lay still, listening. There wasn't much to hear: Muted birdsongs, faint rustling, an occasional wooden creak. She felt no movement of air on her skin, and although she could smell the loamy scent of the woods, the odor seemed attenuated. She had no idea what sort of structures or buildings existed in the village—houses, sheds, hollow trees—but she must be inside one of them. Realizing that she had not yet seen an elven house, she wondered what they looked like. They were probably quite small. She hoped she was taking up a lot of floor space and enormously inconveniencing the resident.

Who had clobbered her? It must have been another elf, she thought; after all the security she'd seen, the secret stairs, the high fence, the archers, the patrols, the magical wards, she found it hard to believe an intruder could sneak into the village, make his way to the clearing, and wait there for the opportunity to hit her over the head and drag her away. But why? She'd been in the village for less than a day, hardly long enough to make enemies. Maybe Glorian had been the real target, and she'd merely had the misfortune to be with him. Maybe he was here too, trussed up like her. Immobilized, blinded, and silenced, she had no way to find out.

Ambrosia heard something then, a rustling, whisking sound, that made her think of dry grass in the wind. This was followed by soft footsteps that came over to her. Although she couldn't see anything, she felt herself being inspected. Fingers touched her throat, the back of her head; they brushed a tender lump, making her squeak. The fingers withdrew and a voice said: "Is she getting enough air with that thing in her mouth?"

"She can breathe," a female voice answered tartly.

A male and a female. A couple? Nebandalex and Shelliyan?

"This is risky," the male voice said.

"And leaving a rogue sorceress free is not? We've no idea why she's here or what she can do. She might try to stop us."

"You think so?"

"Is it a coincidence that she arrived *now*?"

"It could be."

"I say it's not."

Uncomfortable silence ensued. Ambrosia felt their eyes on her.

"We only have to keep her here until tomorrow evening," the female said. "After that, her presence will no longer be a threat."

"I mislike this."

"Yes, you have made that clear. It changes nothing." Then: "Glorian?"

"Humiliated and angry, of course. He has assembled the trackers into groups to start searching for her immediately."

She gave a small, brittle laugh. "Of course. What of Yexandor?"

"I am told he is doing divinations. Casting twigs."

"More problematic than Glorian hunting for footprints and bent branches, but my glamours will hinder his finding her."

"Are you sure? He has watcher glyphs inscribed everywhere, you know."

"And I have spent months studying and subverting them," she said. "His glyphs will show him nothing."

No reply.

"You have trusted me for nearly a year while we worked toward this day. Trust me a little longer. Tonight, it will be rectified."

Long pause. "All right," he said at last.

"Thank you," she said.

"I should go. Glorian will want me to aid in the search."

"Go, then. I will remain here a while."

"You are not going to … ?"

"Harm her? No. You have my word." She laughed again, then said: "Go and join Glorian's little search band; throw him off the trail if you feel the need. Just be sure to meet me at the hill come nightfall."

"I will." Ambrosia heard him depart.

There was a brief quiet, then footsteps once again scuffed across the floor toward where Ambrosia lay, stopping beside her. She felt a toe nudge her gently in the side. "Very interesting," the female voice said. "Under other circumstances I should be pleased to explore you from the inside, but as this shall be my last day in this benighted village—indeed, the last day this village will exist—I will not get the chance. A pity, really." Her captor murmured something inaudible, a chant, a spell; when she spoke again, her words seemed to be drifting in from far away. "A great, great pity, indeed."

~~~~

In the end, Bernard agreed to do what Filothandiar asked. After all, it wasn't as if he really had a choice; there were a hundred different ways that he could die here in the dwarven city, but, it seemed, only
~~~~

one way that he could leave alive.

Once he accepted their generous offer, the dwarves became his buddies. Copper demonstrated this by finally introducing himself properly; his name was Ardegain. In a further display of trust, Ardegain traveled with only one hefty bodyguard instead of two when he escorted Bernard out of the skybox and away from the arena. Along the way, the newly-loquacious dwarf discoursed at length about the legendary Brisindeld. The thing sounded like a nuclear-reactor-in-a-can. It had been installed in some sort of underground chamber safely away from the dwarven city of Dolvendelve; from there it had provided power, carried over copper transmission lines, to the smelting furnaces, elevators, glow-lights, ventilators, and other machinery that helped the city function. Unfortunately, that endless flow of free energy had come to an end several centuries ago, when the dwarves lost the Brisindeld in what sounded like a pair of cataclysmic meteor impacts. These destroyed the power station and its access tunnel and rewrote the surrounding geography, leaving the dwarves trapped in their city behind tons of rubble and debris. By the time they burrowed their way out, looters had moved through the area and absconded with the gem. Eventually they discovered that the thieves were the elves, who had renamed the stone the Illata and put it to use transforming a nearby wetland into a forest, and who had ever since steadfastly refused to return it to its rightful owners.

"But we dwarves not give up," Ardegain said, as they entered a warren of residential tunnels and rooms. "We find new ways to run our machines, and we rebuild what was broken, and now we are ready to take back what is ours."

"Uh-huh," Bernard said. "But where did *you* get the Brisindeld?"

"What?"

"Where did the dwarves get it?"

"Why that matters?"

"Well it sounds like a pretty singular thing. I'm curious where it came from. Originally."

"We find it in our mines. You dig deep enough, who knows what you come across?"

"Can't you just dig up another one, then?"

Ardegain snorted. "Is ours. We need it back."

"You seem to be doing all right without it."

"Things have changed," Ardegain said. They stopped at a low side tunnel that ran back a few feet, then bent ninety degrees to the left. "This is where you stay for now. All you need is inside. When time for you to leave, I come get you."

"Okay," Bernard said, eyeing the rocky gullet.   It didn't look promising. He hunched over and waddled his way in, turning left and then right again, at which point the tunnel opened up into a large and well-appointed chamber bigger than his room back home. He was surprised to see that it boasted human-scale furniture carved out of the stone: A bed with an actual, albeit lumpy, mattress; a writing desk and bench; a table already set with food; even a large raised tub in the corner in which water steamed and bubbled. An alcove off to the left appeared to house a latrine. Gas jets in the walls provided bright, pallid illumination.   All things considered, it looked at least as comfortable as many of the motel rooms to which his (in his opinion) excessively budget-conscious parents had subjected him on their infrequent family vacations.

He went to the table first.   The meal was hardly extravagant—bread, cheese, beer—but he was famished and didn't care. The beer was gross, stale and flat, so he only took a few sips of that as he inhaled everything else. After he had eaten, he examined some documents that were waiting for him, held down by a round, smooth stone with a curious carving on it, a set of concentric circles passing over a cross. He wasn't sure why they needed a paperweight; there wasn't the slightest breeze in this subterranean place, and the scrolls, which were sheets of leathery hide scratched with runic script, didn't seem inclined to curl. He couldn't make sense out of any of the writing, but spent a good deal of time studying what was clearly a map. It bore no compass rose and the surrounding letters had no clear orientation, so for all he knew he was looking at it upside-down, but he could tell what it represented. On the right, a thick wall of jagged angles must be mountains, curving in a semicircle around a region of cottony squiggles that probably represented the forest. At about the midpoint of the woods the entire top layer of the leather had been excised, creating either a lake or a hole in the world; next to that was a small representation of a stockaded village and, in its center, a hill that resembled the lump on the head of some unlucky cartoon character after a safe had bounced off his noggin.

The map sported many other details; clearly some cartographer had spent a good deal of time etching it with tiny knives. Bernard appreciated the craftsmanship, but was too tired to concentrate on it any longer.   He went to the tub and felt the water; hot, but not scalding, and swirling with current. It flowed in through a small hole where it met the wall, and exited through a grilled aperture in the bottom center. The water looked perfectly clear; he wondered if it recirculated the same water all the time, like a fountain, or if it was part of some vast central plumbing system.

He glanced at the entrance. The room was doorless, and he was certain that a guard remained station outside, but the sharply angled hallway gave him privacy in an airport-bathroom sort of way. He stripped off his noisome garments and climbed into the tub, soaking for a while, feeling his muscles unkink. He followed this up with a soapless scrub-down, much to Brannoc's dismay; apparently the rogue believed that bathing removed one's protective layer of grime, and should be avoided.

After getting out of the tub, Bernard considered trying to wash his clothes, but worried that the material would either fail to dry or would shrink and become constrictive. Instead he used the lantern-style knobs on the wall spigots to turn down the gaslights, then crawled beneath the thin, scratchy blanket, hoping to get some sleep before the dwarves rousted him for his mission to retrieve their precious magical battery pack. He closed his eyes for a moment, and when he opened them again, he was back in his own bed, at home. But he wasn't himself; instead, he was Brannoc.

He lay there for a moment, disoriented and puzzled; then he threw off the covers and stood. He went to his dresser and opened the top drawer. His leathers were inside, washed and neatly folded. He put them on over his undergarments, marveling at how soft and supple they felt, how fragrant they smelled, as if they'd been boiled in a soup of flower petals, then dried, stretched, and beaten with rods until the fibers loosened up. His hat was on the dresser as well, perched atop a mannequin head painted to look like a rather fleshy, bespectacled adolescent. He donned the chapeau, then examined himself in a reflecting glass that hung on the wall. He couldn't remember the last time he'd been so clean. In the reflection, he could see his boots sticking out from underneath the bed, so he went and put those on too.

Now that he was fully dressed, he cast about the room for his quarterstaff. There it was, leaning against the wall next to his bed. He took it and fitted it into the holster on his back. That done, he felt as if he needed to go somewhere. He left the house, emerging onto a flat, hard walkway made of some kind of rolled stone. He followed this to a wide road made of similar material, though it was a darker color, slate-grey, like a winter river that had been turned into rock. He looked left and right, feeling as if there should be someone here waiting for him, or coming to join him; but the street was quiet and deserted, and eventually he moved on. He walked alongside the street until he came to a path that led into the woods. He turned onto it, following it under the trees, emerging at the edge of a large, well-clipped meadow. Ahead, the grassy slope rose gently to a squat brick manor. He made his way toward it, eyeing the various odd structures he passed. There were several triangular apparatuses made of metal pipes, with seats suspended by chains, swaying slightly in a cool, damp breeze; he suspected these were punishment devices, though at the moment, there were no thieves or criminals hanging from them. He saw rows of bleachers arranged around what had to be tourney fields, and fenced-in rectangular pens where metal hoops stood atop iron poles. Those were the oddest gibbets he had ever seen, and he had escaped more than a few.

He reached the manor and, feeling compelled to enter, jaunted up the steps and pushed through a large metal gate. Beyond, a wide central corridor led straight back, lined with lockers and closed doors. He ignored these, following a dim babble of voices toward the center of the structure, eventually reaching a broad room with a tall ceiling. It was full of tables and chairs, nearly all of them occupied. The place smelled strongly of food; clearly it was some sort of dining hall. Most of the tables were arranged around the perimeter, but one stood alone in the center. Two thuggish youngsters sat there, staring at the door, as if waiting for someone.

As Brannoc entered, the crowd fell silent, all faces turning to look at him. The watchful pair rose and came around to stand in front of their table. He saw that they wore matching uniforms, striped pants and shirts with large numbers emblazoned on them. Each shirt had writing over the left breast; one said *Kinsey*, the other *Oates*. Clearly these were vassals, so perhaps that was the uniform of their lord.

Brannoc took a step forward. The two youths reached behind them and snatched up their food trays, sending plates and cutlery flying. They slid their arms through hidden straps on the bottoms, using the trays as shields. Someone in the crowd tossed them weapons, which they caught out of the air. One was a staff similar to Brannoc's, but split at the end, with a rope net between the forks; an iron ball sat in the webbing, giving it weight and heft. The other was a short metal club that didn't have much reach, but looked capable of doing significant damage if it connected.

Brannoc wasn't sure who these two were, but he somehow knew that they desperately required a sound thrashing. He slipped his quarterstaff out and spun it in front of himself like a baton, then caught it, holding it horizontally.   His opponents bellowed and charged; he drew his staff back, and——

"Round ears!"

Bernard opened his eyes. Ardegain stood beside the bed.

"Time to go," the dwarf said.

Chapter 7

GLORIAN AND THE other trackers had spent most of the night and much of the morning combing the village and the surrounding woods, fruitlessly searching for some trace of Ambrosia, but she had vanished as utterly as the lost forest of Torgon. In a few hundred years there would still be stories told of the ancient trees, but who would recall the pretty elf who came and went in a single day, never to be seen again? No one, Glorian thought, except perhaps for himself.

He shook his head. No, it was much too soon to sing Ambrosia's death song; she *had* to be here somewhere. It might seem as if some fell hand had descended to pluck her off the face of the world, but of course no such thing had happened; no fingers had reached down from the clouds to snatch her, no mystical wind had carried her off. This mischief came from the forest, not from the sky. The aching lump on the back of his head, as well as the heavy branch that had been used to inflict it, told him that.

After coming to his senses, he had taken the makeshift weapon up to Yexandor so he could read it and discern who had handled it; but this had proved fruitless. The old elf believed it was interference, some force meddling with the longstanding enchantments he had put in place to keep him informed of what went on in the village. He was still at work in his hollow tree, trying to pierce whatever veil had been set against him. Glorian had little confidence that he would succeed; so far, Yexandor's spells had proven ineffective when applied to Ambrosia, sliding off her like rainfall from a waxy leaf.

Now Glorian had returned to the scene of the attack, and stood there staring at the place where he had fallen. That, at least, was completely obvious; the disturbed leaves and bracken made plain that something large had lain there. But there was no sign that Ambrosia had ever hit the ground. She must have been caught before she could collapse, slung over a shoulder, perhaps, and spirited off. Nor was there any trail to show that someone had carried a burden away from here. The villain had either taken the risk of staying on the hard-packed path or had done an astonishingly skillful job of obscuring his tracks through the underbrush.

His tracks? Or *their* tracks? It seemed likely that there had been more than one attacker waiting in ambush for them. It would have been impossible to knock both him and Ambrosia out, catch her before she toppled over, and then disappear. Not without magic, anyway, and if they had used magic openly, Yexandor should have detected it.

Should have.

He stepped off the path to allow a small group of dispirited searchers to pass, Orindel among them. Glorian had joined and left and rejoined most of the tracking parties during the night, but this was the first time he'd encountered Orindel. He caught the leader's eye and looked a question at him, but the other elf shook his head. Nothing. Orindel left the others to stand with Glorian, while the rest of the group moved on.

"How could she just *disappear*?" Glorian said.

"Whoever took her is better than we are," Orindel said. "How is your head?"

"Chewing hurt-bark makes it feel better."

"So you have not had it looked at properly yet, then."

"There is little need for that, and less time."

"You are not required to lead each search group personally, you know," Orindel said. "You are permitted to stop and rest for a little while. You are even permitted to *sleep*."

"I slept."

"Lying senseless on the ground is not sleeping. Really, Glorian, there are others in the village who equal you in tracking ability. We can fail to find Ambrosia without your assistance as well as we can with it."

"That sounds like something Nebandalex would say."

"Nebandalex says a lot of things."

"Yes, he ..." Glorian trailed off. *Nebandalex.* He had not encountered Nebandalex at all this morning, neither in any of the search parties nor on patrol with the other archers nor in the leafy hall having breakfast.

Orindel cocked his head. "What?"

"Have you seen Nebandalex today? Or Shelliyan?"

"Not that I recall." Then: "You think *they* were involved?"

"Some elf took her," Glorian said. "Not me. Not you. Why not them?"

"Why would they? Why would *any* of us? Perhaps whoever enchanted her returned to claim his prize."

"Anyone capable of an enchantment like that would not have needed to club me." Glorian stroked his ear nervously, then said: "I am going to go talk to Yexandor about them."

"Is this really an accusation you want to make?"

"It is not an accusation, it is just an idea."

"That is a fine distinction. I will be interested in hearing you try to explain the difference."

"All right," Glorian said. "I will not go to Yexandor yet, but I *will* go to their house and see if anyone is there."

"I hope your plan is not to shoot them on sight," Orindel said drily.

"Of course not." Glorian reached back and touched his bow. Although normally only wall guards carried their weapons in the village, he had kept it strapped to his back since the attack; no one had remarked on this breach of etiquette until now. "I will do nothing rash. If I find anything of a suspicious nature I will report it to Yexandor."

"Really? Your reputation for impulsivity is pure myth then? As I recall, Yexandor partnered you with Meliander so he could teach you to restrain your enthusiasm."

"Meliander is busy helping Yexandor with his divinations. You can come with me, if you fear I may become overly *enthusiastic*."

"I would, but I have commitments to the village watch. You know that." Orindel looked thoughtful, then reached out and snatched the arrows out of Glorian's quiver, moving so quickly that Glorian didn't have time to protest. Tucking the shafts into the crook of his elbow, he said: "But even so, I will restrain your enthusiasm as best I can."

<div align="center">~~~~</div>

Ardegain sat Bernard down at the table to go over his mission. The dwarf peered at and then ignored most of the documents; perhaps he couldn't read the runes either. However, he spent quite a lot of time on the map—which, it turned out, Bernard *had* positioned upside-down—estimating distances, pointing out landmarks and obstacles, suggesting paths. Ardegain thought Bernard would reach the village by nightfall if he kept up a reasonable pace. Once Bernard agreed that he understood the map and knew the route he was to take, Ardegain made a great show of presenting Bernard with both the map and the stone paperweight that had held everything down. The stone, it turned out, was some sort of pass, to be presented in the unlikely event that he encountered a dwarven patrol that hadn't gotten the message not to attack any strange, gangly humans they might find wandering in the forest.

After that, Ardegain called in his bruisers. They put a leather sack on Bernard's head—or, more accurately, obliged him to put the sack on his own head while they stood around smirking—and then guided him on a long, winding journey through echoing corridors that ranged wildly on a triple axis of damp and dry, hot and cold, silent and noisy. Eventually *damp, cold, and noisy* became dominant, as the distant hiss of a small waterfall grew steadily louder. At last they emerged into an icy spray and swirling wind, at which point Ardegain told him he could remove the sack. He did so immediately. They were at the top of a slick, steep trail carved into the side of a narrow and heavily shadowed crevasse. It seemed to be a new path; the way down was strewn with stone chips and jagged pieces of broken flint, and had not been worn smooth by the passage of water, feet, or time. He couldn't see the cataract from here, but it had to be nearby, judging from the mist that coated the black rock with a glistening sheen of water.

They clambered down the ledge, emerging into a rubble-strewn cavity at the bottom of a tall triangular cleft in the cliff, where three ribbony cascades spilled from different channels high above and gathered in a single large splash pool. The sides of the pool were chiseled into vertical walls, and the gap through which it flowed out to become a small river had been straightened and fortified with a series of gleaming silver chains and a sliding iron gate that was currently drawn to the side. Leftover rubble, packed and graded, formed low wharves, among which a fleet of miniature galleons with shallow drafts and no sails rocked and bobbed in the chop created by the torrents. The dwarves had obviously been working here for some time, building a tiny, hidden marina. But what did they need ships for? It didn't look like they had the infrastructure to load cargo. Were they planning to sail to somewhere with better caves?

"When you get the gem, you bring it back here," Ardegain said, as they moved along a walkway on the opposite side of the water from the boats. "If the gate is closed, show the stone. Guards will know what to do."

"All right," Bernard said, eyeing the vessels, half expecting to see pint-sized pirates swarming the decks. He was having significant difficulty with the idea of dwarves as sailors.

"This is your horse," Ardegain said, as they approached the mouth in the rock wall. A couple of flunkies waited there, holding the reins of a large pony that bore on its back an almost human-sized saddle with accompanying bags.

"Why do I need a horse?" Bernard's earliest memory involving hoofed animals dated back to a circus or carnival many years earlier. There had been a pony ride, where for a few dollars you could put your kid on the hairy little beast and watch it walk around in a circle. Sensing a photo opportunity, his parents had dragged him over to this attraction, paid their money, and handed him over to the attendants; he'd started screaming the moment they put him on the creature's back and hadn't stopped until he'd gotten off of it. Time had done little to reduce his distaste for saddlery.

"Carries supplies," Ardegain said. "Faster to get you to deep woods."

Eyeing the animal, he said: "What's its name?"

"Its name? Name is *your horse*. Go on, go on, sit."

Reluctantly, Bernard made several attempts to climb into the saddle, finally succeeding when several of the milling dwarves came over to immobilize the creature by clustering around it and holding it at strategic points. The pony was so short and his Brannoc-legs so long that his feet touched the ground if he straightened his knees; it was like riding a bicycle that was several sizes too small. He must look absurd, Bernard thought, and he was pretty sure the dwarves were snickering at him. "Now what?"

"Now you go. Make good time on horse, should reach elf city by middle of afternoon. Make bad time, then not until dark. Be careful; elves have eyes you will not see." Ardegain gave the animal a whack on the rump. It startled and cantered away, Bernard clinging to its neck, the rattle of dwarven laughter seeing him off on his journey.

Well, let them laugh. Bernard had concluded that Mercy was correct when she'd speculated, back when this had just been a game, that his character was at the edge of the same forest through which hers had been wandering. He had ended up in the dwarven caves, so it stood to reason that Mercy may have made it to the elven city; and if he managed to find her, they could partner up and figure out what the hell was going on and how to get home. The dwarves and elves could squabble over their trinket all they wanted once Mercy and he were out of here.

Of course, that assumed Mercy would *want* to go home. For all he knew she was out there shooting fireballs, turning herself invisible, flying through the air, having the time of her life. He wouldn't be at all surprised to find that she'd been slated to be born somewhere like this and had only gotten stuck on plain old boring Earth due to some sort of cosmic clerical error, like a misdirected piece of luggage that had ended up in Outer Bumguat instead of its intended destination.

Brannoc said, *Where is Outer Bumguat?*

"Nowhere," Bernard said.

Ah. In that case, we have arrived.

~~~~

Nebandalex and Shelliyan shared a small dwelling in a thicket of young trees, well away from the main footpaths. Like many of the huts
~~~~

that stood on the periphery of the village, theirs was made of living saplings lashed together into walls, their boughs woven into a dome layered with waterproof leaves harvested from the forest. Glorian supposed this sort of living was acceptable to some, but he found it too constrained, too earthbound. He much preferred his platform high up in the branches, with its retractable screens of reeds and vines and a bed that gently swayed with the motion of the tree. If one was going to live in a ground-level hovel with walls and a roof, one might as well be a human.

He circled their shack warily, moving without a sound. He put his ear to the saplings at various spots but heard nothing; if anyone was inside, he or she was being very quiet. He returned to the door, where the thin trees were folded back into an archway similar to those that led into the commons. This one, though, did not stand open and welcoming; a door had been fitted into it, branches planed and lashed together and then stuck into place to form a barrier.

Walls, walls, walls. You couldn't trust elves who hid behind so many walls.

The door had a handle, a forked, curving branch that had been cut short and left as a place to grip. He took hold of it and tugged gently, but the door didn't move. Pushing on it had no effect either. He saw no lock or keyhole, which meant it must be barred or latched on the other side, so someone had to be within. He drew his dagger and rapped on the door with the hilt. "Nebandalex?" he called. "Shelliyan? Are you there?" No answer, of course. He flipped his dagger around and, holding it at the ready, stepped back and spoke a few words to coerce the door to open.

But the door resisted.

He knew he had spoken properly; something held the door in place, denying the power of the glamour he had used to compel it to open. If it were a simple bar, the spell should have released it; if it were a mechanical lock—something which, as far as he knew, did not even *exist* in the village—the spell should have turned the tumblers. So some contrary force was keeping the door shut. It could be countervailing magic, or it could be Nebandalex standing in there with his feet braced against the wall, hanging onto the door with all his strength. Or both.

Orindel had chided him for lack of evidence; well, here it was. He knew he should bring this information up the hill to Yexandor so that the old elf could turns his own resources to bear on the situation; but that would take time, and now that the occupants of the hut knew he had been here, they could get into all manner of mischief while he was gone. So instead of leaving, he spoke the words again, altering them to add more force. The door bowed outward, dark gaps appearing and widening between the branches as they bent away from each other; then, with the sound of wood splintering, it broke. Pieces of wood and torn scraps of vine exploded outward. He flinched and thew a protective arm across his face as bits of broken door pelted him.

When Glorian lowered his arm and looked at the door, he saw no Nebandalex looking shocked, no Ambrosia looking grateful, no Shelliyan looking annoyed. In fact, he didn't even see the interior of the small, rude house. He only saw darkness. He moved forward cautiously, baffled by this unexpected development, and stopped a few paces from the opening. He was not mistaken; this wasn't a trick of the shadows. Beyond the entrance to the house there was simply nothing, matte black, a void. He tentatively stretched his hand out across the threshold; it vanished as if he'd dunked it in a pot of pitch. He felt nothing, no resistance, no frisson of energy, and when he pulled his hand out and counted his fingers, they were all still there.

He knew what this was: A misdirection glamour, just like the one on Yexandor's fallen tree. For all he knew there was a time dilation glamour in there too. Neither spell was trivially invoked; how had Nebandalex and Shelliyan learned them? Why hadn't Yexandor's glyphs detected the magic? He was out of his depth here. He had to tell the others about this at once.

But before he could back away someone pushed him hard from behind, shoving him into the darkness.

~~~~

Bernard had been concerned about orienteering through the wilderness, with no park rangers and no roadside assistance or, for that matter, roads; but the landmarks etched into his leather map proved to be excellent representations of their real-world counterparts, and they were close enough together that he never had to go too far from one before sighting the next. The map also indicated which paths and woodland roads were traversed by elves and humans; these had been marked with ear-like symbols with either a pointed or rounded tip, respectively. The larger the ear, the busier the trail. The route Ardegain had planned mostly kept him well off the riskiest ones, and where they could not be avoided, he was on them for the briefest period possible. Not bad for a bunch of cave-dwelling, xenophobic shut-ins; his father's auto club could hardly have plotted a more efficient journey.
~~~~

One of the last landmarks on the map was a rocky clearing strewn with moss-grown boulders. It seemed like a good place to pause and take stock. While he unrolled the map to its full extent, the pony wandered a little ways off to munch contentedly on the thin-bladed grasses that grew from the gaps and pockets among the megaliths. The enormous stones—squat rectangles with rounded corners, thick disks ribbed along the outer edges like worn and ancient cogs, fallen pylons pierced with circular holes—were too regular to be natural, but whatever structure or henge had once stood here was long since destroyed, the constituent blocks scattered and half-sunken into the earth, and whatever power or significance had once inhered within the site had dissipated.

It was getting dark, and Bernard had begun to have difficulty reading the map; lighter brown on darker brown didn't provide the greatest contrast in the world. Too bad the dwarves hadn't given him a miner's helmet with a built-in light. They probably had those, he thought. He wished the map had a legend to give it some scale. There weren't that many landmarks left between him and the village, but how far apart were they? And how could he find them in the dark? Maybe he should call it a night, find a defensible place to camp. Like here, for instance. The dwarves had waited all those years to get their stone back, they could wait a little longer. And it wasn't like he actually planned to bring it back to them anyway.

We would have made better time if you had stayed on the horse, Brannoc chided. *We would have reached the village by now, and you would know if your precious* Mercy *is there.*

Bernard considered this. Brannoc might be a sarcastic pain, but he wasn't wrong. Even the smaller paths along his route were wide and level enough for him to manage on the pony, which had proven to be remarkably tractable, as if it, too, had studied the map and knew where to go. But after several hours of riding, Bernard's posterior had started to get sore, so he'd decided to get off and walk for a while. After that, he couldn't seem to figure out how to get back on the little beast without dwarves to keep it from thwarting him simply by walking away. Brannoc, no doubt, could have vaulted onto its back like a circus monkey, but Bernard had been reluctant to invite him back into control of their body lest he simply abandon the mission and leave Mercy to her fate.

Well, done was done.

He consulted the map again, but it was too dim to read it in the shadow of the stones. As he rummaged in the pony's saddlebags for a lantern that he knew was there somewhere, he heard a low, brief, distant rumble from the direction of the mountains. Thunder? Great. He didn't suppose the dwarves had thought to supply him with an umbrella.

He found the lantern and carried it over to the map. As he did so, he realized that he had begun to cast a very faint shadow. At first he thought it might be from moonlight; but it shifted and shortened before his eyes, and the color that imbued the surrounding grass was wrong. Puzzled, he searched the darkling sky, and spotted a ball of fire in the distance, spitting a drizzle of embers as it rose. Lantern and map forgotten, he stared while the blazing projectile reached an apex and fell, becoming lost to sight some distance behind him. He couldn't hear the impact, but seconds later the horizon erupted in a flare of red and orange.

As Bernard tried to make sense of what he had just seen, he heard another distant report; it didn't sound like thunder anymore, but like the muzzle roar of a cannon. A second fireball came into view, soaring up from the mountains, following a similar but slightly different trajectory as the first. He could tell that this one was going to travel farther. It was if someone were practicing gunnery skills. Firing experimental shots. Calibrating. Targeting.

Realization dawned.

The dwarves had *artillery*.

Bernard snatched up the map, grabbed the pony's reins, and fled.

<div align="center">~~~~</div>

The blackness inside the tiny house was so complete, Glorian might as well have stumbled down the deepest mineshaft the dwarves had ever dug. If, as he feared, this was a copy of Yexandor's enchantment on the log, and a time dilation glamour was layered on the misdirection, then hours could already have passed since he had been pushed over the threshold; hours in which Nebandalex and Shelliyan could be getting up to even more mischief, with no one the wiser.

He tried to remember what he knew about this spell. Yexandor had explained it to him once; it had something to do with folding space and time. The old elf had scratched pictures in the gravel out in front of his home, a straight line to represent regular space and time and a curved one to represent space and time within the glamour. The glamour's line oscillated up and down across the regular one, and might be ten times as long as the other, yet both arrived at the same end point.

Unfortunately, grasping the glamour's underlying concept went no distance whatsoever toward helping him escape from it. Feeling even more impotent now than he had during the fruitless search of the village and the forest, he decided to start shouting. "Ambrosia! Are you here?" His voice seemed muffled, as if the gloom had enfolded and smothered it; the words came out of his mouth and fluttered to the ground like dead leaves. No one was going to hear him.

To his surprise, a distant voice answered: "Who is there?"

After a moment, Glorian said: "Nebandalex? Is that you?"

There was another long pause before the reply came back. "Who else would it be? This is my house. I think. Is that you, Glorian?"

The delay in Nebandalex's answers and the faint echoing quality of his voice must be caused by the distance the sound had to travel between them, Glorian realized. How far apart were they? Just how tightly had space been warped in this tiny shack? "Yes!" he said. "What have you done with Ambrosia?"

"Ambrosia? I have done nothing with Ambrosia! You were the one charged with squiring her around. Have you lost her?"

"She was taken, and you know it!"

The pause before Nebandalex answered seemed rather longer this time, and when he spoke again, his tone had changed. "I know it *now*," he said. "Is that why you came here? You think *I* took her?"

"Did you?"

"Of course not! I have been wandering in this darkness since I returned from dinner last night!"

"Why is your house enchanted, then?"

"I have no idea," Nebandalex said. "You are the dabbler in magic—what manner of craft would turn our home into a black maze?"

He wasn't familiar with the misdirection glamour, Glorian realized; likely he had never been tested by Yexandor's doorway. Glorian opened his mouth to name the spell, then stopped and, instead, asked, "How long do you think you have been here?"

"I am not sure. Dawn has not come yet, so not very long."

"It was well into afternoon when I came here," Glorian said.

"Afternoon? Absurd! It has been an hour or two, no more."

"It has been more. Much more." There *was* a time-dilation glamour, then; this grew yet more worrisome. "You asked me what craft this was? This is a layered misdirection and time dilation glamour."

Long pause. "Oh, of course."

"Is Shelliyan with you?"

"No, she forgot her pack at the leafy hall and went back for it." Pause. "She insisted on getting it herself. She would not let me do it." Another pause. "She told me she would meet me back here, but … she never did."

Realization dawned. "*She* did this, then," Glorian said. "This is Shelliyan's enchantment."

"Shelliyan studies plants, not sorcery."

"Shelliyan may not have cast the spell, but she must have known about it, or she would be trapped in here as well." He waited a moment for Nebandalex to respond, and when he did not, added: "I thought this was a trap for me, but it was a trap for *you*. To keep you out of the way."

For a little while, Nebandalex was silent.

Then he said: "Keep me out of the way of what?"

~~~~

So far, all the fireballs had fallen short of his position; Bernard was beginning to think they didn't have sufficient range to actually reach him, but they had done a more than adequate job of setting the forest ablaze.

He could no longer hear the cannons firing, although he could tell when a projectile hit the ground; there would be a muffled *whump*, then a wheezy roar, and finally a fresh crimson flower blooming into the night sky. He didn't know what sort of shells were being launched, but they caused one hell of an explosion on impact.

Speaking of shells, one was coming in right now. He could hear it, a faint whistling sound. Turning, he spotted it arcing down from the sky, much closer than he would have liked. It smashed into the trees a few hundred yards behind him, close enough for him to feel the shockwave, the rush of heat. His pony had grown increasingly agitated as the smell of fire thickened in the air and now, finally terrified beyond endurance, it reared, tore the reins from Bernard's hands, and bolted off the path. Cursing, Bernard took off after it. He knew he had little chance of catching the panicked beast, but it carried all his supplies, his food, his water, his stupid lucky stone.

Lucky stone. Ha, that was a good one. Look how lucky he'd been so far.

Still in futile pursuit of the fleeing quadruped, Bernard stumbled onto a wide, well-used path that, if he remembered the map correctly, ran in the general direction of the elven city and was the sort of road the route had him avoiding. He cast a glance back at the mountains. With the clear view that the break in the trees afforded, he saw what
~~~~

amounted to a wall of fire stretching in an arc from left to right across the horizon. He stopped and stared, suffused in ruddy light, sweat trickling down the sides of his face.

He didn't have time to waste chasing ponies. He didn't have time to do anything, except get to the village as fast as he could.

Aside from his quarterstaff and other personal gear, the leather map was the only thing he hadn't lost when the horse took off. He unrolled it and held it up in the firelight, trying to figure out where he was. It didn't look like this particular road actually went into the village, but it brushed up against a surrounding ridge. The ridge had a circle drawn on it, with a square-edged crooked line inside. An arrow connected the circle to the city. Stairs?

Bernard memorized the route as best he could, then rolled up the map and, with one last look at the roaring inferno at his back, turned and started running.

Behind him, the forest burned.

~~~~

Ambrosia was almost certain she was alone.

It was hard to be sure; the blindfold was thick and drawn tight over her eyes, shutting out any view of her surroundings, and her captors—when not talking about her or to her—made as little noise as ants crawling along a leaf. Still, she'd been listening attentively for a long while now, and had heard nothing; not a breath, not the rustle of clothing, not the pop of a joint.

Seemed like a good time to attempt an escape.

It was obvious that she couldn't free herself physically; the ropes that bound her were too tight, the knots too cunningly tied. She might be able to loosen them with a spell, if she remembered any, but she couldn't speak the words or perform the gestures needed to cast even the simplest glamour. A different approach was required. Yexandor had talked about trying to read her strings; it had sounded like he was referring to something inside her, something that stitched her together, like the myriad threads that, when woven just so, could form a shirt, a blanket, a tapestry. She didn't know if that was exactly how he'd meant it, but she'd had a lot of time, lying here tied up with nothing else to do, to think about it, and she had realized one thing.

Strings could be pulled.

Not sure how to transform this idea into something useful, she started by turning inward, searching for the strings that Yexandor had been looking for. He'd been blocked from reaching them, but they were *her* strings, and whatever had stopped him had no standing to
~~~~

deny her in such a fashion. That was what she told herself, anyway, as she tried to visualize what they might look like, glistening threads through the darkness, white spider silk, variegated motley yarn. If one could play music on them there must be a whole set, in different lengths and thicknesses and degrees of tension, like the metal strands of a guitar. No, that wasn't right; a guitar only had a few strings, hardly sufficient to describe an entire being. She was more than that. She was a piano, a zither, a harp as wide as the world, no frame in sight, just the strings, one after another, luminous, and herself standing silent and still in the pale wash of their glow, staring, until she finally reached out with an arm as massive as Yexandor's tree, not her own lithe white limb but a strange, wiry one, differently muscled, sprinkled with freckles, furred with coarse, dark hair rather than a dusting of invisibly fine platinum. She was so startled by this alien appendage that she faltered for a moment, her concentration slipping. The tableau began to fade and she wrenched it back to solidity, focused, transformed her arm so it looked the way she remembered it, even if, as some distant part of her whispered, the way she remembered it was wrong. She couldn't concern herself with that, not now, not if she was to have any chance at all of figuring this out. Ignoring her doubts, she reached out again, touched the strings, ran her fingers across them. She heard or imagined something like music, tones so deep and strong they seemed to vibrate right through her, shimmering into the vast nothing, bouncing off distant unseen surfaces, clashing, combining, fading. She strummed them again and the sound took hold of her, picked her up and carried her, flotsam in the surf, until she crashed through an invisible barrier and found herself washed up on a shore of phosphorescent threads running every which-way, flat or angled or vertical, curved or straight, smooth or jagged, or all of those at once, a crayon palimpsest of a world. She didn't think these were her own strings anymore. The force she had plucked into existence had surged over her and pushed her consciousness out of herself and into the wider world. Might these be the strings that ran through everything around her, through the ropes and the gag and the board at her back, through the walls of the place where she was hidden, the trees outside, the earth, the sky? The lines of energy or matter or potential that constituted her surroundings seemed thinner, more sparse, than those she'd seen within her; but they had to spread across a far wider reality, so perhaps that made sense. As much sense as anything else did, anyway.

She turned or caused the world to rotate around her in a slow circle, strings snaking in and out of view, until she saw something, a small tight tangle of furiously glowing threads, lit up from within by a shifting kaleidoscopic brilliance. Was she looking at herself now? No wonder Yexandor hadn't been able to get through; there was no gap between the warp and weft, no weave loose enough to admit a probing thought; she was surprised she'd been able to escape from inside that incandescent chrysalis. The coruscation obscured whatever bonds held her body immobile, but she knew they were there. She didn't need to see them, just to sever them. And for that, she needed a blade.

Ambrosia raised her right hand. She needed a blade, yes, but not one made of steel or stone; she wouldn't be cutting on a physical level. Extending her forefinger, she concentrated on it, willing it into sharpness. It grew before her eyes, stretched out like a scalpel. A shimmer spread across its edge, similar to Yexandor's hand when he'd tried and failed to reach inside her. When her ethereal knife seemed sufficiently charged, she lowered it toward the Ambrosia-shaped skein of threads, touched it gently to what she thought was the forehead, and slowly slid the tip of it downward; but before she had gotten even to where her nose might be, she realized that the cocoon-like wad was already opening up where she had sliced it, emitting a light that dazzled and blinded even in her imagination. She gasped and withdrew her finger, but too late; the energy that had been contained started ripping free, forcing the split wider, until it burst like a firework and tore the world to pieces.

~~~~

"This is not like Yexandor's misdirection glamour," Glorian said, as he tried to find his way to Nebandalex. How long had he been in here? Hours? Days? Within the confines of the glamour, the minutes seemed to flow by as they had always done, but he had no idea how much time had gone by on the outside.

"How so?" Nebandalex said.

"Yexandor's spell is linear. This one is in three dimensions. Right now you sound close, but above me."

"Do I? I walked up no hills that I recall."

"The glamour presents no true inclines or declines. Its purpose is to confuse and contain."

"Well, it certainly does that well enough." Nebandalex was silent for a while, then said: "Where am I now, in relation to you?"

Glorian considered this. "Down and to my left."

"Really? How curious."

"I am glad you find this so interesting."
~~~~

"I have little else to do at the moment, since you told me not to move." Pause. "Where am I now?"

"Right next to me." Glorian stretched out his arms and turned in a circle; Nebandalex wasn't there. "This glamour is severely twisted on itself." That someone in the village had been able to increase the complexity of the misdirection glamour in such a fashion rather than merely copying the original, and had then deployed it without being detected, unnerved him more than he cared to admit. "It could be a single endless path. There may be no way out at all."

"But there must be a way out," Nebandalex said.

"Why?"

"Because there was a way in."

"If Shelliyan devised a means to connect the ends together, the way out and the way in could be the same thing."

"I told you, Shelliyan does not cast glamours."

"Yes, I know," Glorian said, suppressing a sigh of impatience at Nebandalex's obstinate belief in his partner's innocence. "She may have an accomplice who does."

"Impossible. More likely she has béen taken as well. Perhaps she saw what she was not meant to see."

"But why would she insist on going back for her pack instead of—"

"Ah. Yes. That."

Glorian waited, said nothing. Nebandalex proceeded to fill the silence with a confession that his story about Shelliyan's forgetting her pack had been a fabrication; that, in fact, the two of them had argued after leaving the leafy hall and that she had subsequently stalked off into the forest by herself, leaving him to return home alone. He had not seen her since.

Much as Glorian wanted to believe in his fellow-prisoner's villainy, he had concluded that Nebandalex was most likely telling the truth; he really seemed to have been unaware of Ambrosia's disappearance until Glorian had informed him, and to have no idea how or why his home had been enchanted. Shelliyan, though, had had ample opportunity to arrange or participate in Ambrosia's abduction; but was jealousy really a sufficient motive for so extreme a transgression? Shelliyan was not some human, ruled by impulse and short-term passion, and even if she were, the caliber of the enchantment on this house bespoke a scheme with long-standing roots. What was *really* going on here? Glorian had no idea; and so he kept walking through the dark, hands outstretched, knowing that every step he took meant that any number of minutes had passed out in the real world, and that the plan—whatever it was—was that much closer to fruition.

The feeling that he was about to trip over something or run into a wall still hadn't really faded, causing him to move carefully, even though he knew that there were no such obstacles here. There was *nothing* here; the misdirection glamour isolated those within it from any details of the physical world. Which was why, when he suddenly noticed a thin ripple of light spreading across the vast black nothing, as if a knife blade were cutting open an ebon curtain to reveal the sun blazing on the other side, he had no idea what it might be. He stopped and said, "Nebandalex, do you see that?"

"Yes. What is it?"

"I am not sure. Whatever it is should not—" Glorian broke off as the darkness suddenly splintered into a spiderweb of radiant lines flashing out from the original luminous ribbon. He felt pressure against his face and body, as if in a stiff wind, though not a hair on his head stirred. The network of cracks curved and bowed outward, accompanied by a sound like an entire forest of trees being bent toward their breaking point.

Then the misdirection glamour exploded in a riot of light and sound and spiraling shards of infinite black.

~~~~

Ambrosia woke up on her back, in the dark, in a briar patch.

The way the brambles grabbed and clung to her clothing, it felt as if she were still bound. She extricated one arm, then the other, then carefully unwound the spiky tendrils from her legs and body, wincing every time the thorns bit through her dress to etch red lines across her skin. How had she managed to get herself so entangled without being scratched horribly in the first place? It was like she'd just *materialized* here or something.

Once she had finally worked free of the ensnaring vines, she rolled over onto her stomach and crawled forward, squirming through brambles that plucked and grabbed. The canes sported large, soft berries that burst as she crushed them, leaving dark stains on her hands and clothes; by the time the brush thinned out at the edge of a narrow trail through the trees, she was filthy with juice and pulp and more than a little blood. She inhaled deeply, letting her lungs fill completely for the first time in hours; she would never take breathing for granted again, she thought. The air was redolent of wood smoke, reminding her of the atmosphere in the common area where she'd eaten dinner. Was it nearby? If she could find her way there, or anywhere the other
~~~~

elves gathered, she would be safe, as long as she didn't wander off down any dark paths.

Unfortunately, the path she had just found was one of the dark ones. She took a quick look around. The snaky track appeared to be deserted, but she could hear low, agitated voices off to the right, talking quickly in what sounded like an argument or confused discussion. She couldn't identify the speakers or make out the words, but still, best not to go that way.

She hauled herself onto the path, turned left, and ran.

It didn't take long for the trail to emerge from the thicket into a grove of tall trees where the underbrush had been cleared, leaving a parklike open space of low grass and flowers and raked earth pathways. A number of residences stood in and around this area: Small ground-level huts, screened and tented platforms nestled in the branches, even windowed hollows in the largest living trunks. She scurried across the glade, flitting from dwelling to dwelling, searching for any trace of those who lived here, but the place appeared to be completely deserted. No lights, no sounds, no activity. Where were they?

She noticed that one of the larger tracks looked disturbed, as if many feet had recently trod it. Had a group of elves stampeded in that direction? She decided to go that way, thinking she might catch up with them, or at least find out where everyone had gone. Soon this path disbursed her onto the wide central avenue that led to Yexandor's hill. The earth here was packed much harder than in the woods; she couldn't tell which way the footprints went, although she was sure a ranger like Glorian could have followed them. The smell of smoke was stronger here in the open; small black flakes drifted through the air, slowly settling to the ground, where they swirled and skittered in ragged skeins like thin, filthy spindrift. She picked some up, ground it between her fingers. Ash. Fine and gritty, it clung to her skin and clothing, adding a dusky grey film to the drying blood and berry juice from her escape through the creepers. She looked up; glowing embers floated in the sky high overhead, distant firefly lights fading through orange to dull red before vanishing. Clearly these had *not* originated from the bonfire in the leafy hall.

The forest was burning.

Suddenly, Ambrosia remembered what her female captor had whispered in her ear, that this would be the last night the village would exist. Her kidnappers had known the fire was coming; they might even have set it themselves. She turned her gaze left, toward Yexandor's hill. She didn't doubt he was still up there; everyone else in the village may have fled, but not him. She could imagine him sitting on one of those stone benches, watching the fire, reliving the long-ago calamity he'd described to her, as immediate now as when it had happened, as it always would be, for him.

She needed to go to him, and tell him what she knew. He had to know that he had been betrayed, that this had been planned.

Ambrosia ran as fast as she could along the avenue, through the gap in the earthen rampart, up the spiral path. When she couldn't run any more, she walked; and when she stumbled and fell, she crawled. But she never stopped. The drifting haze thinned as she climbed, until finally she could see through it as if through a gauzy veil. The flames weren't as close as she had feared, but they were everywhere, a roaring, wobbling wall of fire that stretched from the southern riverbank to the northern lakeshore. A steady wind from the mountains pushed the line inexorably forward toward the village, leaving char and ruin in its wake.

Yexandor couldn't extinguish this inferno. No one could.

She turned away from the hellish sight, and kept climbing.

~~~~

The rutted track eventually drew alongside what Bernard thought might be the ridge leading up to the elven village. He kept an eye on the steep, weathered slope as he ran, scanning the nooks and chimneys, searching for anything that might conceal the hidden steps indicated on his map. Unfortunately, knowing about a secret stairway and actually *finding* it were two quite different things, and when the path petered out at the muddy shore of a boggy inlet, he was still at the bottom of the ridge.

From here, looking across the lake beyond the marshy shallows, he had a fine view of the conflagration that continued to rage off to the west, reflected in ruddy blurs that spread across the rippled surface. To his surprise, he saw boats out there, a small flotilla of canoes, rafts, and dories clumped together in the middle of the water. He made out figures hunkered down in the miserable regatta. Elves who had abandoned the threatened forest, seeking refuge where they couldn't burn? He must be close to the village, then.

He just had to *locate* the stupid thing.

Bernard assessed the cliff-like ridge, looking for a likely route to the top. Back home he would never have attempted to scale such a sharply-angled slope, but here? Here, Brannoc could climb that rocky wall in his sleep.
~~~~

Good of you to remember I'm here, Brannoc thought, *now that you need me for something.*

"I'm not sure I need you yet," Bernard said. A few more vessels had drifted out to join the others, silhouettes in the orange twilight. They seemed to have been launched from off to his right; perhaps, if he went that way, he could find a way into the village that didn't involve vertical travel.

Keeping low and hoping the waterborne refugees wouldn't see him—although, really, they were much more likely to be watching the fire than a shadow skulking along the lakeside—he hurried along the narrow, rubbly strip of shoreline. Small, round stones rolled under his boots, constantly threatening to send him sprawling; where the ground wasn't rocky, it was sodden, and where it wasn't sodden, it was mucky, and wanted to claim permanent ownership of his feet. The quarterstaff came in handy as both balance pole and lever, although every time he jammed it into the mud or used it to vault some encroaching finger of water Brannoc bitterly denounced him as a ponderous clod.

After some distance, he passed a cleft in the rock that drew his attention; inside, it looked as if rudimentary steps had been chipped into a natural runoff channel. The bit of beach within was sandy and gently sloped, with faint drag marks across it; perhaps this was a spot where the elves left some of their boats when not using them to fish or hide from infernos. He pivoted and darted up the stairs. They curved to the right, then sharply to the left, the gully becoming quite steep and narrow, although overhead the walls curved outward to bring slitted wooden fortifications into view. He emerged into a dish-shaped depression, almost completely surrounded by stockade walls liberally perforated with both horizontal and vertical slots. Some instinct caused him to throw himself to the ground, not that it would have done any good; under other circumstances he would likely have been in the center of a murderous crossfire regardless of how flat he made himself. It seemed, however, that no one would be shooting at him today.

You are more fortunate than you deserve, demon, Brannoc thought, *but I won't begrudge you your luck, as it's my body they would be filling with their arrows.*

"Gee, thanks," Bernard said, as he scrambled up the slope to a gate made from tree limbs lashed together with ropy vines. It hung partially open behind a half-raised weighted net. He ducked and scurried through the entrance, finding himself in a field of scruffy grass and thin, rocky soil. A steep hill loomed directly in front of him behind an earthen rampart, tall and broad, blotting out the infernal sky. This had to be the butte that the dwarves had marked on his map; aside from its isolation, it didn't look like anything special. If anything, it reminded him of the baby slope at a local low-end ski resort during the off season. Bernard wondered if the elven leader was up there, if he was orchestrating a response to the fire. Did they even know it was an attack? Could they summon a storm to put out the flames? A hurricane should suffice.

He didn't see a trail, so he just charged straight ahead, up the outside of the rampart, down the inside, then up the hill proper, going on all fours when necessary, bulling his way through a carpet of grass and flowers. Before long he encountered a path that seemed to wind around and around in a spiral, judging by its lack of incline. Following that would be way too slow, so he ignored it, and by the time he finished his ascent he had crossed the same path at least half a dozen times.

The hilltop was a plateau interrupted by the most massive fallen tree he had ever seen. He'd seen pictures of giant sequoias, big enough that people had hollowed them out into houses; this one was so huge that some enterprising soul could have carved it into a roadside motel. It stood as tall as a two-story house and as long as three or four buses lined up end to end, like something a motorcycle daredevil might kill himself trying to jump. Bernard couldn't go around the tree; it formed a wooden wall across the entire summit. But he could go over it.

He grabbed a couple handfuls of bark and started climbing.

~~~~

Ambrosia finally reached the top of the hill, and collapsed onto a bench to catch her breath. Lying on her side, looking at the hollow tree, at the blackness over the entrance, she knew she had been right, Yexandor was still here, cloistered behind his obfuscating darkness even now, when the world was on fire around him. She dragged herself off the bench and stumbled across the pond of crushed stone, scuffing through the traces of earlier footsteps, perhaps left by others who had previously tried and failed to dislodge Yexandor from his redoubt. She stopped at the ink splotch of an entrance, facing the darkness. Whatever was going on behind it was beyond her sight. She knew better than to enter and lose herself; if the fire came this far, she didn't think the misdirection glamour would protect her while the fallen tree burned to ash around her. She pounded on the bark beside the
~~~~

opening. It was like hammering on a slightly spongy brick wall, solidly unyielding. "Yexandor!" she cried. "Let me in!"

With a shimmer, the glamour on the entrance vanished; she could see into the dim little foyer. Yexandor stood just inside, staring out at her, paper-pale skin and hair shimmering in the red light. Meliander stood beside him, tugging on his sleeve, pointing at the door like a bored child pestering its mother to go to the park. Yexandor gestured her forward and she entered, passing through the opening as if it were nothing more than a hole in a log. The glamour did not return, leaving the way open behind her.

"Ambrosia," Yexandor said. "Where have you been?" His voice was soft, just as it had been before, betraying no trace of anxiety or excitement, as if the encroaching wall of flame did not exist. She noticed her wand and her dagger lying on one of the benches near the archway; had he been using them, as her possessions, to try to locate her?

"Was … kidnapped," she said, still out of breath.

"Yes, I know," Yexandor said, "but why could I not find you? Object-reading, rune-casting, mind-search, all of them failed."

"There is no time to have this discussion," Meliander said. Then, looking to Ambrosia as if she might have some influence over the ancient elf: "Tell him! Tell him we must leave *now*!"

"Magic," she said, ignoring Meliander. "Tampered with your glyphs. She told me."

"She?"

"Yes."

"Who?"

"Never saw. Were two, at least. She told me … she said this would be the last night there was a village."

Meliander gave her a sharp look. "What? The ones who took you *knew* there would be a fire?"

"She didn't *say* fire, but——"

Ambrosia broke off as Yexandor held up a hand. "Someone has entered," he said. He cast a questioning look around the room, his gaze pausing at the door to the Illata's chamber. The gem sat in its accustomed place, its azure glow spilling out across the threshold. Yexandor stared at it, his lips moving almost imperceptibly. For a moment she thought it might a tremor caused by age or anger, but then she realized that he was whispering. A sigh seemed to pass through the foyer, stirring the fine hairs on the back of her neck. The light of the Illata rippled and grew dim; she had the unsettling sensation of a thin film being laid over her eyes, blurring her vision briefly before being peeled away.

When everything came back into focus, she realized that there were now five elves present, rather than three.

Shelliyan stood near the entrance, Glorian's friend Orindel beside her. He clutched a satchel in one hand, Ambrosia's dagger in the other; Shelliyan held Ambrosia's wand. She raised it and pointed it at the three of them. "Really, Yexandor, you should not leave powerful magical objects lying around where just *anyone* could find them and pick them up. You are fortunate that I took possession of them before one less adept at controlling them, such as their owner, did." Then, to Ambrosia: "Thank you for persuading him to lower his glamour. Circumventing it was proving much more difficult than I had anticipated."

For a moment, they all just stared at her; then Yexandor said, "What do you want, child?"

"What do I want?" She indicated the far wall of the chamber with the tip of the wand, which had begun to glow. "I would like the three of you to move over there while Orindel collects the gem."

Ambrosia said: "The Illata?"

Shelliyan looked at her. "What *other* gem do you suppose the elves possess that would be worth taking?" She gave a brittle, mirthless laugh. "You are here for the same thing." Then, in a sharp, almost metallic voice: "Do not insult me by pretending otherwise!"

Ambrosia, who had been about to deny the charge, closed her mouth.

"You want the Illata?" Meliander said. "Take it and go. It has brought us nothing but grief."

This provoked an angry look and a rebuke from Yexandor. "How can you say that? It saved us from extinction!"

"We kept *ourselves* from falling over that precipice. The gem was ever but a crutch. If the dwarves——"

"Enough!" Shelliyan said. "I have heard these tedious arguments ever since I came to this benighted village. They weary me." She turned away and slashed the wand through the air as if it were a sword; a whiplike stream of coruscating plasma uncoiled from the tip, sizzling and crackling, instantly filling the room with a wash of heat and the stink of ozone. The tendril entwined the carven tree that housed the Illata, causing it to explode in a shower of chunks and fragments that bounced and scattered around the room, trailing wisps of smoke. The gem itself simply fell straight down, thudding to the floor as if it were made of lead.

Shelliyan glanced at Orindel, who was staring open-mouthed at the debris. "Well, go and get it," she said.

"Yes, of course," Orindel said, using the other voice Ambrosia had heard during her captivity. He let the strap on his satchel drop and opened the top flap, but before could move to retrieve the Illata, Ambrosia heard the sound of wood thunking against wood. A wiry, leather-clad apparition pole-vaulted into the room, struck Orindel with both feet, and sent him sprawling. The intruder—a *human*—landed, spun his staff, and swept Shelliyan's legs out from under her. She toppled over, lashing out with the wand before she even hit the ground; the stubby device spat lightning into the ceiling, blasting a hole straight through it. Smoldering bits of bark and splinters of wood rained down around her. A furious expression on her face, she pointed the wand at the newcomer, and—

And time slowed down, like a wagon grinding into deep mud.

The patter of shards from the ceiling became like the gentle downward drift of feathery snow; Orindel's effort to rise turned into a glacial struggle against gravity; the jagged bolt emerging from the wand seemed to be a crack slowly spreading across an invisible pane of glass. Yexandor alone remained unaffected. He calmly walked over and nudged the human to the side, positioning himself directly in the path of the slithering energy. It had begun to split as it traveled through the air; he caught one fork in each hand, the incandescent ribbons entwining his palms and wrists. A thin corona spread down his arms and across his body, wrapping him in a luminous shroud. Yexandor had gotten one last use of out of his time dilation glamour, Ambrosia realized, tremendously speeding himself up in relation to everything else in the fallen tree; but that was finished now, the spell's power spent, and she could smell the cost in the stench of burning clothes and flesh and hair.

Time accelerated again, the seconds settling back into their accustomed rhythm. As the last scraps of the enchantment faded, Orindel sprang to his feet, a look of horror on his face. He dropped both pack and dagger—the latter landed point-down and sank into the floor up to its hilt, as if it had been dropped into a pot of warm butter—and lunged toward Yexandor, perhaps hoping to rescue him from the power of the wand, but the ancient elf's wracked body exploded the instant they made contact. Greasy ash and sizzling vapor bloomed in a flash of light that flung Orindel across the room, where he smashed into the wall and collapsed in a blackened heap. At the same time, Shelliyan cried out as the human dealt her wrist a sharp blow with his staff. The wand flew from her hand, spinning end over end and flaring wildly, drawing squiggles of charred wood across the floor and ceiling that, miraculously, didn't hit anyone, until it finally exploded in a shower of sparks and splinters. Shelliyan clasped her hand to her breast and swept the room with a baleful glare.

For a moment, no one moved; no one spoke.

Then the human looked at Ambrosia. An odd quiver crossed his face, as if his eyes, nose, and mouth were being subtly rearranged; afterwards, his features were unchanged, but his expression was completely different, softer. She saw recognition there. He *knew* her.

His mouth stretched into a wide, happy, incongruous grin.

"Hi, Mercy," he said.

Chapter 8

"WHY DID YOU call me Mercy?" Mercy said, eyeing Bernard with grave suspicion.

"Because it's your name," he said. The look on her face informed him that she didn't have the faintest idea who he was or what he was doing there. This wasn't at all how he had expected their reunion to go. "You don't remember? The game in your room? You were playing an elf, and I——"

The female he had knocked down suddenly cried, "You see? I knew there was something wrong with her. I knew it!"

The other elf, the one standing next to Mercy, said, "It was not *Ambrosia* who slew Yexandor, Shelliyan. It was *you*."

"But look! *Him*! Why did she bring a *human* here?"

Mercy and the other elf glanced at him, evidently considering this a fair question.

"She didn't *bring* me, I——" He never finished the sentence; Bernard, catching movement from the corner of his eye, whirled as the one called Shelliyan grabbed the satchel that her companion had dropped and scuttled toward the glowing, baseball-sized gem that lay on the floor in the other room. That had to be the Illata or, depending on your politics, the Brisindeld.

Whatever it was, if she wanted it, Bernard didn't intend to let her to have it.

In the back of his mind, Brannoc howled for control. Bernard had let the rogue take over for his first entry to the room, when there had been at least two opponents and he'd had no idea what to expect. But one female elf, unarmed, injured, crawling? He could easily get to the gem before she could. Ignoring Brannoc, he levered himself into motion and sprinted into the other chamber, bringing his quarterstaff around, ready to knock the stone away if it looked like the female might reach it first; but as he passed her, she rolled over and snapped her fingers. Yellow light flared brilliantly, blinding him. He stumbled over some debris and braced himself with the quarterstaff to keep from falling, only to have it torn from his grip; a moment later something struck him hard across the backs of his knees. He crumpled to the floor, just as the *twang* of a bowstring sliced through the air. He felt something whisk past his ear as he fell.

He heard Mercy shout, "*Stop!*"

Bernard landed hard on his elbow and rolled over onto his side, blinking away tears as his vision returned. He could make out two slim, tall shapes near the door. Archers. The first was nocking an arrow, while the second had one drawn and ready to fire. Nearby, the female elf crouched, palms raised defensively. She squirmed away from him and cried, "What are you waiting for? He attacked me, shoot him, *shoot*!"

"No! Hold!" That was the one who'd been standing near Mercy. "Both of you, hold!"

The archers looked puzzled, but they complied. Keeping his hands where they could be seen, Bernard struggled to a kneeling position. His staff lay nearby—he was pretty sure that Shelliyan had snatched it and whacked him with it while he'd been dazzled—but he made no move to pick it up; reaching for a weapon seemed like a good way to get himself shot. Instead, he behaved as if he were still blind, rubbing his eyes, casting his gaze around at nothing.

Shelliyan pointed at the corpse against the wall and said, "Look. He killed Orindel. *Look*!"

The bowman on the right shifted his gaze for a moment, eyeing the body. The female's expression turned crafty and she bolted toward the gem. Both archers fired, but the one who had been distracted missed completely, and the other obviously wasn't shooting to kill; his projectile took Shelliyan in the left calf, passing partway through before stopping, like a bloody prank arrow a jokester might wear on his head. Her jagged shriek was anything but jokey, though; it was more like panes of glass being fed into a wood chipper. She went down, rolled over, and came up in a sitting position, glaring at the archers, her face a mask of fury, almond eyes narrowed and dark, weird streaks of mottled blue and grey momentarily marring her alabaster skin, then quickly fading.

Blue? Did elves turn *blue* when they were angry?

No. They did not.

Suddenly Bernard realized what they were dealing with. This was no elf; this must be the Rittandic sorcerer the dwarves had sent, who had gone undercover, then gone rogue. But before he could warn the others, he noticed that the debris littering the room—including the arrows that had missed their targets—had started to shiver; an instant later they began firing themselves with cannonball force at everyone who was still standing. The elves were forced to scatter before the fusillade; the first archer went down when a hunk of wood the size of a yule log bounced off his head, and the second fell with an arrow in his neck. He couldn't see what happened to Mercy or the elf who had been at her side.

Something was rattling nearby: His quarterstaff, shivering, slowly rotating, getting ready to fly. He lunged and grabbed it off the floor. Whatever force animated it didn't survive his touch; it went with him as easily as any inert piece of wood as he rolled back to his feet, loping toward the Illata. The Rittandic had almost reached the gem, holding the satchel open to scoop it up, but Bernard moved a lot faster than she could with that arrow in her leg and got there just ahead of her. He didn't have time to grab the stone himself, so he swung his staff at it like a polo club. Striking the Illata felt like hitting a booby-trapped cinderblock with a hockey stick. There was an explosion of blue light; his hands went numb; his forearms tingled; and, as if he had detonated a bomb underneath it, the jewel went flying toward the door.

Where Mercy, who had just ventured to show herself, caught it with both hands.

~~~~

Once the barrage of broken wood stopped, Ambrosia cautiously stepped into the archway to see if she could do anything to help, only to find the Illata flying straight at her. Catching it had been an automatic reaction; now her fingers were clenched around the thing as if glued there, while the power of the stone throbbed up her arms and throughout her body, a feeling of prickly heat, unbearable pressure, crackling energy. She felt she might burst into flames, or pop like a bubble, or, perhaps, merely fall down dead.

Instead, the world exploded in an eruption of strings and streamers of light, flares and showers of sparks, a whirling, swirling cacophony of noise and fire and smoke and glitter. She found herself caught up in it as if it were a storm, a hurricane raging beneath her feet. The chaotic upwelling lifted her into an endless sky. The sensation was not unlike how it had felt when she'd used the energy of her own strings to free herself from her fetters; and although there was something alien here, something foreign and powerful beyond what she'd managed to conjure out of her own essence, she seemed to be at the center of the violence, the eye around which it spun.

As soon as that thought occurred to her, the luminous mass slowed in its rotation. It began to contract, collapsing inward, layer after layer slamming into her, each imparting a little bit of momentum until she was spinning so fast she felt she might fly to pieces, until—

Until it all stopped.

She floated in a cold dark empty silence, somewhere outside of herself, outside of the world, outside of *everything*; and alone, so utterly alone. She had no idea how long she spent drifting in the nowhere; in
~~~~

this void the concept of hours and minutes seemed absurd. Her senses glazed over like water skinned with ice beneath a winter wind. Something began to stir inside her belly, a faint rumble as of approaching hunger, slowly drawing her from the fugue into which she had slipped. She reached down to touch her abdomen; it felt stretched and hot, and something roiled beneath the skin. Her flesh opened up as if her fingers were knives; her body erupted, disgorging everything that had coalesced into her, an explosion of strings in every hue imaginable, a spectrum as wide as the universe. She had absorbed them in layers and she emitted them the same way, each flash becoming a spherical shell that drifted away, solidified, then was blocked off from view by another, smaller sphere that formed inside it. The outer ones were loosely porous, like a knit stretched too far, but the weaving—that was the only thing she think to could call it—became tighter as the spheres became smaller, until finally she could no longer see through from one to the next. This continued until, at last, she had nothing more to donate to the layering process, leaving her there in the middle, a dust mote at the center of a hailstone, encased in an unbreakable shell. But the shell *could* break, and did, starting with a crack that formed in front of her and spread in either direction, one jag racing upwards to curve over her head, the other arcing down beneath her feet. Light spilled in through the break, filling the interior up like seeping water, drowning her in the glow, until it grew so bright that everything turned black.

~~~~

Bernard watched, aghast, as Mercy's body went rigid, as if she had become the channel for a massive electrical current from the gem to the floor. Never taking his gaze off her, he knelt down and fumbled for his weapon, which he had dropped when the shock of striking the Illata had passed through it. He thought he would pick his staff up and go help her somehow, but instead he lost his balance and collapsed in a heap on the floor. He felt weak, wobbly, cored like an apple. The stone had done that, he realized, and he hadn't even touched it, while Mercy was standing there with her fingers wrapped around it. So what must it be doing to her?

He finally got hold of his quarterstaff and, using it as a crutch, struggled back to his feet. A stained arrow on the ground nearby drew his attention; a thin, jagged, crimson dribble ran across the floor from where it lay, leading his gaze back toward Mercy. As he watched, the bloody trail grew longer, drawing closer to her, but he saw no one; the sanguine droplets simply materialized out of nowhere, nearly black
~~~~

against the brown wood, occasionally smeared into ruddy streaks.

Obviously, the fake elf had removed the arrow from her leg, then turned herself invisible. A few days ago he would have cheerfully derided that as one of Mercy's nutty fantasy confections, but things had changed, hadn't they?

It didn't look like any help would be coming from the other elves, who were still recovering from being pummeled by flying pieces of wood. The unarmed one who had been standing with Mercy seemed to be dead, or at least unconscious, his face bruised and covered with blood from a gash in his forehead. The archer with the arrow in his neck was dead, too, staring at the hole in the ceiling with wide eyes, as if astonished to see such damage; the other archer was awake, but his bow was broken. Evidently oblivious to Mercy's plight, he was attempting with feeble determination to extricate his fallen companion's weapon from beneath his corpse without damaging it. By the time he got it out, it would be too late to do any good.

Bernard tried to take a step, stumbled, and collapsed in a heap on the floor. He managed to push himself upright, but couldn't put together enough coordination to stand up again, and could only watch as the air in front of Mercy flickered and parted like a curtain. A long, narrow finger of shadow spread across the floor and solidified, dimming the light of the Illata. The creature throwing the shadow was no longer a pretty elf, though it was still clad in her clothes, absurdly ill-fitting now. Sleeves which had been long reached to just past the elbow of its skinny arms; likewise, what had been a full skirt dangled barely to its knees, while the green leggings beneath had stretched and torn such that they looked like they had blue polka-dots. The elf's golden tresses had vanished, leaving behind a bare, vertically-elongated skull; her creamy skin had gone cyanotic grey, mottled by dark blue veins beneath. Bernard found himself reminded of an alien antagonist from some paranoiac Cold War space invader film. He wondered if there was a flying saucer parked outside, just waiting to have the Illata plugged into its engine so that it could take off for the stars.

The creature still carried its satchel, dangling by the strap. It stood there for a moment, studying Mercy, perhaps trying to figure out how it could pry the jewel away from her without actually touching the stone; then it positioned the open mouth of the pack below the Illata and made a gesture with its free hand. Seemingly in response, the gem quivered within the cage of Mercy's fingers, but it didn't fall.

"Leave her alone," Bernard said, his voice a humiliating squeak.

The Rittandic glanced at him appraisingly, letting him see its long, flat face, its slit of a nose, its wide, thin-lipped mouth. Its vast black eyes narrowed; the edges of its lips twitched into what may have been a smile. It gave a faint, contemptuous snort, and turned away. Its gaze landed on the hilt of a dagger that protruded from the floor nearby nearby. It opened its palm; the weapon slid free, easy as a knife from a well-baked cake, and flew into its grip. It eyed the weapon, then turned and held it over Mercy's wrist, evidently intending to saw through her hands and free the Illata that way.

"No," Bernard said. Then, louder: "Mercy, *wake up!*"

Mercy blinked. Her eyes came back into focus.

"You can't have this," she said.

The Rittandic shrieked as a shimmering disc of light appeared between it and Mercy. The center of the field flickered collapsed in on itself, forming what looked like a tunnel, endlessly deep yet perfectly flat. The gangly creature was pulled bodily into the opening, as if something within had reached out and yanked it in. Surrounding debris shivered on the floor, and a few smaller pieces began bumping and scraping toward where Mercy stood, until she crumpled to the floor and lay still. The portal shrank to a pinpoint, then to nothing.

The remaining archer finally freed his companion's bow and nocked an arrow, but couldn't seem to decide where to aim it. He eventually settled on the floor in the vicinity of the doorway, though it would obviously take less than a moment to retarget it at Bernard if necessary. Deciding to ignore the bowman, Bernard half-stumbled, half-crawled to where Mercy lay. He studied her for a moment, then rolled her over. An electric tingle washed across her skin, rippled into his fingers, startling him into pulling back. She still clutched the gem with both hands, pressing it into her stomach.

A worn, groggy voice said, "Be careful."

Bernard looked around. The speaker was the elf who'd been standing with Mercy earlier; he had pushed himself up on one elbow, and now regarded Mercy with a mournful look on his face. "Do not touch the Illata," the elf said. "To touch the Illata with bare flesh is fatal, and there has been enough death this night."

Bernard said: "She isn't dead."

"But she must ..." The elf trailed off as Mercy's lashes fluttered, her eyelids opened. She sat up, shook her head, looked down at the jewel in her hands, then, finally, at Bernard.

"About time you showed up," she said.

<div align="center">~~~~</div>

Meliander was right. There had been enough death tonight.

Ambrosia watched Bernard and Nebandalex carry Orindel over to where Glorian lay; they had suffered the least damage, so that job had fallen to them. Meliander had managed to drag himself to one of the benches, where he now sat, head in hands. Blood had stopped flowing from his head wound, but it obviously still pained him significantly. She herself, although unharmed physically, felt that if she tried to do too much, move too much, she might evaporate. She wanted to go to Glorian, thank him, shut his eyes for him, but she didn't dare.

The Illata had not killed her, but it had *changed* her, and the effects of that change were still roiling around inside her. It had found some dormant or forgotten aspect of her psyche and activated it, brought it forward, stitching it into her consciousness. This, she had realized, must be what the enchantment had excised from her mind. The restored memories and persona belonged not to an elf, but to a young female human; it had recognized the red-haired intruder and, somehow, he had recognized her, seen through the form she wore now to the other one inside. He had called her *Mercy*.

Meliander rose and shuffled over, his hands and sleeves smeared with blood he had wiped away from his face. "How are you?"

"Well enough, I suppose," she said, "considering. What about you?"

"Sore in many places, especially my head." He did not move nearer; she still held the Illata in her hands, after all, and the gem was supposed to kill anyone who touched it or spent too much time in its immediate vicinity. He wouldn't want to get too close to it, or to her. "But *you* should be dead."

"Yes. I've heard."

"The Illata has chosen not to destroy you, but for what reason?"

"It *chose* not to destroy me? Yexandor said it wasn't sentient."

"I know what Yexandor said." He turned his eyes toward the burned spot on the floor. "I wish he could see you here, holding it."

"Me too." Her gaze strayed to the blackened spot on the floor where the ancient elf had been immolated. Three dead; two corpses; and one sent … away. She had a vague recollection of opening, for lack of a better term, a door to elsewhere; but she couldn't say for sure where that door led or what awaited Shelliyan on the other side. The Illata had, perhaps, delivered her to a destination of its own choosing, if it had come to be in the habit of making choices.

The others joined them then. Bernard, evidently unconcerned about the Illata's purported instant-death properties, came up close to her, while Nebandalex hung back. "Mercy?" Bernard said. "You know who I am now, right?"

"Yes. You're Bernard." He smiled. "You're also Brannoc." His smile faltered. She squinted at him. "Mostly Bernard, I think. At least at the moment." At that, his smile vanished completely, and she realized with some surprise that he didn't *want* to be Brannoc. Considering that most of the skills they would need going forward belonged to Brannoc, that could be problematic; she would have to keep it in mind. "Bernard, meet Meliander and Nebandalex. I'm afraid it's too late to introduce you to Glorian, Orindel, Yexandor, or Shelliyan."

Meliander and Nebandalex exchanged a glance; then Meliander said, "And you are … *Mercy*, was it?"

"Part of me is."

"The elf," Bernard said, "Shelliyan? She … I think she was something called a Rittandic. A sorcerer sent by the dwarves to steal the Brisindeld."

Ambrosia stared at him. So did the others.

"But, um, she double-crossed them," he said. "I think."

"And you think this because … ?" Ambrosia asked.

"When they were holding me prisoner, they told me they sent a Rittandic sorcerer to infiltrate your village about a year ago, but after a few months they lost contact." When no one said anything, he touched his nose, which she recognized as one of Bernard's nervous gestures; he was pushing up glasses he no longer wore. "They thought you had caught her, but I guess she went rogue. I mean, it sure looked like she wanted the gem for herself."

For several seconds, no one spoke; finally, Meliander said: "The *dwarves* told you this."

"Um, yes."

More silence. Meliander said: "Further elaboration *will* be required."

"Oh right. Yeah. So, they caught me and made me fight in their arena, and when I … um, when I won, they gave me a map and sent me here to fetch the stone for them." He looked at Ambrosia. "But I was never going to steal the Illata! I just wanted to find you, so we could get home, and I … I thought you would be here maybe."

"If this sorcerer was imitating her," Nebandalex said, "where is the real Shelliyan?" No one said anything, and after a moment he turned to Bernard, arms spread wide. "What else did the dwarves say? Do they have Shelliyan captive in their city?"

"I don't think so. They seemed to be completely in the dark about what the Rittandic up to. Listen, about the——"

"What does that mean, *in the dark*?"

"It means they didn't know what the Rittandic was doing. She told them she could infiltrate the village, but I don't think they knew how she was planning to do that. But there's more. The fire——"

"I will go to their city and find——"

"No, listen! The dwarves started the fire!" Bernard said. "They have artillery, they've been shooting firebombs into the forest!"

Meliander said: "What is artillery?"

"Guns! Cannons! Really big ones."

Ambrosia sensed alarm emanating from the Mercy persona. She knew what Bernard was talking about, what *cannons* were, what *artillery* was, and it wasn't good.

"They're trying to burn you out, don't you see? Then they can just come in and take the Brisindeld themselves."

"Shelliyan must have known they were going to attack today. That was what she meant when she said this would be the last night the village would exist," Ambrosia said.

"How could she know that? She was out of touch with the dwarves——"

"Not exactly," Ambrosia said. "The *dwarves* were out of touch with *her*. That doesn't mean she didn't have ways to find out what they were doing."

"Okay, maybe so, but——"

"What she did or did not know does not matter," Meliander said. "What matters at this moment is that the forest is burning." He looked at Ambrosia. "Can you stop the fire? Can you bring the rain, or change the wind?"

"I don't think I'm strong enough."

"Not on your own. But with the Illata … ?"

She hefted the gem, peered at it like a potentially delicious, potentially poisonous apple that she was thinking about eating. "I don't know. Maybe." She looked at him. "I can try."

"Please. We would be grateful."

She nodded, then pressed her hands into either side of the gem, rolling its smooth, warm, glassy facets between her palms, feeling the energy within. Meliander wanted rain? Mercy knew where she could find rain.

Ambrosia visualized the nook outside her Mercy-self's room, imagined she was looking out the window as an enormous storm spent its fury outside. Wind-driven water spattered against the glass, coursed down in sheets from the sky, soaking the yard, the woods, the street. She went to the window on the opposite side of the room. From this window Mercy would normally see the street as it curved away from her house, but now it overlooked the burning forest of Torgonderrer instead, stretching out below her, as if the room floated on a cloud high above the ground. The fire had already scorched much of the woodland, leaving behind smoldering ruins and flaring hotspots, and was beginning to burn into areas where the trees were special, grown from seeds and stock that had survived the destruction of the ancient forest. If the flames were to be stopped, now was the time to do it, when the heart of the elven territory was singed but not blackened. Turning away, she padded across the warm, dry room, back to the window that blocked the storm. She took hold of the sash and flung it upward. A chill wind surged forward eagerly, carrying its load of moisture, filling the room with swirling wind and icy spray.

She returned to the window that overlooked the fire. The carpet, sodden now, squished beneath her feet. Water soaked into her slippers; her saturated, freezing robe clung to her like the shroud that wrapped a body buried at sea. She stood there for a moment, shivering, then threw the window wide. The powerful storm rushed out; the room became a conduit channeling clouds and wind and rain from one world into another.

Ambrosia stepped away from the windows, out of the direct line of the maelstrom. That was when she noticed a trapdoor nearby. The Mercy part of her consciousness told her that it opened onto spiral stairs descending into the kitchen of the house where she lived. She plodded over to it, knelt down, fumbled with the handle; the cold had begun to seep into her hands and fingers, making them stiff and clumsy. Finally, though, she got it open, flipping it over to bang flat against the floor. Spiral stairs went down, all right, but they didn't go to a kitchen; instead they kept going, around and around and around, vanishing into what seemed to be a limitless void.

Well, why not?

She lowered herself through the opening, pulled the door shut on the howling wind, and started descending.

~~~~

Mercy seemed to have gone inside the gem again; Bernard stayed at her side for a little while and then, feeling useless, limped over to the entrance. Now that the fighting was over and the adrenaline rush was wearing off, he had begun to feel battered and sore. He was sure he'd feel worse in the morning, and there'd be no running to the medicine
~~~~

cabinet for ibuprofen.

The remaining archer, Nebandalex, stood just outside the arch, staring moodily at the fire. His lips were moving. Bernard couldn't hear what he was saying; maybe it was a prayer, maybe a curse. Whatever it was, he stopped when Bernard came over, but gave no other sign that he knew someone else was there.

"I'm sorry about your friends," Bernard said after a moment.

No response.

"You and … Glorian, was it? You got here just in time."

"Sooner would have been better," Nebandalex said, "but we were … delayed."

"Oh?"

"Glorian said it was a misdirection glamour."

"What's a misdir—"

"We could not get out until something destroyed the enchantment. I cannot say what broke the spell, but it destroyed my house and threw us into the woods. We had to run to the armory so I could get a new bow and Glorian could get arrows. Orindel had taken his, to keep him from doing anything *rash*." He finally looked at Bernard. "Did you say the dwarves sent that creature to the village over a *year* ago?"

Bernard, who had been having some difficulty following the elf's rambling stream of thought, didn't realize right away that he'd been asked a question. "Um, that's what they told me."

"A year." Nebandalex shook his head. "How could I have failed to realize she was not herself anymore?"

"It was a very convincing illusion."

"That was no illusion. That was … something else." Nebandalex turned away, staring off into the darkness again.

Bernard stood there for a little while, not sure what else to say; so he wandered back to where Mercy stood, rigid and insensible, under Meliander's careful gaze. The elf glanced at Bernard as he approached. "You are from Banderlund," he said.

"So I've been told."

"This is a long way from Banderlund. You would have had to make your way down the entire length of the Slash to get here, unless you came over the Fists." Meliander examined him as if looking for rope and pitons. "*Did* you come over the mountains? Is that how you came to be captured by the dwarves?"

"No. They caught me outside their city. They thought I was planning to rob them."

"Were you?"

"Possibly," Bernard said.

"And your friend?" Meliander indicated Mercy. "Did she plan to steal from us, as you possibly planned to steal from the dwarves?"

"Absolutely not. My character is the thief; hers is the sorceress. Hers is *always* the sorceress."

The elf gave him a quizzical look. "I do not understand."

"Join the club," Bernard said.

"What club?"

Nebandalex stuck his head in the doorway. "Rain," he said.

~~~~

The spiral staircase seemed to corkscrew on forever, a slender, faintly lambent iron column dropping through the void. She'd gotten over her initial caution and was taking the steps much faster now, not quite *running* down them—they were wound in too tight of a circle for that—but definitely not walking, either. Despite this, she still didn't seem to be getting anywhere, although the total lack of reference points made it difficult to gauge her progress. She wished the steps would just fold themselves into a slide; it would make the descent go a lot faster.

As that thought fleeted through her mind, a series of metallic clangs began to ring out from somewhere far below. The sounds grew rapidly louder; for a moment she feared that an iron-shod something had come across the distant terminus of the staircase and decided to charge up it. She gripped the central post that supported the steps, felt it thrum beneath her her hand. The vibrations seemed too steady to be footsteps. Besides, this was *her* place; she had made it; there were no monsters here, no bogeymen, nothing but what she had brought with her. At least, she thought so.

So what *was* happening, then?

She got an answer when the clattering reached her, not long after it started. The ridged treads of the visible steps below the one where she stood retracted, then pivoted forward in sequence, each locking itself at a seamless angle against the next one down, forming a smooth, continuous surface. Afterwards, thin metal flaps folded out from their undersides, swung up and around, and snapped into place against the railing, creating a solid outer wall. Then the stairway gave one last shudder; the noises and vibration stopped. The transformation was over.

Ambrosia eyed the gleaming ramp at her feet. She had wished for a slide? Well now she had one. But did she really want to use it? Undecided, she sat down and probed the slide with her foot. It felt
~~~~

solid enough, and slippery; not greased, exactly, but she didn't think she needed to worry that it would peel her skin off. Of course, that also meant she would have difficulty even slowing down, let alone stopping, if for some reason she didn't like where the slide was taking her.

She could feel the Mercy part of her growing impatient. The idea of a slide had originated with her, and Ambrosia could feel that Mercy wanted to get going; the others were waiting for her, for them, but she couldn't quite bring herself to give the push that would propel her on her way. As she dithered, the step on which she sat suddenly shivered and tipped forward, dumping her into the chute. She shot downward in a dizzying spiral, around and around and around, faster and faster, terrified and cackling with glee at the same time, as if this were the realization of some longstanding ambition. Before long the spinning void around her started to lighten, details appearing as the background faded into view. She was moving so fast that it was largely a blur, but she thought she recognized the interior of Yexandor's huge fallen tree, so was not surprised when the end of the slide came into view and, at the bottom, she saw herself standing there, holding the Illata. Her body loomed massively large as she exited the slide and slammed into it.

She blinked and looked around. Her upper lip felt wet. She touched it, saw bright blood on her fingertips; she must have taken a shot to the face during the fight. She didn't remember being hit, but it had all been happening very fast.

Bernard stood nearby, watching her. "You're back," he said.

She nodded.

He pointed at the ceiling. "Look. Listen."

She looked. She listened. Rain thrummed overhead, blew in through the archway, fell through the hole in the roof. She grinned at him. "I did it."

"Yes," he said. Then: "You're bleeding." He produced a rather disreputable-looking rag from somewhere and reached out to sop up the blood, but she recoiled and shook her head, not ready to be touched. He seemed taken aback, and after a moment stuffed the scrap of cloth back into whatever hidden pocket it had come from.

"Sorry," she said.

"Forget it."

"I just … I didn't—"

"So who are you now? Mercy, or Ambrosia?"

"Yes," she said.

"Yes?"

"I'm both, the same way that you're both Bernard and Brannoc."

"I'm just *Bernard*," he said. "Brannoc is only a character, the same way Ambrosia is *only a character*. You're not Ambrosia, you're *Mercy*. You're just … confused."

"I see. And *Bernard* knows how to handle a quarterstaff, then?"

"I—"

"*Bernard* knows how to speak Elvish?"

"No, but—"

"Don't tell me who to be and I won't tell you, all right?" Leaving him there, Ambrosia swept off to join Meliander and Nebandalex at the door. Rain fell heavily all around, soaking up the fading glow of the fire. After a little while she heard Bernard come up next to her, but he didn't speak; the four of them just stood just inside the entrance, in a silence that was not exactly companionable, watching the sky weep. At length, she touched Meliander's elbow; he started and looked at her hand as if he thought it might be electrified.

"We need to go," she said.

"Who is *we?*"

"Bernard and me."

From behind her, Bernard said: "Us?"

She held up the Illata; it seemed quiescent now, its glow muted but still present, a ghostly light flickering in its depths. "I have to take this. It doesn't belong here."

Meliander scarcely glanced at the gem before shrugging and turning back to face the rain. "Take it, then," he said. "It has brought us conflict and death. It was useful once, perhaps, but ..." He shook his head. "I told Yexandor many times we would be better rid of it."

Nebandalex said: "You are just going to *give* it to her?"

"Look at her, standing there, holding it in her hand. Yexandor could never use it the way she did, not even after all those years."

"But it belongs to the dwarves. If we return it to them, they will stop—"

"It doesn't belong to the dwarves, either," she said.

"So it belongs to no one," Nebandalex said after a moment. "How convenient."

"It doesn't belong to *no one*," she said, "it belongs to *everyone*. And I have to put it back together."

"Put what back together?"

"The Heart," Bernard said. "You think it's a piece of that Heart thing, don't you?"

"What else would it be?"

"What *heart*? Meliander, what are they talking about?"

"Ambrosia believes the Illata is part of a broken god," Meliander said. Then, to Bernard: "It seems that you have also heard of this Heart. What do *you* believe?"

"I don't believe anything." Bernard shrugged. "The dwarves claimed they found it while they were digging a tunnel."

"And the elves tripped over it out in the hills," Ambrosia said. "That doesn't mean it's not the Heart."

"Gods just leave pieces of themselves all over the place here, I guess?"

"When they get shattered by other gods, yes. But I can find the other pieces. I can fix it."

"What makes you think that?"

She held the Illata up. "Because *I* can use it."

"Okay, fair enough," Bernard said. "But why should we?"

"You know why, Bernard! This is just *one piece*, and you just saw how powerful it is. If the Rittandic gets hold of one, that will lead it to the others. If it gets hold of all of them, it'll——"

"It'll what? Destroy the world? Turn everything purple? Make itself President-For-Life? Why is that *our* problem? We aren't even *from* here! Have you forgotten that?"

"What makes you so sure it'll stop with *this* world? You saw what I just did. The Illata can open doors between dimensions."

"Oh, I saw it all right," he said. "So let's open one that goes home, and get out of here."

"No."

After a moment Bernard said: "What?"

"You heard me."

"Fine, you stay here and play fantasy heroine," he said. "*I* want to go home."

The part of Ambrosia that was Mercy knew Bernard well enough to have expected some resistance, but this flat-out refusal surprised her. "But … Bernard, I need your help. You wouldn't abandon your friend Mercy, would you?"

"You're not Mercy," he said. "You told me so yourself."

"Enough," Meliander said. "If you would take the Illata, take it now and go. You may send your …" He looked Bernard over. "Your *friend* home once you are away from the village." He turned to Nebandalex. "Guide them to the river gate. It should be deserted; Yexandor sent everyone to the lake when the scale of the fire became clear."

"What will you tell the others about the Illata?" Nebandalex asked.

"The truth," Meliander said. "I will say a sorceress took it."

Chapter 9

THE DOWNPOUR HAD turned the spiral path into a morass of sludge and gravel, so they descended with relative care. No doubt agile Brannoc could swarm down it with the surefootedness of a mountain goat, but Bernard wanted to prove that he didn't need Brannoc just to get down a stupid muddy slope. Besides, keeping the Illata away from the Rittandic had left all of them injured; even if the trail had been completely dry and easily passable, he doubted they'd be moving much faster than they were now.

He wasn't in a big hurry to get off the hill anyway, because that would put him that much closer to having to make a serious decision. He knew that Mercy or Ambrosia or whoever she was must be furious with him for wanting to leave, but what did she expect? He'd never signed up for any of this. Getting captured and beaten up by dwarves and forced to fight in their arena like some sort of gladiator? Nearly being incinerated by firebombs? Getting beaten up *again* by some weird blue thing disguised as an elf? It made high school seem positively paradisiacal. Who *wouldn't* want out after all that?

Mercy, of course.

He'd hoped that if he insisted on leaving, she would agree to go with him, but clearly that wasn't going to happen; she had convinced herself they'd been brought here for a reason, to fix what no one else could fix, and whether from some misplaced sense of responsibility or a long-frustrated wish to be a heroine or simply boredom with the humdrum world from which they came, she had decided to take ownership of this supposed crisis. She had even convinced herself she wasn't Mercy, that she was, in reality, an elf with a human streak. Talk about an identity crisis! The fact that they were actually in the bodies of their game characters certainly didn't help.

At length they reached the bottom of the hill and paused there, soaked and shivering. "Nebandalex, I'll need supplies," Mercy said. Bernard thought he heard a subtle emphasis on the *I'll*. Was that a dig at him?

Of course it was.

"We can stop by the common area for food and water," Nebandalex said. "The river gate is in that direction anyway."

The downpour didn't let up at all as they moved beneath the dripping leaves. Frigid rain entered Bernard's collar and flowed down his back, exiting from his pant legs and into his boots. He began to feel a tug on his neck, which he eventually realized was because the hood of his cloak had filled up like a water balloon. All this time and he hadn't even known his cloak *had* a hood. He emptied it and then pulled it up over his head, which made things marginally better. Marginally.

The common area turned out to be an elf-style cafeteria, which meant trees for walls and stumps for tables and, of course, no roof to keep out precipitation, either because it never rained here or because elves though rain was cool. Circular puddles dotted the ground; it took him a moment to realize these were submerged fire pits. The tables were bedecked with abandoned hollowware that had turned into birdbaths. Obviously the place had been evacuated in a hurry. Bernard followed the others to a section where a few lean-tos woven from branches and leaves kept piles of supplies dry, sort of. Mercy harvested a few leathery sacks from a heap beneath one shelter and started filling them with goods that Nebandalex pointed out as suitable for taking on the trail. Soon Nebandalex picked up a couple of bags and began stuffing them with dried fruit, jerky, hard bread, and the like; feeling guilty and a bit left out, Bernard did the same. By the time they had finished gathering rations, they looked like thieves staging a heist from a tannery.

As they moved away from the shacks, Bernard said: "Okay, we've raided the fridge, now what?"

"To the river," Nebandalex said. He took the lead again, guiding them along minor trails toward the river gate. Being narrow and twisty and therefore more sheltered by overhanging trees, these were slightly less rain-soaked and wind-blasted than the ways they had taken before. It took no time at all for Bernard to become completely disoriented. Finally they emerged onto a larger path, where they turned left. The trail sloped downward while the land around it rose, then it suddenly reversed and bent skyward. They scrambled up the muddy slope to a saddle in the ridge, the gap blocked by a tall, arrow-slitted stockade wall with a relatively narrow gate. Mercy headed for the door, but Nebandalex put his arm in front of her to stop her. "Wait."

"What?"

"I hear something." Motioning for them to stay where they were, he went to the wall and peered through one of the arrow slits.

"Do you see anything?" she asked.

He looked back at them. "Dwarves. In *boats.* Come look."

They joined him at the fence. Bernard squinted through one of the apertures. He could see where the river flowed by at the bottom of a steep, rocky embankment, carrying a procession of miniature warships along in its slow current. He recognized it as the flotilla that had been bobbing in the small marina where he'd exited the dwarven city via the cleft in the mountain; they must have launched it after the forest fire had gotten going, as an expeditionary force to take the village, drive out the elves, and reclaim the Brisindeld. On one of the vessels that had just passed, two dwarven sailors were arguing in loud, rumbling voices; that must be what Nebandalex had heard. Or maybe they weren't arguing, maybe they were just having a conversation. Bernard wasn't sure he could tell the difference, when it came to dwarves.

"They look like they're made of stone and metal," Mercy said. "Are they?"

"No, that's just their skin," Bernard said. "It's tough, but not as tough as it looks. It's not armor. You can knock them out if you hit them hard enough."

"The river will take them to the lake," Nebandalex said. "They must plan to come ashore on the eastern beach and enter through the gate behind Yexandor's ... behind the hill." He looked over his shoulder, as if he might be able to see the invasion from here. "I must go and warn the others."

"You can't fight them," Bernard said. "See those hollow tubes on the decks? Those are called *cannons*. If they open fire on your rowboats, it'll be a slaughter."

Nebandalex said: "Our archers will—"

"Your archers will nothing. You have to surrender." Nebandalex just stared at him. "Don't you understand? When they get to the lake, they'll sink every boat you've got."

"Then we can't let them make it to the lake," Mercy said, taking the Illata out of her pack.

~~~~

Ambrosia held the gem in her palm, concentrating, willing it awake. Thunder rumbled overhead as the stone's glow intensified. She was vaguely aware that Bernard and Nebandalex stood nearby gawking at her, but her attention was on the Illata. She had used it to summon this storm. The storm remembered that. It remembered *her*.

Lightning flashed out of the sky, streaked through the rain, striking the lead ship as it rounded a bend some distance away. The vessel blossomed into an orange flower; something aboard detonated, flinging fiery shrapnel in every direction. A second blast reduced it to a swiftly sinking raft of flaming debris. The next boat in line came to a halt as it ground into the burning wreckage. Its hull, swabbed with
~~~~

inflammable waterproofing material, ignited, turning it into a massive floating torch. It slowly turned sideways, then stopped and jammed up against the bank, a flaming wall blocking the river. The remaining ships dropped anchors on short lines, arresting their forward motion. They swung around in the current at the end of their tethers, turning broadside to the ridge. Small, dark shapes scurried along the decks; sparkling lights flared as they gathered behind the cannons, lit the fuses.

Bernard said: "How do they know where to ..." He trailed off and, wide-eyed, turned to look at Ambrosia. She glanced down at the glowing gem in her hands. Its light spilled out through the arrow slits, broadcasting long blue-white strips of illumination into the night, telling the dwarves exactly where they were and, perhaps, what they had with them.

Oh crap.

"Get down!" Ambrosia shouted, jumping back from the wall. She flattened herself on the ground as a series of concussions shook the air. Cannon fire blasted chunks from the top of the stockade, thudded into the sodden slope and forest behind them. Muffled explosions ensued, followed by a patter of mud and sand and steaming leaf litter.

"It's all right," Bernard said, still crouching at the base of the wall with one eye to the slit.

Ambrosia and Nebandalex—who had hit the dirt the same time she had—exchanged a glance. "What about this could possibly be *all right*?" Nebandalex said.

"Physics," Bernard said, not turning. "They can't get a clear shot at us here. They're trying to figure it out, but the embankment is too steep. Their cannons won't point at the right angle. They either have to fire way over our heads, or into the ridge below the wall." He jerked his thumb over his shoulder, indicating the cratered terrain behind them. "We're safer here than we would be back there."

Ambrosia eyed the splintered wood at the top of the stockade, and didn't feel particularly safe at all.

Then Bernard said, "Uh-oh. They're coming ashore."

"Please tell me they don't have guns," Ambrosia said.

"Um. Well they don't look like the sort of guns we're used to. More like flintlocks."

"Flintlocks? Those don't work in the rain."

"Oh, *these* flintlocks will work, or I don't know anything about dwarves." Bernard abandoned his position at the wall to join them. "They have axes too. They're going to hack their way in and then start shooting. What was that you said before about me being able to dodge bullets?"

"I wouldn't actually count on that if I were you. How many dwarves are coming?"

"I counted five boats left, maybe ten or eleven to a boat."

"Nebandalex, how many arrows do you have?"

"Not enough," Nebandalex said.

"There's no way we can hold the stockade," Bernard said. "We have to——" He broke off as Ambrosia hefted the Illata, holding it in front of her, denser than leaded crystal. In its cold light, the three of them cast long shadows in different directions, each separated by a wedge of rain-slicked grass.

"We don't have to hold the stockade," she said. "You two stay here. Be ready to run in case this doesn't work."

"In case *what* doesn't work?" Bernard asked.

Without answering, she left the others and went to stand in front of the gate, which had begun to shudder as axe-blows struck in time with shouted commands. She held the Illata out in front of her like a witch offering an apple to an unsuspecting princess.

Bernard appeared on her left side, Nebandalex on her right.

"I thought I told you to stay back there," she said.

Bernard snorted. "Fat chance."

As the Illata glowed brighter, she couldn't quite suppress a smile.

~~~~

Bernard wasn't sure what she was planning to do; although he was trying not to show it, he was still rather shocked at how she had destroyed the first two ships in the dwarven armada, blowing up or drowning the occupants as if they were of no more consequence than hornets annoying her at a picnic. True, the dwarves had sent the Rittandic, had set the forest on fire, had come in their tiny warships to take the village by force; but even so, he never would have guessed that Mercy could be that casually lethal. Or should he call her Ambrosia? Even though she was Mercy, she wasn't Mercy, and he needed to stop thinking of her as if she were the same girl he knew back home.

Nebandalex drew an arrow and nocked it; figuring he ought to get ready for a fight as well, Bernard slipped his quarterstaff out of its holster, gave it a propeller-style spin, and caught it with both hands. He was starting to get the hang of this thing; when he got home, maybe he could have a career as a baton twirler. Ambrosia stood motionless in between them, her eyes closed, her arm slightly outstretched, the gem luminous in her hand. The gate shuddered from
~~~~

the blows of dwarven axes; whatever she hoped to accomplish, she was almost out of time.

Suddenly he noticed a faint, flickering illumination appear along the outside of the gate, like dawn's light seeping around the edges of a door. As he watched, the glow seeped inward, forming a small disk; then the interior of the circle went black, turning it into a ring. A moment later the gate failed, destroyed not by the invaders but by the singularity that Ambrosia had created; it simply crumpled in on itself as if being wadded up by an invisible hand, then vanished, leaving an opening in the fence. On the other side stood a contingent of startled-looking dwarves. They appeared oddly twisted, as if viewed through a funhouse prism.

Nebandalex fired an arrow, which struck the shimmer and, rejected, fell to the ground in front of it. He did not ready another.

The dwarves nearest the wall slipped and fell as their axes were wrenched from their hands and vanished; they clutched with stubby fingers at the yielding mud as the twist in space dragged them forward. Then they went into the warp and were gone, their cries for help cut off, leaving behind nothing but oozing furrows in the muck. The remaining ranks tried to fall back, but the strengthening suction took hold of them and halted their retreat, then reversed it. They slid uphill, shouting, reaching back toward their fellows, until they too entered the portal and evaporated.

The entire landing party had vanished, but the maw's ravening, unidirectional hunger continued to grow. The typical detritus of a forest—fallen branches, sloughed bark, leaf litter—came flying at it and was devoured; every loose thing on the ships shuddered and scraped across the decks, then tumbled through the air into the rift; this included those few dwarves who had remained aboard. The ships themselves began drifting toward them, pulling their anchor lines tight. Water sloshed over the riverbank, mixed with the muck to form a viscous brown mass slurping up the hill toward where they stood. Ambrosia didn't seem to be aware of this, or of anything else; she just stood there, immobile, holding the Illata as it ate everything on the other side of the fence.

"I think that's enough," Bernard said. She didn't respond. He gave her a gentle shake; no reaction. Her shoulder seemed to thrum beneath his fingers. Beyond the gate, the upper layers of earth had begun to peel away, clumps of rock and viscous sludge dribbling into the devouring hole she had created.

"What do we do?" Nebandalex looked and sounded very worried.

"How do we make her stop?"

"I think … I think we have to …" They had to separate her from the gem, that's what they had to do. Bernard thought for a moment, then inserted his quarterstaff between Ambrosia's body and the Illata and gave the stone a little flick. Once again he felt that jolt of force travel up the wood to make his arms thrum; his muscles involuntarily contracted, causing him to jerk the quarterstaff back, striking her and knocking her down. The Illata fell to the ground on his left, Ambrosia on his right. The warp folded and vanished. The listing ships righted themselves; the mud collapsed in a sheet; the river returned to its channel.

Ambrosia said, in a very small voice: "Ouch."

~~~~

She found herself sprawled in the mud, nursing another nosebleed, with Bernard standing over her leaning on his quarterstaff and looking embarrassed. He proffered a hand and helped her to her feet. "Are you all right?"

"I think so. Did you *hit* me?"

"Um. Not on purpose." He pointed one end of the quarterstaff at the Illata, which sat in the muck nearby. Wisps of steam rose from around it, as if it were boiling away the moisture in the surrounding mud. "I was trying to stop you before the whole forest got sucked into that … that thing you made."

"What thing … ? Oh. *That* thing." She remembered opening a wormhole to send the dwarves back where they had come from or, at least, somewhere other than here; even now they were probably picking themselves up off the floor in some dusty cavern or distant plain, wondering what the hell had just happened. "Couldn't you just yell in my ear or something?"

"You weren't listening."

She grunted and wiped her nose on her sleeve, replacing a smear of muddy blood with a smear of bloody mud, then retrieved the Illata and returned it to the small pack she had appropriated from the Rittandic. "It worked?" she said. "They're gone?"

"Looks like it," Bernard said.

Nebandalex had gone to the open gate to peer at the now-deserted ships. "What did you do with them?"

"She wished them to the cornfield," Bernard said.

"What cornfield?"

"Don't listen to him. There isn't any cornfield." Then: "I told the Illata to send them back to where they came from."
~~~~

"And where's that?" Bernard asked.

"I …" She had no real idea where that wormhole had ended. "I'm not sure. But they're not here anymore. Is the river clear?"

"Yes. The boats are empty."

"You're sure?"

"If any dwarves are left aboard, they are being very still."

"All right." She joined him at the gate; Bernard tagged along behind. "So how do we get across?"

"There was a rope bridge here." Nebandalex pointed at a couple of wooden posts, one tilted upward at a crazy angle toward where the gate had stood, the other lying flat in the mud. "They must have cut it so their ships could pass."

"Is there another way?"

"You could take a skiff across the water; there are several beached nearby. But across the river is just wilderness. Where do you really want to go?"

"I don't know yet," she said. "I have to … consult the Illata, find out where the next closest shard is." She indicated Bernard with a tip of her head. "And I have to figure out how to send this one home."

Bernard raised an eyebrow, but didn't say anything.

"You believe there are other gems like the Illata, stones of a similar nature?"

"I do."

Nebandalex studied her for a thoughtful moment, then tipped his bow toward a limp, dripping thicket at the water's edge. "You will find boats hidden in those bushes. Take one. Go across and camp near the riverbank. I will find you by first light."

He pivoted, but before he could leave she said: "Wait."

Nebandalex stopped, looked back at her over his shoulder.

"Are you coming with me?"

"Yes."

He turned to go. Again, she said: "Wait!"

He stopped, looked at her once more.

"When I see you again, how will I know it's really you?"

"Use a password," Bernard said. "How about *suicide mission*?"

She glared at him. "Fine, we'll use a password," she said, "but not *that* one." She looked at Nebandalex. "The next time we meet, the password will be … will be *ribbit*."

Nebandalex nodded and touched his ear, then ran down the slope to vanish into the woods. She stood there looking at the spot where he had disappeared, until Bernard said, "Why *ribbit*?"

She shrugged. "No reason. Let's go find a boat."

Chapter 10

THE MORNING DAWNED unusually cold for this time of year; a side effect, perhaps, of the storm Ambrosia had summoned. It had blown itself out overnight, leaving behind a sky bleached of color, as if the portals she had opened had drained the blue away. As he poled his canoe across the river, shivering beneath a frosted slate heaven streaked with clouds thin as wisps of faded memory, Nebandalex thought about how warm he would be right now in his little house, with Shelliyan. If, of course, the house had not been destroyed; if Shelliyan had not been taken by the impostor; if he had not chosen to go with Ambrosia, to learn if she was right about the existence of other gems, if the Rittandic was still alive and if it might, like Ambrosia, go in search of the next shard.

He hoped it would.

When he'd run back to Yexandor's hill last night to convey the news about the dwarven fleet, he had thought Meliander would try to dissuade him from leaving the village; but Meliander had only offered vague thanks for returning with the information, and to caution him against letting the desire for revenge blind him. Nebandalex knew that he was thinking of the other elves in the village as he spoke, of how they would react when they learned what the dwarves had done. Would Meliander be able to stay every hand on every bowstring? He had always eschewed leadership of the village, and now that it had fallen to him by default, Nebandalex suspected he would be unable or unwilling to exercise it; but Meliander would need to face that challenge on his own.

He landed near where the others should have come ashore last night. He spotted their trail at once; they had dragged their boat away from the bank and made a clumsy attempt to conceal it behind some bushes, but had failed at camouflage almost as spectacularly as they had at erasing the furrow left behind when they'd pulled it out of the water. He permitted himself a smile at their naivete, even as he made a mental note to rectify it. The dinghy they had taken was larger than his canoe, and better suited for the river voyage that, he thought, must be waiting in their future; so he transferred his supplies to it, then pushed the canoe out into the current. It would most likely end up caught on one of the dwarven ships that still strained their anchor ropes downstream, or in the wreckage of the ones Ambrosia had destroyed; otherwise, his fellow-elves would find it drifting among the cattails in the lake and bring it back to the village. In the confused aftermath of the evacuation, no one would think it unusual to find an abandoned vessel in the reeds.

He left the riverbank, picking up the trail where the others had moved away from the river. Before long he found their things, in a little clearing just out of sight of the water. As he'd expected, they had found the ranging gear stored with the boats; they'd made a crude tent from a large oilcloth, their blankets flat, rumpled, and empty beneath it. The soggy remains of what looked like a failed attempt at a fire sat on the ground just in front of the opening. So here was the camp; where were the campers? He looked around and noticed a gap in the surrounding brush. The trail beyond led back toward the river; perhaps they had gone to look for him, or to take care of necessary business; or perhaps Ambrosia was trying to send her recalcitrant friend home, and wanted to avoid accidentally dispatching the contents of their campsite with him. Whatever they were doing, he would wait for them here.

He settled down near the tent and went to work fixing their fire.

~~~~

Bernard pushed through the final tangle of river's-edge growth, emerging cold and damp from slogging through the dewy forest. Ambrosia was down by the water, facing the opposite bank, sitting on an old log that some flood had jammed into the mud and been unable to retrieve. He picked his way across loose rock and twisted driftwood to sit beside her. She didn't appear to register his arrival; her attention was reserved for what was left of the woods across the river. An occasional tree stood amidst the ruin, here and there an entire copse that the flames had missed, but much of what they could see had been reduced to a charred tumbledown wasteland. Here and there, hotspots continued to leach smoke into the air despite the fierce rain that she had summoned last night. At least the trees in and around the village had been spared.

After a few minutes, he said: "Aren't you cold, Mercy?"

Instead of answering, she pointed at the blackened land across the river. "It's all gone, Bernard," she said.

"It's not *all* gone. The village is still there. Plenty of ... well, some of the trees are still there." Then: "There's enough left. It'll grow back. Probably."

"We should have been able to prevent it."

"Prevent it? How? We didn't know the dwarves had artillery. And even if we did, what could we do about it?"

"The Rittandic knew," she said. "She was going to steal the Illata
~~~~

and escape in the chaos."

"And look what happened instead."

"Look what happened? Everything happened exactly the way she planned, except that you showed up."

"Yes, and *you* got the Illata, not her. So really, her plan didn't work at all, did it?"

She finally looked at him. Hair like spun silver fluttered across her face, stirred by a breath of air Bernard could hardly feel. "All her life, Mercy dreamed of coming to a place like this," she said, "and when she did, it got destroyed."

He didn't like that reference to Mercy in the third person and the past tense, as if she were someone else, someone who was no longer around. "Come on, Mercy," he said. "*You* didn't destroy it. Just imagine how much worse it would've been if you hadn't been here to bring that storm."

She shrugged, picked up a flat rock, tried to skip it across the water. It vanished with a quick *ploop* instead.

"So, I was wondering—"

"You're going to ask me to send you home now." She flung another rock at the water, hard. It hit and disappeared.

"Well, I thought you might have changed your mind. About, you know, about staying here."

"Why would I change my mind? I have to find the next piece of the Heart."

"Can't Nebandalex can do it?"

"No, he can't."

"Why not? Why does it have to be *you*, Mercy?"

"Ambrosia."

"*Mercy*. You're just … confused right now, is all."

"I'm not confused. I know who and what I am."

"Do you?"

"Yes. Do you know who *you* are, *Brannoc*?"

Bernard said nothing; after a moment she found another flat stone and threw it. This one skipped five or six times before sinking, leaving a series of ripples to mark its passage. As the ripples faded, he said: "When we first came here, and we were separated, and I got captured by the dwarves, all I could think about was escaping and—"

"How did you escape?"

"What?"

"From the dwarves. How did you escape?"

"I … I didn't. They made me fight in an arena like some kind of gladiator, and after I, um, proved myself——" She raised an eyebrow at that, probably remembering that yesterday he had claimed to have won the fight, but she didn't comment. "——They gave me a map and a pony and sent me to the village to steal that jewel of yours."

"Why would they send you to steal the Illata if they were already planning to burn the forest?"

"I ..." He hadn't thought about that before, but it seemed like a reasonable question. "I don't know."

She gave him a long, appraising look. Finally she said, "That was all they gave you? A map and a pony?"

"Yes. I mean, no, they gave me some supplies too, but I lost most of them when the pony ran away. And they gave me a carved stone that I was supposed to show if I ran into any dwarven patrols in the woods."

"They didn't have any dwarven patrols in the woods."

"Look, Mercy, what I'm trying to tell you is——"

"What did it look like? This carved stone?"

"I don't know. A bunch of circles with a cross through them." She stared at him and slowly shook her head. "What?"

"Circles and a cross? That's the symbol for a target."

"It was just a——"

"The Rittandic knew the dwarves were going to start shooting, right? She must have been able to tell you were coming. I bet she made that rock for them. In fact I bet they used you to do what was supposed to be *her* job. Your position told them where to aim their guns."

He stared at her. "But ... no, that isn't what they told me, they said——"

"Of course it isn't. Do you really think they would tell you they were going to send you into the forest and shoot cannons at you?" She shook her head. "They played you, Brannoc."

"*Bernard*," he said. "I'm *Bernard*. Anyway, I lost the stone when the pony ran away. That was way before I got to the village."

"And they never hit the village, did they? They were probably dropping bombs along that pony's trail until they either blew it up or ran out of ammunition."

"Well, I ..." He trailed off. "Do you really think——"

"Yeah, I do," she said. Then: "But it's not your fault. If you hadn't come they just would've sent someone else." Then, her voice softening: "Probably someone less friendly."

He grunted. "Well, the only reason I did what they asked was because I thought you might be in the village."

"That, and they would've killed you if you didn't."

"Okay, that too. But I didn't care about their stupid gem. I still don't. I just wanted to find *you.*" He took her hand; it was icy cold, smaller and softer than her real one. She looked down at it, then at him, an expression of mild surprise on her face, as if she knew he had never taken Mercy's hand, not even once. "And now that we're back together, let's just go home and leave the world-saving to someone else, okay?"

"Home." She looked away from him, across the river, at the smoldering husk of the forest. "What's so great about *home?* What does it even mean?"

"Home means home. Where we came from. Land of snow and ice and study hall. You can use the Illata to open doors? Just open one that puts us back in your bedroom. Bring the Illata along if you don't want the Rittandic to get it. Let's just not be *here* anymore."

"I can't do that."

"Can't, or won't?"

"I don't know how to open a window that goes somewhere specific. I'm afraid I could leave you someplace you'd like even less than here. In the middle of the ocean, a thousand feet in the air. It's too risky."

"But you said you could control the Illata——"

"No, I said I could *use* it. You saw what happened to the dwarves yesterday. Did it look like I was in control?"

"Well, no, but——"

"No. You had to hit me with your staff to stop me."

"Do you ... you'll learn, though, right? How to use it without losing control of it?"

"I hope so. But we were brought here for a *reason*, Brannoc."

"Bernard." He rubbed his chin, and realized he felt no stubble despite having gone a few days without a shave; in his own body, he was hardly a heavy beard-grower, but even so he would normally be feeling a little less than smooth by now. Why no facial hair? Because Brannoc had been created beardless and, like the video game character he was, he would stay that way? "The reason we're here is that stupid game, that's all."

She shook her head. "It wasn't a game. It was a summons. A spell that took the form of something that Mercy would be sure to invoke."

"By playing it?"

"There are all kinds of ways to invoke things. Flags, wheels, bells. Why not by putting a disc in a machine?"

"Why did it pick you?"

She shrugged. "I don't know. Maybe it really did want me—I mean, Mercy—or maybe it was random. Maybe if someone else found it, it would have been something different. A music player, a camera, a phone. Who knows?"

"Hmm," he said, noticing but not pointing out that she had identified herself as Mercy, if only for a moment. If he called it to her attention she would just deny it and claim to be Ambrosia, but he knew better; she was still Mercy inside. She just didn't remember yet. "Well. I know you believe we're on like a sacred mission to put some benevolent heart thing back together, but I just want you to think about how we got here. Would a nice god really trick people into transporting themselves into another dimension to fight evil?"

"Good is not always nice, Brannoc." She stood up. "Come on, let's get back to camp. Maybe we can try again to start a fire and get warmed up while we're waiting for Nebandalex."

She insisted on calling him *Brannoc*. Trying to prove some sort of point, of course, but it made him realize he didn't even know the face that accompanied that name. He went to the river's edge and got down on his hands and knees in the muddy sand to examine himself in the rippling water; a hollow-cheeked, carrot-topped apparition stared back at him. Dark, distrustful eyes gleamed from deep sockets over a protuberant nose; freckles spattered his cheeks and the curve of his ears. Bernard thought he detected a hint of anger in his visage, as if Brannoc were somewhere beneath his skin, gently tugging his features into a glare of futile dismay. And he was dirty; so, so dirty. Only the icy chill kept him from plunging his head into the water and shaking loose some of the mud and God knew what else that was stuck in that shock of orange hair.

But at least he wasn't wearing broken glasses.

~~~~

They returned to camp along the same narrow path they'd taken to the river. Brush crowded close on either side, the small curled leaves sprinkling them with drops of collected condensation or leftover rain as they passed. When they reached the spot where they had spent the night, they found Nebandalex sitting near a low, smoky fire, heating water in a small kettle. He glanced their way as they emerged from the woods and, before either of them spoke, said: "Ribbit." Then, turning to poke at the fire with a stick, he added, "I was not sure there would still be three of us, but I see that your friend has not departed yet. Has he changed his mind?"
~~~~

"We … decided I need more practice before I try to send him anywhere," Ambrosia said, as they settled around the fire.

Nebandalex gave a sage nod. "Prudent."

"That's me," Bernard said. "Mister prudent. How'd you manage to get a fire going?"

"I raided one of the dwarven ships. They had little worth taking; their blankets are short and rough, their cloaks would scarce fit a child, and their food is difficult to distinguish from their stoneware." He held up a device that resembled a baroque lighter. "They did have a tool that proved quite excellent at making things burn, though."

"We have things like those back home," Bernard said. "We use them to start barbecues and stuff."

"Barbecues?"

"Yeah. You know. Cookouts."

The elf cocked his head.

Bernard sighed. "We use them to start fires."

"Yes, as I said, it makes things burn. Have you eaten?"

"No, we were talking," Ambrosia said.

"I made soup. It will be ready in a few minutes."

Bernard eyed the putative soup; it looked like boiled lawn clippings, he thought, and smelled like a plate of wet leaves that had been put through a microwave oven. "What's, um, what's in it?"

"Roots, bark, berries, mushrooms. I foraged a bit."

"Are you sure this won't, like, kill us or give us the runs?"

"What are *the runs*?"

"They're … never mind. Why can't we just eat the food we took from the village?"

"That food will keep. We should save it for the journey." He gave Ambrosia a pointed look. "There *will* be a journey, yes?"

"Yes. The Illata told me we should go downriver."

"The Illata told you that?" Bernard said. "I didn't know it was a Magic 8 Ball, too."

Nebandalex said, "A Magic 8 Ball?"

"Where we come from, it's, um, it's a fortune-telling device."

"Why is it called an eight ball? Is that how many times it can be used?"

"No, it looks like the eight ball in pool."

"They are found in pools in groups of eight?"

After a moment, Bernard said: "Yes. Yes they are."

"All right, that's enough of *This Week in Nonexistent Magical Artifacts*," Ambrosia said. "Eat your soup."

Nebandalex gave Bernard a narrow, appraising look, then turned to Ambrosia. "Going downriver will take us north into the Slash, then to Abacar and the sea," he said.

She shrugged. "That's where we're going, then."

"Those lands are dominated by humans." He tilted his head in Bernard's direction. "Like this one."

"Why is it called the Slash? Is it a violent area?"

"There was once a good deal of fighting there, before the lords of Abacar unified the region, but that was centuries ago. No, it is an ancient flood plain with a steep central valley that some say looks like a long cut from a knife. That is where the name comes from. The humans grow their crops and graze their animals along almost the entire length. We have had occasion to discourage them from felling trees in the outskirts of Torgonderrer."

"I'm supposed to be from Banderlund," Bernard said. "Is that part of the Slash?"

"Supposed to be?" Nebandalex appeared to think about this for a moment, then shrugged and said, "No. Banderlund is still farther north, beyond the mountains and the Free Coast." He eyed Bernard. "Your nationality may be problematic. Banderlund and Abacar are not on good terms. After we leave the forest, you should avoid telling people where you are from."

"You think we'll have a problem traveling through the Slash?" Ambrosia said. "Are Abacar and Banderlund at war?"

"As far as I know they are not actively fighting. Not yet. But there are tensions. I do not expect we will be attacked just because of your friend's face, but we will probably wish to stay on the river, camp in the countryside, avoid towns and taverns."

"All right, then," Ambrosia said. "We'll follow the river."

"And when the river ends?" Bernard asked.

"We'll play it by ear."

Nebandalex gave her an odd look, then reached up and touched the tip of his ear.

"I mean we'll improvise," she said.

"Oh good," Bernard said. "Improvisation. Because planning things out in advance is so very boring."

FIRST INTERLUDE

ABACAR

Chapter 11

KORRIN BLACKHAWK, LORD of Abacar, was worried that he would be the last to hold that title. This concern had nothing to do with the matter of an heir; it had everything to do with the empire of Banderlund, which lay a steadily-decreasing distance to the north. For the last few weeks Lord Korrin's agents in the kingdom of Rorik had been returning from beyond the massive mountain range known as the Fists, each with a tale more dire than the one before, as if they were engaged in a contest to see who could bring the worst news. Banderlund's forces had landed along Rorik's northern beaches; Banderlund's forces were pushing southward through the scrublands, toward Rorik's population centers; the Banderlundi had routed Rorik's shaggy regulars at the Kaard River, and routed them again at Silver Canyon, taking the bridges there; a second Banderlundi fleet had landed just south of the king's city of Leogrand and begun moving north; and finally, with timing so precise that some might call it sorcery, the two armies had closed like a pincer around the capital. The siege had begun at dawn, and had ended before dusk with the utter collapse of Leogrand's defenders. With that, the pocket of oceanside plains once known as the Free Coast vanished, and Banderlund gained a staging area between the Thumb and the Fingers from which it could strike yet further south.

Lord Korrin did not fear Banderlund's military power, formidable as it was; they couldn't cross the mountains with so much as a caravan, let alone an invading army, without being harried and destroyed in the narrow passes and steep-sided valleys. Nor did he fear that they would land their fleets along Abacar's shores and spew men and materiel at him from multiple directions; the only harbor within a thousand miles was Chasm Bay, at the bottom of the cliff beneath Lord Korrin's feet, and the only way into the Slash from there was the narrow, tortuous, switchbacked Harbor Road. He almost wished they would try to invade by that route; it would be most gratifying to rain stones and arrows and burning pitch down upon the 'Lundi horde as they attempted to crawl from sea to sky, to hear them howl as they were driven back again and again and again.

But that was just an idle daydream of victory; Banderlund would not give him the satisfaction of throwing troops at his walls. Why would they, when they could simply tie a cord around his neck and wait for him to choke?

Granted, the Free Coast had sheltered rabble and pirates, but those were a mere nuisance; far many more legitimate ships had plied Rorik's waters to reach Abacar, bringing rare woods and exotic spices from the steaming jungles of Zuiea, precious ores from the mines of mountainous Hen-Ten, furs from the icy, unsettled polar wastes. In taking Rorik, Banderlund gained unfettered control of the sea along the entirety of the north, which meant trade through those lanes now existed only at their sufferance. The alternative route? A long, risky, *unprofitable* voyage all the way down the wild western coast, around the stormy southern peninsula where the Fists dipped a knuckle into the water, through the dangerously turbulent reach between the Ravels and the Æther, across the Boiling Sea, and, finally, back up the eastern coast. Only the maddest freebooter would undertake such a journey, just to reach the single harbor in the Slash that could receive them; not when they could just sail north and trade with Banderlund instead.

Abacar—indeed, the entire Slash—had just become a backwater. And backwaters eventually silted up.

Korrin and his advisors had seen this coming, of course, and had taken what steps they could. A year earlier, when Banderlund had gained a new empress and began to move against its small neighbors to the south and east, farmers in the rich floodplains of the Gilded Downs had been under instructions to plant crops suitable for storage, drying, and pickling: Root vegetables, squashes and gourds, nuts and hard fruits. Unnecessary expenditures had been cut in all areas so that coin could be stockpiled for ransoms or to raise levies; punishments for crimes were toughened, to prepare for martial law should it need to be imposed; diplomatic feelers had been extended to the other peoples of the Slash, from the secretive elves in their woodlands to the mercantile dwarves beneath their mountains, from the inscrutable Rittandics who studied the Ravels to the wild Pelts who roamed the low mountain slopes west of Abacar, across the chasm. And while he waited for those efforts to bear flowers, Lord Korrin sat through one emergency meeting after another, meetings that went on so long that they finally seemed to meld into a single giant planning session that went on for days. Discussions of food became arguments over trade, over the practicality of negotiation, of assassination, of war, fraught with temporizing speech, nervous looks, furtive glances between allied advisors, and, early on, suggestions that their only choice was to join Banderlund voluntarily, perhaps as an autonomous province. The counselors who favored *that* option had been replaced; Lord Korrin would not willingly don the yoke of a thrall to the Empress of Banderlund. Not until things in the Slash got a lot worse. Which, he knew, they would.

Korrin was sometimes called Skullcrusher, for his prowess with the mace and cudgel; deeming it expedient to appear ready to live up to his moniker, he had lately taken to wearing full, albeit ceremonial, combat gear when he moved about in places where he might be seen by the public. This regalia included a decorative replica of the Maul, that fabled weapon Korrin's ancestors had wielded when they unified the Slash; the original, which had not seen the light for centuries, remained safely hidden away. There were those who believed the Maul contained a power that could, perhaps, be wielded against Banderlund to secure Abacar and the Slash against predation, but if such potential existed Korrin did not know how to unlock it. Perhaps Jordneh, the Rittandic queen, whose predecessors had centuries earlier laid down the wards that protected the Maul from detection and theft, could tell him; but like the elves and dwarves and Pelts, she had yet to respond to his request for aid.

And now, as if all that were not enough, Rumad Kram had begun having visions.

~~~~

"I grow bored, Kram," Lord Korrin said.

Rumad Kram, Korrin's astrologer, gave him a mildly annoyed glance, then turned back to gaze up at the sky, as he had been doing since before Korrin had arrived, and would probably still be doing after Korrin left.

Korrin waited in a state of sweaty impatience. Ceremonial though it was, his armor was still heavy; and he didn't care for being summoned from his bed and then, after clanking up the spiral stairs to the very top of the old man's tower, being made to stand around as if he were a page to be conjured and idled on a whim. He absently fingered the handle of his paste scepter, and wondered if it would break were he to use it to knock Kram off the spire.

"Great things are afoot," Kram said, his voice low and sly.

"Are they?" Korrin said. "I had not noticed, what with my being so preoccupied with Banderlund conquering everything north of here. Really, Kram, you are much more useful when you are informing me of things I do not know already."

Kram accused the heavens with a gnarled and spotty finger. "A powerful wind has risen, and aught may stand against it."

"That is merely another way of saying the same thing." Korrin sighed. "Did you call me here for a *reason*, Kram, or just to prove that you could make me dance on a string?"
~~~~

"We all have strings that make us dance. Some are easier to play than others. Some we can see, others we can know only by the motions they provoke. Some——"

"Enough. Make yourself plain, if you can."

"Make myself *plain*, my lord?" Kram said. "How can I make myself *plain*, when all that is revealed to me is a shadow of an outline of a mystery?"

"A *shadow* of an *outline* of a … So you have nothing of value to say? You dragged me out of a warm bed to tell me the sun will rise in the morning, is that it?"

"So it shall," Kram said, as if this comment were sagacious. Then, in an entirely different tone: "And when it does, it will bring with it players in a great game. Players new to the board, never before seen."

At last, the old man had uttered something of possible interest. "New players? Agents of Banderlund, or something of the like?"

"Agents, yes," Kram said, "though it is not yet apparent who or what they serve. I must study the stars further; I should be able to speak with greater clarity come the morrow."

"The morrow? That same *morrow* when these *agents* are due to arrive? More notice than that would have been appreciated."

"I can but pass along what is revealed, when it is revealed," Kram said with bovine placidity.

"Yes, so you remind me regularly." Korrin sighed again; he seemed to sigh so frequently in Kram's presence. "Very well. I will have my half-brother instruct the watch to be more vigilant and less receptive to bribery for the next few days, particularly those assigned to the outer wall. The threat of public flogging should focus their minds."

The old man shrugged. "As you say."

"We are finished, then. Come to me in the morning, and bring me more information about these agents. Oh, and, Kram?"

"Yes, my lord?"

"The next time you wish to purvey vague information to me in the middle of the night, just send it with a wench. Preferably an attractive one."

<div align="center">~~~~</div>

Rumad Kram watched the sky and listened to Lord Korrin clatter down the roofed stairs that circled the outside of the tower. He sounded like a jostling crate of pots and pans, the way he clanked around in his absurd ceremonial mail. Kram understood that wearing the armor made Lord Korrin hot and irritable—not to mention frequently late; it took a long time to dress when one's clothes were made of fitted metal—and he didn't really grasp the point of wearing it all the time. Perhaps it was to impress the young ladies.

When the night had grown quiet again, Kram sighed, turned, and shuffled across to the open trapdoor in the center of the tower roof. Steep wooden steps descended to his quarters down below. He took them carefully, counting the steps as he went. The sixth one squeaked beneath his weight, as it always did; one of these days, he would prevail upon a carpenter to fix that. He did not pull the door shut behind him. It promised to be a clear and pleasant night, and he enjoyed the cool air that flowed down into his chamber through the hole in the roof. In Kram's younger days, when he had served during the long reign of Korrin's father, he had often spent the night up on the deck of his tower beneath the stars; but when he had started awakening stiff and unable to move from the cold, he knew it was time to stop sleeping outdoors.

His large, circular bedchamber was lit by candles that sat on flat metal disks inserted at regular intervals into the walls. These corresponded to the arrows of a compass, with the largest candles at the cardinal points and smaller ones in between. Stifling a yawn, he tottered around the perimeter, extinguishing them one by one. He always used his fingers to snuff the flames; he found the *tssst* of each fire's tiny death much more satisfying than the silence when he simply blew them out.

Bang.

The old man paused, fingers ready to snuff another candle. That sound had been his trapdoor closing. The wind? No, there was no wind, and he had left it fully open and flat against the roof, so how could it—

Creak.

That was the sixth step. Kram turned and peered into the semidark, wondering who was invading his apartment, seeing no one.

Tssst. The flame of the candle beside him went out. Turning, he saw the tall, thin, ragged, faintly luminous form of a Rittandic, fingers still pinching the wick, staring at him with eyes like two globes of black ice. Shocked, Kram took a step back. "Who are you?" he said.

"My name is unimportant at the moment," the Rittandic said in that metallic voice of theirs, iron nails scraping the blade of a sword. "Sometimes I forget it myself."

"Why are you here? What do you want from me?"

The Rittandic's long arms flashed out. Powerful narrow fingers caught Kram's shoulders. "What I want from you is you."

Kram tried to pull away, but the grip that held him was uncannily strong and his own muscles were weak with age. The Rittandic's lips moved, soundlessly; its bony hands and forearms began to glow as if lit up from within, its delicate bones dark lines like young roots. Its skin was marked with fading bruises, dark smudges against the luminosity, as if from a recent beating. The air crackled and smelled like lightning. A shock went through Kram's body, collarbone to toes; he felt the intruder drinking in the essence that made him what he was.

The last face Kram saw before darkness fell was his own, looking back at him.

~~~~

The newly-created duplicate of Rumad Kram stood a moment, looking down at the blue-grey corpse at his feet. Few could say that they had gazed upon their own dead selves; fewer still could say they had done it more than once.

The body still wore the old man's clothes, but they no longer fit. They were tailored for the small, wizened human Rumad Kram had been, not the tall, slender, deceased Rittandic he now appeared to be. With a glance at the trapdoor, the false Kram squirmed out of his ragged garb, then stripped the astrologer and put on his garments. Everything, of course, fit perfectly. That done, he dragged the naked corpse over to the large fireplace and heaved it in; the gangly arms and legs didn't quite fit, but a few strategic slashes from Ambrosia's knife——which he had managed to retain when she had opened the portal and banished him to the foothills of the Fists, beyond the Peltish Downs——took them off easily and, thanks to a spell to constrict the blood vessels in the vicinity of the cuts, cleanly. He piled the severed limbs like kindling, then spoke a few words to intensify the flames and ensure that the body was completely incinerated. Thin, light Rittandic bones burned much more easily than dense human ones, but it would not do to leave any fragments behind to be discovered by a nosy housekeeper. Not that Kram had one.

That done, he turned. A small, dark shape sat on the bottom step of the stairs, waiting for him. When his gaze fell upon it, it jumped to its feet and, like a shadow given form and mobility, did a little dance around the chamber. He watched it roll and tumble and walk on its hands like an acrobat, until finally it stopped in front of him and said, in a voice like a bonfire fluttering in the wind: "A new form, Kihantroh? We preferred your elf-shape."

"I am Rumad Kram now," he said. "You will refer to me by that name."
~~~~

"As you wish."

"I did not know your kind had partialities among mortal bodies."

"We Tellehi can appreciate beauty when we it."

"I see no beauty in smug, mincing elves," Kram said.

"Yes, we remember your distaste for the long-lived ones. It must have been a sore trial to wear that flesh for so long."

"It was," Kram said. "And I have nothing to show for it."

"*Nothing?* You have the coin the dwarves paid you."

"Feh. I can earn coin a hundred different ways."

"You forced your enemy into the open."

"Ambrosia and her pet human, you mean?"

"They are only agents. Proxies. Your true foe is the one who brought them here."

Kram grumbled in his throat. "And who is that?" he said.

"We are not sure, but mean to learn."

He grumbled again. It felt comfortable, characteristic; clearly the old man made this sound frequently. "See that you do." He rubbed his hands, feeling odd shooting pains from the stiff joints in his fingers and wrists. "Why is it so accursedly *cold* in in this room?" The shadow's shoulders rippled in what may have been a shrug; then it sprang into the air, landing on the bent digits of its left hand, holding its right arm out straight. The creature began rotating slowly, fingers skittering over the floor like the legs of a large, spindly insect. Kram had grown accustomed to such antics, though he had no idea why all the Tellehi indulged in them. He watched for a little while, then said: "Why are you here? Merely to entertain me with circus acrobatics? Or do you have something to tell me?"

It stopped spinning, did a little backflip, ended up sitting on the stairs again. "I was sent to warn you."

"About what?"

"Three come downriver from the elven lands. They seek what you seek."

"Three from the elven lands?" Kram thought for a moment. "Ambrosia, of course, and the Banderlundi. Who is the third? Surely not Meliander; I killed Glorian and Orindel; Nebandalex, perhaps? He will desire revenge for what I did to his mate." The shadow did not answer, which could mean that it did not know, or that he had guessed correctly, or merely that it amused the Tellehi to withhold that information. "Do they know I am here?"

"Even if they do, they will not know what form you have taken."

That was certainly true. Kram glanced at the roaring fire, at the noisome smoke wafting up the chimney; soon, the only remaining evidence of his crime would be slightly greasy ashes.

"What of the dwarves? Do they still think me dead?"

Silence.

Kram looked at the stairs, and found that he was alone; the blot of midnight had vanished. He inhaled, then sighed, feeling an odd, constrictive pain in the deepness of his lungs. He had never taken a body as old as this one, hadn't anticipated the aches, the infirmities that came with it. Younger, stronger Lord Korrin would have been a more favorable target, but as a lad he had been fostered in the Ravels by Queen Jordneh. Kram knew the sort of protections she had woven around the youngster and dared not risk attempting the absorbance glamour against him. Nor did he need to; after all, his goal was to gain the Jewel in the Maul, not to find the most robust body he could steal. Rumad Kram did not know where the Maul was hidden, but Lord Korrin did; and in the old man's skin, disguised as a trusted advisor, he had Lord Korrin's ear. That was worth some transitory discomfort.

After all, having a man's ear was only one step shy of having his mind.

~~~~

The three wanderers reached the outer wall of Abacar early that morning, in the small hours when the sea wind was still and the birds were quiet and the dust lay thick and settled on the broad dirt road that led to the landward gates. At this time of night, those massive doors—two huge iron-bound wooden panels that, at nearly twenty feet high and half that wide, dwarfed and made ridiculous the entrance to the village of the elves—stood shut. A small passage pierced the wall nearby, a tunnel that burrowed through masonry twice as thick as a man was tall. A series of three spiky portcullises blocked the dim corridor, one after the other; in front of it, two stout armed guards stood watch, sheltering beneath a torchlit overhang. Each held a halberd, the hooked axeheads dull grey in the guttering light. The one on the right seemed to be half asleep, but as they approached, his colleague nudged him to alertness. The men tilted their weapons together so that the handles crossed, forming a redundant conceptual barrier in front of the three lowered grates. The weary, mud-spattered travelers stopped well out of reach of the pole-arms.

For a few moments, the two groups regarded each other; then the sentry on the right said: "So what do *you* lot want?"

The lead traveler, a female elf, said: "We'd like to come in."

"Very well. Five falcons each."
~~~~

"We have to *pay* to enter the city?"

"From dusk until dawn, you do." He examined the dirty, dusty, unkempt supplicants. "Helps to keep the criminals out."

"We're not criminals," the gangly, hooded human said.

"Of course you are not. You are good and honest citizens. And that is why you will pay five falcons each, or go away and come back after daybreak, instead of doing something stupid like trying to sneak by us or force your way in."

The grubby strangers held a quiet, whispered conference; then the male elf said: "And what is a *falcon*, exactly?"

Clearly these were bumpkins.

"A falcon is a copper coin," the guard said, patient as a teacher talking to a slow but sweet student. "They are near enough to worthless that children throw them into the waterfall to make wishes come true. Surely you must have fifteen to spare."

The two elves and the human passed a glance among them like an empty purse. The female said, "We haven't got it."

"Pity. Come back after sunrise, then."

"Must we be so quick to send them away?" the heretofore silent guard said. He looked the elf maid up and down. "Might be we can work out a trade."

Beneath the dirt, the Banderlundi's face turned red to match his hair, a few locks of which peeked from under his hood. "She's not for sale."

"I am not looking to *buy* the wench. I just want to rent her."

The human's wiry, stick-thin arm moved toward the quarterstaff on his back. "She's not for *rent*, either, you——"

"You will want to take your *hand* away from your *stick*," the sentry on the left growled, "or you are like to lose both."

The traveler, wisely, complied.

"Enough," the guard on the right said. "There will be no *trading* here tonight. Pay and enter, or do not pay and leave."

The travelers turned and started to shuffle away.

"Oh, and, when you come back?" he called.

They stopped.

"Leave those weapons wherever it was you found them."

PART THREE

THE SECOND SHARD

Chapter 12

SHE DREAMED SHE was drifting far above Abacar, so high that it looked like little more than a whitish-grey smudge in a field of green and blue and black. Somewhere within those walls of stone, the next piece of the Heart awaited discovery; but she didn't know how to get down to it, she just kept floating upward, blown on the wind like a scrap of parchment until, without warning, the world pivoted around her. Sky became earth; earth became sky; she felt a wrenching sensation, then found herself standing atop a splintered butte in the middle of a vast desert. The broiling rock beneath her feet was the color of dried blood, with clotted black dirt ground into its innumerable cracks. Her mesa stood alone in an oceanic expanse of sand and rubble, rolling hills and dunes littered with eddies of broken scree, jagged volcanic tuff surfacing here and there like dark whales frozen in mid-breach. The sun, directly overhead, baked the world with a harsh infection-red glare, so hot it seemed the stone itself should melt and flow beneath it. She lifted a hand to shade her eyes against the infernal glow from above, noticing as she did that it was Mercy's hand, small and dark and dusted with fine black hair, rather than Ambrosia's pale and rather plump one. She looked at both her hands, down at her body. She was human again, herself, the self that had been subsumed and combined when she came here, when she'd touched the Illata, into the character of Ambrosia.

Foolish girl, a soft voice said. Ambrosia's voice. *Look around you.*

She looked around. "There's nothing here."

Nothing? the voice said. *This is* desolation. *It is not* nothing.

The world pivoted again, a swirl, a smear, as of a curtain swiftly drawn and opened again, too fast for her eye to follow the fabric, but slow enough for her to register that something had moved across her vision. When it was gone, so was everything else.

This *is nothing,* Ambrosia's voice whispered.

She was right; though it was a wasteland with no water, no life, and no hope of either, the desert had, at least, been a *place*. But *this*, this vast absence, a uniform dull grey except for occasional sickly flickers of distant dismal light to hint that anything might have existed once, somewhere else, a long time ago ... This was nothing. Less than nothing.

A smudgy blemish in the grey became a figure walking toward her through the nothing; which, she supposed, meant the nothing was *something*, or else how could it be walked through? Trying to figure that out made her head hurt a little. She shut her eyes and pressed her palms against her closed lids; when she took her hands away and looked once more, she saw Ambrosia the sorceress standing in front of her. The elf wore a loose white garment, bound at the waist with a yellow sash. Her arms were bare; she wore a golden band around each wrist. Each bracelet was lightly scaled, engraved to resemble a serpent eating its own tail. Ouroboros. Mercy had seen nothing like that during her admittedly-brief time with the elves; although they were not connected by a chain and did not appear to fetter Ambrosia in any way, Mercy still had the impression that they were manacles.

She said: "Why are you showing me this?"

"You're not trying hard enough," Ambrosia said.

"I almost *died* in that hollow tree! Who are *you* to tell me I'm not *trying* hard enough?"

"You can't succeed on your own. You need Brannoc's help."

"Brannoc ... Bernard *is* helping. If he hadn't come when he did—"

"He would help more if he touched the Heart. Like you did."

"He doesn't want to touch it."

"That's what he says now. But once he and Brannoc are integrated like we are, he'll understand it's better this way. *Our* way."

"To tell the truth I'm not feeling all that integrated just now."

"Don't try to be coy. You are me and I am you. Isn't this the way you always wanted it?"

"What are you talking about?"

"Weren't you tired of just being you? Isn't that what you were always thinking?"

Mercy suddenly felt a cold, stabbing doubt in her stomach. "Is *that* why you picked me? Because you thought I wouldn't mind being ... *combined* with you?"

Ambrosia's expression turned cold as the eyes of her graven snake bracelets. She wavered and faded away, but spoke once more, her voice coming from nowhere, from everywhere, here in this place where nowhere and everywhere were the same thing. *I didn't pick you,* she said. *You picked yourself. Now do what you know you must, and stop wasting my time.*

The grey shattered like breaking glass, and she was awake.

~~~~

She lay there for a few minutes, then turned over and crawled out of the oilcloth drapery that served as their makeshift tent. Before she had really decided where she was going, she found herself a short distance upstream, at a small, flat-topped boulder where Bernard had
~~~~

been sitting. When the guards at the gate had turned them away and they'd made their way back to the trees along the river where they'd hidden their boat, he had volunteered for the first watch. He was wound up, he'd said, and couldn't sleep. Evidently his assessment of his own mental state had not been completely accurate; instead of being perched on the rock keeping an eye on things, he had slid off and lay on the ground beside it, arms and legs akimbo, snoring loudly. She shook her head and knelt down to wake him, and found to her own surprise that the Illata had somehow found its way into her hand, and she was holding it over Bernard's head as if it were an egg she was about to crack. Its blue glow suffused him, made his freckles look black. All she had to do was touch it to his forehead, his cheek, his nose, anywhere. He would become like her. Like them.

Which meant … what, exactly?

Do it, the voice from her dream said. *Why are you hesitating?*

Bernard had made it clear that he did not want to touch the Illata, that was why. He didn't like it, didn't trust it, didn't understand what it had done to her, didn't want it doing the same thing to him.

He only doesn't trust it because he doesn't know it. Once you do it, he'll thank you.

Would he? She wasn't so sure about that.

You want to see this world destroyed, and your world, and every world in between, just because your friend is squeamish?

Of course she didn't want that.

Then do this, and get it over with.

She lowered the gem toward his forehead, stopped again. She couldn't shake the feeling she was about to do him some grievous harm, almost like murdering him or something.

Foolish girl. That's ridiculous.

Her hand trembled. *Was* it ridiculous? If she touched him with the Illata, Bernard would become fused with another personality. That might not be murder, exactly, but it would still be the end of Bernard as he had been. It would be the creation of someone new.

He's already fused with Brannoc, but he's resisting it and that makes him less effective. Do it. Help him help us.

Her fingers closed tightly around the gem. It thrummed slightly in her grip, warm as a freshly-laid egg. She slid it into the pack at her waist, closed the flap. The straps on the front buckled themselves, tightened, locked the Illata away behind enchanted fabric and leather. The stone itself had shown her how to turn the pack into a vault; it wanted to be protected, shielded, as it had been in the carved column in Yexandor's fallen tree of a home. She expected the next shard to be similarly concealed, but hoped the fragment she possessed would allow her to find the others.

The voice in her head whispered, *This is a mistake. You will regret it.*

Maybe so; maybe it was a mistake. But it was the right thing to do. She leaned over and tapped Bernard on the nose. He stirred and muttered, then lay still. "You goof," she said. "I remember when you thought broken glasses were your biggest prob——"

Suddenly a rough hand clamped over her mouth, cutting off her speech; a strong arm went around her waist and pulled her away from Bernard. A man's voice whispered in her ear, "You should have bought your way into the city when you had the chance, pretty elf."

Her attacker hauled her off her feet and half-carried, half-dragged her to a nearby tree. He spun around and flung her hard against the young trunk. She slammed into it with her back. Lights exploded in her head and she slid to the ground; she regained her senses a few moments later, but her attacker had already pulled her arms back around the trunk and was tying them together at the wrists with a length of cord. Another went around her waist. He was quick with knots, like a boatman.

Then he drew a knife, and went for Bernard.

<p style="text-align:center">~~~~</p>

Bernard felt something cold and sharp touching his throat.

He reached up and tried to push whatever it was away, but his fingers found a thick hairy wrist that didn't want to move. He opened his eyes and found himself looking up at a face hovering directly above his, staring down at him and breathing noisily through a bandit-style kerchief that covered everything below the eyes. He reeked of cheap alcohol, reminding Bernard of the smell that used to cling to his grandfather during bloodshot Saturday morning visits.

"Be still," the man said, the concealing fabric rippling as the mouth beneath it moved. He pressed the sharp thing a little harder. Bernard couldn't see it, but obviously it was the edge of a blade. Stupid, stupid! He had volunteered to take the watch, and had fallen asleep! Floating downriver through empty forests and fallow croplands had made him complacent; he should have known that a city would attract criminals and highwaymen. Hadn't the guards at the gate said as much, when they'd asked for an entrance fee?

"We haven't got any money," Bernard said.

The intruder snorted, making his mask flutter. "I know *that*," he said. "Any fool could see you have not got three falcons between you, else you would not be sleeping in the riverside woods." The eyes flicked left. "Money is not what I came here to find."

Bernard glanced the direction the man had looked, and saw Ambrosia tied up against a tree, her arms drawn back around the trunk, a rag in her mouth. "You—"

"Uh-uh. No." The blade moved a little, left and right, with not quite enough pressure to slice through flesh. "I *could* cut your throat right now, but that would make an awful mess and I would rather not dirty myself. Now, where is the third—"

"The third is here," Nebandalex said from somewhere in front of them. Although there was little in the way of brush, the elf was well-concealed; Bernard had not heard him approaching, couldn't see where he stood. "Sheathe your blade and go, villain. You need not die tonight."

The man's sodden gaze returned to Bernard. "On your feet."

"You are behaving foolishly," the elf said, as Bernard hauled himself upright and stood. The thug maneuvered to put Bernard between himself and the origin of Nebandalex's voice. "What do you expect to gain from this?"

"I want the woman," he said.

"You will not have her."

"I have got a knife to your friend's throat."

"Yes, I see that. It makes no difference."

The man made a contemptuous sound. "You think you can shoot me before I water the ground with his blood?"

"Of course I can. I am an elf, and an archer." Nebandalex was still moving; now he seemed to be off to their left. Bernard felt the masked man's hesitation, then found himself forcefully repositioned, once more putting him between his captor and the sound of Nebandalex's voice.

"You dare not kill me," the bandit told the darkness. "Not if you want to get into the city."

"Why?" Nebandalex said. "Are you the only one who knows where the keys are hidden?"

The man said nothing.

"You appear to be alone," Nebandalex said. "You cannot see me, but I can see you. I can put an arrow into any part of your body that is not concealed, and you are much larger than the person you are trying to hide behind." Bernard heard the creak of a bowstring being pulled back. "There is no way that this ends well for you. Once more I say, sheathe your blade and go."

For a moment, there was silence; then the knife was slowly withdrawn from Bernard's throat. "All right," the man said. "I——"

Nebandalex shot him through the neck.

Bernard scrambled away as the highwayman swayed on his feet, apparently not yet realizing he was a dead man. The dagger fell from his hand, buried itself in the moist dirt. He took a step backward, then collapsed to lie supine on the bank, the fingers of one hand trailing in the icy river.

"Oh, wow," Bernard said.

Nebandalex came out of the darkness, holding his bow loosely. He leaned it up against the big rock, knelt to examine the body.

"You *shot* him!"

"Of course I did," the elf said; then, sounding vexed: "I seem to have lost my arrow in the water."

"Oh, wow," Bernard said again. He stumbled over to Ambrosia and pulled the rag out of her mouth. She coughed and spat. "Are you all right? He didn't hurt you?" She shook her head and said she was fine while he went around behind the tree and went to work on the knot. It was some sort of crazy nautical tangle, but his hands seemed to know what to do on their own.

Nebandalex picked up his bow and came over just as the rope came apart. Ambrosia stood, rubbed her wrists, gave the other elf a hug and a kiss on the cheek, and wandered over to look at the corpse. Nebandalex stared after her, looking bemused.

"You didn't have to shoot him," Bernard said. "He was going to leave."

"Why would I have let him leave? So he could choose his prey more carefully, less drunkenly, next time? Is that the way things are done where you come from?"

"Yes. I mean, no. I mean, we have *trials* for people before we, we, we don't just *execute* them——"

"We're not back home, Bernard," Ambrosia said. "Things are different here."

"I don't think they're *that* different. They have laws here, too. They must. You can't build a city like this if you don't have laws."

"We're not in the city yet," she said. Then, returning to where they stood: "What should we do with the body?"

"Why not bury him?"

"No shovels. Besides, that would take too long. I could just use the Illata to send him away."

"Remember what happened the last time you used the Illata,"

Nebandalex said. "We wish to avoid attracting attention. Creating a gaping hole in the world is not the way to do that."

"What's your suggestion?"

"Push him the rest of the way out and let the river take him."

"Isn't the city downstream? What if they find him?"

"What if they do? Nothing connects him to us. In any case there is a large waterfall where the river empties into the sea; no one will find him after he goes over that."

Ambrosia thought for a moment, then nodded. "All right, that sounds reasonable."

Bernard couldn't get his head around it, talking about the dead man as if he were a candy bar they were trying to hide from their weight-loss coach. He found himself wondering how many people Nebandalex had killed, and what they had done to deserve it; he wondered what Ambrosia had *really* done with the Rittandic and the dwarves, if, as she said, she had sent them away, or if those magic doors had dropped them into some volcanic hell. Maybe that was the real reason she wouldn't send him home. "Shouldn't we ... I don't know, say something over him first?" Bernard asked.

Ambrosia shrugged. "Okay." She looked at the body. "Bye," she said.

Well, no one cared about the niceties, and Bernard couldn't think of anything to say anyway. He retrieved his staff from where it lay beside the boulder and used it to lever the body away from the bank. He took a few steps out, walking into cold water up to his ankles, then to his shins, prodding the corpse ahead with his staff to make sure it didn't get caught in any riverside tangles of roots and weeds, until suddenly there was no more solid ground under his feet and he toppled forward, freezing water closing over his head, so icy it stunned him. He felt the current begin to take him but his brain couldn't seem to coordinate his limbs to swim or clamber back to shore; then someone grabbed him by the holster for his staff and hauled him, gasping and sputtering, out of the river. He flopped on his back, chilled to his core, mouth opening and closing like a reeled-in fish.

Nebandalex, standing over him, said: "That was rather dramatic."

"Gets ... deep ... *fast.*"

"We noticed." The elf pulled Bernard to his feet. Shivering like a terribly frightened animal, he looked at the river; the highwayman's body was well downstream already, a small black smudge in the wide dark river.

"Good riddance," Ambrosia said. "Come on, it'll be dawn soon.

Let's start a fire and get you warmed up."

~~~~

As he jerked open the door of his bedroom, Lord Korrin bellowed: "*What* do you *want?*"

The page who had been pounding on his door, a young man Korrin had never seen before, flinched as if expecting a blow. Korrin could imagine why; when the hammering had begun, he had been quite occupied with the girl who had poured wine at dinner, and who had continued her service well into the night. Stumbling out of bed, Korrin had thrown on a tattered purple dressing gown to cover his nakedness, and in his harried irritation at this *second* interruption of the evening, when he had reached for the ceremonial Maul he had instead snatched up the battle maul with which, at the young lady's request, he had been striking poses earlier, and had subsequently left lying beside the bed. He was *almost* irate enough to use the weapon; so if this intruding dunce feared for the structural integrity of his skull, it was not utterly without reason.

And *still* the page stood there, dumbfounded, which only increased Korrin's annoyance; he'd thought they trained these simpletons to retain their composure regardless of who answered their knocks in whatever state of rage or dishabille. "Well? *Speak*, boy, or begone!"

"I … I beg your pardon, my lord, but the astrologer, Rumad Kram—"

"I know who Kram is, fool! What of him? Has he finally died?"

"No, my lord. I mean, not yet. He says he must see you. He says he has had a revelation and you—"

"Damned old man," Korrin said. "I was *just* there! Why can his *revelations* never arrive according to *my* schedule?"

"I am sure I know not, my lord—"

"Of course you know not. Go and tell that ancient troll I will be along in good time."

Korrin slammed the door in the page's face, then turned and strode across the bedroom toward the wicker doors that opened onto his balcony. With winter coming, his attendants had brought out the furs and strung them along the inside, blocking out most of the breeze that would otherwise flow freely through the glossy weave; this had the unfortunate side effect of making his room smell vaguely of rabbit, but that was what incense was for. He glanced to his left, toward the bed; the wench was just pulling up her stockings. "You need not do that," he said. "I am sure I will not be gone long."

"Yes, my lord."
~~~~

She disrobed and, naked once more, made to crawl back beneath the covers, but he raised a hand and stopped her. He pointed to the fireplace, which ran almost the whole length of the wall, separated by masonry into three distinct hearths beneath a single long mantle. Only the box nearest the bed cradled a flame; it had burned low, and the room had grown chilly. "Before you become too cozy, fetch some wood for the fire."

"Of course, my lord," she said. The fireplace sported a number of niches for storing wood; she went to the closest one, knelt down, and began removing logs from the brickwork chamber. Ordinarily Korrin would have watched and enjoyed her movements, but the message from Kram had spoiled his mood. He pushed the wicker doors open and stepped out onto the balcony. The wind off the sea, as it was most nights this time of year, carried a hint of the winter chill to come. That same wind should have been filling the sails of many ships seeking one last round of trading before the snows; however, in the last three weeks only four ships had arrived at the harbor, and of those, two had been carrying refugees from the Free Coast rather than goods for sale or barter. He had let the refugees in, of course, over the tight-lipped objections of most of his advisors; it was either that or let them bob in Chasm Bay until they starved or sank in full view of his own citizens, or drive them back out into the open sea so they could die out there instead. From a utilitarian perspective it would perhaps have been prudent to allow them to perish, but he could hardly do that and still claim any sort of moral superiority over his predaceous neighbor to the north. Which was really the only superiority left to him at this point.

Below, the city was mostly dark; the major avenues remained lit by oil lamps at regular intervals, but he had halted the use of fuel for illuminating side streets and alleys and had ordered that every other lantern along the main ways be left dark. Those lamps had been Kram's idea; each was a hollow iron post about four feet high, topped with a barrel-shaped glass. Within, a long, thick, flat rope descended into a small drum of oil distilled from the blubber of the whales that summered in the sea off the northwestern coast of the Slash. Since the lights had been burning, street crime in Abacar had steadily declined, reducing the number of guards needed for night patrols which, in the long run, meant more money in the city's coffers.

Unfortunately, the best whaling was in Rorik's waters. Which were now Banderlund's waters. Which was why he had been forced to order his brother to stop lighting most of the lamps, collect the unburned oil, and save it for——

"Is my Lord Korrin enjoying the night air?"

"Gods and dogs!" Korrin exclaimed, whirling, leaning up against the stone railing of the balcony. Rumad Kram stood just within the wicker doors, hands clasped behind his back in his habitual manner, face bearing his usual smirk of mildly amused condescension that suggested the aged astrologer was continually comparing Lord Korrin to his ancestors and finding him lacking. "Damn you, Kram! Did that page not tell you I would be along in good time?"

"Forgive me, my lord," Kram purred. "The page was but a runner, sent ahead as I made my own way to your chambers; this vision could not wait. What if the gods saw fit to snatch back the knowledge they had imparted? What if the gods saw fit to strike me down as I waited for you? What if the gods——"

"What if they see fit to strike you down *now,* as you blather on about them?"

The old man tipped his head. "As you say."

"So tell me, then, what is this latest *vision* of yours?"

"I informed you earlier that new players were coming," Kram said. "Agents with an important role in the course of events shaping our fate."

"Yes?"

"Since then, more has been revealed to me. They are three: Two elves, and a human."

"Elves? Has old Yexandor finally responded to my request, then?"

"I fear not, my lord," Kram said. "These are not diplomats come to hear and give counsel. These are rogue elves, and the human who travels with them … The human is a Banderlundi."

Kram paused, and Korrin knew he was being given time to consider the implications of what he had just heard. "For what reason would elves be traveling with a Banderlundi? Have our neighbors to the south thrown in their lot with our enemies to the north?"

"Elves live long, and lay plans that may take centuries to bear fruit," Kram said. "As a man might plant a seed in the hope that one day his children might harvest, so the elves may——"

"I have little patience for metaphor at this hour, old man."

Kram shrugged. "It is well-known that the elves would like to reestablish their ancient woodland. Hemmed in as they are between the mountains and the sea, where else would they look to grow their absurdly large trees but in the fertile ground of the Slash?"

Korrin eyed his advisor for a moment, then said: "That is

dangerous speculation. The elves have never given any indication that they have designs on our lands. Understand that until I lay hands on these so-called agents and find proof of his involvement, I will not have it bruited about that Yexandor is in league with the 'Lundi. Have you any *other* information?"

"Oh, indeed I do, my lord. I have seen them, in my vision. One elf, plain, unremarkable; another elf, pale, with hair the color of silver; and one man, ruddy and speckled, with hair like the autumn leaf-fall."

In the distance, at the far edge of the sea, the sky had begun to glow. "Anything else? What they want, where they are?"

"Their plans were not revealed to me, my lord, but they can only mean ill toward—"

"A simple *no, I do not know what they want* will suffice. Now. You said, or rather *implied*, that they would be arriving this morning. Does that schedule still hold? Do you know which gate, what hour?"

"So many gates, my lord. So many hours."

Korrin grunted. "You have me waving my sword at shadows, old man."

"All I can tell you is that they will be here soon, in our city. *Your* city." Rumad Kram gestured at the darkened streets that sprawled beneath them. "They may be here already, hiding in the shadows, waiting to strike."

"You make them out to be serpents, but tell me you do not know their plans," Korrin said. "I see a contradiction."

"They are surrounded by a mist of red intent," Kram said. "That much is certain. Ignore my words at your peril, my lord."

"Oh, I have no intention of ignoring your words. If my brother's men find travelers such as you describe, they will be apprehended and brought for questioning. But what happens after that will much depend on how *their* words fare against yours." Korrin turned away from his advisor, toward his city. "You may show yourself out."

Kram went.

~~~~

As the night slid toward daybreak, Nebandalex moved along the river, until the trees ended at a cleared area several hundred paces wide at the southwestern wall of the city. This was the gate from which they had been turned away earlier. It looked like the authorities had increased their presence around it, perhaps in anticipation of the morning's rush of entrants; he could see the dark shapes of wall-walkers, spotters and archers such as himself, moving behind the crenellated topside lip, watching for furtive movement along the
~~~~

perimeter. Of course, despite their vigilance they had no chance of noticing a single elf moving through the trees in the darkness; but single elves were not what they were looking for anyway.

Confident that he had gone undetected, Nebandalex stationed himself at the edge of the trees and waited.

People had already been gathered when he got there, waiting to be permitted to enter; their numbers swelled steadily as the sky lightened. Workers and servants, he supposed, arriving from nearby villages and hamlets and, he guessed, less official dwelling places, tents and camps among the trees, as well as wanderers hoping to earn some coin in the city. They sprouted like a crop planted by their betters, bored and motley, milling around in the cold, idling on the sufferance of whoever controlled the gates.

He was glad he didn't have to live here, like that, every day a supplicant.

At last the gates trundled open, each giant panel withdrawing into a thickly reinforced hollow in the walls. The crowd began to stream in, scrutinized by a number of ground-level guards as well as the archers up on the ramparts. Not being familiar with this daily ritual, Nebandalex couldn't tell if this constituted a heightened level of security or was merely routine, but in any case, it was evident that they could not enter without attracting notice; none of them remotely fit the general profile of the surging rabble, insofar as any such profile could be developed; besides, the night watchman had told them to come back without their weapons, and obviously *that* was not an acceptable condition of entrance.

He'd seen enough; his companions were waiting. Nebandalex retreated silently from the city, moving ghostlike through the trees. He found the others where he'd left them, in a thicket at a bend in the road not far from where the wooded area ended. "The gates are being watched quite closely," he said. "We will not be able to slip in without being observed."

"And without getting our weapons confiscated?" Bernard said.

"That is a certainty."

Ambrosia said, "Is it busy enough that they won't notice a little ripple in the air?"

He considered this. "Probably."

"All right, we'll use a veil glamour, then."

"What's that?" Bernard asked.

She glanced at Bernard. "It's like an invisibility spell. It makes people not want to see us, so they don't."

"There is a crowd," Nebandalex said. "Even if they cannot see us, someone may blunder into us."

"Okay. I'll change it a little, make people want to stay away from it. They won't see us, but they'll still avoid us."

Bernard looked suspicious. "Do you need the Illata for that?"

She shrugged. "I *do* have a few tricks of my own, now that my brain isn't broken. Having the Illata helps though. Gather close." Nebandalex and Bernard moved in, one on either side of her. "Closer. Smaller is better when it comes to veils." They pressed in tighter while Ambrosia mumbled and fluttered her fingers. The trees around them shimmered for a moment, then returned to normal, except for a slight softness that Nebandalex only noticed from his peripheral vision, that vanished when he looked at something straight on.

Bernard said: "Is that it?"

"That's it. Let's go."

They exited the trees and, skulking along the edge of the main road, joined the flow of people entering the city. Nebandalex noted that this later traffic differed somewhat from the crowd that had gathered earlier to wait for the gates to open. That group had consisted mainly of individuals bearing nothing but the clothes on their backs and the occasional set of tools; now they found themselves sidling along with such peasants and domestic workers, but also craftsmen hauling samples of their products, peddlers with carts laden with clanging junk, farmers pushing wheelbarrows full of produce, and other agents of local commerce. Abacar seemed to get as many visitors in a day as Torgonderrer had received in the entire time he had lived there.

They positioned themselves between a couple of wagons and, staying close together and unseen within the protective wrapper of Ambrosia's veil, slipped through the gate and into the city. Immediately inside the walls, in a large open square, a collection of ramshackle semipermanent shops stood scattered haphazardly on either side of the wide dirt street. Some ordinance must have prohibited them from abutting the wall directly, Nebandalex thought, or they would have been blooming there, too, like scabrous mushrooms on a fallen tree. Unlike in Torgonderrer, there were no clear trails here, no paths through tree and brush to indicate where to walk; unleashed from the channel that restricted had their entrance, the pedestrian traffic became somewhat random, making it more difficult for their party to move through the crowd without a collision. If someone blundered into them now, detection would be much more likely than when they'd funneled through the gates, where a sense of presence or an unexpected contact could be blamed on some other nearby entrant rather than a flicker in the air.

Ambrosia guided them into an odoriferous cavity formed by three large barrels full of pickled fish and a melon-laden wagon with a broken wheel. The combination of brine, scale, and fruit was aromatic in all the wrong ways, and probably explained why no one had set up shop in this particular niche. Otherwise the open space appeared to be a free-for-all; entering tradespeople would claim a vacant patch of street, halt, and start loudly extolling the virtues of their wares or services, while aggressively defending their patch of turf from others. It all seemed rather unnecessarily adversarial and competitive, and indeed, it was only moments before a scuffle broke out near the gate; a newly-arrived vendor had begun hawking bolts of cloth that were, apparently, too nearby to those being peddled by another, rather grubby fellow who had entered earlier. This drew a crowd of idlers hoping to see a fight, but they were disappointed: A group of guards quickly descended and terminated the argument before blows could ensue. As it happened, these men had been stationed at the mouth of the alley between the wall and the backside of the tents and shops that constituted the bazaar; noticing this, Nebandalex gave Ambrosia a nudge, and the three of them scurried into the gap thus opened, leaving the souk behind.

They retreated some distance, stopping in a dim, sheltered spot behind a tarpaulin-covered pile of rolled-up carpets; voices were approaching from somewhere up ahead of them, and the passage was too narrow to comfortably allow two groups to pass without stumbling over each other. They wedged themselves into a shadowed pocket overhung with drooping rug cylinders and dangling fringe, and waited. The atmosphere was redolent of mildew and damp fabric; Nebandalex wasn't sure if the odor emanated from the tarpaulin, its contents, or both, but in any case it was an improvement, however slight, over the stink of their last rathole. Before long three watchmen passed, loudly debating the merits of the breakfast they had recently finished consuming. After they went by, Nebandalex stuck his head out and peered after them. He could tell he was outside the protection of the veil by the shimmer that passed across his vision, but it was dark here and no one was looking his way. The three men had joined their fellows at the edge of the bazaar, where the fracas had fizzled out; two guards were dragging the squirming disputants out through the front gate, while the others, having evidently confiscated all the fabric in question, returned to their original positions. They dumped the cloth in a heap, and one of the newly-arrived patrollers lifted one corner after another like a merchant inspecting a shipment of wares.

Nebandalex concluded that anyone who started a fight here must be very new, or especially dense, or, perhaps, a stalking-horse sponsored by the guards when they wanted to relieve some seller of his goods. He withdrew into their little alcove, back into the protection of the veil. The three of them crouched together like highway robbers waiting for some unguarded jewel-laden traveler to pass. "They didn't notice us?" Bernard said.

"It appears not."

"I'm sure we're not supposed to be here," Bernard said. "This is, like, a restricted area."

"You mean we are not allowed to camp amongst the moldy rugs?" Nebandalex sighed elaborately. "What a pity."

"They were talking about an inn where they got food," Ambrosia said. "If we keep going we'll probably come out near it."

"What good is an inn if we don't have any money?"

"Perhaps we could work in exchange for lodging," Nebandalex said.

"*Work?*" Bernard said.

Nebandalex shrugged. "Surely inns need things done just like anywhere else."

"With all those people coming into the city, why would they hire *us* to wash dishes or sweep floors?"

"There are other services we could perform. Things peasants from the fields cannot do."

"Such as?"

The elf thought for a moment, then said: "Can either of you sing?"

Bernard said: "Can *you?*"

"Of course. But I cannot harmonize with myself."

"We'll worry about that later," Ambrosia said. "For now, this looks like a good place to hide our weapons." She indicated a dark gap in the mound of carpets.

Nebandalex bent over, looked at the niche. "You want me to put my bow and arrows in there? What if someone desires to buy the rugs? What if the merchant packs them up and moves?"

"These have been here so long the colors are bleeding into the pallet," she said, pointing at the wooden platform on which the carpets rested. "I don't think they're going to be disturbed any time soon."

Bernard poked his staff into the opening, then slid it in all the way. It lay in the shadowed hollow, quite unnoticeable. "I guess that works," he said.

"I am not leaving my bow here unattended."

"Look." By partially unrolling various surrounding bundles, she camouflaged the opening. "See? As good as a veil." She moved the carpets aside. "We *have* to hide the weapons. We can't carry them around town freely, and we can't stay veiled forever." Then, when he continued to hesitate: "It's only for a little while, all right? Just until we find a place to stay. Then we can come back and get them and stash them in our room."

"And if we fail to find a place to stay?"

"Then we might be camping amongst the moldy rugs after all," Ambrosia said.

~~~~

"This bodes ill, my lord," Rumad Kram said, as a recovery team fished the dead man out of the Round Pool.

Lord Korrin ignored the comment. If he jumped out of his skin every time Kram told him something boded ill, he would shed more epidermis in a day than a snake did over the course of its entire scaly life.

The Round Pool was a semicircular backwater of the Elbion, formed by a natural rocky extrusion that calmed the river shortly before its final plunge into Chasm Bay. A number of small, rugged islands broke the water throughout the pool, grey-veined black stone stained white, green, and yellow with bird droppings; an even larger number of failed islands lurked just below the surface, ready to rip the bottom out of any ship that drifted over. These obstructions rendered the pool worthless for navigation by ships of any commercial size, but made it a popular spot for fishermen seeking sport and protein. The corpse that they had come for had been found by one such angler, an aged blacksmith, who like so many other elderly retired men had taken up the rod and reel to pass the time. Most of his shriveled contemporaries cast their lines from shore or from one of the rickety docks, but this fellow had been prosperous enough to afford his own small boat, which he would row out into the deeper part of the pool, carefully guiding it through the treacherous rock field to get to the center, where bigger specimens hid in submerged caves and hollows. But today, instead of a fish, the old smith had found a body out there, come to rest on one of the small islands. Nothing very unusual in that; in general, at least one body came out of the river every week, and no
~~~~

one thought much of it. However, this body had been pierced through the throat, which was slightly more notable; it was relatively uncommon for floaters to show such obvious signs of violence.

And there was one more unusual thing about the body, the thing that had brought Korrin and Kram to join the commander of the city watch at the waterfront. Giving his half-brother a sidelong glance, Korrin said: "He is definitely one of yours?"

Arran Blackhawk grunted affirmation.

"Why is he dressed up like a bandit, then?" The man wore a kerchief partially covering his face, gloves, a black cloak that billowed in the water around him: Just the sort of garb one would expect to find on a highwayman seeking to waylay travelers at night.

"Unauthorized income enhancement, most likely." Then: "As you know, the men have been complaining about their wages for some time."

"Yes. We have discussed this," Korrin said. "A war is coming. I will need coin to—"

A splash from the river drew his attention. The men charged with recovering the body had swarmed out into the Pool with ropes and canoes, and had set up a little staging post on the jagged island where the corpse had gotten stuck; one of them must have lost his footing and now floundered in the dark, icy water, much to the amusement of the crowd of fishmongers, whores, and sailors who had wandered over from the taverns and inns near the Harbor Road to gawk at the recovery operation from behind the perimeter Arran Blackhawk's men had set up.

"They are already at work," Kram said. "See how they murder those under your command, the defenders of the city?"

Korrin glanced at the astrologer, then returned his gaze to the water. Fine mist from the nearby cataract blurred the sun's outline as it rode low over the Peltish Downs across the river, making a soft-edged red circle out of it.

"Who is this *they*?" Arran Blackhawk said.

That got Korrin's attention. "I sent a message. Did you not receive it?"

"That was from you? It was marked with Kram's seal and I was called away before I read it."

Korrin turned to the astrologer. "*Your* seal?"

"After my vision became clearer," Kram said, "I intercepted the courier and amended the message."

Korrin raised an eyebrow. "You cracked *my* seal and changed *my* message?"

"I merely added a description of those shown in my vision." Pause. "I judged it imperative that your half-brother receive the most correct information avail—"

"He received *no* information."

"Only because he failed to open the letter."

"Kram, you send me worthless letters all the time," Arran Blackhawk said. "You warn me that the alignment of the stars is going to cause an increase in public drunkenness. You warn me that the color of the sun is going to cause—"

"Enough," Korrin said. To Arran: "You will read the message immediately upon your return, and take appropriate measures." To Kram: "*You* will stop making a pest of yourself."

Arran Blackhawk muttered something unintelligible; Kram merely grunted.

Out in the Pool, the recovery crew had gotten a rope looped under the dead man's armpits and were preparing to haul him out of the river and into the blacksmith's dory, which had been appropriated for the operation. Behind him, Korrin was quite sure he heard someone taking bets as to whether or not the boat would capsize and how many more people would fall into the water. And indeed, another of the retrieval crew nearly lost his footing on the slick, mossy rock island; a disappointed sigh rippled through the crowd as he caught himself before toppling over. Still, he did lose his hold on his end of the rope, and as a result the corpse splashed back into the water and began to drift away, pulling a different rope-holder in after it. The crowd greeted this development with cheers and catcalls, as if they were watching some sort of sporting event, a tug-of-war perhaps, which was being won by a corpse. "Do not lose the body!" Arran Blackhawk shouted. The team leader made placating gestures toward shore with one hand, while signaling more men into the water with the other. They plunged in, much to the crowd's amusement, and quickly rounded up the wayward corpse.

"If these interlopers are so stealthy, so cunning, why would they kill a guard and toss him into the river for us to find?" Korrin said, murmuring from the side of his mouth.

Kram responded in kind, his voice a low purr. "You said yourself that he looks the part of a bandit. Like as not they had no idea he was of the city watch." The old man shrugged. "Perhaps the poor fool waylaid them, and learned to his cost that they are not to be idly assaulted."

Despite Kram's low tone, Arran Blackhawk had heard him. "I will thank you not to refer to my men as fools," he said.

"If you had read and disseminated my message, your men would have known——"

"If *you* had not tampered with the seal——"

"I said *enough*!" Korrin said. "Your squabbling is tedious."

"Yes, my lord," they said simultaneously; then they glowered at each other. Korrin rolled his eyes.

"It may be that he stumbled upon them as they plotted and so they killed him, then dressed him thusly as a diversion," Kram said, after a brief silence.

"Save your sops for someone who wants them."

"It may be a sop, but Kram makes a point," Korrin said. "You will check the duty roster and find out where he was assigned and who he was with.   Others might also have seen what they should not have seen."

"An excellent plan, my lord," Kram said. He beamed at Arran Blackhawk, who made a face as if someone had waved a cup of curdled milk under his nose.

The swimmers had gotten control of the body, and were now laboring to heave it into the blacksmith's little boat without capsizing it or running it aground on one of the nearby rocks. Arran Blackhawk shouted: "Forget the boat, just bring him back to shore!"

"Perhaps the commander of the watch would permit me to suggest an additional course of action?"

"You *request permission* before offering a suggestion?" he said. "If I did not know better, I would think you were an impostor. Perhaps I should bring *you* in for questioning."

The astrologer's response was a glance at Lord Korrin, accompanied by a nervous titter.

"You know my half-brother speaks in jest, old man," Korrin said. "Make your suggestion."

"Assign a detail to search the town for our enemies. Two elves and a Banderlundi. You will find more detailed descriptions in my ... I mean, Lord Korrin's letter. Surely anyone who sees such a trio will remember them."

"Really," Arran Blackhawk said. "A search detail, you say?"

"They may be being abetted by elements within the city. It may be necessary to go house to house turning over stones until we find the one that hides the serpent."

"What a novel idea." He shook his head. "You think I need an *astrologer* to suggest this strategy? I understand that you are entering your dotage, Kram, but please do not mistake my brother and me for the children you once knew."

"I would never mistake you and my Lord Korrin for children," Kram said, as the recovery team finally dragged their lifeless quarry out of the water. "Were *you* one, you should not be permitted to handle sharp objects such as that sword; and were *he* one, half the young ladies in the castle should be jailed as corrupters of the innocent."

"Only half?" Korrin said. "You give me too little credit."

"And he gives himself too much," Arran Blackhawk muttered.

~~~~

Once Ambrosia finally convinced Nebandalex to cache his bow for a few hours, they left the carpet alcove and headed along the base of the wall, passing unnoticed behind more tents and shops before entering an alley where the open bazaar ended and real buildings began. One bored-looking sentry was stationed at the far end of the alley, but they slunk by him undetected to emerge into a sprawling business district. Several inns stood nearby, along with a somewhat larger number of taverns, various shops selling things like footwear or hats or leather goods, a long low building that looked and smelled like a stable, and, set well apart from everything else, a blacksmith and farriery. On the far side of the smith was a large and rather ramshackle house, set behind a rail fence that served no purpose but decoration; a sign out in front, which looked rather new, identified it as *The Goldsmith Inn*. Ambrosia eyed this place, which seemed rather out of accord with the other, more clearly commercial, structures in the area; and, getting a feeling, said: "There."

"Why there?" Bernard said.

"Because it's out of place," she said, "just like us. Let's go."

They crossed the street and turned right. Fortunately foot traffic was relatively light, and the few pedestrians who came near them felt a mild compulsion to move to the portion of the broad sidewalk nearest the street or to pause for a few seconds, perhaps to scratch, perhaps to adjust a shoe, thus avoiding the veil.

After passing through a cloud of metal-scented smoke that issued from the smith, they reached the inn, where a gap in the fence invited them to enter the yard; they accepted the invitation, crunching up a freshly-raked gravel walk to a wide, deep porch where scattered benches and chairs provided places to sit and observe the street. No one was doing so at the moment. Once they were in the shadows,
~~~~

Ambrosia took the opportunity to drop the veil, which was a relief; maintaining it had started to give her a headache. She wasn't going to tell the others that, though; Bernard would just worry, and find a way to blame it on the Illata.

They entered the building to the tinkling accompaniment of an unseen bell. The interior was much as the exterior had suggested: Cool and dim, with a lot of dark, polished wood and gilt paint. There was no foyer or waiting room, no hostess or bouncer; they went directly from the porch into a large room well-stocked with tables and chairs and lined along the walls by booths with hard bench seats. A large pyramidal fireplace, open on all four sides, formed the centerpiece of the dining area, doing double duty as both hearth and, with its thick iron framework, ceiling support. A low fire burned there, filling the room with a pleasantly nutty aroma unlike any woodsmoke Ambrosia could remember. None of the tables or booths was occupied; in fact, the place appeared to be deserted.

"This looks less than promising," Nebandalex said.

"It looks like a restaurant that hasn't opened yet."

"There's a fire, so someone is here," Ambrosia said. "Come on."

They crossed to the bar. It was the same dark wood as the tables, so highly polished that it glowed. A shiny brass rail across the front provided a place to rest one's elbows while one contemplated the massive mirror attached to the wall behind the bar. It reflected three dirty, disheveled faces; they all looked like they'd just wandered in from a fortnight spent roughing it out in the woods. It occurred to her that a mirror of such size must have cost a small fortune, especially in a place like this, with, presumably, no mass production or cheap imports. She glanced down at the rail, thinking of the name of the inn, reevaluating the material, wondering if it might, in fact, be gold. Bernard seemed to be thinking the same thing; he had taken hold of it and was giving it little tugs as if trying to see if he could pull it free. "What are you doing?" she whispered.

"Huh?" He looked at her, then down at his hands. He pulled them back as if the metal had given him a shock. "I didn't—"

He broke off as a small man in late middle age emerged from a drape-shrouded doorway at the far end of the bar. The fellow stood about five feet tall, with short curly hair that was brown at the top of his head but grey all around, making the portion that retained its color look like an island floating in a foggy sea. He toddled over to a padded stool near where they stood, climbed up onto it, picked up a rag from somewhere, and began busily polishing wood that didn't seem capable of becoming any shinier. He did all this without even looking at them; after a moment, Bernard said: "You did dispel the veil, right?"

"Yes." She eyed the bartender, who continued to ignore them, and finally said: "Excuse me … this *is* an inn, isn't it?"

"Yes, it is." He finally looked at them, his eyes quick and studying. "You seem unlikely to be paying for food or lodging."

"We can work," Bernard said.

"Plenty of people can work," the little man said. "We have all the staff we require. We have a man to supervise the kitchen. We have more men to cook the food and put it on plates. We have girls to carry the plates back and forth. We have boys to wash the plates. We—" He broke off as something shot out of the gap in the curtains, skittered along the bar, and, using the man's head as a platform, launched itself up to an exposed rafter, clinging upside down with tiny claws dug into the wood and a long, furry tail wrapped around the beam. It peered at Ambrosia with huge yellow eyes, then at Bernard, then at Nebandalex, making a soft chittering sound in the back of its throat. Its fur, which had been whitish-grey when it emerged, slowly darkened to match the tone of its surroundings.

"What's *that* thing's job, then?" Bernard said.

The curtain parted again and a man came through, much younger than the barkeep. His son? No, they looked nothing alike; the newcomer was tall and broad and blond, with a completely different face. His gaze bounced around the room and quickly located the acrobatic creature on the ceiling, then dropped to Nebandalex, who had reflexively reached for the bow he was no longer carrying. He raised an amber eyebrow. "If you are going to pretend to shoot, please pretend to miss."

Nebandalex, looking sheepish, lowered his arm.

The man issued a chattery whistle; in response, the cat-thing let go of the beam, turned over in mid-fall, and bounded off Bernard's shoulder, knocking his hat off as it went. He caught it before it hit the floor, and slipped it back into place with a single fluid motion; by the time he had done that, the little beast was sitting on the blond man's shoulder, sending comically enormous blinks in every direction as its head swiveled this way and that.

"I thought we had agreed, Aldric," the bartender said in carefully even tones, "that in the new building, she would not be allowed in the dining room anymore. She steals from the guests."

Aldric shrugged. "I was cleaning her cage and she escaped." He eyed their little band. "Who have we here? Early patrons?"

"No. They claim to be looking for work."

"Mmm. Work? Well then." He rubbed his chin with a long forefinger, the nail making faint scratching noises on invisible stubble; his cat-creature yawned, displaying a row of small, needle-sharp teeth. Still looking at them, he said: "What sort of work can they do, Bertram?"

"I did not get so far as to find out. I was preparing to dash their hopes when your cat jumped on my head."

The creature cheeped pointedly. "You know she hates it when you call her a cat," Aldric said.

Bertram went back to his polishing duties, muttering something under his breath that Ambrosia didn't quite catch; Bertram must be a consummate mutterer, she thought.

"We can help around the inn," Bernard said. "Washing, sweeping, busing—"

Aldric held up a hand. "Stop. Of dish-washers and floor-sweepers and plate-carriers, I have no need." He looked at Bertram and said, in a disappointed tone, "Why are they still here when they are so dull?"

"Perhaps if you had better control over your *cat*, I would have already have sent them away, and you would not now find yourself being bored by their tediousness," Bertram said.

"Mmm." Then, to their group: "We have not been at this location very long, and are still building up a clientele. Therefore I am far more interested in finding someone who can bring in new customers than I am in someone who can serve customers who are already here." He looked them up and down. "Which sort of someones are you?"

Ambrosia opened her mouth to mention Nebandalex's purported singing abilities, but Bernard jumped in ahead of her. "Actually, Ambrosia here is a bit of a storyteller."

"Is she, then?" The owner gave her an appraising look. "You tell stories?"

"Maybe," she said.

"Mmm. *Maybe*? I can hardly advertise that I *may* have a storyteller." He looked at Bertram. "Bertram, have we good food and drink here? Excellent service? Friendly staff?"

"Maybe," Bertram said,

He turned back to them. "You see? Less than compelling."

"Yes," she said. "Okay, yes, I'm a storyteller."

"You are sure? Because it rather seems as if you decided that just this moment."

"Yes, I'm sure."

"Very well. Tell us a story."

Ambrosia said: "Right now?"

"Right now. If I present a storyteller who turns out to be terrible, and all my patrons leave, I shall be most unhappy. Better to find out ahead of time."

"Um. All right." She would have to kill Bernard later. "What kind of story do you want to hear?"

"A storyteller does not *ask* what story to tell," Aldric said. "She just *tells* one."

On second thought, maybe she should kill Bernard now. That would make a good story, wouldn't it?

~~~~

A knock at the door was followed by Arran Blackhawk's voice. "My lord?"

"Come in," Korrin said, his voice muffled by the pillow in which his face rested.

A pause; another knock. "Korrin? Are you there?"

His half-brother couldn't hear him, obviously. Korrin lifted his head just long enough to repeat his invitation to enter, then let it drop again. He heard the door open; footsteps crossed to the bed. The door closed. The wench continued kneading Korrin's back. No one spoke. After a moment Lord Korrin said, into the pillow: "Have you brought news, or do you just want to go next?"

"News. My men have gone through all the buildings near the Round Pool, interviewed everyone they found. There is no trace of the suspects Kram's letter mentions."

"Really." Korrin cracked one eye open and looked at Arran. "Surely no one believes that they dumped the body *directly* into the Pool? It could only have come from upstream."

"As you say. The men are working their way in that direction as we speak."

"Of course you did not disturb me just to tell me no progress has been made."

"Of course." Arran sighed. "A sentry on evening duty at the front gate did see three wanderers who matched their descriptions; they wanted to enter overnight, but could not pay the fee. His partner at the gate, name of Marjack, propositioned the female, which nearly provoked a fight. The strangers left and, as far as can be determined, did not return. Not that way, anyhow."

"Sentries are not supposed to dally with visitors."

"I am aware of that."
~~~~

Korrin grunted. "And what excuse did Marjack offer for his behavior?"

"None. He is the man we pulled out of the Pond this morning."

Korrin raised his head at that, then rolled over onto his back and sat up. "This cannot be coincidence."

"By most accounts Marjack was a lout and a bully, especially when he drank. He got off duty shortly after the travelers came and went. He visited several taverns, then exited by the night gate and never returned."

"You think he went looking for the elf-woman?"

Arran Blackhawk shrugged. "It is possible; one of the elves carried a bow, as they often do, and the injury to Marjack's throat is consistent with having been shot. A bit of fletching was found embedded in the wound, I am told."

"Then there is every reason to believe that these three killed him, and little reason to believe that they did not."

Arran said nothing.

"You have another opinion?"

"You know what I think of those who read meaning in the stars."

"There *is* a difference between Rumad Kram and some street magician armed with a map of the heavens," Korrin said. "He may have a touch of the charlatan to him, but how would you explain the appearance of three strangers matching the description of those he warned me against?"

"They could be in cahoots."

Korrin could only guffaw at that idea. "Please, brother, be serious. The only time the old man leaves the tower is to come and pester me with visions. I doubt he has been beyond the city walls in the entire time I have sat upon the hawk throne. He would hardly have the opportunity to go out and hire a whore, let alone engage in clandestine meetings with far-flung conspirators."

"He could have other means of communicating with them. A scrying mirror, remote writing——"

"Make up your mind. Is the old man a fraud, or a clairvoyant?" Korrin shook his head. "We waste time. Have you informed Kram about this incident at the gate?"

"I report to you, not to him."

"Find him and tell him. I would know what his response is."

"Yes, my lord." Arran bowed stiffly, turned, and exited, his sword bouncing against his hip. He closed the door with a bang.

The wench made to resume her ministrations, but Korrin waved her away, put on his robe, and crossed the small chamber to stand near the window. This room—one of a number of similar bolt-holes scattered throughout the castle to which he would repair when he craved relaxation, or simply wanted to make it difficult for a casual seeker to locate his august presence—was at a lower elevation than his apartment, but still commanded a serviceable view of the city and the sea out below the cliffs, where the high sun sparkled on the swells. He searched the ocean but, of course, espied nothing but the endless glimmer of open water and lack of commerce.

He heard the door open behind him. Glancing over his shoulder, he saw Rumad Kram shuffle in, leaning on his staff, his bags of trinkets swinging at his belt. "I just told my brother you rarely left your tower," Korrin said, "and yet here you are, giving the lie to my words." Korrin nodded to the wench, who gathered her things and departed. Turning back to the window, he said: "You have begun to make a habit of interrupting me when I am alone with the fair maidens of the castle."

"My apologies, my lord," Kram said. "Shall I fetch her back for you? Perhaps ask her to bring along a sister or two?"

"That will not be necessary," Korrin said. "I have seen her sisters and they are all quite plain. My brother informed you?"

"I encountered him in the hallway not ten paces from here—ten of *his* paces, not mine—but in fact I had already received the tale from one of his men. I have been looking for you, to share my thoughts on the matter."

"Which are?"

"The same as yours, Lord Korrin. If this man was not killed by the three we seek, I will eat one of my books every day for a year."

"Perhaps you should do that anyway," Korrin said. "It might add some bulk to your frame."

"Leather and parchment is notably lacking in nutrition," Kram said, as if this were something of which he had direct experience. "In any case, there can be no doubt now. They are here."

"So it would seem. Yet aside from two sentries, one of whom is dead, no one has seen them."

"Yes," Kram said. "A pity my warning did not reach all ears that should have heard it until it was too late."

"The city watch is spreading the description of your outlaws to the innkeepers and fish mongers and alehouse bartenders and the like. That will suffice." Korrin cocked his head. "Unless you would have me post handbills and send criers to roam the streets shouting about it? I am sure that would hardly drive our quarries deeper underground."

"My lord Korrin is wise to avoid making these criminals more wary than they already are," Kram said, "but it may be more prudent to spread the word far and wide. After all, the searchers of the city watch are not necessarily the most … discreet of men."

"Perhaps not. But once it gets around that they are looking for Marjack's killers, they will certainly be the most motivated."

<div align="center">~~~~</div>

Bernard knew he was taking several chances when he volunteered Ambrosia as a storyteller: First, that she wouldn't simply refuse; second, that there was enough of Mercy in her to remember those stories she used to peck out on that computer; and third, that the innkeeper would find her material worthy of giving them boarding for the night. He'd been pretty confident about the first two, but since Mercy had never shared a single paragraph—never even a single *sentence*—he had no idea about the third. He was, he supposed, about to find out.

Looking nervous, Ambrosia started to speak, then cleared her throat and asked for some water. Bertram provided this in a metal cup. She took a small sip. "Give her something stronger," Aldric said, not taking his eyes off her. "We do not want her drying out in the middle of her tale." The intensity of his gaze caused Bernard to add a fourth item to his list of gambles: That Aldric was in fact even *considering* hiring Ambrosia as an entertainer, rather than plotting how to get her in the sack. He certainly looked like the type who would have a coterie of women that he picked from, the way Bernard's father might choose a suit from his closet.

Bertram handed over another drink. Ambrosia sipped that one, too, coughed, turned red, coughed some more, picked up the cup of water, and drained it. Then, with one last furious and panic-stricken glance at Bernard, she began telling them a tale about a girl named Cardella, who lived in an icebound castle under siege, high in the mountains, where she was a serving wench to a thoroughly unpleasant king named Lahr. Lahr had been driven in retreat to this craggy redoubt by the handsome and noble Prince Faundren over the course of a war that began, as wars so often did, as a real estate squabble involving a disputed province. It had turned personal when Lahr's assassins bumbled their assignment to kill Faundren, leaving him alive and mourning his murdered bride.

Bernard expected the story to end with Faundren's forces storming the castle, followed by a one-on-one showdown between the prince and the king, followed by Cardella and Faundren falling in love and living happily ever after; but instead, Lahr's forces triumphed at the last moment and Faundren was taken prisoner.   Bernard adjusted his expectations, anticipating that Faundren would escape and things would then proceed to the showdown, the happily ever after, and so forth, but he was wrong again; instead, the odious Lahr personally chopped Faundren's head off, then carried it around his throne room for a while as a trophy.   Then Lahr ordered up a huge feast to celebrate his triumph and, out of arrogance or stupidity or, most likely, both, gave his food taster the evening off and assigned the job to Faundren's severed head instead.   Not surprisingly, the head was less than effective in this position; being unattached to a living body, it suffered no ill effects after Lahr tipped a goblet full of wine into its mouth—wine which, unfortunately for Lahr, Cardella had spiked with poison that she'd stolen from the apothecary.   The king died writhing and coughing up blood; Cardella fled, was cornered by Lahr's champion atop one of the tall towers, and jumped to her death rather than accept capture.

The end.

Wow, what a downer. Bernard hoped their own quest or whatever it was didn't end that way.

The room was silent for a moment; then Aldric clapped his hands and said, "Poor Cardella, driven to her death! There's nothing like a good tragedy to encourage patrons to order more ale! Do you have other stories?"

"Some," she said.

"Good, good. You should work on your delivery a bit. Take different tones of voice for different characters, if you can. Perhaps one of your servants here can provide some background music or sound effects, you know, bang a spoon against a plate to simulate the sound of the siege engines, that sort of thing."   Bernard and Nebandalex traded glances.   The elf raised an eyebrow; Bernard shrugged and shook his head.   Aldric, apparently picking up on this unspoken exchange, said: "Or I could find a minstrel to accompany the tale with music." He snapped his fingers loudly. "Yes. We shall have a minstrel!" He pointed at Bertram. "Find that fellow, the one who used to play the harp and the horn at our old place, and have him spread the word that we have a new, never-before-heard storyteller this evening. Tell him that if there are no wives around, he should mention that she is stunningly beautiful."

"I shall tell him that right away," Bertram said, not looking up from whatever it was he was doing back there.

Returning his attention to Ambrosia, Aldric said, "In exchange for your story, I will give you and your servants ... er, that is, your *companions* ... a spare room, and breakfast in the morning. And you and the minstrel can split whatever coins are thrown into your hat, according to whatever formula you decide. Fair enough?"

Ambrosia glanced at Bernard and Nebandalex for approval, and when neither objected, said: "Fair enough."

"Very good." Aldric reached behind the bar and produced a large, battered, shockingly blue hat. "Here is your hat." He tossed it at Ambrosia as if it were a flying disk, but it never reached her; the monkey-cat-thing launched itself from Aldric's shoulder and snatched the chapeau out of the air. Animal and headpiece hit the floor in a tangle of fur and claws and fabric; then, its prize clutched in its clever tail, the creature scampered back to the bar and vanished through the curtain into the back room.

"So much for their hat," the bartender said.

"I have four more just like it," Aldric said. Then, as he followed his pet: "Bertram, get them something to eat, would you?"

Bernard saw Ambrosia looking at him and said, "That was a good—" He broke off when she grabbed him by the ear and dragged him to a nearby table. "Ow! Let go! Ow! Who are you, my grandmother?"

"Stop it, you big baby," she said, letting go of him. He dropped onto a chair. She sat down across from him; Nebandalex ambled over and stood nearby, looking amused. "You've got a lot of nerve throwing me under the bus like that, Bernard."

Bernard couldn't suppress a grin, hearing her talk like Mercy again. Maybe telling the story had brought that part of her a little bit closer to the foreground. "Sorry, but, you heard him—he was looking for an entertainer, and—"

"And Nebandalex said he could sing."

"He's already got a minstrel."

"Which you didn't know when you volunteered me—" Ambrosia broke off as Bertram came over with a tray of warm bread, cheese, three cups of dark liquid, and what appeared to be chartreuse eggs, with a side of some sort of similarly-colored meat that vaguely resembled pork chops. Ambrosia eyed the platter. "Green eggs and ham? Really?"

"It is quite popular," Bertram said.

"Is it? Do you get a lot of customers named Sam?"

"No." Bertram looked Ambrosia up and down. "A storyteller you may be, but you are still dirty, not to mention smelly. Aldric will want you cleaned up before you perform. I will have the girls begin heating water so you can bathe." He spun and marched back toward the bar without waiting for a reply, vanishing through a swinging door with a kitchen behind it.

"Yeah, I bet Aldric would just *love* to watch the girls give her a bath," Bernard said.

Ambrosia shot him a glare. "What was that, Bernard?"

"Mmm, green eggs and ham," he said.

~~~~

After they finished their breakfast, Aldric reappeared from behind the curtain—without his furry little friend this time—and showed them to their room. No wonder it was vacant; hardly premium, it amounted to little more than a closet-like chamber behind the kitchen, wedged between the angling slope of the rear roof and a crook in the chimney. It was loud, hot, cramped, and dark, stuffy and windowless, and the three cots were about as wide as church pews; but it was free.

Or rather, it was being paid for, but not with money; Ambrosia was reminded of this when, immediately after Aldric dropped them off, two female employees arrived to pick her up. They took her to a nearby outbuilding, evidently formerly part of the blacksmith's shop, where a large bellows that had once served to melt iron had been adapted into some sort of bathwater-heating device. She was a little bit surprised to see the elaborate spa that had been constructed in the old forge, and wondered again exactly how wealthy Aldric was. Clearly he felt no need to take any percentage of whatever proceeds went into his crazy blue hat.

As instructed by the ladies, she removed her rather filthy garments and settled into a broad, deep basin of smooth black rock. The hot water felt wonderful; she had been in a near-constant state of chill, damp, or both ever since she came here. Soap and a scrub brush materialized nearby and she set to work cleaning herself up. Meanwhile, one of the ladies collected the clothes Ambrosia had discarded and, holding them like they were some sort of creepy gelatinous creatures that given the opportunity would flow up her arms and eat her brain, carried them to the forge and tossed them into the voracious orange glow. "Hey, those are my clothes!" Ambrosia said, alarmed; was she going to be expected to perform naked or something?

From behind her, Aldric's voice said: "They are beyond salvage, I fear." With a little gasp, she looked over her shoulder. The innkeeper
~~~~

stood there, mostly hidden behind a gigantic armload of ladies' clothing, as if he had been ambushed by the display rack at a haberdashery. "Something in here should fit you, I think," he said, dumping the pile on a wooden bench nearby.

"Where … where did you get all *that*?"

Aldric shrugged. "Here and there. The girls will help you select an appropriate outfit." He sat down on the bench next to the heap. "I have got a lad out advertising tonight's event. I had thought to send you out as well, but now I see it is going to take a goodly portion of the day just getting you cleaned up. Besides, not showing you off ahead of time will only add to the mystery." He looked her over. "I am pleased to see that you do not subscribe to the silly belief that bathing causes illness."

"Um," she said. Then: "Are you … that is, how long have you been watching——"

"You need not worry about me in that regard," he said.

"Oh." She thought about that for a moment. "Okay. My friends——"

"Do not get access to the baths with their free room and board," Aldric said. "I did send a wash basin to your room, though, and a set of decent clothes for each of them. Males are easier to fit than females. Fewer variables. Are you planning to do something about your hair?" It took a second for that last comment to register; when it did, she ducked her head underwater and shook it vigorously. When she surfaced, a cloud of dirty water was slowly dispersing around her.

"You may need to repeat that a few more times."

"Mmm. What's expected of me tonight?"

"Just do what you did this afternoon. You will have musical accompaniment, if I can locate a suitable player. The fellow I used to hire seems to have moved on. Why do you not have your own minstrel or play an instrument yourself, like other bards do?"

"Being a bard is not my main gig," she said.

"I see." If Aldric wondered what a *gig* was, he didn't ask. "Well, finding a musician is another of my lad's tasks. It is somewhat late notice, but there is no shortage of lute strummers looking for engagements in reputable establishments." He grinned, making him look very young; then he got to his feet. "Enjoy the rest of your bath. Once the grooming commences, you might find the experience less than pleasant."

Aldric exited through a narrow door in the back wall. How had he managed to squeeze through there with that huge armload of clothes?

The ladies reappeared shortly thereafter, one carrying a large and rather dangerous-looking comb, a brush, and a box that resembled a medieval torture kit but, when opened, turned out to contain makeup in various forms and hues.   Meanwhile, the other one started rummaging through the mound of clothes Aldric had left, holding pieces up, inspecting them, and either tossing them over her shoulder or sorting them into piles based on some criteria Ambrosia couldn't immediately identify.

The girl with the comb came over and held it up in a way that, while perfectly innocent, managed to seem threatening.

"This is going to hurt," she said.

Chapter 13

ALDRIC'S ASSESSMENT HAD been accurate; Ambrosia's makeover lasted most of the day. Progress was slowed once other guests started wandering into the baths; apparently under orders to keep her presence a secret, Aldric's girls had set up a divider, and kept her hidden behind it whenever the spa was occupied. She took the opportunity to sleep back there for several hours, too, swaddled as she was in warmth and soft blankets, relaxed from her bath, exhausted from her journey, not waking up until it was time for an afternoon lunch break. She knew she was supposed to be out looking for the next piece of the Heart, but surely she had earned a day to recuperate from her long trip and the beating that had preceded it. Besides, none of this had been *her* idea; it was Bernard who'd put her forward as some sort of bard, after all. She doubted Aldric would have put this much effort into prettying up a crooning Nebandalex. Anyway, tomorrow, after she had told her story and they had some money, they would get back to the reason they had come here.

By the time she finally left the spa, the sun hung low over the walls of the city. She got to spend a few minutes with Bernard and Nebandalex in their closet of a room, just long enough to collect some astonished remarks from Bernard regarding the fact that she was not only wearing new, fancy clothes but *had had her hair styled* and was wearing *makeup*—he half-jokingly made her say the password, *ribbit*, to prove it was really her and not some impostor—and to learn that the others, too, had slept for much of the morning, had received dry bread and cheese for lunch, and had only ventured out of the room to use the privy. The clothes Aldric had mentioned sending were still neatly stacked in the corner, unused, evidently having been found wanting.

Nebandalex asked about retrieving their weapons. "After dark," she said. "There isn't time now." This was confirmed a few moments later when Aldric announced himself with a perfunctory knock, then breezed in. Suddenly the room smelled like sandalwood. He greeted the others politely even though they still wore their filthy old garments, but fawned over her as if she were a favorite little sister he hadn't seen since she was a child, and look, now she was all grown up! He rather grandly announced that he had already fielded a number of inquiries from people who had heard about his new storyteller and wanted to know more about her: What sort of tales she spun, what she looked like, if she was as lovely as had been claimed. Aldric, cagey promoter that he was, would only allow that she was an exotic beauty from the forest; any who wished to know more than that must come and see for themselves, and drop a few coins in the hat. Which reminded him, he had to fetch a new hat for her to use. Did she need anything else? Perhaps she would like to come and see how he had arranged the dining area for her and the minstrel he'd hired? And before she quite realized what he was doing, she found herself peeled away from the group and squirreled away in his apartment so that she could make her big entrance from there.

Aldric's room seemed to be mostly office, though there was a living area off to the side with a small cot, a couple of wardrobes, and a few other pieces of domestic furniture. One of the wardrobes was partially open; she was sure she saw the garments rejected during her makeover hanging inside, but decided not to ask why he had a closet full of women's clothing. An odd piece of furniture, like a cross between a rabbit hutch and a giant hamster pen, stood against the wall opposite the wardrobes; that was where Aldric's pet creature, whose name, he said, was Trouble, lived when she wasn't brachiating around the rafters in the dining area. At the moment, Trouble was draped across the innkeeper's shoulders like a boneless stole, half asleep, enjoying a light ear-scratching from his almost Aldric's fingers. Her fur was mostly dark, matching his shirt, but where she lay against his blonde hair it was a shade of muddy gold.

At length, strains of music began to drift from the room beyond the curtain. A musician——not, unfortunately, the legendary and possibly mythical fellow with a harp and a horn, who had proven unobtainable——had arrived, and was plucking out a tune on his mandolin or lute or whatever it was that he played. Before long, the tenor of the notes became freighted, expectant; Aldric cocked his head, listening. "I think you are being cued," he said.

"Does that mean … is it time?"

"Shortly." He went to the curtain, peered through the gap. "A good crowd."

"I hope it's a *friendly* crowd."

"You'll be fine," Aldric said. "Remember, don't just *tell* the story, *be* the story. Be the characters, be the scenery, be the setting." He flashed her a dazzling smile; his teeth were white and even and perfect, which made her wonder what sort of dental care he had access to. "If all else fails, be beautiful. You shouldn't have any difficulty doing *that*." Chuckling, he carried Trouble over to the hutch and took out a leather harness with an attached leash. This, he explained, was to keep her from roaming the inn like a small marauder, causing patrons' food, plates, and purses to disappear when they weren't looking; apparently some found that sort of behavior less than amusing. He poured the drowsy animal into the strappy apparatus and secured it in a few places, then returned her to his shoulders and rejoined Ambrosia at the curtain. Trouble blinked her huge eyes and emitted a soft meeping sound. Ambrosia reached out and scratched behind her ears the way Aldric had done earlier, eliciting something like a purr. The creature might object to being referred to as a cat—or, more likely, Aldric objected to it, and attributed the objection to Trouble—but she certainly sounded like one.

The innkeeper gave Ambrosia a reassuring pat on the shoulder, then exited through the curtain to make introductions. First he announced the minstrel's name, which was Korben, and then he proceeded to some puffery about how good music paired with a good story could aid in digestion, and by the way, had everyone tried the ale? A smattering of laughter followed; then he gave them Ambrosia's name and told them that, yes, everything they may have heard about her was true. Light applause told her it was time to make her entrance, and she went out to face the audience.

Two padded stools had been erected in a cleared space in front of the bar. Trying not to look at the crowd, she took the vacant one next to the musician, a doughy, pie-faced fellow dressed in foppish greens and reds. The applause picked up and a few hoots were added as she adjusted her skirts, inadvertently revealing, then hiding, a length of leg; Aldric made a comment to the effect that if anyone was expecting a burlesque show they had come to the wrong establishment, eliciting more amusement from the crowd.

Story time. She took a deep breath, swallowed, and got on with it, once again relating the tale of King Lahr, Prince Faundren, and Cardella the wench. She tried to use a different voice for each of the main characters, as Aldric had suggested, and no one laughed at her; the minstrel strummed his mandolin at appropriate moments, gauging the tone and intensity to fit the scene: Not an easy task, she realized, given that he didn't know how the story would go. But after a little while she sort of forgot the audience and the minstrel and just lost herself in the story; it almost seemed to be telling itself, moving inexorably to Prince Faundren's execution, King Lahr's death, Cardella's ultimate act of fatal defiance. When it was over, she didn't say *the end*; she simply bowed her head and fell silent.

After a moment, her listeners began to applaud. She chanced a look at them; most were clapping, some sat stone-faced, while others were busy eating or chatting and seemed not to have listened to her at all. The minstrel gave her a wink, then put his mandolin across his knees and began tuning it. As she wondered what was supposed to happen next, Aldric came over, carrying one of his absurd floppy hats. This one had not, as far as she could tell, been used as a chew toy by his cat-thing. He placed it upside-down on the nearest table and said, "Ambrosia and Korben humbly request that if you enjoyed their performance, you express your appreciation in the customary manner." The guests there dropped a few coins into the hat, then passed it along to another table; Aldric smiled in their direction and retreated back to the bar.

Korben jumped off the stool, his jowly cheeks and chin rippling as he landed. He offered Ambrosia a fleshy hand to help her to her feet. "Well told," he said.

"Thanks," she said. "Um, well-played."

He shrugged. "I know I was not Aldric's first choice, or even his second, but I hope I did credibly well." He looked around. "I heard you were here with two friends. Where are they?"

"In the back," she said.

"What? They did not come out to hear your tale? Shameful! I must meet them and make them feel the guilt they deserve. Go and fetch them, and I will get us all something to drink."

He headed for the bar. A bit nonplussed, Ambrosia went to the back hall that led to the guest rooms, which was separated from the dining area by a curtain made of highly-polished wooden beads that clicked and clattered as she passed through. She almost walked right into Bernard and Nebandalex, who were standing immediately behind it. Startled, she said: "What are you two doing here?"

Nebandalex said, "Listening, of course."

"I was hoping for a happier ending this time," Bernard added.

"Sorry, that would be selling out," she said. "Come on, the minstrel wants to meet you."

Bernard looked suspicious. "What for?"

"He says he wants to make you feel guilty for not being in the audience to support me."

"Great," Bernard said. "Like I don't get enough guilt from my parents."

~~~~

They followed Ambrosia into the dining area, over to a small table that Aldric had set aside for her and the minstrel near the bar. Korben was already there, drinking from a wooden mug; three others, all
~~~~

metal, were arranged around him. He smiled as they came over, lifted his cup in greeting, and took a swig.

"What is that?" Bernard said as they sat down.

"Ale, of course," the minstrel said.

"Ale? You mean, like, beer?"

"If you say so."

Bernard picked up a mug, sipped from it, made a face, and put it down.

"You do not care for it?" Korben said. "Goldshine's ale is supposed to be among the best in Abacar."

"It's fine. It's just not carbonated."

Korben and Nebandalex both appeared mystified; Nebandalex said: "You and your words. What does *carbonated* mean?"

Bernard pointed at the flagon. "No bubbles."

Korben picked up his mug and examined it, as if looking for a list of ingredients. "Why would you want bubbles in your ale?"

Ambrosia took a sip. "And since when are you an expert on ale, anyway?"

"Well, since never," he said, "but beer is supposed to have bubbles. It's supposed to be cold, too. Everyone knows that."

"Just to remind you," Ambrosia said, "we are not back home. They don't have refrigerators here."

"And they don't have carbon dioxide either?"

"You're being a pill."

Bernard shrugged. "Whatever."

Nebandalex, who had already finished his own beverage, pointed at Bernard's and said, "May I?" Without waiting for a reply, the elf reached over, picked up Bernard's mug, and started quaffing the contents.

"Um, sure, be my guest," Bernard said.

Korben, shaking his head in evident bemusement, went to the stool where he had left his mandolin and started doing something with the strings.

"Pace yourself, Nebandalex," Ambrosia said.

"Pace *your* self," Bernard said. "You're slurring your words."

"Am I am not?"

It took Bernard a second to parse that one. "Yes you are. You're supposed to tell another story. You can't tell a story if you're drunk."

"Sure I can," she said. "I can tell a story about a couple of stupid foosball … I mean, football … players who try and mess with a girl in the forest, and she beats them up and … wait, let me remember how it ends …" She trailed off, her face screwed up in concentration.

Bernard said: "Mercy?"

"I said wait. I'm thinking. I'm …" She flopped face-down on the table.

"*Mercy!*" Bernard exclaimed.

Aldric, across the room glad-handing his customers, looked over with a frown on his face.

Suddenly Bernard felt a cord around his neck, cutting off his breath. The room exploded in an uproar as he scrabbled at the wire. In the vast mirror behind the bar, he saw that Korben, the minstrel, had come up behind him and was strangling him with what looked like a guitar string. As his vision faded, the mirror showed the door of the inn bursting open. A squad of armed men barged in, forging a path through the customers toward their table; and some of the customers weren't even customers, but more watchmen, apparently undercover, who joined the incoming authorities to pacify the room from various spots within it.

Bernard heard Aldric shouting something, but couldn't make out the words; the innkeeper moved to intercept the men, but one of the sentries checked him with an arm across his chest. The innkeeper, his face stormy, began arguing with the guard, but no one else paid him any attention.

Bernard felt blood trickling down his neck from where the wire was biting into his skin. His head felt thick and full and heavy, like a sponge that could neither drain nor absorb more liquid. He moved his eyes off the mirror, looking for help from Lex, from anyone, but the other elf had drunk even more than Ambrosia and lay sprawled beneath the table, unconscious and drooling. Whatever was in the ale, it was powerful and quick.

Then the roaring in Bernard's ears overtook the riot of the crowd, and silence overtook the roaring, and everything went black.

~~~~

Aldric watched in dismay as fully a quarter of his so-called patrons jumped to their feet and revealed themselves to be members of the city watch. Such a thing would never have happened at his old location; there, he had known all the men who patrolled that part of town, and would have recognized them in the crowd. But here, he was a relative newcomer, without the connections to learn that such an action was being planned, to know which gears should be jammed to stop it, to negotiate something more subtle, something that didn't make him look like a stooge of the watchmen who was only too happy to open his
~~~~

doors to displays of law-and-order thuggery.

The men had started actively shepherding his *real* guests out the door, giving him an opportunity to make his way to the table, where Korben was gleefully garroting the one called Bernard. As Aldric approached, the minstrel—if minstrel he was, and not another disguised guardsman who happened to be able to strum a little—finally released his hold and allowed the orange-haired fellow to slump sideways in his chair, then fall off it, thudding to the floor.

"What in the name of all the false gods of Abacar is going on here?" Aldric said.

"Official business of the city watch." Korben produced a gilt badge and displayed it like a child showing off a new toy to a friend who could not afford one, waggling it for effect before pocketing it. Turning to his instrument, he casually reattached the string, as if strangling people with it were just a routine component of his performances. "I would advise you and your staff to stay out of it."

The obvious pleasure Korben derived from flourishing his little tin star led Aldric to conclude that he really *was* a minstrel, albeit one who had been temporarily breveted to official status. He surveyed the man's three victims. "Are they dead?"

"That is no concern of yours."

"It is a concern of mine if people are being murdered in my dining room."

"It cannot be *murder* as long as I carry that mark from Lord Korrin," Korben said, "but if it will ease your mind, they are not dead. They are wanted for questioning."

"In regard to what crime—" A crash from behind him drew Aldric's attention; the watchmen were clearing a path to haul off their prisoners, and rather than bother to drag his tables out of the way were just flipping them over, sending food and flatware scattering across the floor. "By the bells on my mother's toes," he muttered, stepping back as three large men came over. Each picked up a limp body, slung it over his shoulder, and departed; a pair of archers stood nearby, arrows nocked and ready, as if fearing that one of their captives might suddenly awaken and start tearing everyone in the room to pieces.

A man wearing an officer's colors approached. "You. Innkeeper. You gave them rooms?"

"I gave them *a* room, in exchange for the lady's services."

The fellow snorted and said, "Which I am sure were duly rendered. Which room is it?"

"Under the common inn charter, my rooms are secure from search except by——"

The man whipped out a piece of paper and thrust it at Aldric. He examined the document; it was an official writ, stamped with Lord Korrin's seal, ordering the search of his guests' room and the seizure of their property. He sighed, then looked over his shoulder. "Bertram, show these fine gentlemen the room we gave to Ambrosia and her friends."

Bertram nodded, took the skeleton key out from behind the bar, crossed the room, and vanished through the bead curtain. The officer gestured to a couple of his men; they followed the bartender into the back hall. "Remember, we are to bring everything back exactly as we find it," he called after them. "No dumping out bags or purses!"

Someone tapped Aldric on the shoulder. Turning, he saw Korben standing there ready to depart, mandolin stowed in its case, coat on, giving him an expectant look. "What do *you* want?" Aldric asked.

"My share from the money hat."

Aldric pointed at the door. "Get out."

<div align="center">~~~~</div>

Arran Blackhawk wondered when he had started taking orders from Rumad Kram.

True, the old man had been an advisor to the Blackhawk family—which was to say, *Korrin's* family—for longer than Arran had been alive. But lately it seemed that Kram had wearied of merely dispensing advice. There could be no better example than this elaborate plan of his to send several dozen of Arran's men, many disguised as ordinary citizens, to apprehend three criminals. *Alleged* criminals. *Alleged criminals* who were, if things proceeded according to plan, going to be *drugged* and *unconscious* before the watch even moved to arrest them.

Why did Kram need so many men for such an operation? Had the old man finally gone paranoid and senile? Or was there something else afoot?

Whatever the underlying facts, it seemed the astrologer's scheme had gone off as expected; Arran had received a runner not long ago informing him that the prisoners were going to be arriving by wagon at the small postern gate in the south wall. This message was the first Arran had heard of the entire operation, and he had only received it because the runner had gotten confused over certain details; he had somehow formed the impression that Arran had arranged the whole charade and was therefore the man to be notified of its success. By the time he had finished grilling the youth for details, he probably felt like a criminal himself, but a few copper kestrels had eased the lad's misgivings and ensured that Kram would not find out about the impending delivery until Arran had had a chance to deal with it. He counted himself fortunate that the boy had made that mistake; it was far past time that he inserted himself into Kram's security-related machinations. By, for instance, waiting at the postern gate to intercept a cartload of unconscious thugs.

Soon enough, the prisoner wagon announced its arrival in a cacophony of squeaking wheels and clattering hooves. When it hove into sight, the conveyance was so top-heavy with guards that it put him in mind of a flock of vultures devouring the remains of a steer. One in particular stood out: A pudgy fellow who rode on the buckboard, dressed in an only slightly less absurd version of a court jester's motley, a gaudily-plumed parrot among the carrion birds. Were some assassin perched on a nearby rooftop with instructions to kill someone but no description of the target, the man would already have an arrow in his eye.

As the vehicle quivered to a halt, the variegated fop clambered down from it and wobbled over to stand in front of him. The man carried no weapon, only a mandolin case; clearly this was *not* one of Arran Blackhawk's sentries. "You are not Rumad Kram," he said, looking around, as if the elderly astrologer, notorious prankster that he was, might be hiding nearby waiting to jump out at him.

"No I am not, thank the gods. Who are you, who is so observant?"

"I was told to deliver the prisoners directly to Rumad Kram."

"I am Arran Blackhawk." He spared a glance for the wagon; the *real* guards were already unloading it, ignoring, as well they should, his conversation with what was evidently a musician harboring delusions of importance. Returning his attention to the dandy, he continued: "These men are under *my* command, not Kram's, and I say the prisoners will be delivered here, and now, and to me. Answer my question: Who are you?"

"I am Korben," he said. "You may have heard of—"

"And you are a ... performer?"

"Of some repute," Korben said stiffly.

"Your repute does not extend to here." Arran looked the fellow up and down. "What is your involvement in this?"

"Goldshine's barman retained me to provide accompaniment to a storyteller at his new inn. Not long after I was hired, Rumad Kram approached me with a draught and a badge. The draughts were for them." Here he indicated the limp prisoners, who were being carried from the wagon like so many sacks of barley. "And the badge was for me." He licked his lips and added, "The old man gave me a silver hawk, too, and promised me another upon completion of the—"

"*Rumad Kram* approached you."

"Yes."

"In person."

"Of course."

Arran gestured at the surrounding darkness. "Somewhere out there, in the city."

"Where else would he—"

"Rumad Kram rarely leaves the castle," Arran Blackhawk said. "He certainly does not wander about on his own, offering potions and silver and badges to purveyors of doggerel."

"*Doggerel?* I—"

"How did he even know to seek you out? How did he learn you had been hired?"

"I believe there was a crier advertising the—"

Arran Blackhawk snorted. "Unless the cryer broke into the keep and climbed the stairs to the top of the tall tower and shouted it into his ear-horn, I do not believe Kram would have heard about your good fortune *that* way. Well, I suppose it matters not." He held out his hand. "I will have the badge."

The minstrel hesitated, then reached into his pocket and pulled out a thin scrap of amber-colored metal. Blackhawk took it and examined it, then said: "You are not a member of the watch, not even when carrying this token in your pocket. Kram is not authorized to brevet musicians and mummers who have nothing better to do with their time than facilitate his schemes. Consider yourself fortunate that I am not confiscating the hawk he gave you and having you clapped in chains for impersonating a guardsman." He turned to the captain of the squad, who had remained nearby after the prisoners had been taken away. "Get this idiot out of my sight."

"Right away, sir."

Turning his back as the protesting minstrel was removed from the castle, Arran Blackhawk made for the cells.

It would not be long before Kram learned that his prey had been snared, and the last thing Arran Blackhawk wanted was for the astrologer to get them alone before *he* did.

~~~~

Rumad Kram had been pacing in a circle around his chambers for
~~~~

most of the evening, waiting for word that Ambrosia and her cohorts had been captured; he was beginning to worry that something had gone wrong, that she and the others had somehow detected the subterfuge, overpowered the guards, escaped his trap. He had hoped to neutralize them before they even realized they were under threat, but it would not pay to underestimate them. Not after what they had done the first time they met, atop the hill in Torgonderrer.

Kram understood that it was a mistake to compare the situations; things were much different this time. When he had first gone to the village of the elves, it had been as an agent of the dwarves, who had hired him to infiltrate the village. Months of effort had proven that Yexandor's wards around the perimeter were inviolate, and could not be breached or crossed without triggering detection; but then the Tellehi had revealed themselves, and brought with them such arcane knowledge as the absorbance glamour, which could make of oneself a perfect simulacrum of another—at the cost of the target's life, of course. One could not create so perfect a replica without consuming every scrap of the original. Thus armed, Kram had returned and stolen the form of the one called Shelliyan simply because she had been alone outside the village, foraging for shoots and fungus, rooting in the loam like some sort of animal. Shelliyan could pass through the protections around the village. She was an elf; she belonged there. It was only later that Kram-as-Shelliyan realized she had erred, and was trapped in that body, unable to trade it for a better target, such as Meliander. Using the absorbance glamour inside the village would have set off every alarm Yexandor had, and using it outside the village, while not impossible, would have resulted in a missing elf, and there were few enough elves that this would, again, have put the entire village on alert. So she had bided her time, and made slow, steady preparations, only to have Ambrosia arrive to disrupt them just as they were coming to fruition.

After Ambrosia had banished Shelliyan to the mountains, she had made her way through the Peltish Downs to Abacar, where the Tellehi had told her she might find the Jewel in the Maul. This time, she chose her vessels much more strategically, as stepping stones to reach her ultimate target: Rumad Kram. A highly placed figure with direct access to the top echelon of local power, he possessed little defense against sorcery. For all his supposed knowledge and foresight, the ancient astrologer was nothing but an ordinary human who thought he could read the future in the patterns of the stars. His isolation in the tower and, external to that, within the walls of Korrin's fortress, were his only protections—and they were little deterrent to one such as Kihantroh, who had stolen the shape of a merchant, then a scullery maid, and, finally, a page, then slunk invisibly up the spiral stairs. He had even been passed by Lord Korrin—an ideal target, but protected by Jordneh's magic, and therefore unassailable—who was on his way down, and clanked by in ignorance, his attention turned aside by a veil glamour.

And thus the one who had been Shelliyan had now become Rumad Kram, trusted advisor to Lord Korrin. Other personalities murmured inside Kram's mind; they were quiet, mostly, but they were there, mumbling, muttering underneath the loudest layer, the topmost persona, which belonged to the flesh he currently wore. The true power of the absorbance glamour, and what set it apart from merely imitative or illusory enchantments, was that he did not *pretend* to be the old man, did not merely *look like* the astrologer; in all ways that mattered, he *was* Rumad Kram. For the moment, the original Kihantroh barely existed; it lay beneath Kram's crotchety self, subsumed and submerged, even as it informed and directed his actions.

Yes, this time, Ambrosia did not know who he was, or where he was, or what he planned. This time, all advantages were his.

A rapping from the overhead trapdoor drew Kram's thoughts back to present concerns. Ignoring the complaints of his aging joints, he climbed the steps, threw back the bolt, and clambered onto the rooftop. A wide-eyed page stood nearby, looking at him with fearful indecision, as if thinking he should offer assistance to the old man but worrying that, if he did, Kram might take it as an insult and fling him off the tower. This fear was not unfounded.

"Well?" the astrologer said.

"What?" the page said. Then, as if suddenly remembering he was there for a reason: "Oh! Yes. I am to tell you that you are needed in the cells."

"They have been captured, then? The three intruders?"

"I do not know. Arran Blackhawk told me to tell you that you are needed in the cells. He did not tell me why."

"Very well, I … wait. *Blackhawk* sent you?"

"Yes."

"Lord Korrin's brother?"

"*Half*-brother," the page said, evidently accustomed to correcting people on this topic. "Yes. He awaits your presence."

"Feh. What is *he* doing down in the dungeon?"

"I believe he is in charge of security for the town and castle, sir," the boy said, "and so he maintains an office there."

"I know that, you nit." Kram considered this information. The whole point of his waiting in the tower rather than lurking near the cells or at the gate had been to keep the Blackhawks from realizing something was going on; but if Arran Blackhawk knew the prisoners were here, then so did Lord Korrin——or at least, he would, once he and his wench-of-the-moment could be located. Kram had understood that he would not have Ambrosia and the others to himself forever, but he had hoped for at least a little bit of time to probe and interrogate. They should still be unconscious from the draught, at least; Arran Blackhawk would have learned nothing from them. With any luck, his instructions not to rifle their belongings would have been obeyed, and even if it had not, he was confident that Ambrosia would have secured the Illata from being easily taken. That was what *he* would have done.

The page said: "Sir?"

"Yes, yes, I know," Kram said. "I am needed in the cells, and we must not keep our Lord's *half*-brother waiting." He extended an arm. "Be of some use, then, and help an old man down these accursed stairs."

~~~~

Arran Blackhawk sat on a high, hard wooden stool near the heavy iron door of the cells. He hoped Kram would arrive soon, so they could get this farce over with. He shifted around, trying to find a better position; the stool was a highly uncomfortable perch, and because it was bolted to the floor, it could not be brought into the proximity of a nearby table, also bolted to the floor, that would otherwise have been the perfect height to use as a footrest. This was all by design, of course; whoever sat here was not supposed to be able to find a comfortable position and, having done so, fall asleep; and, being on what most would consider the *wrong* side of the dungeon gate, immobilizing the furniture prevented any escaping prisoners from picking up a chair or a bench and using it as a blunt instrument to help them get to the *right* side.

None of which changed the fact that Arran's back hurt.

He heard a key turning in the lock and got to his feet, but when the door opened it was just one of the guards from the lower levels arriving for his shift. The man appeared startled to find Arran standing there, and paused to gape. "You are not who I am waiting for," Arran said, waving the fellow by.

A thin voice said: "Perhaps I am?" The call was followed by
~~~~

Rumad Kram, hobbling down the corridor while leaning on a page. Arran studied the astrologer as he approached. Something about him had changed recently, and Arran could not figure out what it was; he seemed even more slyly self-amused than usual, if that were possible, like some sardonic court fop telling a long, ironic anecdote that reflected poorly on everyone else. Arran had long suspected that Kram's lameness to be at least partly affected—if he were truly so rheumatic, why did he insist on continuing to live at the top of one of the tallest staircases the castle had to offer?—but this was something different.

Whatever was going on, Arran Blackhawk misliked it.

He stepped aside and held the door open until the old man and his escort finally arrived. Arran ordered the page away, to the boy's obvious relief; he was gone before the echo of his dismissal had faded from the rock-walled chamber. Kram stepped into the anteroom as Arran closed the door, then sent the lingering guard off with nothing but a sidelong glance. When they were alone, he studied Kram for a few seconds; the astrologer withstood the scrutiny with an enigmatic smile, then said, "Surely you did not call me down here just to admire my visage?"

"Surely not." Whatever was different about Rumad Kram, his prickly demeanor had stayed constant. "Your three arch-villains are here. What were you thinking, giving poison and a badge to that lute-playing miscreant?"

"It was not poison," Kram said. "Poisons are forbidden. It was merely a draught crafted to make a man want to drink more of it, and then to sleep for a goodly number of hours."

"You are a brewer of potions now?"

"I am on good terms with the alchemist. Is that a crime?"

"Would that it were. Then I could arrest you." Blackhawk shook his head. "Your philtre did not entirely work as advertised. One of them declined to continue drinking it, and so your pet minstrel took it upon himself to strangle the fool half to death with a mandolin cord. We cannot have common folk brandishing the mark of the watch and thinking they can go around garroting people."

"I would hardly characterize this as *going around garroting people*," the astrologer said.

"Well, the people who saw it will."

"Let them." The old man began idly picking at a cuticle on his left hand. "I did what was necessary to apprehend the criminals, since *you* didn't seem interested in the job."

Resisting the urge to whip out his sword and detach Kram's head from the rest of him, Arran said: "You knew where they were and did not see fit to tell me. This charade was dangerous and unnecessary. Do not do its like again."

"Why would I, when they have been captured?" Kram grinned like a skull that had just received the cheerful news that it would soon receive a fresh coating of skin. "Where are they?"

"They are in the first oubliette."

"Ah, very good. A wise choice for such criminals as these. I would like to see them, if I may."

"Follow me," Blackhawk said. He led the astrologer down a side corridor into what looked like, and in fact was, a storeroom. Going to an unlabeled barrel in the far left corner, he hooked his thumbs into a couple of knotholes in the wood and began to twist, unscrewing it from the floor until it came loose. He lifted it away and set it aside, revealing a threaded iron collar over a stone throat that descended into darkness. He had put them in this hole rather than in one of the regular cells to make sure they could not be spirited away without his finding out; extracting a prisoner from the oubliette was a production only slightly less laborious than giving birth. If the old man thought it was because he considered the prisoners extremely dangerous, Blackhawk would not disabuse him.

"I said I wanted to *see* them," Kram said, "not look down into a black pit. How do I know they are even there?"

"Perhaps you could consult your stars," Blackhawk said, taking a lantern from the wall, "as they seem so knowledgeable about the whereabouts of these villains, and about other things, such as the employment status of minstrels." As he spoke he tied the lantern to a nearby string; when it was secure, he lowered it into the opening so that Kram could observe the three prisoners lying in the straw below, stripped of their possessions, still unconscious. An angry red welt across the Banderlundi's throat marked where Korben's cord had bit into his skin.

Kram, delighted as a child being given a new pet, pointed at the female elf. "Bring that one up," he said. "The others can stay down there until they are removed for execution."

"Have we already decided to execute them, then?"

"What else would one do with thieves and murderers?"

"I thought it might be interesting to interrogate them first."

"To what end?"

"To find out what they are doing here, perhaps? Aside from telling stories in inns, I mean, which is to all accounts the extent of nefarious activity they had gotten up to before your clever little trap was sprung."

"She is a sorceress," Kram said. "She probably hoped to enslave her audience using the sound of her voice."

"Really? In that case, I should be remiss in my duty if I let you speak to her. My half-brother would be most cross should you come under her baleful influence."

"Her wiles will not work on me. Bring her up, I tell you."

Arran Blackhawk sighed. "As you wish." He whistled loudly, using the melody that indicated he wanted a pair of guards but that there was no urgency. Before long, two men entered and joined him at the mouth of the oubliette. "Rumad Kram wishes to make a withdrawal." He indicated one of the men. "You, fetch the block and tackle crew. Bring up the female, and *only* the female."

"Yes, sir." The fellow pivoted on his heel and exited.

To the other he said: "You, stay here and keep an eye on our esteemed astrologer. Make sure he does not fall into the hole."

"As you say, sir."

Blackhawk turned. "Where are you going?" Kram asked.

"I do not wish to be here when the witch starts talking," he said. "You may be immune to her charms, but some of us are not so strong-willed."

This appeared to alarm the guard, who looked at him and said: "Sir? *Witch*, sir?"

"Do not worry," Arran said as he departed. "If she wakes up and begins to speak, just put your fingers in your ears and hum."

~~~~

Arran Blackhawk did not return after leaving the room, but eventually a couple more guards arrived, rolling a pyramidal winch-like contraption between them. Three more men slouched along behind; these were unarmed, and looked more like common laborers than sentries. After positioning the pyramid above the hole, the extra men folded down two pairs of angled legs, one from the front face of the pyramid and one from the back, which slotted into unobtrusive notches in the floor. They locked in place with the twist of a sturdy wing-nut, acting as braces to further stabilize the winch. Once the device was thus secured, two of the men turned the crank a bit, lowering a sling on the end of a thin iron cable partway into the hole. Another man settled into the sling and was lowered out of sight.

This was quite an elaborate process; little wonder that those who went into the oubliette rarely came out again. It was simply more
~~~~

convenient to leave them in the hole. Rumad Kram eyed the winch, fascinated, quite sure that it bore the marks of dwarven workmanship. Appropriate, was it not, that a dwarven machine would be used to retrieve the Brisindeld's thief from her prison?

The cable shook and jiggled as the guard at the end of it did something; then it gave two sharp jerks. The crank operators wound the drum back up, and before long Ambrosia rose out of the pit. She had been stripped down to a thin shift, eliciting appreciative remarks from those performing the extraction.

"Who is *that?*"

Rumad Kram whirled, startled to hear that voice right beside him. "Lord Korrin!" he exclaimed.

Korrin gave a curt little nod. "Rumad Kram."

"I thought you were in your bed, my lord."

"I was in *a* bed," Korrin said, "until my half-brother found me and informed me that I should come here at once."

Accursed meddler. So *that* was where the other Blackhawk had gone, in search of Korrin. "How kind of him to do that himself and let the pages get their rest."

"Very droll. Tell me who this is, Kram."

The astrologer glanced at Ambrosia. The men were swiveling the winch at the base, rotating her away from the hole; she slowly swung past them, gently swaying back and forth as she moved. Korrin's eyes tracked every movement she made. "This one? You need not trouble yourself with her, my lord."

"Oh, I think perhaps I do need to trouble myself with her," he said. "What do you have planned?"

"Interrogation, of course."

"Why?"

"To learn her purpose here."

"As I have heard it," Korrin said, "her *purpose* was to tell stories at an inn. The owner, who evidently never received the message that we were looking for an elf of this description—a matter I will be taking up with my half-brother, before you begin to bleat about the insufficiency of our efforts to spread this net of yours—had a crier going around *advertising* her presence. That hardly seems like the act of someone who is trying to avoid notice."

"She is a sorceress, my lord," Kram said. "No doubt she hoped to use her voice to entrance those who came to listen—"

"Yes, my brother relayed your theory. I believe it no more than he did." Korrin looked Ambrosia up and down. "If enchantment is her goal, she need not use her voice to achieve it." Then, to the operators of the winch: "You will have her cleaned up and delivered to my chambers."

Kram gaped at him. This simply could not be happening.

"Close your mouth, Kram," Korrin said. "I can count your teeth, and a disturbing number of them are missing."

"My lord, think about this! Even if you do not believe she is a sorceress, she is implicated in the murder of a man of the watch!"

"Is she? Where is the bow, Kram? None was found in their room."

"Elves *always* carry bows. Obviously they cached their weapons elsewhere."

"Obviously," Korrin said, rolling his eyes.

Korrin's weakness for comely females was widely known, of course, but Kram had never considered that the man would pluck a prisoner out of the dungeon and deposit her in his bed. "I cannot allow you to take this, this, this *witch* to your room! Who knows what manner of spell she might—"

"You know my rooms are proofed against enchantment. And I have devices to prevent witches from casting spells."

"But—"

"*Enough!*" Lord Korrin's voice boomed in the tiny room, causing all the other men to flinch, then begin finding things to do that involved studiously looking anywhere but at Kram and Korrin. "Marjack died of an arrow wound. Very well. All elves are archers, you say? You have your archer there in the pit." He stepped over to where Ambrosia lay unconscious, lifted her hand by the wrist, turned it so Kram could see her soft white palm. "These fingers have never plucked a bowstring."

"One need not hold the bow to cause the arrow to be loosed."

Korrin snorted. "Save your platitudes for your apprentice, should you ever get one."

"Is my lord quite certain he is thinking clearly, and is not under the influence of drink or—"

"Have a care, old man," Korrin said. "You are not my father, and I am not bound by familial duty to tolerate you." To the guards: "You have your instructions. Let the other two face the chasm, but this one is mine." Back to Kram: "You have exceeded your authority in this matter. There will be no more meddling from you in the operation of the city watch. Is that understood?"

Kram said nothing.

"Is that *understood*, old man? My brother is agitating for *you* to face the chasm as well, for what you have done. Do not give me cause to take him seriously."

"It is understood, my lord," Kram said.

"Good. These other prisoners will be given to the cable like any common criminal, nothing more. Remember, Kram, if anything further happens that should not, I will learn of it." Korrin let the astrologer marinate in the heat of his glare for a few moments, then turned and left, his footfalls fading up the corridor.

The men had begun to screw the barrel back into place, shutting the others up in the oubliette again. Calling one of the idle fellows over, Kram said: "Where are their things?"

"Whose things?"

"Them."

"Who?"

"The prisoners!"

"Oh. Them." He shrugged. "Should be in the vault, if they have not been divvied up already."

"I gave orders that their goods were not to be rifled." In response, the man just favored him with an insolent look; that last exchange with Lord Korrin had done serious damage to his standing here. "Their possessions had best be intact," Kram said, "or they will not be the only ones swinging over the chasm by day's end. Show me this vault."

Conveying his disdain for Kram's empty threats by moving with ostentatious slowness, the fellow took him back up the hallway to the hub-like guardroom, then through a door and down another dim corridor. Kram could smell where they were going before they got there. "I asked to visit the vault," he said, "not the latrine."

"What better place for a vault?" the guard said.

They reached the toilets that the sentries used, a small room with a partially tiled floor. Against the back wall was a slanted trough, crossed by a wooden plank with rough holes sawn in it. River water sluiced through the trough, entering and exiting through a pair of rusted iron grilles. Off to the right a small, battered armoire stood against the wall, one door hanging partway open to reveal clean rags and other crude toiletries; a mound of dirty ones near the trough was the source of the odor. The guard went to the armoire, produced a key, opened the door a little more, and reached inside. His arm twisted one way, then the other, giving Kram to understand that he was unlocking something; then he pulled an unseen handle, causing the armoire to swing away from the wall, revealing a small cavity beyond. Kram tottered over and peered through the opening; the chamber might have been the closet of an impoverished hoarder, but he would hardly have labeled it a *vault*. Vaults concealed items of value, not rubbish.

The guard stepped aside. "Will that be all, your lordship?"

"Yes," Kram said. "Go."

"Have a care not to let the door close on you," the man said, "or you might find yourself spending more time in there than you expected."

"Yes yes." Kram waved his hand. "Get gone."

He waited for the man to depart, then took a nearby lantern off its hook and shuffled into the junk room. He let the door mostly close behind him, wedging it open with his walking staff. He set the lantern on the floor and looked around. They didn't appear to bother with any such frills as labels or identification or, indeed, any sort of organization whatsoever, and so he had no idea which items might have belonged to Ambrosia and the others. But still, he knew.

The Illata was here.

He had sensed it as they'd approached the latrine, concealing his excitement behind a facade of irascibility. Obviously the guards had not realized what lay within their grasp, or they would have alerted the Blackhawks. Of course, they were dull and thick-witted, unattuned to the stone's mystical emanations; and, as he had expected, Ambrosia had done something to dull its radiance, had sealed and hidden it. He could be quite sure the jailers were unaware of the treasure they had captured along with their prisoners.

Kram turned in a slow circle around the small chamber, finally stopping at a small leather pack thrown haphazardly against the wall. Startled, he recognized it as belonging to Shelliyan; she had been filling it with scraps of moss at the very moment he had taken her. Her submerged consciousness recognized it as well—it was the last thing she had seen before she died—and resurged momentarily, forcing him to quash her back to silence. This took more effort than he'd expected; when it was over he was surprised to find himself lying on the floor, clutching a few strands of long, honey-colored hair, as if it had sprouted from his scalp and he had torn it out with his fingers. Worse, he lacked any memory of having done so.

That was bad, very bad. He needed to find a way to jettison these personalities once he was done with them. Perhaps the Illata could help him with that.

Hands trembling slightly, he took the pack and fumbled with the strap and buckle. It quickly became apparent that the accursed thing was actively resisting his efforts to open it; he would get it partially undone, only to have the leather thong slip from his fingers and bind itself closed again. Ambrosia's work, no doubt; a spell to protect the pack's contents from detection and theft. Frustrated, he picked up a nearby knife and tried slashing through the material, and found himself thwarted once more; either the blade was incredibly dull (which, he discovered by testing it with his finger, it was), or the leather was woven through with steel, or his muscles were even more feeble than he had realized. He still had Ambrosia's preternaturally sharp blade hidden away in his chambers; perhaps its enchantment would be adequate to the task of cutting through the material. And if not … well, he would think of something. A few scraps of fabric would not keep him from his prize, no matter what the witch had done to it.

Kram opened his robes and tied the pack around his waist; then, almost as an afterthought, he snatched up a nearby belt that, if he remembered correctly, also belonged to Ambrosia. Festooned with little leather sacks and cases, it might contain something of interest; more importantly, it gave him something to carry in his hands that he could hand over if challenged, distracting attention from the one item he *really* wanted to smuggle out of here. Rising painfully to his feet, he grabbed his walking stick and headed out of the vault, giving the armoire a solid whack with the knobby head of his staff to send it swinging shut.

And if he rather childishly pretended it was Arran Blackhawk's head he was smacking, no one ever needed to know.

<center>~~~~</center>

Bernard woke up face-down on a thick layer of noisome mildewed straw, surrounded by utter darkness. He rolled over and sat up, spitting bedding out of his mouth. His neck felt as if someone had dribbled a ring of lighter fluid around it and then tossed a match. He explored it carefully with his fingers, discovering the beginnings of a long, thin, sticky scab across the front, cutting into the flesh over his windpipe. Bits of fusty grass clung to the wound; as he gingerly picked them off, he tried not to imagine what sort of nasty bacteria they might be leaving behind.

He supposed this must be another prison cell. How had he gotten here? They'd been at the inn, he remembered. The minstrel had bought them ale. Mercy and Lex had drunk it and passed out; Bernard had declined, and had nearly gotten strangled instead. Perhaps he should be less fussy in the future. Not to mention that, after battling the dwarven champion and the Rittandic sorcerer, he had let a *minstrel* get the drop on him. How humiliating. It was the highwayman all over again, except this time Nebandalex hadn't been available to rescue him. But perhaps the others were here, or at least nearby. "Hello?" he said, his voice a froggy croak. "Is anyone there?"

"Yes."

"Nebandalex?"

"Of course." The elf sounded strained, exhausted. "We were just discussing how we might escape. Have you forgotten?"

"We were?" Bernard leaned forward and rubbed his temples. Being choked half to death seemed have left him with a blazing headache. "I don't remember."

After a moment, Nebandalex said: "Am I still talking to Brannoc?"

Bernard's fingers stopped moving. "No. This is Bernard." Then: "You were talking to *Brannoc*?"

"That was what he told me."

"He said that out loud?"

"That is generally how talking is done."

"How were you planning to escape?"

"He was checking the walls, looking for a door. When he found none he said we must be in an oubliette—that they must have dropped us in through a hole in the ceiling. Evidently he is experienced in such matters." Bernard heard Nebandalex shifting around on the straw, though of course he couldn't see a thing. "We were both too short to reach the ceiling, so he was going to give me a boost up."

Wow, Brannoc sure had been busy while Bernard was unconscious. It had been several days since he'd had one of those internal dialogs with Brannoc that had been common when he'd first landed in this hellhole of a world; evidently his brush with asphyxiation had allowed the rogue to reassert control over the body they shared. He would have to think through the implications of that. "Where's Mercy?"

"Ambrosia? She is … not here."

"What do you mean, she's not here?"

"I mean she is somewhere else."

"Where is she?"

"Somewhere. Else." Then: "Could you bring Brannoc back, at least until we get out of here?"

"Sorry, Brannoc doesn't come and go at my beck and call," Bernard said, stung by the implication, justified though it might be, that Brannoc was of more value in this sort of situation than he was. "I'm afraid you're stuck with me."

"Mmm," Lex said. "Well. He seemed to think the ceiling would be out of reach anyway, and that it was likely to be blocked from the other side. And my head still hurts. Perhaps we should just rest."

In the ensuing silence, Bernard considered what Nebandalex had said. Korben had choked him into insensibility, and Brannoc had come back, just like how Bernard had been returned to their body when the dwarves had pummeled Brannoc. But what if Korben had actually killed him instead of just forcing him into unconsciousness? Would Brannoc have moved back in permanently, or would they both be gone? What did that imply about the real Mercy, who, like Brannoc, emerged mainly in hints and flashes and the occasional turn of phrase? Did that mean that the only way to bring her back for real was to kill Ambrosia? Now that was something Bernard *really* didn't want to think about. Unfortunately, there wasn't anything to do down here besides thinking and sleeping; and he doubted he would be falling asleep any time soon.

Ten minutes later, he was snoring.

<div align="center">~~~~</div>

In his room at the top of the tall spire, Rumad Kram sat at an ancient writing table, staring at Ambrosia's enchanted pack. It lay on the battered wooden surface, nothing but cloth and leather, yet it had proven invulnerable. The Illata was almost within his grasp, but this accursed satchel was keeping it away from him.

He had gotten both the pack and the belt out of the cells unchallenged and, when he'd rifled the contents of the small pouches and containers that were attached to the belt, he'd found trinkets and gewgaws of the lowest order, totemic foci that only the most mundane conjurer would carry. This had convinced him that Ambrosia was, at best, a sorceress of only minor accomplishment; the use of such materials could make certain invocations easier to effect, but skilled workers of magic—even the lazy ones—eschewed them, mainly because they were too easily lost or stolen, as amply demonstrated by the fact that he now had Ambrosia's meager possessions in one of his desk drawers. When the witch awakened in Korrin's bed, she would find herself crippled by their lack as much as by the protective enchantments woven around his lordship's chambers.

No, Kram thought, although she and her allies had managed to drive him empty-handed from Yexandor's hilltop hovel, Ambrosia was no true magician. Any *real* power she now wielded came from the Illata. Doubtless she had used it to seal itself in this bag, and she could open and close it at will as if it were any random container; but Kram, unauthorized person that he was, could not undo the strap, or cut it, or burn it, or crush it. Even Ambrosia's knife, which had previously been able to cut through *anything* he tested it against, did not avail him here.

Kram had hoped to have time alone with Ambrosia, either to use the absorbance glamour on her and learn what she knew directly or, if that failed, to compel her to speak by using coercive sorceries or threats against her friends; but the meddling Blackhawks had scuttled any chance of either plan working. He could hardly invade Lord Korrin's chambers and work enchantments on Ambrosia there; nor could he countermand the orders that had been given to the guards in the dungeon. He was fortunate to have been able to secure possession of the satchel, but it was not enough. He needed to get the Illata out of it.

He put his hands on the bag, feeling the radiance within, a hint of a quiver of a ripple of its power seeping through the material; some of it had to be escaping, after all, if only to provide the energy that made the bag impervious to attack. And that energy must have some connection to Ambrosia, else she would be as powerless to open it as he was. Struck by that thought, he cupped his hands around the pack, closed his eyes, and explored the way the currents flowed around its surface; before long, he he was able to sense the individual strings of the glamour, the strands of magic, that gave force to the enchantment. Most were tightly bound and far too strong to unwind; these were the ones involved in protecting the Illata's container from harm. But a few trailed off into the Æther like the unraveling fringe of a knit garment. He sent his mind along these lines, searching for and, eventually, finding a connection to the enchanter.

Ambrosia.

He could feel her presence, as if she were there in the room with him rather than ensconced in Lord Korrin's chamber. He could sense that the narcotic draught she'd been given had begun to wear off, but for the moment she remained in twilight. Kram took the opportunity to study her with senses other than sight, but his attempts to probe beyond the surface were rebuffed, as if he were trying to stick a butter knife into a brick wall. There was something odd about her, something dense and impenetrable, and he quickly realized what it was.

She comprised far too many Strings.

This so-called elf was wound more tightly than anything else he had ever explored. That might explain why she was able handle the Illata, which killed everyone else who came into contact with it. Its energy was such that, if not carefully contained, it eroded the threads of the reality that surrounded it. In the case of inert things like stone and earth, this effect of steady degradation might not be particularly noticeable, but when a living creature's essential stitching was pulled apart, death would ensue with dramatic swiftness.

But not Ambrosia. Any hope he had harbored of attacking her at this level, of finding a loose thread and simply unraveling her out of the world, faded; he could neither summon nor control the energy that would be required to pull her apart, certainly not on his own, and probably not even with the Illata at his disposal. Which it was not. Yet.

He was about to retreat when he realized something even more surprising: There were *two* sets of Strings within her, interwoven like the variegated threads of a tapestry. Was there more than one being occupying the corpus that called itself Ambrosia? Kram understood, as few others did in this benighted realm of ignorance and superstition, that even the solidest-seeming object was mostly empty space; even so, it was not possible to merge two bodies and make them one, any more than one could push two stones together and create a single rock of the same size but twice the mass. The more fragile one would be destroyed, leaving nothing but rubble.

Which of these two Ambrosias was the more fragile?

If only he could exploit this discovery somehow! But as Korrin had said, his apartment had longstanding spells of protection on it, refreshed and rewoven by Jordneh herself, that interfered with the active invocation of glamours. Kram had been able to follow the passive threads of enchantment back to their source, and once there could observe and inspect Ambrosia, but if he tried to cast anything that affected the room or those within it the attempt would fail or, worse, backfire. In any case, he sensed that she had begun waking up; he had to withdraw, or risk discovery. Lord Korrin was already in a suspicious frame of mind, and it would hardly do for Ambrosia to begin babbling that the phantom of his astrologer was hovering around his bedchamber staring at her. Kram pulled his consciousness back into his body, found himself in his chair, still staring at the pack; except now his nose was bleeding, dripping brilliant crimson onto the thirsty surface of the wood, where it soaked in and quickly turned black.

Cursing, Kram wiped his upper lip, then went in search of a rag.

~~~~

Bernard awoke to the sound of grinding metal. For a moment he thought he had fallen asleep in shop class again, but in shop class he normally didn't sprawl on the floor or have a piece of dry grass poking
~~~~

him in the eye.   Rolling over onto his back, he saw a sliver of light appear in the ceiling, widening into an entire circle as a plug in the top of the room was removed.   The interior of the cell became visible, blindingly bright at first, then, as his eyes adjusted, revealed as roughly circular, ten or fifteen feet in diameter.   In the center, a stone platform rose mushroom-like from the bedding, flat-topped and covered with myriad small scratches.   The walls curved inward overhead, then bent up again, ending in a masonry dome perhaps half as wide as the dungeon.   It was as if they were being held inside a stubby inverted light bulb half full of musty straw.

Almost directly opposite him, Nebandalex sat against the wall, looking up at the roof of their prison, where a head had appeared in the opening, peering down at them.   After a moment this head barked out a few words, conveying to other, unseen, heads the information that the prisoners were awake; then it withdrew.   Various creaking, whining, and groaning noises ensued, drifting into the pit from the room above.   Before long, a narrow, cylindrical cage descended on a greased rope of braided metal.   It was open on one side, with a curved door mounted on a rail.   As this rather unpromising conveyance came to rest on the stone platform directly underneath the opening, a voice from above shouted, "Into the cage, one at a time!   Close the door behind you!"

The two of them exchanged a look; Nebandalex rolled his eyes and shook his head.   Bernard called back, "Why should we?"

After a moment, a head appeared in the hole again, but this time it was accompanied by an arm.   The hand at the end of the arm held a small crossbow, which it waggled first at Nebandalex, then at the cage. The elf sighed and clambered across the deep straw toward the capsule; the threatening weapon withdrew, though the head did not. Bernard watched Lex climb into the enclosure; he examined the door briefly, figured out how to work it, and rolled it sideways along its curved track.   It snapped into place at the end of its run, locking with an audible click.   The squeaking sounds resumed; the Lex-laden cage trundled up through the hole and out of sight.   A metallic clatter echoed and faded.   Before long another cage of identical design, or possibly the original one emptied of its contents, descended in the same fashion as before.   Bernard went inside, gave the door a yank, and watched the floor recede through the bars beneath his feet.   He wondered where they were taking him, and if he would like it any better than the place from which he was being removed.   He doubted it.

The barred capsule fit precisely through the circular opening, with scarcely an inch to spare around its perimeter; clearly it had been designed for the sole purpose of hauling prisoners from the depths without actually releasing them from captivity. Topside, Bernard found that the cable ran up to an iron cranelike device operated by half a dozen men, passing through a series of heavy pulleys before winding around a large hand-cranked winch. Once the bottom of his cage had cleared the door, they locked the winch in place, then swung the boom around and deposited his cage on the floor. As they performed this maneuver, he said: "The dwarves would have had one that operated on steam power." This comment was ignored by the operators, but earned him a sidelong look from Nebandalex, who remained confined in an identical cage right next to Bernard's.

While some of the men set about closing up the pit, others wheeled over a pair of what looked like the bastard offspring of a hand truck and a forklift. Each had three flat, narrow prongs on the bottom that slid into gaps in the base of the cage; then one man pushed from the front while two more pulled from the back, tipping the entire apparatus until the capsules slid into a rounded catch in the vertical portion of the cart. A metallic snap vibrated through the floor and bars as an unseen latch engaged, securing the cage in place. Bernard found himself lying against the bars at an angle of about forty degrees, watching the ceiling scroll by overhead as they squeaked and jostled their way up a dim corridor, through an austere-looking guardroom, and out into a larger, upward-sloping passageway. Eventually they exited through a small door and entered a courtyard, where they were turned around and restored to a vertical orientation. It seemed to be around dawn; the early-morning light gave a bluish cast to the cream-colored flagstones and walls, but the horses and cart that stood waiting for them remained resolutely black. A couple of men had been hanging around grooming the horses, but now they left off that task and came over to the cages, pausing to collect a couple of thick leather straps from the back of the cart. They stopped in front of Bernard's cage first, and opened a small panel in the door. "Give me your hands," the one holding the leather said.

"Sorry," Bernard said, "I'm still using them." No one appeared to find this amusing. He sighed and put his hands out through the slot; the men bound his wrists with the leather thong, making it tighter than he thought absolutely necessary given the fact that he was still imprisoned. As they moved on to Lex's cage and Bernard pulled his hands back inside, he found himself abruptly tilted again, causing him to slam against the bars to his back. His mobile prison was wheeled over to the back of the cart and put level. A muscular fellow started pumping a lever at the back of the hand truck, causing the three-pronged fork to rise up a track inside the half-cylinder of the dolly. Bernard found himself wondering what would happen if he tried to rock the cage to make it fall off the fork. He gave it a half-hearted try; the cage didn't go anywhere, but a gruff, javelin-toting guard materialized next to it and ordered him to stop. The spear looked quite capable of skewering him through the bars like an hors d'oeuvre, so he complied.

As the bottom of his cell drew even with the floor of the wagon, he realized that the cart sported wooden rollers and, riding on top of those, rails that lined up with the slots in the bottom of the capsule. He felt a shudder run through the cage as they ejected it from the hand truck and onto the tracks. It rolled forward along them railroad-style until a bumper attached to the buckboard stopped it. The attendants placed a wooden spacer behind his cage, turned a couple of thumbscrews to secure it, then repeated the entire procedure with Nebandalex. The wagon quivered as his cell rattled down and came to a halt on the far side of the spacer, just out of arm's reach. An identical spacer, placed behind it, secured the second prisoner in place.

"This apparatus is quite clever," the elf said, as a couple of the men settled onto the seat in front of Bernard. "I am impressed."

The driver grunted. "I did not build it," he said.

"I realize that. My friend says it has the hallmark of dwarven design and manufacture. May I ask where you are taking us?"

The man who had spoken looked over his shoulder at them. "You are to be let go," he said. Then, as his companion guffawed in a rather derisive fashion, he turned away and shook the reins, starting them in motion.

Nebandalex looked at Bernard through the two sets of bars that separated them. "Did you hear that? We are to be let go."

"For some reason, that doesn't make me feel any better," Bernard said.

~~~~

Ambrosia awoke to the cool, bright light of morning. The events of the previous evening were vague and fuzzy, like the fading memory of a dream. She had told a story, the minstrel had brought them beer, and then ... what? She couldn't remember. Had she gotten sloshed on ale? Was she hung over? Her eyes felt dry and grainy, and her mouth seemed to be full of thistledown. She coughed and dry-spat a
~~~~

few times, which didn't really help; she tried blinking really fast to produce tears, which helped a little.

A wonderful aroma suffused the air. What was it? Cinnamon? Cloves? Were Aldric's cooks making pancakes in the kitchen? Mmm, pancakes. She could go for some of those. She sat up, but that made everything go all rotational and she quickly lay back down, panting, waiting for her head to reattach itself. Eventually she tried sitting up again, taking it much more slowly this time, and more or less succeeded.

Okay, where was she? This wasn't the closet-sized room Aldric had given them; the bed in which she lay wouldn't even have fit into it. It stretched out around her like a plateau, flanked by six massive posts supporting a thickly embroidered canopy from which a gigantic woven raptor face glared down at her. Ornate wooden end tables stood on either side, heavily carved and inlaid with what looked like gold leaf; each table supported a silver burner, and each burner leached a thick, aromatic plume of smoke into the air. That was what she had smelled: Not the spices in cooking food, but smoldering incense.

What was she wearing? It was some sort of nightdress, its gauzy material so diaphanous it may as well have been invisible. She certainly didn't remember ever owning such a garment. Had her tale been such a smashing success that Aldric had moved her to the honeymoon suite, complete with sexy nightwear? She reflexively pulled the blanket up to her shoulders, then cast a furtive look around to see if anyone was watching her.

"You are awake. Good."

The unexpected voice made her jump; it didn't belong to Aldric, or Bernard, or any other males she recalled knowing. She couldn't make out who had spoken, as objects more than a few yards away were still rather blurry and it was a vastly large room. But she picked up movement, a violet, person-shaped smear approaching the bed. As this blob got closer it resolved itself into a large, tawny-haired man clad in a purple robe. He carried himself as if he were someone important. She had never seen him before; or maybe she had and just didn't remember.

"I'm not so sure I am," she said. "Awake, I mean."

"You are, else we would not be talking." He stopped at the foot of the bed. "I am Lord Korrin. You are safe here."

Lord Korrin? Maybe he actually *was* someone important, then. "Where's here?"

He cocked his head, as if the answer to this should be obvious.

"My bedchamber," he said.

"How did I get here?"

"I had you brought up from the dungeon."

"From the ... dungeon?"

"Yes." He came around the footboard and sat down on the foot of the bed, which still put him at least a yard away from her toes. "After you were arrested, you were taken to the oubliette. You would not remember that; you were ... asleep."

"After I was *arrested?*"

He nodded.

"Was I doing something wrong?"

He shrugged. "You were telling stories at an inn."

"That much I *do* remember." She looked around; the room was beginning to come into better focus. "Where are my friends?"

"They are not here. I do not make a habit of bringing *all* murderers to my rooms."

"Murderers?"

"Yes. Your cohorts murdered one of the men of the city watch." He frowned. "Well, so Rumad Kram says."

"What? We never——"

"Your group got into a minor argument with a guard at the city gate. Words were exchanged. The man was later found dead in the river, slain by an arrow through the throat. Although we found no weapons in your room, Rumad Kram is quite certain that your elf companion is the archer who fired the killing shot." Korrin paused significantly, as if waiting for her to comment on the topic; when she didn't, he said: "You do not recall that either?"

"No. I mean ... There was a man who attacked us in our camp. He tied me up, and ..." She trailed off. "That was a *guard?*"

"Yes."

"Then why was he dressed like a robber?"

Lord Korrin sat there a moment as if contemplating his answer; then he stood and walked across the room to a door in the wall opposite the bed. He stopped, turned, and motioned for her to join him; he didn't look like a blob at that distance anymore, which was an improvement. She shook her head, reluctant to pad around in the absurdly thin garment she had on. Perhaps realizing this, her host indicated a nearby wardrobe with a tilt of his head. She eyed it, then scurried over and found a number of robes in a variety of sizes, shades, and weights, all of them apparently meant to be worn by a woman. Why was she not surprised? She chose the thickest one she could find, a sort of terrycloth the color of a dusty lemon, and slipped it on. It was too long for her, dragging along the floor, but it was warm and modest; Lord Korrin looked a little disappointed by her selection, but did not attempt to dissuade her.

When she joined him at the door, he opened it and guided her through with a hand on the small of her back. They stepped out onto what appeared to be a wraparound balcony, partway up a tower, high above a labyrinthine city. A greasy porridge of clouds thickened in the sky overhead; below, the streets stretched out into the blue light of early morning, illuminated by widely-spaced lamps that burned with steady light like a scattering of ruddy pearls. Moving his hand farther across her back and placing his fingers on her opposite hip, Korrin steered her to the left, leading her in a circular stroll along the windswept deck.

"Abacar is the greatest city in the Slash," he said. With his free hand, he gestured expansively at the landscape that surrounded them; his other hand stayed on her back, scant inches above the danger zone. "Like my father, and my father's father, and all the rest who came before them, it is my lot to govern here, and ensure that the city and the realm prosper."

"It's your lot?" She looked around. "Your *lot* seems to be treating you pretty well."

"There are benefits, of course," he said; then, a bit absently: "Some are quite pleasant indeed." After a moment, he reverted to his oratorical tone of voice. "Preserving the legacy of my ancestors and keeping the Slash free from the dominion of outsiders is a grave responsibility; I do it to the best of my ability, taking advantage of good counsel when I can, making my own way when necessary. I understand that some may question the decisions I make, or disagree with my actions, and seek redress, some by violence, others by, perhaps, donning the mantle of the outlaw."

"So it's *your* fault the guard attacked us?"

"Some would say so, because I was forced to cut their wages, in preparation to defend the Slash against the Banderlundi." Then: "I am told one of your companions is, in fact, a Banderlundi. Would you care to explain how that came about?"

"He's just someone I've known for a long time. He showed up in Torgonderrer to help me out of a … a tight spot." By now they were perhaps halfway around the tower. She heard the faint crash of the sea, far off beyond the craggy bluffs. She ran her hand along the waist-high railing that stood between her and a significant drop; the stone was rough and cold, and slightly damp from condensation. "Where are they? My friends?"

"They are on their way to be punished for their crime. And for yours."

"We're not allowed to defend ourselves?"

"Deadly force is my prerogative within the walls of Abacar, not yours."

"We weren't in Abacar then."

"You are now."

"What about me? Why am *I* not on my way to be punished?"

"I thought you and I might talk." The door to his chamber came back into view; he guided her inside. While they had been circumnavigating the balcony, someone had evidently brought in an outfit for her and left it folded on the nightstand. The neat pile of clothes was held in place by a large, gaudy necklace set with a blue stone nearly as big as her fist, sitting on it like a paperweight. "Please, dress yourself," Korrin said.

What was it with the men around here, telling her what to wear and when to wear it? At least Aldric had had a reason, sort of. This seemed to be strictly for Korrin's amusement. "While you stand there and watch? I don't think so."

He sighed elaborately, then grinned; it made him look like a teenager. "Such is my lot," he said.

"Is that a fit pastime for a king?"

"I am not a king," he said, "and expect to see nothing I have not seen before."

"Fine," she said. She transferred the jewelry to the table, picked up the clothes, and went to the wardrobe. She swung the door wide and positioned it between herself and Korrin, then tried to get dressed without actually removing her robe. It was clumsy work, and it took a while for her to figure out how all the apparel went together—there were many laces to tie, many buttons to hook—but eventually she managed it and stepped back into view. Korrin looked suspiciously pleased with himself, which she quickly realized was due to a large, strategically-placed floor mirror on the opposite wall; he'd probably been observing her reflection the entire time.

Lords. Always doing whatever they wanted.

Annoyed, she returned to the bed and sat down to pull on the moccasin-like footwear that had been left beside it; like everything else, they fit perfectly. She made to stand, but Korrin held up a hand to stop her. "And the necklace," he said.

Oh, of course; she couldn't go about without the finery he had picked out for her. Wondering what this was really all about—she didn't believe he was expending all this effort merely to seduce her, but nor did she believe he was only interested in *talking*—she ducked her head and slid the chain over her hair, feeling a momentary head rush as she straightened up and the gem bounced against her chest; a lingering effect of the potion that had been used to knock her out, no doubt.

Korrin, considerate fellow that he was, was at her elbow in a flash, steadying her. "Are you all right?"

She pulled back from him. "I'm all right. Just dizzy for a second."

"Good. Very good. Now that you are dressed, I would like to show you something."

"About my friends——"

"This *is* about your friends. Come." He went to a narrow door beside the hearth and opened it, urging her forward into a small wedge-shaped room. What the chamber lacked in size, it made up for in square footage of battle gear; the place was crammed full of armor, shields, swords, axes, and other manly items. She wondered if he was going to take down a couple of blades and challenge her to a sparring match; but no, he led her to the pointed end of the wedge, where the floor dropped away in a steep flight of narrow, switchbacked stairs. The descent ended at an iron door barely wider than her shoulders, barred on this side. He removed the bar, opened the door, and ushered her on ahead; he had to turn sideways to squeeze through after her, and past her, out to the center of a tiny scrap of greenery jutting out over an abyss. Turning, he said: "Welcome to my garden."

Her back pressed flat against the stone wall of the castle, Ambrosia said: "Okay."

Lord Korrin might label this a garden, but it was little more than a wide, narrow ledge where the castle wall bowed inward, allowing a section of the cliff-edge to remain exposed. It couldn't be more than ten or fifteen feet long and, at most, eight feet wide. The ground was rocky, glistening and slick with moisture from the drifting mist of the nearby falls; narrow beds of ornamental vegetation snaked between the protuberant stones, none of it currently in bloom, though she could see that some of the stalks had been deadheaded not long before. Creeping ivy with star-shaped leaves edged in white grew in a clump from the far side of the ledge; some of it climbed a little way up the stone wall of the castle, but most of it dribbled down the cliff. Small succulents grew in decorative mounds in the sheltered spots around short, flat-topped columns; Korrin sat down on one of these, looking out at the massive split in the rock formed by the roaring cataract to their left.

"Shouldn't there be a … a wall or something around this?" she asked. She had to shout to be heard over the waterfall.

"It is quite safe." He patted the seat beside him.

"Of course it is. I'll just stay here though."

"Are you afraid of heights?"

"I'm afraid of depths."

He seemed to find this amusing; or maybe he was just smiling because of how she clung to the wall like some sort of gaudy beetle. "I come here when I need to think," he said. "I have spent much time here in recent weeks, but I find that solutions to my problems still escape me."

"Maybe the solutions are afraid that if they come out here, they'll fall."

"Perhaps, but they are wrong. Please, come away from the wall and sit with me."

It seemed they weren't going to go back inside, and she wasn't going to find out what had happened to the others, until she humored him. She picked her way along the least spray-slicked path she could find, then lowered herself onto the stone next to him. A few feet away, the ground curved downward as it entered the vast chasm. Her gaze followed it, then moved along it toward the city wall, then past that to where a thin black line ran from one side of the chasm to the other, bridging the vast empty space like a suture that hadn't figured out its task was hopeless, that the two edges could never be brought back together. The line bowed in the center, where a few small shapes dangled. She peered at this mysterious thread, tracing back it to a small building that stuck even farther out of the cliff than the castle did. There was some sort of activity going on down there, but she couldn't tell what it was.

"This is also where I come to watch executions," Korrin said.

Chapter 14

THE CART BEARING Bernard and Nebandalex in their cages trundled along a narrow road that ran between the outer wall of the city, tall and massive to their left, and an inner wall to their right, lower but still formidable enough that it wouldn't have seemed out of place enclosing a prison yard. The surface was poorly cobbled but the heavy wagon, evidently well-equipped with shock absorbers, rode it smoothly. Aside from the creaking of the wheels and the clattering of the horses' hooves, there wasn't much to hear, except for the ever-present rumble of the unseen cataract. Bernard couldn't decide if he should feel like water in a sluice or a beef cow on its last journey, but was leaning toward beef cow.

Presently they drew abreast of a wide, low door in the outer wall. Bored-looking men waited there; they slid the gate open as the conveyance approached, then went back to their ennui. The roar of the waterfall boomed through the gap with such force that Bernard imagined it might physically stop their progress, but of course no such thing happened and they passed through without incident. On the other side, a stony outcropping jutted far out into a vast gulf, obviously formed by the waterfall they had been hearing; it was out of sight somewhere to the left, filling the air with mist and sound. They proceeded out onto the massive promontory, past a small stone building built so close to the edge that it looked ready to slide off at the slightest provocation. The spit of land narrowed as they went, the abyss encroaching on either side, drawing so much of Bernard's attention that he didn't notice a vertical stone finger near the tip of the headland until the cart clattered to a stop beside it.

"Are they going to throw us off the cliff?" Nebandalex said, rather casually, as if inquiring whether or not Bernard had ever read a particular book.

"That seems too simple," Bernard said. He eyed a hefty black iron ring screwed into the rocky column; a thick, heavily greased cable of twisted metal fiber was attached to the ring by the biggest eyelet he had ever seen. This was sunk into a barrel screw as big around as a telephone pole, and then to a set of massive pressure clamps. From there, like a giant's clothesline, the cable ran out over the chasm, dipping parabolically before rising again and becoming obscured by the foggy spray. In the middle, at the lowest spot of the cable, several dark shapes hung high above the water, swaying in the morning breeze. "I think they have something else in mind."

Another forklift-style hand truck emerged from the building they had passed, pushed by a group of men who rolled it down to the cart and used it to remove the cages, lowering each one to the ground. Then the crossbows came out. Covered from every angle except above, Bernard didn't try any funny business when they unlocked and opened the door of his capsule, but he did press himself against the bars on the opposite side and refused to budge. The fellow who had opened the cage, obviously accustomed to this sort of behavior, just sighed and gestured impatiently for him to get moving; in response, Bernard shook his head. The man clucked his tongue, which inspired an unseen person to jab something pointy into Bernard's backside. He jumped forward with a yelp, enabling the man in front to catch him by the wrists and haul him the rest of the way out. In short order Bernard found himself picked up, spun around, frog-marched over to the stone finger, spun around again, and put into a chokehold. Someone stepped up in front of him and tied an additional strap around one of his wrists; it had a thick, broad midsection and long narrow ends, sort of like a weightlifter's belt. The wide portion was heavily studded with slick-looking nubs of oily metal. With a practiced flick the guard sent the free end of the big strap over the cable, catching it on the other side and giving it a twist so that it landed with its studs against the metal of the cable. The man's hands moved in a knot-tying blur; when they stopped, each of Bernard's wrists had become one with the thong.

Evidently satisfied with his work, the man nodded, stepped back, and said, "Goodbye."

Strong arms picked Bernard up and flung him forward with vigor. The earth fell away as he shot out over empty space. Far below his dangling feet, water frothed and foamed against the tumbled and jagged shoreline, black rocks streaked with the droppings of untold generations of sea birds. He could hear them faintly screeching, and fancied that they were jeering at him, way up there in the sky where he didn't belong. Drifting mist from the waterfall filmed him with chill moisture. The sound of metal whisking against metal whispered in his ears as gravity worked with his initial momentum to carry him along, eased by the lack of friction between the greased cable and the metal studs. If this were a tourist zip line, people would be lining up to pay good money for a ride, and here he was getting one for free. Lucky him.

As he neared the low point of the cable, the slope moderated and he began to slow down. He twisted his arms, trying to get a look back the way he had come, and felt a sudden braking action as the strap tightened and the dry leather came into contact with the cable. After that, he continued to twist it deliberately in short bursts; he wanted to avoid crashing into the other prisoners who were currently hanging out here, but not at the cost of the cable's chewing through the strap. He wasn't sure if a fall into water from this height would be fatal, but it would certainly hurt.

He eventually slid to a stop a yard or two away from the beginning of the prisoner line, and dangled there swaying back and forth while the first one in line—a woman, human, apparently—eyed him for a moment, then grinned in a manner that was strangely predatory for someone swinging from her wrists over the sea. Maybe she wasn't quite right in the head; no normal person would grin like that, given their current predicament. Aside from her, it looked like all the others hanging out here were men. A couple were alive, but most were dead, or nearly so. The deceased were in varying stages of putrefaction, the process of decay helped along by the moist air and the chattering carrion birds that clustered around the more distant ones, tearing off scraps. They stayed away from the corpses that adjoined the living, not willing to risk taking a blow for a mouthful of meat; they understood that patience would be rewarded.

Behind him, Bernard heard a rapidly-approaching skittering noise. That had to be Nebandalex coming to join them. Momentarily, the elf thumped into Bernard's backside and knocked him closer to the grinning woman.

"I wonder how many they plan to pile on today," she said, sounding just as blasé as Nebandalex had when he'd speculated that they were going to be thrown off the cliff. Didn't anyone around here know when they should start to panic?

"I think I may vomit," Nebandalex said in a thick voice.

"If you do," the woman said, "try to aim for the water."

~~~~

Ambrosia and Korrin had spent perhaps fifteen minutes sitting on the rock in Korrin's so-called garden, watching as a tiny wagon pulled up alongside that distant finger of stone, disbursing even tinier people who went about the business of attaching other, equally tiny but infinitely less fortunate, people to what Korrin had explained was a metal rope that had been created for Abacar by the dwarves during some bygone era of friendliness and cooperation. Enchanted to resist wear and corrosion, it had spanned the gap in the cliffs for centuries.

"So you just send them out there to hang by their arms?" she
~~~~

asked, watching first one dot, then another, get sent out to join several other dots already depending from the middle of the parabola.

"Yes."

"How long do you leave them there?"

"Until they die, of course."

"Until they … What?"

"Until they die." He gave her an amused look. "I did tell you I came here to watch executions, did I not?"

"But that's … It's torture! To just *leave* them out there until they——"

"Leaving them there is *precisely* the point," he said. "This has been our method of public execution for centuries, since the time of the …" He trailed off, then said: "I suppose you elves have no need to concern yourselves with making an example of the guilty, but we are not so fortunate here. Everyone sees, and no one wants to suffer such a fate himself. There are viewing platforms along the walls on that side, where parents take their children, and point, and say, *do not do what they did.*"

"You have *viewing platforms?*"

"Are you surprised? There is no point to public justice if the public cannot see it, or if it occurs at such a remove that none can tell what is happening." Then, in a reflective tone: "It *is* some considerable distance from here, is it not?"

"I … suppose."

"It would be difficult to recognize a face from so far." He was watching her carefully now. "Even one that you might know very well."

"Yes, it would … Wait. Those were my friends?"

He said nothing.

"You brought me here so I could watch my friends be sent out to die?"

"No, I brought you out here that you might save them. I can dispatch a man with a rope to draw them back. Is there anything you wish to tell me that would inspire me to do so?"

Was this some sort of test? What did he want her to say? "I already told you everything."

"Did you?" Korrin turned to look at the distant cable. "Pity."

"You can't do this."

"Of course I can. What sort of trouble did your Banderlundi friend help you with?"

Was *that* what he wanted to know? "Someone tried to steal the

Illata from the elves. That's a gem that——"

"I know of the Illata. The dwarves name it the Brisindeld. They have been squabbling over it with your kind for years."

"Oh." That surprised her. "I thought it was a secret."

He shrugged. "Not from me."

"Well, this thief timed her attack to coincide with a dwarven invasion. Bernard—the Banderlundi—arrived in time to help us stop her, but she killed Yexandor, and the dwarves burned a lot of the forest with——"

"Wait. Slow down."

"But my friends——"

"Are not going anywhere. You say Yexandor is dead?"

"Yes."

"But this attacker you speak of did not obtain the Illata."

"No."

"And the dwarves burned Torgonderrer?"

"Some of it. A storm put the fire out before it got to the village."

"And you say they sent in an invasion force after the fire started?"

"Yes. They sailed down the river in little ships."

"Little ships?"

"Yes. What?"

"Some time ago I received a message from Filothandiar, the leader of the dwarves, claiming that their western tunnels had reached all the way to the sea, and that they had established a small harbor there, from which they wished to sail in order to trade gold and other material of the mountains. The dwarves are extraordinarily clever with rock and metal, much less so with wood, and they requested our assistance in designing craft that they could operate. Our shipwrights created plans for scaled-down vessels, which we sold to them."

"I guess they took your plans and added guns and cannons to turn them into war boats."

"Guns? Cannons?"

"Like … Think catapults or ballistas," she said. "But cannons are iron tubes, and instead of rocks or big arrows they shoot metal balls that explode when they hit, for knocking down walls. And guns are like little cannons, for killing people."

Now he was just staring at her.

"Oh, and, they used artillery—even bigger cannons, fired from the mountains—to burn the forest. It was a diversion, I guess."

"The *dwarves* did all this."

"Yes. But they never entered the village; their boats were lost in the storm. So they didn't——"

"And they were in league with this individual who attempted to steal the Illata?"

"Yes, once. But not really, at the end. She played the elves and dwarves against each other so she could get the gem and get away in the chaos."

"And you? How did you get away?"

"The new leader of the elves gave us the Illata and … kicked us out, basically. We took a boat and floated north on the river, to here."

"When did these momentous events happen?"

"Three days ago."

"Three days." Korrin looked thoughtful, then, briefly, crafty; then determined. He stood, extended a hand. "I am receiving an envoy from the small folk of the mountains shortly. He arrived in the city this morning in, I'm told, a state of some agitation. I'd hoped that Filothandiar had sent him to discuss the situation with Banderlund, but now it seems he may have another agenda in mind. You will attend the public reception."

She let him pull her to her feet. "I'm sure I have no business at——"

"You made it your business when you spun the tale I just heard. I would hear the dwarf's version of these events."

"You don't believe me?"

"I would hear the dwarf's version," he said again, "and compare it to yours. For you *are* a storyteller, are you not?"

"What about my friends?" She glanced at the distant, dangling figures. "Will you have them brought back?"

"Once I am satisfied that you have told me the truth, yes," Korrin said. Then, when she started to protest: "It is no use arguing. You cannot persuade me otherwise." He showed her that grin again. "Fear not. They will still be there after the audience, I promise."

<center>~~~~</center>

Rumad Kram stood atop his tower, staring at the chasm that yawned beside the city, a lazy jagged mouth slowly splitting the land. The wind shifted and the mist thinned, allowing him a better view of the cable as they sent Nebandalex out to join the Banderlundi high above the sea. They would hang there suffering for a while, then expire, never to vex him again. Ambrosia would be unable to use magic to rescue them; at least, not as long as she remained in Lord Korrin's chambers, or continued to wear the suppression device—which, by dampening her ability to focus, would make it difficult for her to cast any but the simplest sort of glamours—that he had mentioned in the dungeon. And, of course, the cable itself was invested with resistance to sorcerous and physical attack, else the salty mist would have reduced it to rust decades ago. But what if Ambrosia persuaded Korrin to send a slider out with a rope to haul her friends back? The womanizing fool might be protected from enchantment, but he was more than susceptible to the entreaties of a pretty face.

Therefore, the two prisoners needed to be removed from play, permanently, before any such thing could happen.

He had initially thought he might work up a sorcery that would sever the leather bonds that held the prisoners aloft, sending them plunging into the icy waters of Chasm Bay; but then he'd been struck by a better idea, one that would cause a major distraction, if not outright chaos, for Arran Blackhawk's security forces to deal with, while giving Kram the opportunity to operate freely for a little while. And so Kram carried Ambrosia's impenetrable pack, clutching it to his side like a purse; he still could not open the accursed thing, but he had worked out a means to utilize its slow seep of energy to boost the range and potency of his evocations. By bouncing spells off the radiant shell that protected the knapsack, he could achieve a sort of slingshot effect, nowhere near as powerful as having full possession and use of the Illata would be, but still potent. He knew this approach was not unlike the reliance on foci that he had earlier scorned, but he would be foolish not to utilize the tools he had obtained; which was why, in addition to her pack, he also carried Ambrosia's uncannily sharp blade. Although it had failed against the knapsack, it could, he believed, cut through almost anything else.

Including the punishment cable.

He took out the knife one last time, balanced it by its hilt on the wall of his tower, and surrounded it with a small stasis veil to render it invisible and immobile. Then he wove a triggering enchantment, binding it both to his physical location and to the steady ticking of the clock. When he arrived in the great hall, or when sufficient time had passed that he *should* have arrived there, the spell would fire; the knife would fly; the great cable would be severed; and the prisoners would fall.

Perhaps, when he next saw Ambrosia, he should thank her for gifting him with such a weapon.

Chuckling, Kram checked the sun, then hobbled toward the stairs. He was late for Lord Korrin's audience with the dwarf, and it promised to be most interesting.

~~~~
~~~~

Lord Korrin's massive throne, carved to resemble the head of a gigantic bird of prey, utterly dominated the platform at the head of the audience hall.   Glossy grey beaten silver or platinum formed the feathered crest, giving way to carved ebony, burl wood, and ivory for the cheeks and surrounding plumage; two huge globular crystals, black and glistening, served as its eyes. Ambrosia imagined that any vermin blundering into its presence would take one look at that fearsome raptor face and die of fright. The massive relief must be hugely heavy, and obviously it wouldn't do to have the ruler of Abacar crushed in his chair by his own intimidating artwork; this was prevented by a proliferation of bolts, straps, and braces, obviously add-ons, that secured it to the rear wall, partially blocking access to a narrow and obviously little-used aperture that was obscured by a purple curtain. Ambrosia's own chair, which appeared to have been dragged in from a nearby dining room, seemed small, shabby and temporary by comparison, but at least it didn't look capable of eating her.

Lord Korrin sat in the embrace of the enormous golden beak, looking regally powerful in his ceremonial battle garb, clutching a scepter that, unsurprisingly, appeared to be patterned after some sort of weapon.   A large blue gem was set into the head, reminding Ambrosia of an inert version of the Illata.

Ah, the Illata. How to get it back? She still hadn't figured out an approach that was likely to get her stuff back without revealing too much information.   Korrin had told her that all of their possessions—except for their cached weapons, which as far as she knew had not been found—were being kept in a vault in the dungeon, he hadn't shown the slightest inclination to have them brought to her. Why did she need with a ratty old satchel and a belt loaded with trinkets right now? What was so important? She could hardly say that what she *really* wanted was the Illata hidden in her pack, especially not after she'd told him how the Rittandic had killed Yexandor while trying to steal it while leaving out the fact that she had acquired it instead. Explaining how *that* had happened would be awkward at best. The opportunity to sneak off under cover of a glamour had never arisen; Korrin hadn't left her on her own for one minute since she'd awakened in his bed earlier, and now, perched on the edge of a small chair up on the dais, right next to his throne, where literally *everyone* in the hall seemed to be staring at her, pointing at her, whispering about her, or doing all three at once, there was absolutely no way she could simply vanish. If only she knew a glamour that would allow her to melt into the upholstery and disappear, leaving behind an illusion of herself in the chair to fool all the observers! That would be——

For a moment she felt dizzy again, and gave her head a slight shake to clear it. She would be glad when the aftereffects of the toxic draught had worn off completely.

Suddenly an unseen horn blew a series of short, sour notes. The massive doors at the far end of the vast chamber creaked open and four elaborately garbed heralds entered, carrying a large bar from which a fluttering banner hung; emblazoned across the fabric was a stylized representation of a long pick or hammer. Behind the men was what looked like empty space, followed by two more heralds and two guards. After a moment she realized that the empty space must contain the dwarven emissary, not tall enough to be seen over the top of the banner. As they drew closer the top of his head came into view, but no more than that. The effect was unintentionally comical, and under other circumstances she might have permitted herself a grin.

The procession stopped in front of the throne; the rightmost herald cried, "A representative from Dolvendelve comes before you, Korrin, Lord of Abacar. I present Ardegain, speaker for great Filothandiar, King of the Dwarves!"

The four flag-carriers rolled up the banner; two of them went left and the other two, taking the furled standard with them, went right, revealing the remainder of the body of the copper-colored dwarf who had been behind them. For a moment he just stood there, and Ambrosia could almost fancy he was made of metal, not unlike the great hawk's head; but then he moved, approaching the bottom of the platform, clutching his beard with his hands in a manner that pulled his own head down to look at the floor. Clearly this was a gesture of respect or subservience; she could only imagine what his reaction would be when he looked up and saw an elf sitting there above him to receive it.

"You may rise, friend dwarf," Korrin said.

The dwarf released his beard, looked up at Korrin, and opened his mouth to say something; then his gaze flicked to Ambrosia, and his expression morphed into one of open-mouthed gawping.

After a moment, Korrin said: "Do you not wish to speak?"

"I ... You ... Why is *that one* next to your throne?"

"I asked her to sit there."

"Why?"

"Because she has been telling me a *most interesting* story," Korrin said, "and I wanted to hear how it ends. According to her tale, you dwarves burned the elven forest. According to her tale, you took the ship designs we gave you and built war galleons to sail down the river and attack Torgonderrer."

"This—that—I am not here for answering to charges from *elves*!"

"So you deny it? If I send riders to Torgonderrer, they will discover the forest perfectly intact? They will find Yexandor playing the fiddle while the elves hold hands and dance in circles around the trees, or whatever it is they do out there in the woods?"

"Well." Ardegain was silent for a moment. "Well, you see, we were——"

Korrin jumped to his feet. "You *did* burn it!"

"Theft of Brisindeld is *our* business. Not yours!"

"Do you not understand that Banderlund is on *all* our doorsteps? I was counting on you to put your differences aside and consider the whole situation, not just your own vendetta! Instead you have crippled one of the … Did Filothandiar even *read* the message I sent?" Then, visibly composing himself, he sat down again, picked up his ceremonial weapon, and laid it across his knees. "Why now? Why try to take the stone by force *now*?"

"Filothandiar would not want us to discuss this where all these ears can listen," Ardegain said, looking around, as if he might locate Filothandiar's disapproving face in the crowd.

"I assure you, we will have a private audience later," Korrin said, "but why should they not hear? Are you *ashamed* of what your people have done?"

"There is no shame in trying to take back what is ours!" Then: "Very well. You ask, did Filothandiar read your message? Of course he did! And he knows the Slash will fall to Banderlund. You cannot stop them. And then Banderlund will come south into the forest, into our mountains. We even catch one, a Banderlundi scout, snooping around our tunnels. Dwarves can shut ourselves below the ground; dwarves can wait until Banderlund goes away. Elves in their forest cannot. Elves in their forest are vulnerable. Banderlund will take Torgonderrer and when it does, Banderlund will get the Brisindeld. Dwarves cannot let that happen!"

A new voice said: "Why not? What would they do with it?"

Ardegain turned to peer at the gallery, though of course he was too short to see past the first row of attendees, even though most of them were sitting on benches. From her perch on the dais, though, Ambrosia had a view from wall to wall, and could observe a thin elder standing at the back. For a moment she was reminded of Yexandor, although this fellow seemed to have come by his stoop and his wrinkles naturally, the way humans did. He shuffled forward, relying on a staff for support, making his way toward the open space in front of the platform. The people parted in front of him as if he were jabbing at them with the pointed end of his walking stick, though he made no such movements.

"You are *late*, Kram," Lord Korrin said.

"My apologies, my lord," the old man called from the midst of the crowd. "I have grown aged, and am not as sprightly as you may recall from the days of your youth."

"You jest," Korrin said. "You were old when my father was young."

"Indeed." The wizened creature emerged from the throng and stopped before the dais, leaning on his staff, looking at dwarf, man, and elf in turn. His gaze stayed on Ambrosia a moment too long for her liking before returning to and settling on the envoy from beneath the mountain. "Pray do not keep the good people in suspense, friend dwarf," Kram said. "Tell us what the Brisindeld is, and what the Banderlundi would do with it if they laid hands on this treasure the elves stole from you."

Ardegain looked from Kram to Korrin, back to Kram, back to Korrin. Finally he said, "Brisindeld is a gem. Elves call it *Illata*. It is very powerful; it supplied energy for all of Dolvendelve before *they*—" He pointed a stubby finger at Ambrosia. "—took it."

"It must have been a great loss," Kram said, a sympathetic grandfather consoling a small, blameless child over the loss of a favorite toy.

"Yes," Ardegain said. "Took a long time for us to build new ways to make power for heat and light and machines, but we did it. The elves, they hold the Brisindeld, they keep it away from us, they study it, they use it to grow silly kinds of trees, but they not *attack* us with it. If *Banderlund* gets hold of it, they will use it to conquer everything. They will use it to reach even *us*, in the dark underground. You understand?"

"They are doing a rather credible job of conquering everything even *without* the assistance of the Brisindeld," the old man said.

"Hush, Kram," Korrin said. Then, to the dwarf: "And it never occurred to you, I suppose, that you could make common cause with the elves and the rest of us, rather than destroying what they built, snatching back the gem, and shutting yourselves up under the mountain?"

"Elves not interested in working with us," Ardegain said. "Any group we send into forest, they chase out with arrows. Even ones waving truce flags."

"So much conflict over a chunk of mineral," Kram said.

"Not just a mineral!" Ardegain said. "Is not piece of quartz! Is not a stupid *decoration* like what *she* wears, sitting so proud up there with your lord!"

"But you found it in the ground, did you not? You came across it by chance while digging? Is that not how and where minerals are to be found?"

Lord Korrin said: "Kram, have you a point to make?"

"I do." Kram reached into his voluminous robes and pulled out a small leather satchel, raising it over his head as if it were a trophy hard-won in battle. "*This* is my point."

Korrin raised an eyebrow. "Your point is a purse?"

Ambrosia eyed it; it looked familiar.

"Not just any purse. It was taken from your elf, there, when she was captured."

Oh, crap.

"You have taken to rifling prisoners' possessions?" Lord Korrin asked. "Do you need an increase in your wage?"

The toadies in the audience tittered their amusement.

"I was not *rifling* it." Kram sounded wounded. "I was *studying* it."

"You are become a leather-worker now? What is your opinion of its craftsmanship?"

"I was attempting to open it, but was thwarted. The purse is heavily enchanted. It must contain something of great value. A gem, perhaps."

After a moment, Korrin said: "This is why you failed to arrive on time?"

"Yes, my lord. I was in my tower, where I would not be disturbed and where, if something went wrong, no one would be harmed except myself."

"Harmed?"

"Attempting to unravel that which has been bound by strong magic is not without risks. If one pulls the wrong string at the wrong time, the energy released can be ... destructive."

"In that case, I am sure everyone appreciates your consideration."

Kram acknowledged this with a slight bow, then said: "But my precautions proved unnecessary; the enchantment on this object is well beyond my meager capability to unravel. I am a seer, not a sorcerer; I can observe the magic that invests the pack, but not defuse it."

"Understood." Korrin looked from Kram to Ambrosia, back to Kram, back to Ambrosia. Finally he said: "The pack is yours?"

"I …" Crap, crap, crap. She knew what was in there. Somehow, Kram knew it too.

"If is elf's pack, make *elf* open it," Ardegain said.

"A reasonable suggestion." Korrin snapped his fingers. "Bring it."

"But, my lord——"

"*Bring it*, Kram."

The astrologer shuffled over to the bottom of the dais, where he stopped and held out the purse. "Surely you would not make an old man climb yet more stairs?" he said.

Korrin grunted, then set aside his scepter, stood, and clattered down the steps to where Kram waited. Taking the pack, he tried without success to unbuckle the straps that held it shut. He produced a dagger, ornamental but razor-sharp and gleaming, and attempted to cut the leather, failing in this endeavor as well. Finally, he returned to the top of the dais and handed the satchel to Ambrosia. "Open it," he said.

She turned the pack this way and that. Looking up at Korrin, she said, "I don't——"

"No more stories. Open the pack."

He was deadly serious now. She fussed with the strap for a moment, undid the buckle, slid it free. Something shifted within the bag, changing its center of gravity; it turned in her fumbling hands, tipped toward the floor. A large, glowing gem fell out.

The room exploded.

~~~~

"My name is Cynidece," the stringy-haired woman said. "Welcome to the end of the line." Then, looking down: "Or at least, the lowest part of it."

"I'm Bernard." He nodded his head backward. "This is Nebandalex."

Nebandalex, busy staring at the water below the swaying center of the cable, didn't say anything.

"Nebandalex is an elf," Bernard said, unnecessarily.

"I see that. What did you and your elf do to get yourselves sent out here?"

"I'm … not sure," Bernard said.

"You are *not sure*?" She laughed and looked back over her shoulder, "Did you hear that, Poddock? He is not sure why they are here."

"I heard," the man who hung behind her said, his voice dry and
~~~~

rough. "Regardless, he will end up just as dead as the rest of us."

"Poddock is feeling a bit morbid," Cynidece said, "as he has been out here for quite some time."

"Oh," Bernard said. "I'm sorry. Do you two, um, know each other?"

"I met him here last night," she said, as if they had bumped into each other at an art gallery or something.

"So they're just … just going to *leave* us out here?"

"Of course they are. What, did you think this was a prank? This is an *execution*, my friend."

"But … why like this?"

"Think about it," she said. "We die out here, everyone thanks their gods that it is not them, and they think twice about picking a pocket or cutting a purse."

"Is that why you're here? You're a pickpocket?"

"Oh, no," she said. "That is why *Poddock* is here. He stole from the wrong woman in the bazaar."

Poddock coughed and hacked up nothing. "How was I to know she was one of Lord Korrin's favorites?" he croaked.

"As to that, you would be best advised to rob homely ladies, and leave attractive ones alone," Cynidece said. "And if you *are* so foolish as to rob a comely girl from the castle, take care not to knock her down and damage her pretty face."

"For one who professes not to be a robber," Nebandalex said, "you seem to have much knowledge about who should and should not be robbed."

"See, I knew you were listening," Cynidece said; Nebandalex only grunted in response. She grinned, and something in her smile reminded Bernard of Mercy—the old Mercy from back home, before she got all blonde and weird and elvish and fabulous. He wondered where she was, why she wasn't with them; then he thought about what his fellow prisoners had just said, about this Lord Korrin, about pretty girls. Maybe Korrin had looked at Mercy, and had liked what he'd seen. Would that be better or worse than being hung out over the chasm? What did Lord Korrin do to pretty girls?

He wasn't sure he wanted to find out. Instead, he said: "Okay, what about him? The guy in between Poddock and the … the dead ones? What did *he* do?"

"I cannot say," she said. "He does not talk. I suppose that means he has nothing to say, or, more likely, he has lost the ability to say it. It happens, after a few days with no water." Then, in a mock whisper:

"By sunset Poddock will not be saying much either, I fear, so it is a good thing you two have come along to keep me company."

"I can hear you," Poddock said. "I am thirsty, not deaf."

"The dehydration is what kills you," Cynidece said. "They like you to die slowly. Otherwise they would just tie a rock around your neck and throw you into the——"

Before she finished speaking, a sharp metallic twang sliced through the air. They lurched and shuddered, then began to plummet, leaving Bernard's stomach hovering somewhere up where he and the others had been swaying.

The massive cable had snapped.

It seemed that dehydration would not claim them after all.

~~~~

Kram knew that when Ambrosia opened the pack, he would have, at most, a few seconds to move before those in the room—most especially Korrin and Ardegain—realized what it contained. He hoped and believed that the suppressor device she wore around her neck, disguised as a large and rather tacky lump of jewelry, would slow her down enough that he could act before she was able to turn the gem against him; but still, best to take no chances. Fortunately, the elf had become the center of attention in the room, first when Korrin had put her on the dais to provoke the dwarf, then when Kram had maneuvered her into being required to reveal the contents of her satchel. This meant that no one was paying any attention to Kram; and by imploring Korrin to come down the stairs to collect the pack, he had purchased time to ready a few sorceries, keying them to gestures so that he could complete them in an instant.

Now that instant had arrived.

First he invoked a flash glamour aimed at the throne, causing blinding illumination to flare at Lord Korrin's feet, searing the vision of anyone with the misfortune to be looking directly at the platform. This, of course, meant that nearly the entire room had been rendered temporarily sightless. Simultaneously, he launched a battering ram of force against Ambrosia, toppling her chair and sending her flying backwards into the wall; and then, before the flare had faded, before the Illata had hit the ground, he extended his grip with lines of unseen power, snatched the Illata with invisible fingers, and brought it back to himself. The gem vanished into an inner pocket of his robe, undetected in the chaos and the fading afterimage of the flare. He felt it through the fabric, warm and thrumming against his flesh; he wouldn't want it this close to his own body, but any damage it might do
~~~~

to Kram's withered frame would be of less than little consequence once he shed it. And he had, of course, made sure that the pockets of this particular garment did not contain holes.

That done, Kram returned to the role of loyal attendant.

"My lord!" he cried, hobbling with unfeigned difficulty up the stairs. "The witch has tried to blind you!"

Lord Korrin, reacting, as usual, more quickly than everyone else, had managed to turn his head and shield his eyes in the crook of his elbow; now he lowered the protective limb. His eyes were red from the nearness and intensity of the flare; tears streaked his cheeks. At first Kram thought Korrin may have managed to salvage his vision, but as the man cast blindly about he realized that the flare had done its work after all. Those close to the dais were similarly afflicted, most notably the bellowing, stomping, flailing dwarf. His roars of dismay, along with the mingled cries of the assembly, quickly drew sighted guards from surrounding rooms and corridors; as they began shepherding stunned courtiers and sycophants from the chamber, Kram gained the top of the platform. Despite his blindness, Lord Korrin oriented on him at once. "Kram?" he said. "Is that you?"

"Yes, my lord."

"I thought I smelled your liniment," Korrin said. "Can you see?"

"Yes, my lord, my eyes are so old and cloudy that the light had little effect on——"

"Never mind about your complaints! Where is she?"

"The witch? She is——" Kram glanced at where Ambrosia should have been if, as he intended, she had been dashed and shattered against the stone wall; but he broke off, realizing she wasn't there. Had she been prepared for his attack and taken countermeasures?

"What, Kram?" Korrin said. "She is what?"

"Fled, my lord. She is fled." Then, seeing this for the opportunity that it was: "And she has taken the gem with her!"

From behind and below, the blinded dwarf cursed in his native tongue, then shouted: "This is your fault, Lord Korrin! *Your* fault!"

"Silence!" Korrin roared. He put a hand on Kram's shoulder. "Lead me out of here," he said into the astrologer's ear. "She must be found before she escapes."

"Escape is not her goal. It never was."

"Then what is?"

"Is it not yet obvious, my lord? She seeks the Jewel in the Maul."

"The Jewel?"

"Of course," Kram said. "You heard the dwarf speak of the

power of one gem. Just imagine the power of *two.*"

~~~~

The vertigo of Bernard's initial slide out over the abyss was nothing compared to free fall. Except it wasn't free fall, not really; as they plunged toward the foaming black water, they were straightening out the cable, sliding along it again, back toward the end from which they had come. Suddenly he remembered what had happened when he had tried to look behind him on his way out; by twisting his leather fetters, he had managed to produce enough friction to slow himself down. Would that still work? Could he reduce his velocity enough to avoid hitting the water like it was a concrete floor?

He brought his wrists together and hooked his fingers around the straps, then twisted. It tightened on the cable and seemed to slow him down, because Cynidece slammed into him. It was like getting hit by a hunk of timber; her body was hard as stone, every inch of it taut muscle. She reflexively wrapped her legs around Bernard's waist, as if this would somehow arrest their descent, but the impact had forced his wrists apart and they had already begun picking up speed again. They plowed into Nebandalex, whose light frame had less resistance to the sea wind that blew in and curled up from below; the three of them continued their plunge together in a tangle of limbs and bodies.

Over the wind and the screaming—it might have been him doing the screaming or it might have been someone else, he wasn't sure—Bernard heard a ripping sound; one of the other prisoners spun away from their trajectory. He wasn't sure which it was, until he saw that the body was missing an arm; it must be one of the corpses, he realized, decayed enough that it had come apart at the shoulder. The thick strap was still bound to its remaining wrist, and at the end of that, flapping in the wind, was the detached arm; the leather had proven stronger than the rotting flesh and tendons.

The leather!

Bernard shouted, "Twist your straps."

Cynidece yelled something back at him; she didn't understand what he was saying. He jerked his wrists, trying to show her how to bring them together, but he didn't have gravity helping him now and couldn't catch hold the way he'd done before. He tried again, this time crossing his forearms at the elbows and locking his wrists around each other. The position was incredibly uncomfortable, but he managed to get the parts of the leather that weren't clad in metal to intertwine against the cable. The fibers scraped and bit into the tough animal hide. Cynidece watched what he did with narrowed eyes; they
~~~~

widened as understanding dawned. She put her hands together and twined her fingers around the narrow sections of her own strap, left hand on the right, right hand on the left; then she pulled her hands apart, her muscular arms tensing, closing the leather around the cable.

They began to slow down; Nebandalex, who had not mastered this trick, pulled away from them.

"Nebandalex!" Bernard yelled, trying to see the elf over his shoulder. "Make friction! *Friction!*"

A screech of pain caused Bernard to look up, past Cynidece. Trying to arrest his fall, Poddock had locked his legs around the cord, and the metal had sliced through his flesh like a bandsaw. Horrified, Bernard realized that with their leathers tight on the cable, he and Cynidece must be squeegeeing off ancient layers of grease. He only had a moment to think about this before a scalding shower of blood erupted from the man's body as some major artery was severed. Somehow, though, he still clung to the cable; the burrowing wire had gotten stuck somewhere inside his groin, maybe on his hip. He receded as the heavy bone resisted further incursion from the cable; the bodies beyond started piling up on top of him in a gruesome clump of dead and dying flesh, first the prisoner who didn't talk, then the prisoners who couldn't.

Feeling sick, Bernard looked away, and found himself facing the black craggy wall of the cliff opposite the city. It loomed over them like a ship bearing down on the wreckage of a life raft. At first he thought they would be dashed against it, but there was an overhang, a broad, deep hollow that the relentless pounding of the waves and the churning wash of the cataract had carved from the bottom of the palisade. This cavity would eventually cause the rock face to collapse, widening the gulf by another several yards, but that was in the distant geological future; for the present, the overhang acted as a lifesaving pivot. Most of the cable, including the clot of bodies stuck against Poddock——he heard the soft, sodden *crunch* of their impact, and could only assume they had been pulped——twanged flat against the cliffside, but the portion below the lip of the eroded section kept going. The world spun dizzyingly as the abrupt change in momentum threw Bernard into a twist. He glimpsed Nebandalex shoot off the end of the cable, heard a faint splash; then his own fetters slipped the line and he was flung forward, rocketing toward the rubbly debris that had accumulated over the centuries into a rough and shadowed shore. He landed well short of it, knifing into the water at a shallow angle, then curving upward, or maybe downward; he couldn't tell, couldn't see the light, didn't know which way led to the surface. But, amazingly enough, he was alive; either he had slowed himself enough with his straps or the last-minute change in direction had burned enough momentum so that hitting the water was less like hitting pavement and more like doing a belly-flop from the high board. The *extremely* high board. It hurt like nobody's business, but it didn't kill him.

He started kicking, hoping to find his way to the surface, but the currents here were strong and strange, distorted by the collision of ocean waves and tides and the thundering power of the waterfall. He was hopelessly disoriented; the leather strap between his wrists acted like a drag, keeping him from making anything that resembled progress. For all he knew he was swimming sideways or downward or in circles. His fingers touched rock, then slipped and found a broad emptiness. For a moment he thought it might be a pocket in the wall, but then he felt water flowing *into* the hole, as if it drained into something deeper, some subterranean continuation of the sea.

There would be no air that way. No light. No life.

In a panic, he turned and tried to push off the rock, but only succeeded in doing an underwater flip. Unmoored, the current seized him, catching the strap as if it were a sail. It sucked him into the tunnel. He didn't have the strength to resist; he could only watch as the dark world darkened even further around him until, at the last, he wondered if the light was fading, or he was, or both.

Probably both.

~~~~

Ambrosia was sure she was the only one who had noticed Rumad Kram's fingers start moving the second she unraveled the pack. She suspected he had done something to make the gem spill out of it. From what Lord Korrin had told her, she knew the old man was an astrologer and not a sorcerer, but her gut said he was triggering a spell; she'd instinctively called on the Illata to protect her, and it seemed to have done so by opening a doorway to somewhere else; but at the same time a tremendous shockwave had hit her, knocking her into the portal and causing her to lose her grip on the Illata. She had felt the tunnel collapsing around her, the sensation like sinking into water while wrapped in a thick blanket, but just as she started to think she was going to suffocate in the wormhole it spat her out. She slammed into a wall as if she'd been launched from a catapult, slumped to the floor, and just lay there for a moment, gasping for breath.

Where was she?

It was a corridor, long and straight and, at the moment, completely
~~~~

deserted. It looked different from the other areas of the castle that she'd been in, older; the floor consisted of interlocking cobbles in various shapes and colors, worn smooth by years of passing feet, and the walls were arcaded with shallow, whitewashed nooks, inside of which alabaster statues of men and women, many bearing more than a passing likeness to Lord Korrin, stood or sat in postures of confident alertness or stately repose. Nearby, the corridor terminated in a purple curtain that she thought might be the one she had noticed behind the throne. Shouting and other sounds of chaos emanated from it, convincing her that going in that direction would be inadvisable. Instead, she fled down the hallway as fast as she could, which it turned out was not very fast at all; Kram's blast and her subsequent rough transit through the warp had done more damage than she'd thought at first. Her ribs and left side ached terribly, her left knee kept wanting to buckle, and it felt like she was bleeding from at least one of her ears. Her knee finally gave out less than halfway down the corridor, just short of where it took a right turn. She crawled into a nearby niche, wherein the statue of a triumphant warrior leaned contemplatively on his great sword, a splintered shield propped up against his shins. She curled up behind the shield and made herself as small as possible in the shadows. She certainly wasn't going to escape by speed or by stealth; a veil glamour would have done a better job of hiding her, but with her throbbing head she doubted she could focus well enough to cast one. The best she could do at the moment was hide; that spell had very nearly killed her. Kram, the Rittandic sorcerer in a new disguise, had clearly set this whole thing up, had arranged for Bernard and Nebandalex to be sent out onto that cable to die; maybe he'd even sent that guard out in disguise to accost them and get them to commit the crime.

The lazy days of their trip downriver scrolled through her memory, little of consequence happening. She should have spent that time planning, practicing magic, figuring out the Illata, considering their next move and what the Rittandic might be up to; instead she'd been goggling at the landscape, pestering Nebandalex for stories about the elves, putting off Bernard when he asked about going home, when he tried to make her think about the world they'd left behind, what might be going on there, how their parents might be sobbing in some hospital over their unconscious bodies or putting up posters saying they had disappeared. He had accused her, more than once and, she realized now, not unfairly, of treating this world like a game that had been created for her amusement. But it wasn't a game, was it? It hadn't been one since she had awakened in the forest.

A game? Tell that to Glorian, to Orindel, to Yexandor, to the real Shelliyan, the real Rumad Kram; tell them they were dead, but it was okay, because this was just a game. Tell it to Nebandalex and Bernard, hanging by their arms a few hundred feet above the water. Tell it to—

Suddenly Lord Korrin's commanding tone echoed through the hallway, interrupting her self-lacerating reverie. "You really think the witch means to claim the Jewel in the Maul, Kram?"

"Of course she does," Kram said. "It all becomes clear now. She stole the Illata from her fellow elves, who had stolen it from the dwarves; and now she seeks to steal the Jewel from you."

Crap, crap, crap! Hoping they would stay where they were, she squeezed into the back of the alcove. No such luck; she could hear Korrin's metal-shod footsteps approaching, though they sounded oddly unsteady. She held her breath and waited for them to pass.

"Pleased as I am that it all becomes clear *now*," Korrin said, "I would have been greatly more pleased had it become clear much sooner."

"I beseech my lord to excuse an old man's inability to perfectly foresee the future," Kram said. "I *did* warn you not to bring her out of the oubliette, did I not? Rather than recriminate, let us pray we are not already too late to stop her."

Korrin made a dismissive noise. "She will not find the Maul, Kram. You know as well as I that it is shielded from detection. And if she *does* somehow find it, she will be unable to take it from its guardians."

"My lord fails to understand the danger posed by her possession of the Illata," Kram said. "Like calls to like; the Illata and Jewel in the Maul are of a kind. She will use the Illata to find the Maul, and to evade its protections."

As they went by her hiding place, Ambrosia discovered why Korrin's footsteps sounded strange; he wasn't leaning on the old man for support, exactly, but Kram had one hand on his elbow and another on his shoulder, as if guiding him. Korrin's eyes were red, his face streaked with drying tears, and after a moment she realized that Korrin must be blind, or nearly so. She did recall a flash, just before she had fallen into the wormhole, but she had thought it was from the concussive blow of Kram's spell. Perhaps it had been something else, an assault on the vision of everyone in the room, yet another layer of misdirection and attack.

Korrin said: "Have your stars seen fit to tell you *why* she wants the gems?"

Kram shrugged. "A creature such as Ambrosia seeks only power," he said. They stopped just past Ambrosia's niche, at the spot where the corridor bent to the right; his gaze flitted around the hall of echoes as if he was looking for something. Had he sensed her presence? She had already stopped breathing; if only she could stop *thinking*!

"I spoke to her, Kram, spent time with her. Her nature did not seem to be one that sought power for power's own sake."

"One's true nature can be concealed behind a facade and made undetectable," Kram said, "especially when that facade is calculated to inspire trust, desire, or devotion."

Lord Korrin was silent a moment, then grunted. "She will find that whatever power she gains will not satisfy her."

"Perhaps not. And then she will seek more."

Kram appeared to have found what he was looking for: A black, narrow opening in the back of an alcove in the vertex of the corner, almost hidden behind a statue of a weeping woman. He guided Korrin toward this aperture. As they approached it, Korrin said: "Where are we? I feel a draught."

"Just a breeze through the window, my lord. Step carefully, my lord, there are stairs ahead."

There was no window here. Why had Kram lied about the cold breath of air that rose from the depths? Where did the stairs he had mentioned lead? Why did Korrin believe him? Didn't he know the halls of his own castle?

Ambrosia waited for several seconds after Kram and Korrin had disappeared through the narrow archway, then stole to where they had stood, peering down into the dimness. Did she really want to follow them down there, into some dungeon or cellar where she might find herself trapped?

Did she have a choice?

With one last glance at the empty corridor, she turned and hobbled down the stairs, into the chill damp darkness below.

~~~~

As Rumad Kram guided him down the stairs, Lord Korrin's vision slowly returned; and as it did, it dawned upon him that the astrologer was leading him into the catacombs. Of course; they had not descended from the dais in the normal fashion, but rather through the purple curtain, and that was where the corridor beyond it led: Into the statuary hall of Korrin's ancestors, from which one could access the crypts. He should have recognized the fusty odor that always
~~~~

emanated from those dank chambers. But why was the old man taking him this way? There was no reason to descend this low into the castle, except to visit the tomb where Korrin's ancestors were buried, or …

Or to pick up the Maul.

Korrin didn't suppose the old man was in the mood to pay his respect to generations of dead Blackhawks; but Kram did not know the Maul was down here. No one did, except for Jordneh of the Ravels and the current Lord of Abacar. So what was the point of descending *these* steps, at *this* time, when, so Kram claimed, the Jewel was threatened with discovery and theft? It could not be random; he was sure Kram had his reasons. Kram *always* had reasons for what he did, loath though he might be to share them. Did he think the catacombs would be a convenient place to hide while Korrin regained his sight?

Despite what the old man claimed, Korrin did not believe that Ambrosia would be able to locate the Maul. The vault in which it lay was older than Rumad Kram—older, in fact, than ten Krams laid end-to-end—but the bindings woven upon it when the Maul had been laid to rest, after the defeat of the necromantic cult of Daras-Drûm hundreds of years ago, remained as strong as ever. As her predecessors had been doing for centuries, the Rittandic queen came every decade or so to refresh the enchantments on the vault and the seals across the ancient tunnels and warrens of Daras-Drûm on the other side of the chasm. No sane denizen of the Slash wanted to see *those* death-worshiping bastards rise again.

"My lord understands, of course, that we are dealing with a source of incredible power," Kram said, as they reached the bottom of the narrow stars and headed for the crypt.

"I am aware of that, Kram," Korrin said. "You may recall that my ancestors took the jewel from the necromancers, at great cost, to keep them from filling all the lands from here to the southern mountains with walking corpses."

"Indeed, some say I am old enough to remember it first-hand," Kram purred. "That is why the Maul remains hidden and secure, while you bear that replica." Korrin still clutched the ceremonial scepter, made in the shape of the Maul, a pallid and rather shabby imitation of the splendor of the real thing. At least, he supposed it must be; he had never actually seen the original. No one had, not for hundreds of years, not even the sorceress whose magic kept it safe.

They came to the end of the corridor, where it terminated at an ancient, massive iron door flanked by atlantes, heavily muscled and bent with the exertion of holding up the castle. Kram pushed the door with his staff; it creaked inward and they entered the cold isolation of the crypt. Eternal blue flames, jetting from spigot-shaped sconces, shadowed the cantilevered hall with pale illumination; it reminded Korrin of the light that had spilled from the pack at the moment Ambrosia had undone the straps, before the flare had blinded everyone in the room. "What are we *doing* down here, Kram?" he asked.

"She will be looking for you," the old man said.

"Why?"

"To kill you, of course."

"She is an assassin now as well as a thief?"

"Think about it, my lord. You have yet to produce an heir——"

"I have yet to *marry*," Korrin said. "I am quite sure I have an heir."

"I am not merely being pedantic. A bastard and an heir are not the same thing."

"I know that. Just ask my esteemed half-brother."

"*You* ask him. I value my head."

"Yet I fail to see what the status of my progeny has to do with Ambrosia, or with our presence in the tombs." The astrologer had already moved on ahead of him, deeper into the crypt; Korrin clanked along behind. "Get to the *point*, Kram, before I turn around and lock you in here, that you may annoy the statues as you bemoan the effect of cold damp air on your aching joints."

"If she kills you, seizes the Maul, and takes control of Abacar, who will contest it? Who will lay a better claim? Your half-brother, who is, as you alluded, a bastard? Your *heirs*, as you term them?"

"Any of their claims would certainly be better than that of a murdering elven witch. Why are we *really* down here, Kram? Surely you do not intend for us to hide in a mausoleum until the witch is found."

"But, my lord," Kram said, "she is found already." He held up a withered finger and traced a circle in the air, then pointed at the door through which they had passed.

Lord Korrin turned around; Ambrosia stood just inside the entrance to the crypt.

"Oh, crap," she said.

<p style="text-align:center">~~~~</p>

The old man must have known where she was all along; maybe he had even led Lord Korrin past her on purpose, to draw her out and lure her down here, where Korrin could deal with her. In her battered condition she could hardly escape back up the stairs, not before Korrin caught her and bashed her head in. He seemed ready to do that, taking a step toward her, raising his scepter——which didn't look so ceremonial at the moment, which actually looked rather scary, and quite capable of doing some skull-crushing——in a two-handed grip over his head. If it had been a pick-axe he would have been ready to start chipping away at the vast, mossy slabs that made up the floor, to dig her a grave.

"So Kram was right," he said quietly, his voice all the more frightening for its soft tone. "You *did* come here looking for the Maul."

Ambrosia shook her head and started to raise her hands, then stopped, realizing that he would take it as a threatening gesture, as if she were getting ready to cast a spell. "No, I was hiding! I followed you when you went by, and——"

Then Kram said, with elaborate innocence: "Oh, is the Maul concealed within *this* crypt, my lord?"

Korrin's eyes widened. He half-turned. Beyond him, in the shadows, Ambrosia could see that Rumad Kram had somehow, despite his evident lameness, moved a considerable distance farther away, and was now inspecting a smallish, nondescript tomb. It appeared to house the remains of a favored royal pet; instead of depicting some fearsomely armored fighter or wise, proud matriarch, the carving on the lid depicted the curled-up form of a dozing canine.

Korrin said: "Kram?"

The astrologer's hand disappeared into his robe. "Yes, my lord?"

"What are you doing?"

Kram's hand reappeared, holding a thick cloth wadded around something. Even through the obscuring fabric, Ambrosia could see that the wrapped item glowed blue. "I am preventing yon witch from obtaining the Jewel in the Maul," he said.

Lord Korrin acted fast, she had to give him that; as soon as Kram produced what was obviously the Illata, he bolted toward the old man, cudgel at the ready. Unencumbered by ceremonial armor, he may have gotten there in time; but he *was* encumbered, and Kram was too far away to be thwarted. Turning his hand so that the gem faced the floor, he slammed it down against the drab sarcophagus. The lid exploded, sending fragments of stone skittering across the floor. A shockwave rattled the tombs, staggered Lord Korrin, and actually knocked Ambrosia over; she stumbled and fell onto one of the other ossuaries, catching hold of the carven arm of the statue that sat astride it. The cold marble hand held an upraised goblet as if in toast to his fellow dead. Condensed moisture had pooled inside the cup, wine-dark with dissolved minerals and an algal scrim.

Clinging to the arm for support, she turned and saw Kram kneeling over the dog's tomb, one arm in it up to the elbow. Realizing he could not possibly close the remaining distance in time, Korrin flung his scepter at the astrologer, hurling it so mightily that he lost one of his decorative gloves. As this ungainly projectile spun through the air, Kram lifted the hand that held the cloth-wrapped Illata and caused the weapon to be deflected in a lopsided spiral to clatter and vanish among the ancient caskets. Then the old man withdrew his own gaudy weapon, similar in shape to what Korrin had hurled, smaller and even more jewel-encrusted. At the tip, placed in a half-sunken setting, a twin of the Illata radiated light, shining out through the precious stones arranged about the hollow head. Kram swept this device up and thrust it at Korrin just as the big man stretched out his powerful arms to seize the astrologer in a mighty grip. One of Korrin's hands closed around the shaft of the Maul, checking Kram's swing; his other, ungloved, hand landed flat against the end, where the Jewel glowed and thrummed.

Ambrosia could only gape as Lord Korrin cooked inside his own fancy armor. Smoke rose from his mouth and nose and ears; it poured out of the gaps and chinks in his mail and dribbled foamy tendrils across the floor. His hair turned silver, then white, then ash-grey; then it ignited. His skin tightened across his head and exposed hand as the flesh beneath boiled away; his eyes erupted into twin jets of vapor. Lacking muscle, mass, and life, the desiccated remains of Lord Korrin toppled over backwards and broke into pieces on the floor, leaving little more than cracked and roasted bone in a smoldering metal shell.

It was over in a few seconds. Kram rose to stand over the remains, looking rather pleased with himself.

Suddenly Ambrosia felt a cold, stony grip close around her wrist. The cup-holding statue on the tomb—*all* of the statues, in fact—had begun to move; she had grabbed its arm to stop herself from falling, and it, in turned, had grabbed *her*. Kram didn't appear to be responsible for this witchery; he was backing away from the sarcophagi, moving toward the center of the chamber, eyeing the coffins with a mixture of wonder and trepidation. His gaze landed on her again, firmly in the grip of the quickening stone, and he smiled. "So, Ambrosia, this time, you are alone." He held up his hands; one held the Maul, the other the Illata, nestled in its bed of cloth. "And I have two stones, while you have none."

The statue that held her had detached from its base now, and dragged her along as it moved toward Kram. The other statues, too, had begun closing in on the astrologer. These must be the guardians of which Korrin had spoken earlier. She was an incidental target, she realized; they were after the Jewel in the Maul. "Enjoy it while you can," she said, "before they take it away from you."

"Oh, I hardly think so," Kram said. "My prizes are too hard-won to give them up to thoughtless stone. And the dwarf in the audience hall gave me a most *splendid* idea with his ranting." He closed his eyes and whispered, and suddenly the large, gaudy jewel around her neck—a pendant almost as big as the Illata, of a similar cut—grew warm and began to glow. Kram smiled at her, as if she were a dim child performing a stupid trick that she thought was clever; then he drew a luminous circle in the air with the Maul, stepped through it, and was gone.

The statues stopped their lumbering movement; for a moment she thought they had become inanimate again, but no, they were only adjusting to whatever sorcery Kram had just perpetrated, reorienting on the one they thought possessed the Jewel. Reorienting on *her.*

The stone hand around her wrist began to squeeze painfully hard. She closed her eyes, but then, when the statue lifted her off the ground, she opened them again.

If she was going to die, she wanted to see it coming.

Concluded in
Part II of the
"Strings" Duology
Ravels
By James V. Viscosi

"COMFORT"
as told by
MERCEDES VACCARO

~~~~

</div>

BENTWOOD WAS AT war, and had been for the last three seasons. King Lahr, Lord of the Realm, directed his soldiers from the fastness of Humbold's Spire, a black castle at the edge of a chasm. High in the mountains, Humbold's Spire was whipped by winds that always carried snow or the threat of snow, and obscured by great icy fogs that welled up from the chasm like blood from a wound. The road to the Spire was narrow and winding and could be held by a few men even against an entire legion. So, secure in the dark walls of the Spire, Lahr waited for news that his forces had finally routed the armies of Prince Faundren.

As he sat on his throne, his chin cupped in his hand, his arm braced on his knee, his crown sitting at an angle on his head, Lahr thought black thoughts of his foe. Kings of Bentwood had often been at war, and indeed Faundren's realm of Fimble was their favorite opponent. Occasionally a king had been forced to retreat temporarily to Humbold's Spire, there to gather his strength before driving his opponent to ruin. But no other king had spent two seasons in the Spire.

Of course, no other king had had to deal with Faundren.

At the thought of the Prince, with his shining hair and his horse the color of the moon, Lahr spat at the feet of the serving girl, Cardella, who waited quietly near his throne.

"Curse the man," he growled at her bowed head. "Curse him and flay him and feed him to the hogs. What's that stretch of river to him, anyway? It's mine! At least, it would be if old Unglor hadn't lost it two generations ago, the fool."

"Yes, my lord," Cardella said softly.

"Bring me some wine," he muttered, staring out across the vast dark empty room.

"Yes, my lord." Moving on feet accustomed to servility, she did not so much leave the chamber as flee it, vanishing into one of the many dark doorways that gaped on the throne room. Lahr watched her go, watched the movement of her body under the ragged dress. He wondered how old the girl was. He should know, he thought; but he had forgotten. Well, he had more important things to occupy his mind, didn't he?
~~~~

While he waited for his wine, Lahr turned to Toad, his food taster, who lounged on a cushion to his left. Toad's head was tipped back and his mouth was wide, issuing a guttural snore. Lahr judged the distance, gathered a wad of spit in his mouth, and hawked. It vanished down Toad's open gullet. Lahr smiled; he was two for three today.

There came a great pounding at the door of the throne room. One of Lahr's guards looked at him; he said, "Yes yes yes, open it. Who could be invading here? Ah, Cardella. My wine."

The guard walked down from the throne platform, his boots ringing sharply on the stones. He passed the thick columns that supported the distant ceiling, passed the pews on which the occupants of Humbold's Spire sat when their King called them, passed the tapestries of Bentwood's glories of old, and reached the thick wooden doors that opened onto the outer hallway. As he reached for the latch, the pounding came again. Lahr waved an impatient hand.

The guard undid the latch and tugged on the door. It swung on creaky hinges to reveal the battered form of Lortax, the king's Champion. Lortax strode into the room, peremptorily pushing aside the guard with a hand still cased in steel. "My lord," he said as he approached the throne.

"Lortax. "

"I bring ill news, sire."

Lahr eyed his knight. "You may speak."

"Faundren is mounting another attack, sire. He's got more men than he's ever had before. He's pushing his way up the ravine and my soldiers have not been able to stop him." Pause. "He may reach the gates."

"What?" Lahr jumped to his feet. The crown, never secure on his head, came loose and clattered to the floor. Cardella raised a hand to her mouth to hide her smile. "Reach the gates? Impossible!"

"It is true, sire," Lortax said.

Lahr paced back and forth in front of the throne, his robes swishing softly as he spun at each end of his line. He stopped in front of Toad long enough to kick the slumberer in the foot, startling him awake. Toad sat up in surprise, then coughed and gagged and spat a glistening wad on the floor. "Toad!" the king shouted. "You lie there and sleep while my greatest enemy walks to the gates of my castle!" He spun without awaiting a reply and strode to the other side of the dais, where he confronted Cardella. "No one has ever reached the gates of Humbold's Spire. *Ever!*"

"That's true, my lord King," she said.

"How close is he?" Lahr said, whirling to face Lortax.

"A day's march." Lortax removed his mail gloves, ran his fingers through his hair. They came out bloody. "We are slowing him down, but—"

"Do not *slow* him! *Stop* him!"

"His forces are too strong, sire," Lortax said. "Each of his men fights like five. And he fights like ten!"

"But sire," Toad interjected, "even if he reaches the gates, he cannot enter. The walls will stand against him."

"Perhaps," Lortax said.

"*Perhaps?*" Lahr glared at the knight. "Say what you mean."

"In the middle of Faundren's column is a ballista being towed by snow lizards. It is very large and may be strong enough to batter down the gates."

"Snow lizards?"

"Yes, sire."

"Where did Faundren get snow lizards, when Bentwood is the only kingdom which raises them?"

"Treachery, no doubt."

"No doubt. You bring me dire tidings, Champion."

"Aye, sire."

"When Faundren arrives with his lizards and his ballista, we will roast him in boiling oil." He turned to Toad. "Tell the castellan to ready the cauldrons."

Toad cleared his throat.

"Is this a problem?" Lahr said.

"Perhaps my lord King has forgotten that he discarded the stores of siege oil because they took up room which could be better used for casks of wine."

Lahr turned red. "Do you mock me, Toad?" he said, his voice almost a whisper.

"No, my lord."

"You are wise not to." Lahr turned back to Lortax. "Remain here. See to the defenses. When Faundren arrives you will lead the guard against him. Now go from my sight."

"Yes, sire." Lortax bowed his way backwards out of the throne room. The guard pushed the door shut behind him.

"Bad news," Toad said.

"Ah, the toad croaks again," Lahr said. "He should beware, for the croaking toad is found and eaten by the hawk."

"Hawks don't eat toads," Toad said.

"I say they do and that makes it so," Lahr said. "Cardella, bring me more wine.'"

Lahr's lips were shiny with grease and the floor around his throne was littered with bones. In his hands he held a brown haunch of meat that glistened in the light of the torches. He was working it furiously, turning it this way and that, his teeth closing on every bit of flesh he could find.

"… Lahr …"

He paused in his eating and looked around, his eyes narrow and suspicious. His crown slid forward on his head. He looked sharply at Cardella, who stood nearby, holding a platter full of meat, cheese, bread, and wine. "Did you hear that?" the king demanded.

"Hear what, my lord?"

"… Lahr! …"

"That!" the king roared. "That! That!"

She frowned. "I hear nothing, sire, save you enjoying your meal."

"Then *listen*, blast you!" He whirled on Toad and kicked him in the knee. "Toad, wake up!"

Toad sat up blearily. "What—*haaaak!*—what does my lord require?"

"Listen, damn your ears!"

Toad, confused, listened. Lahr listened. Cardella listened.

"Lahr!" The cry was stronger now, closer. "Coward!"

Lahr went ashen. The meat fell from his hands and clumped to the floor, picking up dirt and bits of straw as it bounced down the stairs. "Faundren," he said.

There came, again, a great pounding on the double doors. Lahr looked up, then retreated behind his throne. "Go away!" he shouted wildly, as if the hordes of Faundren were about to pour into the chamber.

The guard at the door peered through a small grate, then said: "It is Lortax, sire."

Lahr stared briefly, seeming to wonder where he had heard that name before. Then, composing himself, he returned to his throne and adjusted his crown. "Yes. Lortax. Of course. Let him in."

"My lord," Lortax said as he strode up the carpet, "Faundren's men are at the gates."

"Well, what are you doing in here?" Lahr cried. "Get out there! Fight them! Drive them off!"

"Of course, my lord. The castle guard is already engaging his army. Your archers are stationed at the battlements." He paused carefully. "I thought perhaps my lord King would like to view the battle?"

Lahr's skin took on a clammy look. "View … the … battle?"

"From the safety of a tower, of course."

"Oh. Oh, yes. Yes, of course." He looked at Cardella. "Bring the food."

Lahr looked out over the sea of men who fought in front of Humbold's Spire. The ravine through which the road traveled opened up before the castle gates, making a field large enough to decamp an army. A low wall protected this area, but Faundren had breached it, and his blue-clad forces had poured through to engage Lahr's men in green. Sword struck sword, mace struck shield; spears thrust and arrows flew; and blood sparkled in the snow.

Lahr watched the battle with a chicken leg clutched in his hand, but he never raised it to his lips and it grew cold. Cardella, standing behind him, scanned the battle for the legendary Prince Faundren, but he was not to be seen. This had not escaped the notice of the king; over the clang of the weapons and the cries of the soldiers, she occasionally heard him mutter, "Where is he, blast him?"

The question was answered as the shadows lengthened, when a column of mounted soldiers charged out of the ravine. At their head was a shining stallion, and on his back rode Prince Faundren. His hair flashed in the sun, streaming out beneath his helmet. The soldiers parted before him; those of Lahr's colors were spitted on his lance as he drove a wedge through the weary footmen.

At the sight of the prince, Lahr rose slowly to his feet. Toad pulled him back down again. "Best you not catch an arrow, sire," he whispered, his thick lips close to Lahr's ear.

Now Faundren had cleared a bloody path to the very gates of Humbold's Spire, and his horsemen kept the path clear. Out of the ravine came the ballista, a huge crossbow on wheels, towed by two massive white reptiles with eyes like crystals of ice. Each lizard bore two riders.

"Lahr!" Faundren shouted. "Lahr! Coward! Come and face me!"

In his portable throne, Lahr trembled.

"Lahr!" Faundren cried. "Are you a man? Bloated child! Come and face me!"

The king jumped to his feet, leaned over the parapet, and hurled his chicken leg at Faundren. It landed in the snow beside the prince's noble horse. Faundren looked up at the king, then down at the chicken leg. He saluted King Lahr and bellowed, "If you will not come and face me, then I will come to you!" He guided his horse away from the gates as the ballista was positioned before it.

Lahr turned away from the battle. "I've seen enough," he said.

The pounding of the ballista resonated throughout the castle, but that was not enough to keep Toad from his slumber. King Lahr sprawled on his throne, wincing every time he heard the thud of the ballista against the gates. It was only a matter of time, he knew, before they were sundered, and then the battle would spill into Humbold's Spire itself.

Damn Faundren to hell, anyway.

"You summoned me?"

He looked over at Cardella, who had appeared from the dark doorway leading to the kitchen. "Yes, child," he said. "Please, come here."

She approached him uncertainly. She came to the front of the throne and stopped. Lahr took her hands and pulled her down to kneel before him. "My lord?" she asked, her eyes wide.

"Cardella," said the King, as if turning the name over on his tongue. "Cardella, this——" He was interrupted by the boom of the siege engine. When the echoes died down, he continued. "This may be my last battle. Faundren may get inside the castle. I am … uneasy." His hand strayed up her arm, toward her breast. His fingers were greasy from the meat. "I require … comfort."

"Your majesty, I——"

Now his finger traced a path across her collarbone, while his other hand gripped her wrist tightly. She gasped at the sudden pressure of his hand. "*Comfort*," he said again, emphasizing the word.

"Sire, I——"

"Your mother used to give me … comfort," he said, licking his lips, "when I was uneasy." He paused. "You look very much like her, you know."

She stared at him. Awed by the honor of his solicitations, he thought. He hooked his finger into the neckline of her grimy dress. "Your mother was … dear to me, in a way," he said. "It saddened me when she cast herself from the high parapet. But you, dear child, are so like her——"

She knocked his hand away from her dress and slipped her hand from his slimy grip, turned and ran off. Lahr stood, his fists clenched, trembling head to toe; and he shouted after her, "Stupid cow! Strumpet!"

Then she was gone. He sank back into his throne, into his stupor; and the siege engine pounded on.

Cardella ran down the dark corridor, panting, her heart racing ahead of her feet, feet unaccustomed to *that* sort of servility. She did not slow until she reached the familiar confines of the kitchen, where blazing fires kept the cold far at bay. One of the cooks saw her come in and handed her a flagon of wine. "Bring this to the alchemist," he said, ignoring or not noticing her condition.

"The … alchemist?" Cardella said.

"Yes, the alchemist," the cook said. "You know, the old man. He's probably forgotten he wanted it, but bring it just the same. Go on, girl!" The cook turned her around and sent her out a different doorway with a pat on her behind.

As she walked to the alchemist's chambers, the pounding in her ears subsided, and by the time she reached the door she felt perfectly calm, unreal almost, as she thought and thought about the conclusion she had reached. *She was the king's daughter.* How could she have lived seventeen years, unknowing? Her mother had said, had *insisted*, that Cardella was fathered by a drunken castle guard; but hadn't she often stood in the shadows staring at the king with an expression not of loyalty or even fear, but as if he had slapped her without reason? The question of Cardella's paternity was one her mother would never speak about in any detail, saying vague things instead of definite ones. It was dark; he took me from behind; I never saw his face. Perhaps these were all true statements, but her mother had used them as shields to hide another truth that she had not wanted to reveal.

But now those shields had been broken, years after her mother's death; now the truth was laid bare, pulsing like Lahr's black heart. *Your mother used to give me comfort,* he'd said. She understood what sort of comfort he spoke of. And Lahr knew she was his child; he must know. Perhaps the whole court knew, and had been silently mocking her all her life, and despising her for an ignorant, foolish, empty-headed girl. *Why, she doesn't even know her own father,* they might say, *when he looks her in the face every day.* Humiliation swept over her, staining her face crimson, followed by a hot tide of anger that scorched her soul.

With a hand that was questioning its servility, she knocked at the alchemist's door and got no answer. She repeated the knock, then pushed open the door and went inside. Xanx, the king's ancient alchemist, was sitting at a table full of vials and bottles, his head forward on the wood, snoring heavily. Cardella walked to the table and put the flagon on it. Absently, she began picking up Xanx's vials and flasks, turning them over in front of her and trying to read the labels.

Boom! The ballista again. Cardella listened to the echoes, and it was as if the projectiles launched by the siege engine were striking her, pounding away at some shell that surrounded her. She left Xanx to his slumber, adopting a slow pace on her way back to the kitchen. When she arrived, one of the cooks—a different one this time—accosted her. "Where have you been?" she demanded, shoving a bowl of fruit into Cardella's hands. "The king has been waiting for this!"

"I don't want to bring it," she said, her arms full with the huge wooden bowl. "Can't someone else do it this time?"

The cook licked her lips and eyed Cardella. "You are the king's favorite serving wench," she said. "Go on, now, and stop asking silly questions."

And so Cardella found herself hustled up the dim corridor that led to the throne room, to the King, her father, the man who required *comfort* from her.

She approached the throne carefully. Lahr sat there, statue-like, staring straight ahead, his hands clenched into flabby fists. When she neared him his head snapped around and he glared at her. She held the bowl out to him. "Your fruit, sire."

He reached out and took an apple and examined it as if the secret of victory were written upon its red skin. "I have these imported," he said, apparently addressing the apple, "from the southern March of Bentwood. Faundren's cut us off from there, so when these are gone, there will be no more. It is my prerogative to have fresh fruit from my orchards in the south, and Faundren is denying me it." He looked up at her with those blue eyes, eyes that should have been steely but that were simply pale and icy. "It is also my prerogative to have comfort from whomever I choose. And *you* are denying me that."

She backed off a step, but his hand—not greasy this time—shot out and grabbed her wrist. She gasped and nearly dropped the bowl of fruit, but a lifetime of servitude had given her a surer grip than that. He pulled on her, not gently, and suddenly something leaped into her mind, something that she hadn't realized before now. "My lord King, wait," she said.

"Wait for what?" he said.

"Listen."

"Listen to *what*?"

"The pounding. It's stopped."

He stared at her, then released her hand and stood, a hand cupped to his ear. His crown tottered unsteadily. He stayed in that position for several minutes, an interval in which there should have been at least one report from the ballista.

Instead, silence.

The King turned to Cardella, and it was obvious from his expression that he intended no more lechery today. His face was pale and pasty and sweat gleamed from his features, making his skin the color of uncooked dough smeared with water. "What does this mean?" he asked, his voice now as unsteady as his crown.

Toad coughed in his sleep. Lahr knotted the fabric of his robe in his hands, twisting it back and forth, waiting. Cardella stood where she was, a marionette holding a bowl of fruit.

When the pounding started again, it was on the doors of the throne room, and it was delivered not by a ballista but by a fist. "Faundren!" Lahr said. "He's come for me!" He scrambled off the dais, leaving his crown where it fell, and scampered toward one of the dark doorways, his robe flying behind him.

"My lord King!"

Lahr froze just before he left the chamber. The voice was Lortax's, and it came from beyond the huge double door.

"Can it be?" Lahr said.

"My lord King! Open the door! I bring great news!"

Lahr hurried back to the dais, fumbled the crown back onto his head, and sat. Then, as if he had been there calmly awaiting the arrival of Faundren and his men, Lahr waved his hand to the guard and said, "Admit him."

The door swung open. Faundren's hair gleamed in the twilight of the torches. King Lahr gasped and drew his legs up onto the throne, hugging himself around his knees; but then Faundren marched forward into the chamber, dragging chains behind him; and holding the end of the chains was Lortax, battered and grimy but grinning widely. Blood darkened his moustache.

Lahr jumped to his feet, elation on his features. "Lortax!" he said. "You shall reap a rich reward for this! How? How did you do it?"

"Prince Faundren offered to end the siege if I engaged him in single combat. I agreed, and——"

"And you defeated him!"

"——and when the arrangements were made and his men stood

down, two squads of your defenders took them from behind, while your archers unleashed such a rain of arrows … even now the attackers are being driven pell-mell back down the ravine. The scavengers will eat well come the spring thaw."

Well-pleased, Lahr said: "This is a great victory, Lortax!"

"*Victory*," Faundren said. "Your *victory* is as hollow and without honor as you are."

"But it is a victory nonetheless," Lahr said. "Toad!"

"*Haaaaak!*"

"Call the pages, call the criers, summon all my subjects, bring them here! We will have a celebration tonight!"

"Yes, my lord." Still coughing, Toad stumbled out of the room.

Lahr turned back to the Prince, who regarded him with black and undisguised hate. "Tell me, brave Prince Faundren," Lahr said, "what inspired this lunacy? Why did you heedlessly throw yourself against the gates of Humbold's Spire when it could only mean your doom?"

"You should know, brave King Lahr," Faundren said. "Or perhaps the assassin you sent to my bed never returned to tell you what he did to my Princess?"

"Oh. That. You came all this way because of a *woman?*" Lahr waved his hand. "You are a romantic fool, Faundren. But now I will grant the request you made of me; now I will face you." He walked slowly down the stairs of the dais. Faundren did not move as Lahr approached, but Lortax and three guards held him firm, just in case. Lahr stopped a few feet from the Prince and raised his hand to strike Faundren; but before he could the captive spat in Lahr's face.

Lahr lowered the hand he had meant to use to strike the Prince and used it to wipe himself off instead.

"You will regret that, fair Prince," he said.

It was an hour or three before all the inhabitants of the castle could be found and directed to the throne room, but it had been done and the chamber was full of people. All eyes were on Prince Faundren, still standing in chains before the King, and the murmurs in the hall were much reduced from their usual noisy babble. As the last of the courtiers arrived, Toad emerged from the shadows and said, "All are here, my lord." He flopped down on his cushion, clearly exhausted.

Lahr adjusted his crown, then stood. "The war is ended!" he cried. "Behold my captive, Prince Faundren!"

There was no roar of approval. The crowd simply stared.

Lahr slowly descended the stairs again, this time wearing the ceremonial scabbard and sword of his fathers. He stopped before the Prince. Faundren's breath came hard, and he stared at Lahr with the restrained fury of a bound whirlwind.

Lahr slid his sword from its sheath and held it up for all to see. The polished blade glimmered in the torchlight. He nodded to Lortax, who nodded to his men, and together they pulled the Prince to his knees. Then Lahr moved around beside the man and, raising up the sword, brought it crashing down on Faundren's neck.

Cardella averted her eyes. The soft chunk of the sword biting into Faundren's flesh nauseated her. The first blow was followed by a second, and then a third. She heard liquid pattering to the floor. Then, finally, the Prince's head came off. It hit the flagstones with a noise like a ripe melon. When she dared to look, she saw the King holding up Faundren's head by the hair, showing his grisly prize to the silent crowd. Blood dripped from the severed neck.

"Well?" the King said. "Victory is ours!"

Taking its cue, the crowd went wild. They cheered and clapped and hooted. Lahr stood there a little while, his expression exultant, then turned and climbed back to his throne. He brought Faundren's head with him, placing it on his lap and stroking its hair as if it were a favorite cat. "Let us celebrate!" he said. Servants appeared among the crowd, carrying plates loaded with the best wares of the kitchen. Lahr said, "Cardella. An apple."

She brought the bowl over. Toad picked up an apple, but Lahr stopped him. "No," Lahr said. "Prince Faundren has agreed to be my food taster this evening. Haven't you, my Prince?" He lifted the head and caused it to nod in agreement. "You are too kind, brave Prince Faundren." He relieved Toad of the apple and held it up to Faundren's dead lips. After a few seconds he said: "The apple does not please you? Oh, forgive me, my lord. Cardella, the Prince desires wine. Bring him some." She turned and walked slowly toward the dark doorway. Lahr called after her, "If you are quick, perhaps the Prince will take a liking to you and allow you in his bed!"

Cardella hesitated a moment, then vanished into the darkness. Soon she returned with a flagon of white wine. The King took it from her, unstoppered it, and forced the lip into Faundren's mouth. Cardella, feeling sick, retreated back into the passage, watching from the shadows.

"Drink," the King said, tipping the flask into the dead mouth. Wine dribbled out of Faundren's severed neck, the yellow liquid streaked with gore. "Is it good?" Lahr asked. He nodded the Prince's head. "Excellent!" He tipped the flagon to his own mouth and took several huge swallows.

"A toast!" he said, jumping to his feet. Faundren's head swung in his grip. "A toast to … to …"

His court stared at him.

Faundren's head slipped from his fingers and bounced down the stairs, coming to rest near his body.

"My lord King?" Lortax said, stepping up to the platform.

"The wench—" Lahr gasped, pointing toward the corridor, toward Cardella. "The wench!" He tore at his throat with his fat fingers, then fell, tumbling down the stairs. He landed on his back, gasping, gurgling, blood running from the corners of his mouth, eyes turning a jaundiced yellow. He rolled over onto his stomach, still gasping, still bleeding; he pushed himself up onto his knees, then fell over again, his eyes wide and staring at the ceiling. Blood welled out of his mouth, oozed into his greying beard.

The chamber fell silent.

Cardella turned and ran.

Lortax knelt beside Lahr, felt his throat, looked into his eyes. There could be no doubt; he was dead. "The King is poisoned!" Lortax shouted, standing up. "Guards! Follow me!" He dashed down the corridor toward the kitchen, three guards behind him. Their footfalls echoed against the walls. As he ran, Lortax felt himself kick something. It bounced and clattered down the hallway in front of him, and when he emerged into the kitchen he found it up against a table leg; it was one of Xanx's bottles, unstoppered and empty. It had a skull engraved upon its side. He snapped his fingers and pointed. "Take that," he said to one of the guards. Then, to the cooks who stared at him: "Where is the wench, Cardella?"

"She's not here," a cook said, his voice as thin as his body was fat. "She took a tray. She said—"

"Which way did she go?"

"There." The cook pointed at one of the many openings that led from the kitchen. "She said the King had ordered her to take food to some prisoner in the high tower. My lord, what's going on?" he shouted at Lortax's back, as he led the guards after Cardella.

The guard post at the base of the tower was deserted, the sentry having been pressed into the defense of Humbold's Spire and either killed or summoned to witness the farce in the throne room. Lortax took the stairs of the high tower two at a time, soon outstripping his men. Around and around he went, past doors of solid oak with barred windows, cells where prisoners wailed and muttered and slowly went insane. Higher and higher he went; the air grew colder and colder. At the top of the tower was a door, and the door was open, and the wind blew snow in gusts through the portal. He pushed against the gale, out onto the high parapet.

A tray was at his feet. On it was a piece of meat, a loaf of bread, a lump of cheese, a clay mug of water. A skin of ice had formed on the water's surface. Lortax kicked it all aside as he strode out onto the snow-slicked flagstones.

Cardella was there. During her flight she had acquired a dark cloak; it billowed around her as she stood on the edge of the high parapet, looking down at the fog and the snow that hid the chasm from view. She reminded Lortax of a raven, black wings spread as it prepared to fly. "Stand down from there," Lortax said gruffly, though he knew she would not.

Cardella turned to him, her cheeks ruddy with cold and exertion but her eyes calm. "Hello, Lortax."

"Stand down," he said again.

She raised her eyebrows. Snow had collected in them. "Have I not given my lord King comfort?" she asked.

The wind gusted and raised a curtain of snow between them. She was an obscure shape, blurred, unreal. "The comfort of the grave," Lortax said.

She smiled faintly, turned back to the chasm. "I hope he finds it lessens his unease," she said. The wind gusted; blinding snow stung Lortax's face and eyes. The guards arrived, their footsteps clanging on the stairs behind him, but he raised a hand and stopped them.

When he could see again, Cardella was gone.

Lortax led his men away, leaving the empty night to howl among the peaks.

About the Author

James V. Viscosi is the author of several horror and fantasy novels. An expatriate New Yorker, he currently resides with his wife and various finned and furry animals in sunny Southern California, where he spends most of his time hiding underneath a very large hat. Visit him online at www.jamesviscosi.com.

www.ingramcontent.com/pod-product-compliance
Lightning Source LLC
Chambersburg PA
CBHW020405110726
47899CB00006B/1863